The Marfa Blues

searching for treasure

John Egenes

A Delta Vee Trade Paperback
Copyright 2025 by John Egenes
Cover and interior art by Pearl Barry

ISBN: 979-8-218-63317-2
15 14 13 12 11 5 4 3 2 1

For more information visit our Facebook Page:
www.facebook.com/TheMarfaBlues/

To the Raven,
the world's contant orphan.

CONTENTS

Prologue - 1867

Part 1

Part 2

Part 3

Part 4

Part 5

Epilogue

La Tierra del Loyah
Sierra Cajon
Las Montañas de la Muerte
monticulo de Chinati
Las Montañas del Aguila
Monticulo de Capote
Rio Cibola
Arroyo Alamo
Fuerte de Laton
El Presidio del Norte
El Rio Bravo
Fuerte de Davis
cañon de tamaño mediano
el tesoro es en el cañon de caja pequeña
cañon grande
La Tierra de los Comancheros
Pequeña cañon
tres cruses en las tumbas de los muertos
rocas grandes
Rio Perdiz
escondite de banditos
moros
dos pinos gigantes
Arroyo Alamito
Arroyo Maronso
los arboles muertos
Pase del Rosa Salvaje
Las colinas de caballo
cascados de los conejos
Las Lajitas

Prologue - 1867

South Texas 1867

The salty water that Fermin Macias scooped from the river earlier that day was now taking its toll as he lay in his blanket on the edge of the camp in the rugged Texas badlands. The light of the waning moon cast long shadows on the desert floor, the nearest ones erased by the glare of the cook fire at the camp's center. He rose from his bedroll to the sounds of men singing and playing *guitarras*, the merrymaking fortified by the mezcal they drank.

Fermin struggled along in the red dirt until he found a place to relieve himself, a large boulder in the surrounds of a hollow that was nestled back into the rock outcropping in the nearby brush. His head was pounding, his stomach churned, and he could think of nothing beyond the pain behind his eyes and the tightening nausea that finally manifested as an uncontrolled stream of vomit and spit.

Why had he ever volunteered for this *pendejo's* journey? When word had come that the soldiers of Benito Juárez were on their way to overthrow the government, Emperor Maximilian was forced to send his valuables north for shipment back to his home in Austria. Belongings were packed hurriedly and the wagon train left the castle at *Chapultepec,* headed north to Texas. At the time, Fermin was honored to be chosen as one of the guards. Now, he wasn't so sure.

Forty-five barrels of flour were loaded onto fifteen wagons, each pulled by a yoked team of oxen. Hidden inside the flour was a treasure worth over $10 million in gold, silver and jewels. The contents were known only to the four *generales* and the nineteen *soldados* that made up the escort party, each one hand picked by *El Emperador* himself. To a man they were loyal *Maximilianos.*

They had chosen a circuitous route to Texas, zig-zagging their way north in a seemingly random manner in order to thwart any plans to attack them. Their intention was to move north into Texas, then turn east toward the Gulf of Mexico. The journey would end at Galveston, where they would load the bounty onto a ship bound for the French coast.

The going was rough and the oxen strained against the loads as the men pulled their bandanas up over their mouths in vain attempts to battle the dust. Outriders rode at the front and to the rear of the wagon train, with others traveling alongside. The days passed slowly and the men fought to stay alert, and by the time they finally crossed the river into Texas they felt a sense of relief, knowing that they were at last free from the *soldados* of Benito Juárez.

They made their way to *Ojinaga* on the bank of *El Río Bravo*, the river the *Americanos* called the Rio Grande. They forded the river into Texas and made camp at *El Presidio del Norte.* There they encountered six gringos— *Americanos*—who told them they came from a place called *Missouri.* They said they were soldiers in the Confederate army but now that the war was over they refused to live under Yankee rule. They were headed south to live free, in Mexico.

The *Americanos* were well armed, with many repeating rifles, needle guns, and pistols. They were a well disciplined group of soldiers, and their leader was a powerful man by the name of Murdock. Impressed with the organization and discipline of the Confederates, and faced with negotiating the unfamiliar territory of the Texas plains, the Mexican generals convinced the Americans to hire on as *guardias* to help protect the party. It felt good to have them along, with their Henry forty-fours and Winchester saddle carbines. These were men experienced in fighting and tempered on the battlefield. They were not told what was in the barrels—only that it was special flour, and that they were taking the wagons across Texas to the port of Galveston. From *El Presidio* the group traveled to the northeast, into the Texas badlands filled with mesquite, sage, and cholla. They were camped in the rugged foothills of the mountains, in a place the ancients called *Toyah.*

Unable to summon the strength to return to camp, Fermin eased himself into the cradle between two large boulders. The cool rock felt good against his skin and eased the throbbing pain in his head. Within minutes he was asleep.

He awoke with a start. He had no idea how much time had passed, but it was darker. The moon had moved far over into the western sky. Fermin could hear rushed sounds of violence coming from the camp, and he forced himself to his feet to peer over the rocks. At first the scene he witnessed made no sense. Men slipped quietly through the camp, stabbing those who were asleep in their bedrolls. He watched in horror as his Mexican *compadres* were dragged from wagons and killed, their bodies dropped casually in the dirt as the American soldiers slipped from one victim to the next with merciless precision. Fermin first thought they were Indians, but these killers worked silently, and they didn't look like any Indians he had ever seen.

He suddenly realized it was the *Americanos* doing the killing. It was over in a few minutes as he watched, frozen in place and shocked at the carnage. The Americans checked the bodies, systematically stabbing them again to make sure they were dead. Fermin knew that they would come looking for him once they figured out the body count was one man short. He looked around for an escape route but he was trapped in the small boxed swale and surrounded by high rocks on three sides. If he tried to run they would hear, and death would be certain. He hunkered back down between the two boulders and waited, unable to think, afraid to breathe.

When the predawn light broke it exposed a grisly scene. Fermin sneaked a look over the rock and was suddenly sick. He turned and threw up again, praying that they wouldn't hear. The six *gringos* were sitting around the fire, making coffee and cooking bacon, laughing and joking as if nothing had happened. He didn't understand their English but he knew what they were talking about.

They had found out about the treasure, that much was clear. And they would come looking for him, he was sure of that. He had to get away, but he would have to wait. He needed to gather his wits about him. And besides, they didn't seem to be in a hurry to find him right now. Maybe they didn't realize he was missing. He would wait.

When they finished their breakfast a couple of them saddled horses and rode off to the west, away from his hiding place. It was mid morning when they returned. Fermin watched as the six of them sat down and began to talk. Their voices gradually grew louder until finally, the leader shouted for them to be silent. They kept still as he spoke softly to them. Fermin could not hear what was said, but he knew that their leader was giving orders. When he finished speaking the men all stood and moved toward the horses and oxen that were tied and staked out at the camp's perimeter. Fermin watched as they harnessed six teams of oxen to wagons. Each of the men climbed up into the driver's seat of a wagon and drove it slowly out of camp.

He crept silently from his hiding spot, afraid they might have left a man behind to search for him. When he was satisfied that no one was there, he made a tentative approach to the campsite. He checked all twenty-two of his *compañeros* and found none alive. Each man had been stabbed through the heart, his throat cut. Fermin would be of no help to them now.

He rummaged through the camp gear and collected some hardtack, dried fruit, and cheese, along with two canteens of water and a large knife. He grabbed a long sabre and slid it into its sheath, then slipped a .50-70 caliber Sharps carbine into a rifle scabbard. He picked up two boxes of cartridges and two pairs of saddlebags, then stuffed the food and the ammunition into the saddlebags, along with some spare clothes.

Fermin found his own .44 caliber Walker Colt pistol and strapped it around his waist. Then he picked up his bedroll and found his saddle and bridle that were neatly laid out, military style, near the picketed horse herd. He chose a sorrel mare from the string and saddled her.

After buckling on his gear and bedroll and stepping up into the saddle, he paused to take a last look at the devastation. Then Fermin Macias turned the mare south, toward Mexico.

Stashing the Treasure

The confederates made three trips, each time driving the fifteen wagonloads of treasure to a hidden canyon about a mile to the southwest of the camp. Killing the soldiers had been easy enough. They hadn't had to fire a shot. No need to waste bullets on a few Mexicans. But this was something else again. This was backbreaking work.

They unloaded the barrels and drove the empty wagons back to camp, where they hitched the oxen to the next six and drove back out to the hiding place, returning to repeat the process. Now, as the last three wagons were driven to the hiding spot, all of the men rode along.

The cache was unimaginable. They had figured there might be one or two barrels with a bit of loot hidden in the flour, but every one of them was filled with treasure. Gold and silver, jewels worth a fortune. More than the men could ever have dreamed of. There was so much bounty that they couldn't carry even a fraction of it. They would have to stash it and come back for it, with more men and better preparation.

The plan was to hide the treasure and ride back to Missouri, where they could regroup and find enough men and equipment to recover the loot. Back in camp they set about erasing the scene of their crime. They gathered the fifteen wagons together, tied the Mexican horses and oxen to the wagons, and shot them all. They piled the bodies of the slain Mexicans against the wagons and doused everything with coal oil. One of them set a match to it, and as it burned he said, "I reckon it'll look like Injuns killed 'em."

It was perfect. No one would be looking for them now. No one but them knew about the treasure. Just before they set off toward Missouri, their leader took a bag of gold coins and divided the contents among the men. It was an act of good faith, and it would quench their greed until they could return from Missouri.

The treasure was hidden in a small cave deep inside a box canyon so narrow that it was barely wide enough to turn the wagons around. The cave was a short way up the side of the canyon wall, and carrying those forty-five barrels of treasure had not been easy, but it would be high enough to stay dry when the summer storms came and the flash floods filled the canyon floor with water. They piled boulders across the entrance so that it was invisible from down below. They would be back soon to open it up.

The sun was low in the west as they watched the fire. The men fell silent, but it was not out of respect for the dead. Each one was considering his own stake in this business and thinking selfishly of how he might grab all the loot for himself. The group remained lost in thought until they finally climbed onto their horses and rode off to the northeast. The stench of death was in the air and they wanted to make camp as far away as possible.

Six miles to the south, in a makeshift camp next to a sheltered spring on top of a rocky mesa, Fermin Macias watched the smoke from the fire and knew that he would have to return.

Fermin Finds the Treasure

The desert wind blew softly from the south as the young mare picked her way steadily down the sloping wall of the mesa to the desert below. Fermin leaned back in the Grimsley saddle and shifted most of his weight to his stirrups. He slacked his reins to give the mare her head and allowed her to choose her own footing down the precarious path. It was slow going, but the horse made steady progress until at last the steep rock gave way to loose gravel on the more gentle slopes at its base. They broke through the chaparral and onto the desert floor. Fermin picked up the reins and turned the mare toward the smoke that was still rising in wisps above the sage and buckbrush.

The horse and rider entered the plundered campsite at a slow walk, the mare nervous at the smell of death. Fermin dismounted and surveyed the charred remains of what was left of the people and livestock. He knew there was nothing he could do for his compatriots, and he didn't have the luxury of burying them because he had a more important job to do. He was sad for the loss of his friends, and he felt guilty that the first thing that had sprung to mind was that it was a terrible waste of good livestock.

He saw the tracks heading out of camp to the east and knew that the *Americanos* had taken the treasure that way, so he stepped back up onto the mare and turned her toward the southwest to follow the wagon ruts from the previous day. The wagons had cleared a winding path by brute force, breaking through mesquite and cholla cactus, crossing a couple of dry arroyos and bludgeoning a crude roadway up into the broken mesas that dominated this part of the Chihuahuan Desert.

Fermin was no tracker but he would have to be blind to lose this trail. He followed it well up into the *arroyos secos* until it was passing through narrow canyon gaps not much wider than the wagons. He was surprised that the *confederales* had made it this far with even a single wagonload of treasure. These slot canyons – *barrancos de renura*—held secrets that few knew. It was rumored that Benito Juárez himself had hidden in these ravines, and that the famous outlaw gangs of the James and Younger brothers had many hideouts salted away within the vast mazes of these remote desert canyons.

The tracks ended in the shadows of a narrow draw whose high sides blocked the sun for much of the day. Dismounting, Fermin struggled to find anything in the hazy afternoon light, but he saw the trampled plants and scuff marks on the rocks and sand, and they pointed in the direction the outlaws had carried their bounty. He followed the path a short way up the slope to the small cave. The entrance was freshly covered by rocks and branches, and further obscured by a large boulder that the gang had dislodged from above. If not for the tracks, Fermin would never have seen the cave from below. He knew that the first storm would erase the tracks, and that no one else would find it.

He dislodged a few of the larger rocks, just enough to slip inside the cave to make sure the treasure was there. Satisfied that it was, he walked back to his horse, keeping an eye out for any sign of the gang. He had no idea when they might return for their loot and he knew what they would do to him if they found him there.

The sun had dried every drop of morning moisture from the ground by the time Macias began the ride south out of the canyon and away from the treasure. The young soldier continually reined the mare in and turned to look back, knowing that a trail going one direction looks completely different when traveling back the other way. He needed to create a map in his head in order to return here. He could find his way back to the area, but he wasn't sure if he would be able to locate the narrow canyon or the cave. He kept track of his route by dead reckoning, memorizing his mental pictures of mesas, large rocks and trees, and other landmarks so he would recognize them later.

At the end of the third day's ride he pitched camp in the shade of a large acacia tree. He climbed up into its canopy and collected a small bag full of seed pods. He scraped off some of the tree's bark, then ground these up into a powder and mixed them together in a pan with water. He set it to heat over a small fire. While this was simmering he whittled the needles of dried cholla cactus into several sharp styluses. Once they were finished he emptied one of the saddlebags and cut it apart with his knife. He sliced away at the bag's goatskin lining until his efforts produced a large piece of the thin goat leather.

The simmering mixture was eventually reduced to a thick paste, the color of blackberries. When he was satisfied that it was ready, Fermin pulled the pan from the fire and set it to cool. He sat down and picked up a stylus, dipped it into the dark blue mixture and began to draw on the goatskin.

Fermin Returns to Mexico

After two more days of winding through the labyrinth of gullies and draws in the Toyah country Fermin Macias emerged onto a high desert plain. There were sandy hills to the east and the jagged crest of the Limpia Mountains rose behind limestone cliffs to the southwest. He rode through a narrow draw for a few miles before it emptied into a wide basin that meandered south toward the fort at *El Presidio del Norte*. He gave the mare her head and allowed her to follow the dry wash, then he turned her toward the east to avoid the fort and the American soldiers there.

The going was slow and he wished he could cover more ground each day. He needed to bring word of the ambush back to Emperor Maximilian, but he would not risk injuring the young mare. She was the only thing keeping him alive in this country, and a misstep could cripple her. Now was not the time to be left afoot.

The map had taken hours to complete. The tedious work left him exhausted by the time he finished. He was satisfied with his rendering and gratified that he had managed to remember so many small details about the trail that led back to the cave and its treasure. He wasn't sure about some of the names and their exact locations, but he was pleased at how his script looked on the smooth leather, with its graceful lines and flourishes that drew the eye toward the small landmarks he had illustrated across the chart.

He was not a *cartógrafo*—a map maker—but he knew the map he had drawn would be useful, and he was anxious for *El Emperador* to see it. Once the map was finished he laid it on a flat rock and allowed the ink to dry for the rest of the night. In the morning he rolled the goatskin tightly and tied it with a piece of leather thong that he had cut from the torn saddlebag. He slipped the small leather tube down into his high top cavalry boot where it now resided.

The mare was honest and surefooted and maintained an even pace through the rocky badlands. The pair headed eastward for another three days before turning south again. They finally crossed *El Río Bravo* near the trading post at *Lajitas* and made their way into Mexico. Fermin turned his horse to the south and headed across the Chihuahuan Desert toward *Chapultepec* and the emperor.

The transfer of the treasure had been kept secret, and none of the soldiers in his group had worn their uniforms. Except for his military boots, Macias was wearing civilian clothes and wasn't sure he would be able to convince any soldiers he met that he was on a mission. He had no papers and no way of proving who he was, so he continued riding south until he got to the village of *Las Mariposas,* where his luck finally ran out.

He was met by a ragtag group of men loyal to Benito Juárez . They arrested him and locked him in the small jail until he could be transported to their headquarters. Knowing his life now forfeit, Fermin asked for paper and pen to write a farewell note to his family. He wrote of his pride in being a soldier for the Emperor, and told his mother and brother that God would surely look after him. When he had finished the letter to his family he wrote another note, and kept it hidden from the guard.

Fermin managed to loosen a nail from the cell's weather beaten window frame and used it to dig away at the adobe wall. He carefully carved out the mud mortar around one of the bricks and freed it from the wall. Using the nail and his hands he broke the brick in two and crumbled half of it back into the adobe dirt it had been made from, scattering it around the dirt floor. He pulled the leather map from his boot, rolled the note inside it, and placed it in the recess, then covered it with the remaining half of the brick. He used his drinking water to make a small amount of mud to mortar the brick back into place.

Fermin Macias prayed that those loyal to Maximilian would find his map. He hoped against hope that *El Emperador* would somehow be reunited with his wealth, and that they would return safely to Austria. He didn't know that the emperor had already been captured and executed by Juárez 's soldiers, or that his map would remain in its hiding place in the *Las Mariposas* jail for a hundred years.

Outlaws

The days following the massacre were not kind to the outlaws. Murdock had cut his hand a couple of weeks earlier, and though it was only a scratch at the time, it became infected and swelled until it grew ugly and septic. During the first day on the trail back to Missouri his hand and arm were swollen and throbbing. His head began to pound and his heart was racing. The palm of his hand was purple, with dark streaks that ran in blotches across his wrist and up his forearm. He was dizzy and disoriented as he rode. He gasped for breath and struggled to stay upright in the saddle. By late in the day he had become delirious. The nearest settlement was Fort Concho, two days ride to the east, so the group changed course and headed there. Their leader needed a doctor.

The doctor took a cursory look at Murdock and instructed the men to carry him into the house, where they deposited him on a bed. The men spent the night camped outside the fort, drinking tequila and taking turns bragging about what each would do with his share of the fortune.

In the morning, foggy-headed and hung over from a night of Mexican liquor, the men stumbled back to the doctor's house, where even their bloodshot eyes could see that Murdock was in no shape to travel. They retired to the front porch and, after some heated deliberation, they agreed that they would head north and leave their leader in the doctor's care.

They discussed the plan with Murdock, who was barely conscious. It was decided that he would follow them in a day or two, once he was able to travel. They made plans to meet back in Missouri. Murdock could hardly sit up in bed, but knowing the others had ridden off without him left him angry and frustrated at being left behind.

The next morning, against the passionate objections of the doctor, Murdock saddled his horse and set off to catch up with his men. It was all he could do to ride, with dizziness and fever overwhelming him, but he wasn't about to allow his men to steal his treasure. Through sheer force of will he managed to ride for most of the day. He did not stop to rest because he knew that if he climbed down from the saddle he wouldn't be able to get back up on his horse again. Each mile he traveled was an eternity, a hell all its own.

Sick as he was, Murdock fared better than his companions did. He came upon them late in the day, lying in a heap, mutilated and scalped at the hands of a Comanche raiding party. They were left to rot in the hot sun. Their horses, saddles, clothing, and weapons were gone. Murdock was shaken by the grisly sight, but he was still so sick that he was unable to truly grasp the horror if it.

Barely able to stay on his horse, he pointed himself toward the northwest and made slow progress into the Texas Hill Country. There, he met a small group of cowboys headed to Denton with a herd of horses to sell. Murdock threw in with them, relieved to have some company.

His relief was short-lived because it turned out that they weren't cowboys at all. They were horse thieves on the run from the law. Just before the group reached Denton they were surrounded and arrested by the local sheriff and his posse, who had been lying in wait for them.

The men were tried and sentenced on the spot and were swiftly and summarily hanged right there on the trail. Murdock was spared because he was not a member of the gang. He was thrown into a jail cell and held for later trial. If found guilty, he would join the rest of the gang.

He grew steadily sicker in his cell. The town's doctor visited him several times and finally implored the sheriff to release him so that he could better care for the outlaw at his office. The request was denied, and as Murdock grew worse he knew he was not going to survive. He was the only person left alive who knew about the treasure, and he knew he was going to die.

Finally, when the doctor returned, Murdock told him about it all. He admitted his crimes during a guilt-ridden confession in a futile attempt at absolution. He managed to draw a crude map and gave it to the doctor. He implored the doctor to find the treasure. The physician listened patiently while Murdock rambled on about mountains of gold, barrels full of diamonds and rubies, and the hidden treasure worth untold millions.

The doctor took the map and made assurances to Murdock that he would find the treasure. This seemed to have a calming effect up the prisoner. Murdock died the next day in the wretched jail cell with no one there to witness his passing.

The doctor didn't believe the tale of treasure and riches. It was obviously the fantasy of a delirious man who was having visions brought on by his advanced malady. But the map he had drawn was compelling, and after considering it for a couple of weeks he decided it wouldn't hurt to check. So, with map in hand, he coaxed his friend, Denton's leading attorney, to accompany him on a trip west in search of the treasure. It would be a good excuse to get away and do a little hunting.

Their explorations bore no fruit, however, and after a three-week journey that consisted mostly of drinking and enlisting the services of local town prostitutes along the way, the pair finally gave up. During the ride home, while sitting in camp one night drinking sour mash whiskey, the doctor tossed the map into the campfire.

Part 1

Berkeley, May 1990

The two friends saw each other often over the years. The younger woman eventually came to live in the bay area, not far from the older woman's home in Berkeley. She had always been the younger woman's best friend.

Maybe the only true friend I ever had, the younger woman reflected, *she's been my sage, my mentor, my compatriot. She guided me through some rough waters and gave me a swift kick in the butt whenever I needed one.*

The previous year, the older woman was diagnosed with pancreatic cancer. She was 46 years old and grew steadily thinner and more frail as the months passed. Her friend visited her every chance she got. They would sit and bask in each other's company, not saying much, just enjoying being near one another. When they did talk they often reminisced about their time in Marfa, Texas back in the nineteen sixties.

"George used to tell us all about riding those freight trains with Sam," the older one mused, "Remember that? He sure could go on and on about things, couldn't he?"

The younger one smiled at the memory. "Yeah, George was one of a kind. Those two made a big impression on me that first day. Remember when him and Sam wandered into the cafe, when was that? Nineteen sixty eight, wasn't it?"

"Yep, the summer of sixty-eight," the older woman replied. "That was a year to beat all years."

"It sure was," the younger woman said.

Las Mariposas, Mexico 1957

Ignacio Santiago felt the heat of the sun on his shoulders as he chopped at the brown dirt with his *azada*, mixing the dark red adobe dirt with water and straw until the mud ran soft, like pudding. There was no breeze, and the Mexican sun baked his tools until they were too hot to touch. It was only May, much too early for the summer heat, but he had to pour water on his hoe just so he could pick it up. Ignacio had done the backbreaking work of the *adobero* his whole life, and over the years the hoe's long handle had grown smooth and taken on the shape of his hands.

He worked the small spade back and forth, pushing and pulling, chopping the dirt and forming it into a high mound. When he finished he carved out a dent at its peak, until it looked like a small volcano. He dragged the garden hose over and ran water into its caldera. By kneading the mud with his hoe and adding bits of straw to the mixture as he worked, the volcano's small crater grew steadily larger until there was enough mud to fill his *carretilla.* He shoveled the mud into the wheelbarrow, tossed his *pala* on top, and pushed the cart up the two-by-twelve ramp and through the front door of the dilapidated structure.

The adobe was built on the main street of Las Mariposas more than a hundred years before and had served as the village jail for most the time since. It was abandoned during the *Gran Depresion* of the nineteen thirties, when the housing of prisoners became a luxury that the small town could no longer afford. The building had been empty for more than twenty years, after the jail was relocated to Santa Rosa. The structure's mud roof no longer kept the rain out, and the *vigas* were sagging badly. It had long since become a home to snakes and scorpions. The occasional centipede fell through the cracks between the ceiling's *latillas,* only to crawl back to the adobe wall in its flowing, snake like cadence, to repeat the process.

Ignacio had been hired to restore the old building by a *gringo* couple from the north. They wanted a holiday home in Mexico and bought the place on a whim, sight unseen. He was glad they were not in a hurry like most *Americanos,* because it allowed him to work alone. Though he usually enjoyed working with his *compañeros*, these days he savored the time spent by himself, alone with his thoughts, and this job would see him through most of the year.

Rosalina, his wife of 38 years, had passed away two years earlier after losing a swift and painful battle with the cancer in her lungs. It was a cruel irony that she didn't smoke, but Ignacio had been *un fumador* his entire life. The loss dealt a crippling blow, and Ignacio gave himself up to his work and labors seven days a week, often for weeks at a time, in an effort to dull the pain. The wind had gone from his sails and he plodded through his workdays uninspired, focused only upon the task at hand, ignoring the quiet beauty of the world around him.

At the end of each day he made the slow walk up the dirt road to the cantina, ordered a beer, and made small talk with his friends. But he no longer sang along to the lively *rancheras* that played on the jukebox the way he did when Rosalina was there with him, back when they danced together on the cantina's porch in the setting sun and sang along to the music that drifted out through the open windows. He had lost himself in those dreams now, and when the dreams faded he walked home to eat dinner alone on the couch.

His daughter Suelita lived nearby, and her son Diego was a great comfort to him. Diego's father left to find work shortly after the boy was born and had never returned. Ignacio became more than just a doting grandfather to him. He was the boy's father figure, the man Diego looked up to. The two were inseparable, and the old man saw to it that Diego learned the things a young man should know.

Ignacio was repairing the mud walls in one of the three jail cells that were to be converted into bedrooms. He pushed the heavy wheelbarrow into the room and sighed as he let it settle gently to the floor. He was sixty-nine years old, too old for this sort of hard labor but determined to keep at it until he could push the cart no longer. It was a chore to get out of bed each morning, but he willed himself to his feet, dressed, and ate a quick breakfast and was out the door every day at dawn. He walked the path into the rising sun to his front gate and listened to the morning sounds of barking dogs in the dirt streets of Las Mariposas.

As the old man applied the mud coating to the interior walls of the old rooms his trowel scraped a loose adobe brick that was set into the wall in a haphazard manner. Its mud mortar has been torn away and gave it a distinctive rounded appearance that looked to Ignacio as if it had been disturbed at some point.

He set his *paleta* down and grabbed at the loose brick, wiggled it free, pulled it away from the wall to find that it was only half a brick, a facade set into the wall for appearance only. He reached into the hole to clean out any dirt and particles and found that it was deeper than it appeared—much larger than the brick that had concealed it. His fingers closed around an object hidden inside, and he pulled it out into the light of day.

It was a small piece of *cuero*—leather—that was rolled up like a cigar and tied with a leather thong. The leather appeared to be the hide of an elk or deer. Ignacio studied it for a moment. He carefully untied the leather string and unrolled the scroll to reveal a map—drawn in ink—with a place and date:

"La Tierra del Toyah"

A piece of paper fell out onto the dirt floor and Ignacio reached to pick it up. He opened the note that had been written ninety years before:

Para el buscador de este mapa -

Yo era un miembro de un grupo de soldados que transportaban las pertenencias del Emperador Maximiliano al Puerto de Galveston en Los Estados Unidos. Fuimos atacados por forajidos y todos fueron asesinados. Escapé escondiéndome. Los carros contenían la fortuna del Emperador. Oro y plata y joyas. La fortuna está escondida en una cueva en las tierras baldías de Texas, donde he dibujado este mapa. He sido capturado por los soldados de Benito Juárez y será enviado a la horca. Ruego a Guadalupe que nuestro Emperador esté todavía a salvo, y que le transmitas este mensaje de alguna manera.

firmado, Fermin Macías 26 de junio de 1867

To the finder of this map –

I was a member of a group of soldiers who were transporting the belongings of Emperor Maximilian to the Port of Galveston in The United States. We were attacked by outlaws and all were killed. I escaped by hiding. The wagons contained the fortune of the Emperor. Gold and silver and jewels. The fortune is hidden in a cave in the badlands of Texas, where I have drawn this map. I have been captured by the soldiers of Benito Juárez and will be sent to the gallows. I pray to Guadalupe that our Emperor is still safe, and that you will pass this message to him somehow.

signed, Fermin Macias 26 June 1867

Ignacio held the leather up to the daylight that shone through the window and studied the drawings on it. It was cut haphazardly into a rough rectangle. The map maker's hand had been that of a practiced artist, and though some of its lines were blurred by a slight running of the ink, the chart contained incredible details and renderings of landmarks and natural features.

Some names of rivers - *Arroyo Alamo, Río Perdiz, Río Cibola* -were familiar to him, though others were not. He recognized a few of the landmarks - *Fuerte de Davis, Fuerte de Laton, Chinali, Montañas de la Muerte, Muscalero, Pase del Rosa Salvaje.* Others were unknown to him - *pozo de agua del Coronel Johnson, agujero del hombre muerto.*

Small drawings of peaks, water springs, and routes through mountain passes have been meticulously recorded on it. And there, toward the upper right, near a place called *Escondite de Banditos*, was a small icon similar to *un Cruz de Hierro*— an Iron Cross— that marked the place where a treasure was hidden. Ignacio didn't know what to make of the map and the note, and he wished that Rosalina were there to explain it to him. She was always the wise one. He was often confounded by God's creation, but his Rosa knew the mysterious ways of the world and how best to deal with puzzles like this. She would have been able to tell him what to do.

He finished plastering the cell walls, then rinsed his tools and *carretilla.* Ignacio picked up the map and the note and walked the short way home. He would not stop at the cantina that evening.

Marfa 1963

The young girl was jerked violently from a sound sleep by the sickening squeal of tires sliding sideways across the two lane highway. The screeching stopped abruptly, replaced by pounding and loud thuds as the car hit the gravel shoulder and plunged off the road and down the embankment. The old Chevy's knee action suspension lost its fight against the sudden assault from the encounter with large rocks and weeds, dead logs, and the hard red dirt of the southwest Texas desert, and the automobile flipped itself end over end several times, cartwheeling until it came to rest upright in the dry creek bed at the bottom of the escarpment, sixty-five feet below the road above.

The girl was thrown forward and down to the floorboards behind the front seat where her mother sat. Her brother was in the back seat next to her, but his body lie twisted at an odd angle. His eyes were open but had a strange blank cast to them. The girl was pinned in place and struggled to free herself, but as was her manner, she remained quiet. She did not cry, did not scream for help. She did not call to her mother or father as she studied her brother for signs of life. She was deathly afraid, but oddly calm and kept her wits about her until she finally managed to free herself.

She was afraid to touch her brother, but she whispered to him, *"Jimmy! Jimmy, are you okay?"* She looked over the seat to her mother and knew that she was dead, crushed from the impact. Her eye caught the glint from the gold Saint Christopher medallion that had been torn from her mother's neck and now rested on the seat next to her, and the girl picked it up.

Her father was lifeless as well, caught behind the wheel and impaled by the steering column. The coupe's passenger door was jammed shut, crumpled beyond repair, and her only escape was to crawl out through the broken glass that clung to the rim of the back window. She walked a short way from the wreck and stumbled over the left front wheel that rested in the tall grama grass along the creek bed, severed from the car. She sat down on the tire, still clutching the small gold medallion, and turned to look back at the twisted wreckage. Alone in the dark with only the stars for company, the girl began to shiver as she waited for someone to come.

Vera DeSoto

Vera picked up the plate and wiped away the ring from beneath the coffee cup left there by the last customer of the day, a trucker who had headed back out to his big rig parked outside. She turned to put the dishes in the sink and saw that the sun still hadn't quite set. The days were still growing longer and the sun would be up for a little while yet, even this late in the day. Amy was busy replacing silverware and napkins, filling the salt and pepper shakers and the sugar jars.

Tired as she was, Vera enjoyed this time of day. It was the time when the locals had all gone home, when there were still a couple of trucks parked out front with their drivers talking on CB radios while their diesel engines idled in the dirt parking lot. Only a few cars and trucks drove by on the two lane highway that ran past the cafe. As a trucker once told her, "Marfa ain't exactly in the middle of nowhere, but anybody driving past ain't goin' anyplace."

She hadn't bought the place so much as inherited it. Three years of opening up in the morning, waiting tables all day, and closing up at night hadn't really prepared her for running it all on her own. Vera always suspected her boss, Johnny Morgan, was participating in illicit activities. She didn't know what, and she didn't really want to know. All she knew was that Johnny was a good man, and that was all that mattered.

Johnny had saved her from herself. He took her in and gave her a job six years before. She was headed down a road that she shouldn't be on, and if she had stayed on it she wouldn't have lasted much longer. Booze and drugs were taking their toll but honestly, they weren't the things that would be the end of her. No, the real threats were the path she had taken, the general direction she allowed herself to be steered, the wretched sorts of people she chose to fall in with, and the pointlessness of it all.

Drinking and drugs were a big part of all that, but they could be discarded. No, it was the people around her that pulled her down to their level and cheated her of her original dreams. She had given up on those dreams and no longer cared about her books, no longer listened to the lyrics of the songs she loved. Hell, she couldn't even remember the last time she read anything back in those days. Life was just a constant search for a party, a hedonistic journey that steadily emptied her of her aspirations, plans, and any goals she once might have had.

But fate had put her there, alone in a Marfa cafe, sitting in a booth and nursing a bottomless cup of coffee for three hours. She had been dropped at a truck stop back in Van Horn and she took the first ride offered, from an oil rig worker on his way down to the gulf coast. As they drove east along the two lane highway his behavior gradually changed from polite to aggressive, and he made his desires and intentions plainly known. When he pulled off the road in Marfa to fill up his pickup truck, Vera grabbed her small satchel and hopped out, and told him to fuck off.

Johnny watched her there in the corner booth, staring down at her coffee and looking like she had reached the end of her rope. And then he came to her rescue. He offered her a way out and she took it, no questions asked.

It started as a job, no strings attached, and for that Vera was grateful. Johnny was a strange one, a single man in his mid-fifties who wasn't looking for a woman and didn't expect anything extra in return for his generosity. He paid her promptly every week and let her live in the small apartment above the cafe. Aside from her work in the cafe, the only thing he required from Vera was that she stay away from drugs and alcohol. Otherwise, he steered clear of her personal life and left her alone.

Johnny had no pets, no close friends, but everybody in the area knew him. He often left for two or three days at a time and when he did he told Vera to open and close as she saw fit. He didn't seem to care if she opened the cafe at all when he was gone, though she was religious about sticking to the posted hours.

Vera never found out where Johnny went on those trips. He didn't offer the information and she never asked. Their relationship was a distant one, at least on the surface. They made small talk about the weather, politics, and the running of the cafe. Johnny taught her how to cook in the ways that short order fry cooks cook, and Vera was good at handling even the roughest truckers and cowboys who came in off the road, knowing all the while that Johnny had her back if things went wrong. They never did, and she was grateful for that. She steadily grew into the job so that by the time Johnny left for good, it just seemed natural to take on the running of the place.

After two and a half years, Johnny came in one day to tell Vera that he had come into some money and wanted to retire. He would be leaving Marfa for places unknown (yet another piece of personal information he declined to share with her). Vera objected when he sat down with her in that corner booth and signed over the cafe to her. She would have none of it and flatly refused. She would not be a charity case. She would stand on her own feet, make her own way in the world. Johnny persisted and finally convinced her to buy the place from him.

"How much do you want for it?" she asked.

He told her she could make payments whenever she could, and not to worry if she missed one. He wouldn't name a price, wouldn't say how much the payments should be. That would be up to her. He said only that she should stop paying whenever she felt she had paid enough. He gave her the number of a bank account in Alpine where she could deposit payments, and that was that.

The next morning his pickup truck was gone, and the keys to the cafe were on the counter when she came downstairs from the apartment. She had not seen or heard from him since then, over three years ago.

After a little more than a year Vera realized that Johnny wasn't coming back. Little by little she moved into his house at the back of the property. It wasn't so much a move from the tiny flat above the cafe as it was a gradual migration. Over a period of months she replaced his furniture with items she bought second hand. She packed his belongings, a few things at a time, and moved them into the shed at the rear of the house.

She kept thinking he would return for them, but after a year she knew that wasn't going to happen. Finally, she stored some of the more fragile things in the apartment above the cafe and got rid of the rest. She painted and cleaned and slowly remade the old adobe house into a real home. It wasn't fancy, but what Vera had done with it revealed more to her about herself than she had ever known.

She was lonesome, but she wasn't lonely. At least, that's how she liked to think of herself. She occasionally took a man home for the night—never more than two or three nights. It helped to break the spell of endless nights of solitude, though she hadn't allowed it to happen for a long time. And with Amy being around a lot Vera kept thoughts of lovers at bay. She didn't yearn for a partner, had no longing for a man in her life, though sex and a warm body were nice once in a while.

Vera liked living alone, enjoyed her independence, and relished the challenges that the cafe and the house offered her. She was thriving. She started reading again, and started listening to the lyrics of the songs on her records. She even started to secretly write some of her own.

She had grown to love the desert and the people in Marfa. They were a respectful lot, a breed who kept to themselves and didn't ask questions. They were people who didn't care who you were in your previous life. And every single one of these desert folk had had previous lives, that was certain. She knew she could always count on them, that they were there for her if she needed them. For the first time in her life Vera felt as though she had found a home.

Marfa, Texas 1966

There wasn't much going on in Marfa that thirteen-year-old Amy Hidalgo didn't know about. Truth be told, there wasn't much going on in Marfa at all in 1966. Still, Amy always knew where the action was, who was playing pigeon in the alley with coins they'd swiped from the news stand, where to score some weed, and how to get into either of the town's movie theaters for free.

Amy didn't hang out with the popular crowd. She was just a skinny mixed-race kid who was trying to hold things together until she was old enough to leave for good. Her Mexican heritage marked her as an undesirable at school, a target for ridicule and bullying by those she viewed as rich white kids whose ranching families controlled everything. Later she would come to realize that, by world standards, they weren't rich at all. And as for the white kids who weren't rich, well, they always fell in line and followed whatever the rich ones did.

Marfa wasn't much of a town then. Amy hated living there, though she would eventually grow to love it. She viewed the town as a feeble old desert queen, a stoic spinster standing silent and proper, an old maid who was too stingy to offer much in the way of entertainment or diversion for a teenager like Rosa Amarilla Hidalgo. She was a small girl, but she always thought her name more than made up for her size. In English it meant *Yellow Rose Gentleman*. She wished her last name had been Hidalga so she could be Yellow Rose Noblewoman. She enjoyed the fantasy of being a rich countess or better yet, an empress.

Marfa didn't offer amenities. TV reception was spotty, which suited Amy because there wasn't a TV at her house. There were no shopping malls or arcades or other places for young people to hang out. Most of the activities for Marfa's teens consisted of school dances, pep rallies, and football games. Amy never felt a part of the school scene, never felt like she belonged. She didn't fit in at these events, and so she avoided them.

Parents in the area let their kids run wild, and Amy figured that was just a part of living so far from civilization. Let the kids be kids. Let them blow off some steam. Harmless fun and all that. They'll grow out of it. At least, most of them will. Amy got into her fair share of trouble and didn't think about the prospect that maybe she would never grow out of it, that trouble would follow her for her entire life. She concentrated on today. She would let others worry about tomorrow.

For Marfa's teenagers Friday nights usually included drinking and driving and making out on the Nopal Road near the old Army airfield. The weekend hours seemed to be filled with young men in pickup trucks, trying to prove to each other how much liquor they could hold. Those trucks often ended up in someone's pasture after being drunkenly steered off the road and through the pasture's barbed wire fence. Other activities included tipping cows, lighting off half-sticks of dynamite stolen from someone's father's barn, and climbing the town's water tower to paint lewd remarks on its sides. The boys got to do all of this while girls sat and watched and cheered them on.

Amy never tipped a cow, mostly because she wasn't included in any of those activities. To be honest, she was just as happy to stay away. For as long as she could remember, she had been a loner, a nonconformist. She was comfortable with only herself for company. Amy was biding her time until she finished high school, though she didn't really know why she felt the need to get a diploma. Maybe it was because she remembered her mother telling her how proud she would be when Amy grew up to be a doctor or a famous painter or maybe even president of the United States. But her mother was gone now, and it didn't really matter anymore. Still, she made a half-hearted effort to stay in school. But to Amy, the best graduation gift you could get for a senior at Marfa High School was a bus ticket out of town, and that was still a few years off. She would only be starting ninth grade in September.

Marfa boasted having two movie theaters, the Palace and the Texas, right across the street from each other. And while the cinematic choices weren't the greatest, each of the air conditioned buildings offered a chance to escape the relentless summer heat. During the summer the movie theaters were crowded in the middle of the day, filled with folks enjoying some relief from the burning sun. At many matinees there were more people asleep than watching the movie. Some of them snored their way through two or three showings of the same film.

Amy didn't really mind sitting through multiple viewings of "The Ghost and Mr. Chicken", or "That Darn Cat". It was worth it. And when Henry, the ham-fisted fat boy who was her brother's age was on duty at the Texas he gave her an endless supply of popcorn and soft drinks. He was two years older than Amy and she knew he had a crush on her. As a street-savvy thirteen year old, Amy didn't hesitate to use it to her advantage.

Movies not only offered escape from the oppressive June heat, they lured Amy away from the hard realities of life at home, from the darkness of the small squatter's shack she shared with her father. It was a depressing place, a closet-sized shanty that felt like a prison, where the interior walls had no sheathing and the framing studs were exposed, where the cracks in the walls let the moonlight and the cold winter wind pass through like water through a sieve. The summer rain pounded across the leaking tin roof and created a jarring, droning dissonance that made Amy want to scream sometimes. The ghosts from her past came to haunt her during those long summer days and those movies provided an escape.

She had no brothers or sisters—not since Jimmy and her mother were killed out on the Fort Davis highway. Her father, Francisco Hildalgo, was drunk at the wheel with his wife beside him and their children in the back seat. Three years later she still couldn't understand why her mother and brother were dead and her poor excuse for a father was still alive, still the drunk he had always been. The ghosts that visited her dreams reminded her that he wasn't the only one who survived. She still had not figured out how to live with her guilt.

Amy's rebellion against authority started soon after the crash. The shock of losing both her brother and her mother sent her deep into a self-protective mode and she began to develop a hardened persona, a shell that protected her from being abandoned again. Of course, her father's absence didn't help, nor did his drinking when he was home. Each one silently blamed the other for the loss of their family.

Jimmy Hidalgo was two years older and Amy idolized him the way little sisters look up to their older brothers. Jimmy seemed to have everything figured out. She never understood how he knew the things he knew. It amazed her, the things he could do.

Jimmy was full of life, always at the center of the group of friends. He told jokes that made everyone laugh. He was the one everyone looked to for ideas about what to do next. And he wasn't afraid to take Amy along with him on his adventures, never afraid of what the others might think about having his little sister with him. She loved him for that.

And Jimmy had given Amy her name.

"Rosa's a Mexican name," he said one day, "and so is Amarilla." He put both hands on her shoulders and looked into her eyes.

"You're American, not Mexican. I am going to call you Amy," he told her. She was five years old and was thrilled at this. Their parents protested, but the name stuck.

Their father had crossed the river from Mexico when he was fourteen, looking to make big money in America. The pay for Mexican nationals turned out to be a lot less than people had said it would be. Francisco Hidalgo labored at countless odd jobs until he signed on as a roughneck on an oil rig near Odessa. The pay was good and the comaraderie of the hard living oil workers seemed to suit him. He met his future wife, Myra in a pool hall in San Angelo. She was a fiery Irish redhead with a free spirit and a flame in her eyes. Francisco was smitten.

He was a mean drunk. His alcoholic rages usually took a turn toward the physical, leaving him with various battle scars on his face and hands, and a twice-broken nose. These were the result of Friday night fights in local honkytonks. Not surprisingly, Myra became another of his conquests, her bruises a testament to her husband's mixture of anger and alcohol.

Francisco had been a functioning alcoholic all of Amy's life, and after the car accident a bitterness took hold of him. It was a resentment that never left. Not surprisingly, he aimed his anger at the only other survivor and convinced himself that somehow the accident had been his daughter's fault. He never threatened his daughter with physical abuse, but the mountain of guilt and emotional baggage he heaped upon her more than made up for it. It didn't take long for Amy to learn to avoid him.

She stayed away from their dilapidated homesteader's shack and wandered the streets of Marfa when he was home from the oil fields. She learned the ins and outs of life on the south side of town. Truth be told, she was grateful that her father had somehow managed to keep his job on the oil rigs up near Midland because it kept him away from her. He left for two or three weeks at a stretch, and Amy knew that he preferred the rigs to being at home with her. Francisco opted for the hard drinking and violence that were the norm up there. His daughter knew he felt more at home with his oilfield buddies than he did with her.

When Francisco headed off to the oil fields he left Amy with a few dollars and a hungover promise to return soon. She hid her loneliness from others and acted as if she lived a normal life. The arrangement suited Amy. She hid the fact that she was living on her own. She didn't want the child welfare people to come for her so she tried to keep her head down and her nose clean. The trouble was, she was her own worst enemy. She was hotheaded and impulsive, and she was living in a world she hadn't chosen.

Deep down, Amy knew that the day would come when her father would not return. She tried her best to put it out of her mind, but when the night grew dark and the clapboard walls of the little shack seemed to press down on her, the isolation crept in and held her captive. It was like being clamped in a vise, alone in the darkness until the gray streaks of dawn lit up the eastern sky and the morning light came to rescue her.

Amy Meets Vera

Amy met Vera in 1966, the year before her father died. Vera had been a casual acquaintance of her mother's. They knew each other the way people often know other people in a small town, the way you know the mechanic at the garage or the checkout lady at the market. Amy remembered eating with her mother at Vera's cafe when she was small, and she had seen "the cafe lady" around town a few times. Their friendship got off to a rocky start. They had never had a proper conversation until Amy was thirteen years old, when Vera caught her stealing a pastry from the case in the cafe.

It was at the end of the day, after the last of the customers had gone and Vera was mopping up and stacking the last of the dishes. Amy crouched in the shadows outside, watching through the front window. When Vera disappeared into the kitchen Amy made her move. She slipped through the front door and quietly tiptoed across the black and white checkerboard linoleum floor to the counter, where she silently lifted the glass lid that covered the slices of cake and pie. Reaching in, she slipped a piece of apple pie into her coat pocket, then as quietly as she could, replaced the pastry cover and turned to leave. She came face to face with Vera, standing between her and the front door, hands on her hips, eyes glaring.

"And just where the hell do you think you're going with that, young lady?"

"No place."

"No place? It looks like you're goin' *SOME* place. You were fixin' to head out of here without payin', weren't ya?"

"It's just a piece of pie." Amy was scared out of her mind but I put on a show of defiance.

"Well now, that might be. But it's *MY* pie. It ain't *YOUR* pie until you pay for it."

Vera stared at Amy a while, until the girl started fidgeting and looked down at her feet.

"So, do you have money to pay for that piece of pie? That'll be eighty cents."

"I don't have any with me."

"Well then, I reckon we'll just have to head over to your house and talk to your father about this."

"He ain't home. He's gone to work," she lied.

"What time does he get home?"

"He won't be back for a couple of weeks, maybe longer. I don't know."

"What?" Vera paused, then lowered her head and looked Amy in the eye.

"Who's taking care of you? Is there someone there we can talk to?"

"Nope. It's just me."

Vera grew quiet. "Just you..." she said, more as a statement than a question.

She looked hard at Amy, studying her face, and noticed for the first time the tattered shirt and blue jeans, the dirty hair and unwashed hands and face. Amy looked back at her defiantly but was suddenly afraid. Vera reached out and grabbed the girl by the shoulders, spun her around, and guided her back to the counter.

"Well, in that case, I reckon you better take a seat. A piece of pie ain't gonna be enough for dinner," she said, and she went back to the kitchen to fire up the grill.

Taylor Brooks 1966

At about the same time Amy Hidalgo was coming face to face with Vera DeSoto in Marfa, Taylor Brooks was checking herself in her mirror before she headed to her meeting. *I look good, even if I do say so myself,* she thought.

Taylor had been an overachiever from an early age, which came as no surprise because her father was a long-tenured Harvard Law Professor and her mother head of Neurosurgery at Brigham and Women's Hospital. Self entitlement was bred into her, though she had to strive constantly to please her parents and to make them proud of her. For the most part, she succeeded.

Neither parent was overjoyed at her choice of Harvard Business School, nor of business as a career path, but they supported her efforts, nevertheless. Shortly after graduation she met Jackson Braun and, to her parents' disdain, she accepted the job he offered her.

Braun was New York's leading art dealer, a high rolling wheeler-dealer who ran in the most elite circles among New York's avant-garde. His wife, Harper, was the heiress to a massive family oil trust. They were young, rich, and powerful, and Taylor lost no time in making herself an invaluable asset to them.

To Jackson Braun, Taylor Brooks was a dream come true. Armed with her Harvard MBA and a steel trap memory, she was a machine when it came to numbers and accounting. She created flowcharts in her mind, and by merely reading the numbers on a P&L sheet she could visualize a company's strengths and weaknesses and could see where it would be in five years' time.

She was far more than just a computational wizard; Taylor had a sixth sense about business, and with it an ability to make bold decisions based on hunches that seemed to come out of thin air. Her intuitive leaps resulted in investments that even the most daring and impetuous hedge funders would shy away from. But those hunches paid off handsomely, and they quickly delivered her from a drab third floor flat to her own penthouse apartment on New York's Upper East Side.

She took the elevator to the lobby, where a driver was waiting to take her to her meeting with Jordan Hayes. She was just getting to know him, but she knew he would fit into her plans quite nicely. Hayes was a full professor at Cambridge, where he was performing groundbreaking research for NovaTrine Labs, a huge multinational pharmaceutical company headquartered in upstate New York. NovaTrine had its fingers in every bioscience pie in existence.

Professor Hayes was one of the world's leading authorities in biogenetics and cloning. So far, his group had managed to clone tree frog guppies, salamanders, and various species of sea urchins. According to Jordan, they were close to cloning a rabbit, and they had their sights set on sheep and cattle. It was the stuff of science fiction, and it excited Taylor.

It had been easy for her to coax Hayes into violating his NDA and getting him to talk about his work. Taylor smiled when she saw how readily he would share trade secrets with her. All she had to do was to flirt a little. Jordan was a nerd, first and foremost. Brilliant though he might be, he couldn't help himself when faced with the opportunity to impress a beautiful woman with his knowledge and ideas.

As the two faced each other over the restaurant table, Hayes was letting on that they had, in fact, cloned a calf that lived for almost two weeks. It was a Guernsey cow, grafted from the cells of a year-old heifer, and its markings and genetic markers were an exact match to those of its mother/sister. Jordan explained to Taylor that a clone had no parents, only siblings. A clone was an exact copy of its predecessor.

The wheels in her head were spinning as she thought about how she could profit from this knowledge. While he was explaining some of the benefits from cloning, Taylor began to formulate a plan.

"You see, Taylor," Hayes was mansplaining, "the cloned individual is a *replica* of the original. It's a lot like making two prints from the same photographic negative."

"But what good does that do?" she asked innocently.

"It's not a matter of *good* or *bad*," he continued, "it has to do with how we can capitalize upon the unique aspects that a cloned birth provides."

Taylor looked at him with her eyes wide, ignoring his condescending explanation. She pretended that his descriptions were far over her head, but she was already fully aware of possible benefits. More so, in fact, than Hayes was.

"The cloning process provides a roadmap for us, one in which the car we drive can be big or small and can carry any manner of passengers."

Taylor was puzzled. "What does that mean?"

"Well, it means that theoretically, we can make the clone as big or as small as we want, depending on how we control the cellular differentiation. We could create a giant mouse or a tiny elephant, at least in theory."

"And just what good would that do, having a tiny elephant?"

"Oh, that's not really the point. You see, another aspect of all of this is the idea of altering a female mammal's genes to produce milk that contains specific pharmaceutical ingredients. These ingredients could be used by humans. For instance, you could milk the cow and get a vaccine for polio. Or, the cow gives milk that has medicine to treat cancer. That sort of thing."

"Wow! You mean you can milk medicine from a cow?"

"Well, it's not as simple as..."

"That would change the world, wouldn't it? I mean, anyone who figured out how to do that would make a fortune... no, they'd make a hundred fortunes, a *thousand.*"

"Again, like I said, it's all very hush-hush and it's in the early stages now. And goats would probably be better candidates for that, but we're making progress. The trouble is, we're having some difficulty with financing, with getting the bigwigs at NovaTrine on board with us."

That last bit struck a nerve with Taylor. She asked, "And you say you can make a cow as big or little as you want?"

"Oh, not yet. That's a little ways off. But there's no reason we couldn't, at least in principle."

Taylor set her dessert spoon down and looked across the table. "Let me ask you this, Jordan. How much money do you need?"

The wheels in Taylor's head were running full throttle and she thought, *What I wouldn't give for a giant cow...*

Cloning Cows

"How much do you know about cloning?" Taylor asked Jackson Braun.

She sat with Braun and his wife, Harper, at their breakfast table on the terrace of their Fifth Avenue penthouse apartment, overlooking Central Park. Taylor watched his expression and stirred her morning coffee as Jackson studied the papers she had given him.

"How would that work?" Braun asked as he looked over the portfolio and prospectus that Taylor had given him. He couldn't make sense of it all. Harper looked on but it was obvious that this discussion held no interest for her. Still, she wanted to play an active role in her husband's business ventures, so she tried to stay focused.

"It's simple," Taylor replied.

"Yeah, simple for you, maybe. But we mortals don't have the brain capacity that you have," he quipped.

Harper laughed. "Wow, Taylor. You are such a brainiac. I don't know how you do it. This looks like... well, I don't know *what* it looks like. But my gawd... it's very impressive." She was mostly looking at the photographs in the portfolio, ignoring the graphs, flow charts, and descriptions that accompanied them.

Taylor looked back and forth between the two, "Jackson? Harper? Okay, it works this way. We buy into the project at a leveraged forty-eight percent, offering to prop up the running costs for the time being, and then we trade for a lion's share of the company later on by issuing blank stock receipts as collateral. They call them 'junk bonds.' It's no problem."

"I don't know what you just said, but I trust that you know what you're doing, Taylor," Jackson said.

"Look, I don't see how we can miss," she said, a bit too excitedly. Taylor had to force herself to slow down here and began to breathe slowly, concentrating on calming herself. This prospect was exhilarating, but she needed to refrain from the hard sell to Jackson. If he thought that she was overeager it might spook him.

"I mean, even if they don't manage to clone a cow, we're looking at millions in tangible assets from the patents and copyrights alone." She paused to let that sink in. When Jackson looked up from the portfolio, she added, "We can also leverage even more equity by moving the lab out to

Texas."

"What? Texas? Why Texas?" he asked.

"Out to your ranch in Marfa. Can't you see?" She opened the portfolio to the back pages and laid it out on the table. She pointed to a large color photo in which a mockup of the lab buildings was superimposed onto a photograph of the dry Texas desert.

"Oooh... so, we'd have a laboratory on our ranch!" Harper exclaimed, "Oh, how exciting!"

"The thing is," Taylor continued, "we have the space there to do the work. A herd of cows won't attract attention there, and the lab people can go about their business undisturbed." She paused for effect, "Plus, it puts the operation in our hands and keeps it away from the prying eyes of NovaTrine."

"Well, I'm pretty sure they're gonna want a say in the whole deal," Jackson said.

"Oh sure, they'll still have a controlling interest at first, but we'll be the hands-on operators and will make the big decisions, especially while we're footing the bill."

Jackson looked at his wife. "Whattaya think, honey?"

"Does this mean that we'll get to have some real cowboys on our ranch?" she asked.

"I think it does," Taylor replied with a smile.

"Far out! This sounds like fun! Let's do it!" she cried.

Orphaned

Amy spent three and a half years mostly alone, after losing her mother and her brother. That was a long time for her, a third of her life back then. Her old man had given up trying to be a father and spent his time away at work in the oil fields up near Midland. He was often gone for weeks at a time.

It was early in 1967 when Amy ran into a man on the street. She knew right away that he was an oil field roughneck, with his denim pants and shirt and his Caterpillar ballcap and cowboy boots like a uniform. His face and hands were darkened by a tan that ended at the shirt collar and cuffs. He towered over her and blocked out the morning sun. She recognized him as one of the men who worked with her father on the rigs.

"Hello, Rosa." He paused as they passed each other on the sidewalk. Amy stopped and looked away awkwardly. She didn't like being called Rosa.

"How are you doing?" he asked.

She looked down at her feet, nervous and a little afraid of the man. Her parents and their friends called her Rosa, and Amy didn't care for it. "Okay," she replied.

"I'm sorry about your father," he said, and Amy turned to look up at him. "Sorry to hear about the accident up in Sweetwater."

It came as a shock, but she wasn't about to let it show, so she quickly erased it from her face and replied, "Thank you."

"Your father was a good worker," he continued, "are you going to be all right? Do you need anything? Do you have family to look after you?"

"No... it's fine," she stammered, "I mean, it's okay, I'm okay." Amy could feel the heat rising in her face. "Sorry, I gotta be going, thanks."

Amy wanted to run away as fast as she could, but she forced herself to walk calmly up the street, away from her father's friend.

She spent the rest of the morning wandering aimlessly, numbly thinking that she should do something, but not knowing what. She considered telling Vera, but then thought better of it. No one needed to know.

He's never around anyway, she thought to herself, *so it's not gonna make any difference to me.*

Finally, she headed to the Texas Theater, where the beguiled Henry let her in. She coaxed some popcorn and Coke from him and walked into the nearly empty theater, where she picked a seat in the center of one of the middle rows. She lit a cigarette and sat down to watch "The Incredible Mr. Limpet," still wondering if she should tell Vera.

Child Services

"Yes ma'am, I will. Yes, that's fine. I'll make sure she does. Thank you." Vera hung up the cafe's wall phone and finished scribbling in her notepad. She looked around.

"Amy, come here for a minute," Vera shouted, "Need to talk to you about something."

She looked into the kitchen but no one was there, then saw that the back door was open. She poked her head outside to see Amy hanging dish towels out to dry.

"Hey, I need to talk to you," Vera said.

"Sure, whatcha need?"

"Come here and sit down," Vera motioned toward the table on the back patio.

"Am I in trouble?" Amy asked tentatively.

"No, nothing like that," Vera replied. Amy joined her and set the rest of the dishcloths down on the table.

"I just got off the phone with the lady from child services," Vera told her, "she's concerned about some of the things you're doing."

"Like what?" Amy replied defensively.

"It seems as though you were caught smoking pot with your friends out behind the Saint George." She waited for Amy to respond. When she didn't, Vera continued.

"Look, it's one thing to be smoking cigarettes at your age—which you *shouldn't,* by the way—but it's another thing to get caught with dope. Are you hearing what I'm saying?"

"Yeah, but heck... I don't see why they don't just leave me alone." Amy's face was scrunched up tightly.

"Listen, you oughta be damned glad that it was Ernie who caught you. Anybody else, and you'd have gone to jail."

"Aw, we weren't hurtin' anyone," Amy said, "I wish they'd just leave us alone."

"Look, Amy... you can't go around doing whatever the hell you want, whenever you like. I've seen the characters you're running around with and I can tell you, they're not the kind of people you ought to be hanging out with."

"But they're my friends!" Amy shouted, a little too loudly, "I should be able to pick my own friends, shouldn't I?"

"Depends on who they are," Vera said, "and I'll tell you this, Amy. Those jokers are *not* your friends. Take it from someone who's been there. I know all about those sorts, and they're not who you think they are."

"That's easy for you to say," Amy said, "You have lots of friends. Everybody knows who you are, and you get to do anything you want." She was becoming visibly upset and Vera tried to head it off.

"Well, I'll tell you a secret, young lady. I don't have as many friends as you might think. How many parties do I go to? How many dates do I go on? Do you see people lining up to ask me over for dinner?"

Amy was taken aback. "Oh, I'm sorry. I didn't mean..."

"Look, that's okay. I'm just saying, I know how it feels to be your age, living in a place with nothing to do except get into trouble. But listen, Amy, you can't go on doing this. You've been ditching school."

Amy looked surprised.

"Yeah, you didn't think I knew, did you?" Vera continued, "You were caught shoplifting from the liquor store. Stealing *cigarettes,* for gawdsakes! And now you're smoking pot out behind the hotel, and doing god only knows what else." She paused to let that sink in. Amy looked down at her hands.

"I've turned a blind eye to some of this, but when they catch you smoking dope, well... I've gotta draw the line, Amy."

"I'm sorry," the girl said, still looking down and not wanting to meet Vera's stare, "I just want to be able to hang out with my friends. Kids in school don't like me because I'm a Mexican. But my friends don't mind and I can hang out and smoke with them, and that's cool."

"I know it *seems* cool right now, Amy, but listen to me. It's gonna lead you down a bad road." When Vera looked at her, she couldn't help but smile.

"Damn, you remind me so much of me," she laughed.

Amy looked up, "Why?"

"Because I was a badass when I was fourteen, just like you." She smiled, "And look where it got me!"

"Well, is that so bad?" Amy replied.

Vera shook her head. "Okay, look. Here's the deal. The child services are gonna come down here and take you away from me if you don't straighten up. That's the long and the short of it, *kapeesh*?"

"What? They can't take me away, can they?" she asked, startled.

"They damned sure can, and they will," Vera said. "Like I said, I just got off the phone with that child services lady and that's pretty much what she's tellin' me."

"Well, maybe I can try not to get in so much trouble anymore." Amy was subdued and sheepish. Vera thought that she was probably more embarrassed than anything.

"How about you don't get into *any* trouble anymore, okay?"

Amy shrugged and looked away.

"Look at me," Vera demanded, "Look here, at *me*!" She waited until Amy reluctantly looked up and met her eyes.

"I've got you, Amy. I'm here for you, and don't ever forget that." She watched as the girl's eyes began to water.

"But listen, you have to meet me halfway, okay? You have to do some of the work here, *comprende*?"

"Si," she said, "Está bien."

Amy and the Law

"Look, Vera… I don't want to be here like this," Ernie Sands said, "I've got a job to do and I just have to do it, that's all."

"Well you don't have to come in here, threatening a little girl like that, Ernie Sands. Shame on you!"

As a sherrif's deputy, Ernie Sands always tried to maintain an air of composure and confidence, but Vera intimidated him. Right now, he was actually a little afraid of her.

"Aw, I didn't mean to scare her, Vera. I was just…"

"You were just what, Ernie?" Vera was furious. "You come in here and threaten to take her away to child services? What the hell, Ernie?"

"Look, Vera. She's fourteen years old. Her parents are gone. She doesn't have any family to take her in. What am I supposed to do?"

"You're supposed to use your heart, Ernie, your *heart! THAT'S* what you're supposed to do!" Vera remained rigid behind the counter, grasping the dish towel with all her might.

Amy was crouched down on the floor in the corner of the kitchen, out of sight. Ernie had barged into the cafe and told her she had to go with him to the county court building. Amy ran into the back and began to sob quietly. That's when Vera had stepped in.

"What the hell's goin' on, Ernie?"

"I have to take her to child services, Vera. You know that. I've got my orders."

"I don't give a damn about your orders, Ernie."

"Look… she can't live in that shack all by herself. I know she hasn't had the easiest time, but she's been gettin' herself into a lot of trouble lately and I don't see…"

"You don't see? You don't *SEE!*" Vera was shaking her fist at him.

"She has no family, Vera. She's…"

"She's got family right *HERE!*" Vera shouted, "You're lookin' at her family. I'm tellin' you, *I'M* her family, and you damn sure ain't gonna take her away, Ernie. You got that?"

This gave him pause, and he considered it for a moment.

"You mean you'd take her in? You'd be her guardian?"

"I reckon I just said as much, didn't I?" Vera snapped.

"Well," Ernie turned toward Vera with a blank look. He was lost in thought.

"Let me see what I can do," he said and turned toward the door.

"And Ernie?" Vera called after him. He turned back to look at her.

She whispered, mouthing the words, "Thank you for that."

When she heard the door close, Amy stood up. She was sobbing, and Vera came back and put her arms around her.

"It's gonna be all right, my little girl. It's gonna be all right." It was the first time that Vera had ever seen Amy cry.

Bovine Clones

Watching Taylor Brooks was a lesson in efficiency. Point her toward a goal and nothing seemed to get in her way. By the spring of 1967 she had organized and engineered the move from New York to Texas. The new lab was already up and running, though it still lacked a few finishing touches.

At Taylor's request Jackson and Harper flew out to the ranch the day before and now stood with Taylor in front of an old hay barn and tractor building on a remote section of the ranch. Taylor was explaining the layout of the new lab as they stood in the doorway, looking at the rundown structure.

"Wouldn't it have been easier just to build a new building rather than try to restore this old wreck?" Jackson asked.

"Well, that's the point, Jackson," Taylor explained, "A big, shiny new building is going to attract a lot of attention, even way out here. Much better to leave the old one intact and build the lab inside it."

Taylor smiled as she opened a small weatherbeaten door and led them in, anticipating the shocked looks on their faces when they saw what was inside.

"I hate to say I told you so, but... well, I told you so," she said with a grin.

"My god, this is unbelievable!" Jackson exclaimed as he looked around. "It's like a nuclear reactor in here! How did... where...? I can't believe this!"

The barn's exterior, the planks of old grey barn siding that were hammered together with square, handmade nails, gave way to a modern interior that no one would have guessed was there. Row upon row of work benches filled with exotic equipment made of stainless steel and glass. Beakers were attached to glass tubing that wound its way across the benches. There were refrigerators filled with jars of various colored liquids, and an entire wall that contained several large reel to reel tape recorders, or what Jackson thought were tape recorders.

"We built a whole new building inside the old one," she explained. She pointed to the of tape recorders, "Those are actually computers," she said, "but I suppose you could play some Jefferson Airplane on them."

Taylor paused to let the enormity of it sink in, then continued, "They're used in sequencing the genome structures that the scientists explore in their research study."

"It's like something from a space movie!" Harper said, her eyes wide and taking it all in.

"Yes it is, isn't it?"

"How is this possible, Taylor? I mean, how did you manage to get all this done so fast?" Jackson was shaking his head in disbelief.

"Oh, I have my ways," she grinned, "I have my ways..."

There were several lab scientists—easily spotted with their white lab coats and pocket protectors that held mechanical pencils and slide rules—mixed with construction workers who were putting the finishing touches on the workspace. Three men stood on a scaffold, working on the overhead lighting system, while two others were attaching wall panels that would conceal the miles of wiring that had been installed in order to operate the state of the art computer systems. It was overwhelming.

"I expected this to take months, or even years, to get to this stage. But you've managed it in just a few weeks! You never cease to amaze me, Taylor."

"Thanks, Jackson. I flew the construction crew in from New York. Local workers would talk too much and we can't have word getting around. The lab boys were very anxious to move out here to the wild west and get to work. And it didn't hurt that I offered a few small incentives here and there to those involved in all of this."

Jackson smiled, "Well, I think this deserves a toast. How about we head back to the house and mix up some margaritas?"

"Sounds like a plan," Taylor replied with a grin.

The Camera

"When you're finished with the side work you can restack the clean dishes."

"Okay."

Vera enjoyed watching Amy as she attended to the small housekeeping chores in the cafe. It took Vera a little while to get used to having someone else around the place, but Amy was fourteen, and she had a way of growing on you. And once she got used to her, Vera couldn't imagine the cafe without the young girl. And to Amy, that felt good.

In some ways Amy was born for the job. She took to it immediately. She felt like she just fit right into the cafe's vibe. Vera never had to tell her twice about how to do something or when to do it. If it needed doing, Amy was on it.

The customers loved her. She took all the ribbing and the jokes in stride and gave back as good as she got, until even the most hardened of the truckers and cowboys had a soft spot in their hearts for her. Vera was amazed at how quickly Amy became "just one of the guys," and it made her heart glad.

After she moved in with Vera, Amy seemed to have given up a lot of her wayward behavior, though Vera knew the young girl still smoked a cigarette or two in secret once in a while. She knew that Amy joined her friends for a toke now and then, but there wasn't much she could do about it. She would have to trust that the girl would find her own way.

"When you're done, come upstairs. I've got something to show you."

Vera climbed the stairs and opened the door to the apartment. There was a little daylight left, but the place was dimly lit and she switched on the light. She opened the large walk-in closet in the living room and searched around in the back behind old clothing and stacks of towels and bedding until she found the box she was looking for. She pulled it out and carried it across the room, then dropped it onto the couch and sat down next to it.

The carton was filled with Johnny's old keepsakes and mementos. Vera had shoved it into the back of the closet when she was cleaning out the old adobe. She rummaged around until she found a leather case with a worn out strap attached, then carefully lifted it out and set it on the small table next to her. She heard Amy's footsteps on the stairs.

"Hi. Whatcha need?"

Vera looked at the girl for a long time, with a sort of considering look on her face, until it made Amy nervous.

"Did I do something wrong?"

"I don't know…. did you?" Vera replied. She enjoyed keeping the girl off balance. Amy shifted nervously as Vera kept a steady gaze on her.

Finally breaking the spell, Vera said, "Nah, don't worry about it. Come here and sit down."

She picked up the case and offered it to the girl. "Here, take a look at this."

Amy reached for it tentatively, then asked, "What is this?"

"Open it up."

She unsnapped the lid, opened the case, looked inside, and saw a camera. It looked pretty fancy to Amy, though she didn't really know what she was looking at.

"Wow, this looks pretty nice. Is it yours? I didn't know you were a photographer!"

"Nope, it ain't mine and nope, I'm not a photographer…least, not so's you'd notice," Vera said. She recognized the way Amy's face crinkled up into a puzzled look. It meant that the girl was hard at work, thinking and concentrating on something in particular. Vera stifled the grin that was forming and kept the stern look on her face.

"It ain't mine," she continued, "It's yours. That is, if you want it."

Amy was confused. "What? Mine? But I don't…."

"Look, I just thought it might be nice for you to have something to do. I know you like to draw, and I thought maybe you might like taking pictures, that's all."

Vera smiled at the girl's puzzled expression.

"Go ahead, take it out of the case."

"Uh… Well… I don't know what to say…" Amy gently picked up the camera and examined it.

"It's something that Johnny left behind, and it's just gonna rot, sitting in that box. And look, it's not just some cheap camera. It's a Nikon F. And if you don't know, that's a really good one. It's like the professionals use. And look here, there's more."

Vera reached into the old box and pulled out two more leather cases. She opened one and retrieved a long camera lens, then lifted it up to show Amy.

"See? There are some extra lenses in here. I don't think Johnny was a photographer... leastways, I've never seen any photographs around here, and he never mentioned it. Maybe he just traded it for something, I don't know."

"This is really cool stuff!" The young girl was becoming excited. "I don't know anything about taking pictures, but it might be fun to try."

Amy felt her face crinkle up again and this time the tears came.

"Nobody's ever given me anything like this before," she said, and started to cry. She wasn't the hugging type, but Amy threw her arms around Vera and clutched her fiercely.

Vera allowed the embrace for a few moments, then gently pushed the girl back. She held her at arm's length and looked at her.

"You know, Amy, if anything ever happens to you... well, I'm here for you. I don't want you to ever think you're alone, because you're not. I wouldn't ever let them take you away, you know that don't you?"

"Yeah," Amy mumbled, trying her hardest not to cry.

"Well then, c'mere." Vera motioned and pulled the girl back into a hug. A smile spread across Vera's face and she said, "We'll get you some film and I reckon we'll make a photographer out of you. And who knows? I bet we'll see one of your pictures on the cover of Life Magazine someday."

Part 2

Baton Rouge 1968

Vagrancy was the most common offense in Louisiana in 1968. Some say that there were more arrests for vagrancy than for all other crimes put together, and so it was that George Willow and Sam Hardwick were not unique in committing this particular crime. Louisiana law, as in most of America's states, equated economic status with crime. This enabled vagrants to be taken from the streets as criminals who were "likely to commit a crime." The lesson that George and Sam learned too late was that they probably shouldn't have tried to hitchhike through Baton Rouge, Louisiana looking like the long haired hippies that they were.

The boys were released after six days in a roach-infested cell. The bailiff tossed two duffle bags and two plastic bags full of clothes across the counter and pushed a slip of paper for the two to sign. He gave them an envelope that contained their money, along with a few bits of paper, pencils, and other items from their pockets.

"We catch you on the street again it's gonna be six months poundin' rocks on the pea farm for you," he warned them.

They emerged from the police station into the bright sunlight and made their way across the street to an alley to hide and to try to figure out their next move. There was a little over eight dollars in the envelope. They knew they couldn't start hitchhiking again or they would end up right back in jail, this time for a lot longer than just six days.

Sam suggested they try the bus. "We might have enough to get us across the river."

George's gaze was focused down the street on a sign with "Blood Bank" in large red letters.

"Look at that," he said, "let's see if we can sell some blood and get a few bucks."

Two hours later the two had another ten dollars in their cash reserves. The nurse gave them a pile of cookies and large cups of heavily sugared coffee and made them sit on a couch in the waiting room afterward. They were still wobbly as they made their way up the street to the bus station.

Nine dollars and change bought two tickets to Lake Charles. The two wouldn't quite make it out of Louisiana but they would figure that out when they got there. For now, they pulled their coats out of the duffel bag, stowed their gear down in the baggage compartment, and climbed up into the Greyhound.

"Just like Promised Land," George said.

"Huh?"

"Promised Land. You know, Chuck Berry."

Sam looked at his friend with a blank stare and George responded, "You mean you don't know *'Promised Land'*?" He shook his head. "Dang, son. How can you *not know* Chuck Berry?"

Sam just shrugged as George continued.

"It's a song about goin' to California, man. You know, he talks about ridin' a Greyhound across Alabam', getting' stuck in Birmingham."

Sam looked at him, "Well, then it's a good thing we're not headed to Alabama."

"You're missin' the point, man. We're goin' to California! We're goin' back to the *city,* man! We're headed back to the promised land, just like Chuck did."

"Yeah, I guess we are at that," Sam said as they headed down the aisle to find a seat.

Ebbets Fields 1968

Ebbets Fields glanced up at the passing Mississippi landscape and leaned back in her seat on the Greyhound bus that carried her down Highway 61. *Bob Dylan wrote a song about this road*, she thought as she took in the bewildering variety of trees and plants that seemed to claim every bit of land that wasn't paved.

She spread herself and her belongings over two seats on the bus. Only one other passenger was aboard, an older man who sat in the seat behind the driver. The two obviously knew each other and had carried on a conversation since the man boarded back in Natchez. She would be coming into Baton Rouge soon, where she would transfer to another bus that would take her home to Texas.

She enjoyed riding the big Greyhound, especially when it was empty like this. She could sit and read her book in silence, and if the road wasn't too rough she could even take out her drawing tools and sketch. She pulled her makeup mirror from her oversized Madras print purse and opened it. The face that looked back at her was pretty, with large green eyes that revealed a sharp intellect and an inquisitive mind. She squinted through her horn rimmed glasses at the small wrinkles that formed around the edges of her eyes.

Her wavy red hair was braided into a long, flowing strand of ginger that bore witness to her Irish ancestry. When she was outdoors she remained mostly covered beneath a large floppy hat because that same Irish legacy rendered her prone to sunburn. She wore several handmade bracelets on her wrists. Some she made herself, and others were made by hippie friends or by artisans she met at craft fairs and festivals.

At almost six feet tall, men found her height both attractive and intimidating at the same time. She learned early on that men don't really like a smart woman—even less if the woman is taller than they are. That fact was, she had never met anyone who could see past her unconventional appearance and into her soul, who saw who she really was. She was all smiles on the outside and mostly a wreck on the inside. She was lonely and alone.

Her relationship with Wayne Guidry had lasted nine months, though it had seemed like nine years to Ebbets. When the emotional abuse turned physical, she tried to leave. Calling the cops had not helped and, in fact, only made things worse. Wayne wanted to dominate her, to control who she was, and though he never really succeeded, Ebbets collected enough bruises that it was sometimes hard to tell.

She was returning to Texas from visiting relatives in Mississippi, where she caused a stir among the Vicksburg locals. She thought her rural Texas home was conservative, but compared with Mississippi, Texas seemed like California. People in Vicksburg didn't glance politely at her out of curiosity, they stared openly, out of shock and horror. How could anyone allow their daughter to dress like that?, they wondered. How could they allow her out in public? And to *Church*, for goodness sakes! She was used to being the odd person out, so Ebbets paid them no mind and enjoyed her stay with her cousins in Vicksburg. Still, she was glad to be on her way back home to Boerne, Texas. As the bus rolled down the two lane toward Baton Rouge Ebbets found herself thinking of her father.

Tom Fields was born and raised in Brooklyn, the son of Irish immigrants and a lifelong Dodgers fan. When Margaret was pregnant, Tom already knew what they would name the child, whether it was a boy or a girl.

"Just think, Maggie... Ebbets!" he told her, "Ebbets Fields. What a name! You can't go wrong with a name like Ebbets Fields". His wife would smile and say, that's fine dear. They both quietly assumed it would be a boy.

Maggie didn't make it through the day of her daughter's birth. When complications set in the doctors gathered in scrub rooms, nurses rushed to prepare the operating theater, the anesthetist assembled his collection of stainless steel gadgetry and attached all manner of hoses and tubing, needles and catheters, dials and meters.

Mrs. Fields was rushed to surgery where all of this expertise and technology was gathered and within minutes a crying ball of ginger haired energy burst forth into the world. In the same moment Ebbets was drawing her first breaths, her mother was gasping her last.

It took three days for Tom Fields to regain any sense of composure, to register that he was a single parent and that Maggie was not going to be there to see her baby girl. When the hospital administrator asked for the child's name he replied with the only thing he could think of. "Ebbets", he said. He and Maggie had not talked about a middle name so when they requested it he replied, "I don't know.... none, I guess."

And so Ebbets Fields, the namesake of the Brooklyn Dodgers' ball yard, came into the world with neither a mother nor a middle name.

Tom Fields took his daughter to ball games when she was small, but when Ebbets was seven he moved the two of them to Texas for a new job. He would never again see his Dodgers play ball. Ebbets had no real interest in baseball growing up, but she loved to listen to her father talk about his beloved team. He was furious when the Dodgers moved to Los Angeles, and he vowed he would never forgive them. But Ebbets knew that he loved them just the same.

In 1965 Tom Fields died of a heart attack at forty-eight years old. Ebbets was devastated. There were no relatives nearby to take her in, but because she was a senior in high school and would be eighteen in a few months, the local authorities allowed her to stay alone in the old house. A government woman from San Antonio stopped by to check on her twice a week.

Ebbets had no heart for school but she forced herself to show up for classes every day just to make it through to graduation. She knew her father would have wanted to see her graduate, and she wanted to make him proud. When graduation day finally arrived she donned her cap and gown and went through the motions of her valediction but stayed away from the parties and celebrations that followed.

Lightning Strikes

Lightning occurs when electricity bounces around inside a cloud, like feelings inside your heart. Some of those electric bits live at the top of the cloud, and others live at the bottom. They move around inside until they build up a charge and come together in a great flash of light and energy. When the energy stays inside the cloud and never touches the earth, it spends itself without leaving a mark, with only that flash of light to mark its passing. This is called sheet lightning.

But sometimes that cloud will sail through the sky until it passes over exactly the right spot on the earth. That place on the ground is filled with its own kind of electricity, like the feelings in someone else's heart, and it develops what is called ground potential. People who know these things say that the two are opposite charges, and that opposites attract.

But that's not really what's going on. The charges aren't really opposite— they're complimentary. They are not alike, but they are drawn to each other. They are two sides of a coin, two covers of a book, two halves of an apple pie. They need each other in order to complete something whole. And when that cloud passes over exactly the right spot, at exactly the right time, it sends some of that energy down, and the spot sends some of its energy up, and a bond is formed because there is ground potential. And then, ZAP! a lightning bolt is sent between the two and there is a tremendous flash and explosion when they finally connect.

Those who knew George Willow knew that he had fallen in love countless times in the past. He was always falling in love. He loved women and he couldn't help himself. He was a hopeless romantic, but his feelings were always sheet lightning. There was the strong attraction and the big flash, but the feelings always spent themselves because there was never ground potential. None, that is, until Ebbets Fields glided past him to take her seat on that Greyhound bus.

For a split second—for the tiniest measurement of time possible—their eyes met as Ebbets made her way toward the back of the bus. And as her cloud floated past George's seat—exactly the right spot—there was ground potential. And as rapid as was the meeting of their eyes, so too was the bolt and the flash and the explosion of the lightning strike.

Louisiana Bus Ride

George let his gaze follow the tall, slender young woman who made her way past and settled into a seat across the aisle, three rows back. He had seen his share of fine looking women but had to admit, she was strikingly beautiful, in a nerdy librarian sort of way. She wore horn rimmed glasses and had braided her red hair, which lent an academic look. This conservative impression was offset by the colorful tie dyed dress she wore, and the big floppy hat that seemed to engulf her.

Sam watched George when she passed. His friend had turned his whole body just to watch her as she took the hat off and placed it in the overhead rack. She retrieved one of the small pillows that you get on buses, and then she settled into her seat, pulled a book out of her bag and began to read, all in one smooth, elegant motion. Several beaded necklaces wound gracefully around her neck and glittered in the late afternoon sun.

George was hypnotized by it all and couldn't keep his eyes off of her. She wore several bracelets on each wrist that jangled together like wind chimes. Outside of New Orleans, she was the first hippie girl the two had seen in Louisiana, and George was instantly smitten.

"It's not polite to stare," Sam said.

"I could get used to this," he said as Sam was pressing the button that tilted the seat back. "Air conditioned, quiet... and we don't have to stand out there with our thumbs out. Plus, the scenery isn't too bad, either."

George waited for her to look up at him, which she took her time doing, and when she slyly returned his gaze he smiled at her, which caused her to blush and quickly look down to the book in her lap.

George stood up and turned to start back toward her.

"Really?" Sam asked, dumbfounded. "Just like that? You're gonna go back and hit on her just like that?"

"Well pard, you know what they say," George replied, "It ain't no use putting your foot down if you ain't got a leg to stand on," and turned to make his way back to sit down in the seat across the aisle from her.

I'll never figure that guy out, Sam thought to himself.

The woman made a show of ignoring him, but it didn't faze George in the least.

"Howdy, my name's George," he said cheerfully. She paused as if considering his statement.

"Ebbets," she finally replied, "Nice to meet you."

"Ebbets?"

"Yes, Ebbets. That's my name. Ebbets."

"Ebbets... hmmm. What kind of name is that?"

"My last name is Fields".

"Uh.... I'm not sure...," George stammered.

"Brooklyn Dodgers," she said. Nothing. George just sat there looking stupefied.

"Ebbets Field. It's where they played."

"Ah, right..." George finally understood. "So your parents named you after a baseball stadium?"

"Well, my dad. He grew up in Brooklyn... a diehard Dodgers fan. Never forgave them for moving to Los Angeles, but he still loved 'em. And since his last name was Fields, well..."

"Wait... I thought it was the LA Dodgers," George said.

She just looked at him, and when she didn't respond he blurted out, "What I mean is, I'm from LA!" She stared blankly at him. "Well, not exactly *from* LA," he said, "But I'm headed there!" He was flustered, but intent upon making an impression. Ebbets Fields just sat there motionless, watching him make a fool of himself.

"So, I guess we have something in common, don't we?" he asked.

"Well, maybe we do and maybe we don't," Ebbets said slyly, "but my dad would tell you that Johnny Roseboro is no Roy Campanella."

George's face twisted into a frown, "Dang, you've lost me. I don't know what that even means, but I'll take your word for it," he said.

He asked if he could join her for a while. Ebbets looked at him thoughtfully, as if appraising him, and finally said, "I guess that would be okay." She moved over to the window seat and made room. George was glad they had taken the bus now. So much better than hitchhiking, and he was already in love.

The bus stopped in Grosse Tete, where Sam got off to buy a candy bar. When he returned with the other passengers he saw his partner happily ensconced with the woman. He stretched out on the two seats, propped his jacket under his head, and as the big diesel bus pulled up onto the two lane he drifted off to sleep for the trip to Lake Charles.

"Where are you headed?" George asked Ebbets.

"I've been visiting my cousin in Vicksburg and now I'm going back home to Boerne, Texas," she answered. "It's a little bit northwest of San Antonio."

"Bernie? Kinda sounds like the name of a pizza place."

Ebbets laughed, "No, it's spelled B-O-E-R-N-E," she said, "It looks like 'Born', but it's pronounced 'Bernie'. Folks get confused with it."

"Well, what's life like in Bernie, Texas?" George joked, "I'll bet you break a lot of hearts there."

Ebbets blushed. "It's a pretty small town," she said. "They say that in Boerne, you don't lose your girlfriend... you just lose your turn." When she smiled at George he thought his world had caught fire.

They talked nonstop all the way to Lafayette, where the bus stopped to take on a couple of passengers. Ebbets found herself drawn to this man, and was surprised that she was telling him things that she normally kept to herself. She was still on her guard, but she really liked talking with George. She had never met anyone quite like him.

Ebbets told him that she had been majoring in art at the university in San Antonio. She said she was a painter, and George listened, entranced, as she rambled excitedly about her artistic influences.

"I'm really into expressionist painters like de Kooning and Jackson Pollock, and of course Pollock's wife Lee Krasner. And I love the big mural stuff by Guston and Kadish, and of course Diego Rivera and Frida." She paused, struck by a thought, "Oh, and did you know, Edward Hopper just passed away! Such lovely prints he made. What a shame."

She waved her hands as she talked, excited to share her passion. At the end of one of its flights her hand came to rest on his forearm and he put his on top of it and the lightning struck again, with the chill and tingling that comes with first contact. Ebbets paused to look at him. She smiled and continued, unshakable in her enthusiasm.

"I started my third year at UT San Antonio but I had to drop out. But I'm hoping I can get into an art school in New York or Chicago or someplace to finish my degree. My dad always wanted me to go to Austin, but I really want to study with people on the cutting edge. You know, in a *real* city, with *real* artists." Her face said it all, and George was caught up in her excitement. He had no idea what she was talking about but he could feel her reaching in and steadily taking ahold of his heart.

"New York?" he asked, a little too anxiously, "That's a long ways away."

"Yeah, I suppose it is."

"Well, what about California? That's where I'm headed." He fumbled and looked down, embarrassed, examining his hands.

"California is nice," she said, "but I really haven't given it any thought."

George looked up, "Well, I know there's UCLA and USC, and there's a school called Cal Arts, I think."

She turned once again to face him. He was obviously nervous. She smiled to herself and found it endearing.

"Well, maybe I'll keep that in mind," she said, "I suppose if I was in California I could go see the Dodgers play sometime." George looked up, hopeful.

"I've been mostly thinkin' about back east." and George felt the wind go out of his sails.

Then Ebbets added, "but Cal Arts is a really good school, too," and he felt another sudden rush of hope. He knew it was ridiculous to think she would have any interest in him, but George lived for his fantasies, and Miss Ebbets Fields was now a full blown fantasy, right there in the seat next to him.

When the bus finally pulled into the depot in Lake Charles, George and Ebbets were holding hands and talking in whispers, occasionally bursting out laughing at a joke, then quickly becoming quiet as they gazed at each other and smiled.

Sam woke up to the rush of wind from the bus's air brakes. When he looked back he saw the two were obviously smitten and unaware that he and George had reached the end of their ride. Sam stood and made his way back to get his partner.

"Hey, c'mon, pard. We've run out of bus ticket. This is our stop."

"Hey, Sam. Meet Ebbets. She's from *BERNIE*, Texas."

"Great to meet you, Ebbets," Sam said. "Really sorry we have to cut out on you, but this is as far as we're paid up." Sam could see the pain in George's eyes. He had seen this look many times before, but he couldn't help feeling a bit sorry for his lovesick friend.

"I'll write to you," George was telling her. "I'll call you long distance. And I'll come visit, I promise."

Sam had to prod George away. "C'mon, bud. The bus is leavin'. Really good to meet you, Ebbets. Hope to see you again sometime."

"And me you," she replied with a grin and a wink at George. As he started to stand up she leaned over and pulled him to her, then kissed him hard on the mouth. When she released him he drew back, gasping.

"God, where have you been all my life?" he said.

"You take care of yourself," she said, "and watch out for all those other girls. Remember, I'll be right there in Boerne. And you haven't lost your turn."

"Damn, that is one fine lady," George remarked as the two stood on the landing and watched the bus doors close. "I feel like a puppy in a room full of rubber balls."

Ebbets blew a kiss from the window, and as George watched the bus pull away, the skies in his world turned a little darker.

Ebbets

It had taken a while for the pain to ease. The loss of her father was devastating, but eventually Ebbets began to think about what might lie ahead. Art and creativity were in her blood, and she spent hours thinking about those things. She finally decided to move to San Antonio, where she could attend college. She was ready for a change, and she was surprised at how excited she was when the University of Texas accepted her application to start in the fall.

Ebbets settled into college and fell in love with academic life. Her eyes were opened to new ideas and new worlds, and to a community of like minded people. She threw herself into drawing and painting. She kept books full of her own drawings of birds and trees and people, and of make-believe places she wished she could visit, and she recounted these things in long passages in the diary she kept.

She met Wayne Guidry in May of 1967, at the end of her second year. What started out as a blossoming romance quickly turned sour. By the time she was halfway through the first semester of her third year Wayne was dominating her life.

He accused her of spying on him, then of cheating on him. His verbal abuse became physical and his violent behavior grew until he no longer cared if he hurt her. Ebbets had collected a fair number of scrapes and bruises by the Christmas holidays. Her grades were slipping and she knew she would have to drop out of school.

In early May she quit school. She kept it from Wayne so she could continue to be away from him during the day. When he found out, he hit her in the face with one of her books. She ran to the bathroom and locked herself in while he stood outside and pleaded with her that he was sorry. It was what he always did. And true to form, Wayne's remorse steadily changed to anger when she didn't respond. Finally, he was pounding on the bathroom door, demanding to be let in.

Ebbets looked at herself in the mirror. The woman who returned her gaze had a bloody nose. Her left eye was swollen and purple. She looked twenty years older than she was.

"It's time to go," she said calmly to her reflection.

She took refuge at a girlfriend's place and collected her belongings while Wayne was away. With nowhere else to go, she left San Antonio and headed back home to Boerne. Once there, she made plans. She would take some time to visit her aunt and uncle in Mississippi. They were forever asking her to come and stay, so she thought she would spend a few weeks with them.

She organized and stored her belongings, withdrew some cash from her small savings, locked up the house and gave the key to the neighbor for safekeeping. On the first of May, 1968 Ebbets bought a bus ticket to Vicksburg and headed north.

Lake Charles

The day had spent itself by the time Sam and George got off the bus in Lake Charles, but what remained of the pale sun still managed to make them sweat, even as it settled below the treetops to the west. It didn't cast itself in humid, feverish waves the way it would in July, but it was enough to cause them to drink water continuously, only to squander it in rivers of perspiration.

Still, after spending six days in the Baton Rouge jail, it was a relief to be outside in the heat of the South Texas day. They grabbed their grips and carried them around to the front of the building. Looking around, Sam pointed out railroad tracks running right beside the bus depot, but neither of them knew which direction led to the train yards. There was a gas station across the street, so they picked up their bags and hiked across to it, where they found a local roadmap and took it back outside to study it. When they found the railyards on it they set off along the tracks toward them.

Half a mile later the pair slipped unseen into the yards, keeping engines and boxcars between them and the railroad office. The boys kept out of sight until they saw a westbound freight train that was being made up. They worked their way along the side of the train until they found an empty car. They tossed their belongings inside and climbed in.

The pair had covered thousands of miles, had enjoyed the views from inside boxcars, and had learned most of their road lessons the hard way. They sometimes shared boxcars with old hobos who told them stories and added to their knowledge of the road. Much of it was nonsensical, and they knew that some of the stories were downright lies, but they always came away with a view of an alternate universe that they could never have imagined. They were well prepared when they found this westbound train and quickly made themselves at home. Twilight settled in as they waited to leave Lake Charles.

Once they were underway, George pulled himself to his feet and maneuvered to the door to sit beside Sam, who was busy waving at the people in the cars that were stopped at the street crossings they passed as the train gathered speed through the town. By the time they reached the city limits they were traveling at a good clip through the warm night air. The train made its way around a gradual curve, where the two could look forward toward the engines and back to the caboose. They saw that the freight train was more than a mile long. Their boxcar was somewhere in the middle.

The temperature dropped as the freight train moved farther into the growing darkness and they felt refreshed, glad to be back on the wanderer's road, happy to be headed back to California. When darkness came the fireflies danced in the night air to the steady clack of the wheels playing their rhythm against the big steel rails below. The music sang the two to sleep.

San Antonio

Darkness had fallen as the train slowed to a crawl, passing through the suburbs and into the main yards in San Antonio. The train would be broken up in there and the train cars reconfigured into new trains that would head north or west to other cities where they would again be broken up yet again into other trains. The process would be repeated forever as boxcars crisscrossed the nation to their destinations or places of origin, with new ones added.

The boys climbed down from the boxcar and tossed their duffels to the ground. They gathered their gear and headed toward the center of the train yards.

"I been thinkin'," George said as they walked along the main line. He was glancing at the roadmap, struggling under the fading light.

"You've been thinkin', huh? That can be a dangerous thing."

"I been thinkin' about Ebbets."

George had been talking about her all the way from Lake Charles, and Sam was getting tired of hearing about her.

"I just want to see her again," George insisted.

Sam sighed, "Yeah, I can see that. She really got under your skin, didn't she? But listen, pard. We can't just jump off this train and go hitchhiking to Boerne, Texas in the middle of the night, tryin' to find your long lost love. What if she's not there? What if she's got a boyfriend? What if her dad's got a shotgun?"

Sam thought about it, then he offered up a compromise.

"I'll tell you what. Maybe you can send her a letter from here, so it gets to her right away."

"Aw, I don't know..."

"Look, it might be better if you *didn't* go up there. Maybe she doesn't want you to see where she lives. Maybe it'd be better if we get to California and you can invite her out to stay with you instead."

"Well, I don't know... I don't want to intrude on her, but damn... I reckon I'm pretty lovesick."

He looked as downcast as Sam had ever seen him. "Yeah, I'd say that's putting it mildly."

As they made their way through the yards they saw a switchman working the track switches.

"Hi," Sam greeted, "We're looking for a westbound. Anything going out soon?"

"Yep," he replied, "Couple of hours or so 'til it gets made up. Runnin' out on three, right over there," he said, pointing to a line four or five tracks over. "Not very many empties on it though, but it's headed for El Paso."

"Good deal," Sam said, "thanks a lot."

The pair found a spot to hide settled in for the wait.

Sam said, "Why don't you write that letter and I'll see if I can get one of these guys to mail it for you."

George shook his head, dejected but resigned to his fate. "Damn... okay, I'll do it. Maybe I can get her to come out to California."

He pulled his pen and paper from the duffle bag and set to work writing the letter. When he finished he took another sheet of paper and folded it into a sort of envelope, then folded the letter and stuffed it inside. He rummaged around in the bag and found a roll of tape and managed to seal the makeshift envelope shut. He addressed it and handed it to Sam.

"I'll take it over to the office," Sam said, "better if there's only one of us."

He took the letter and was aware of George watching him as he walked off toward the small building beneath the yard's watchtower.

He returned a few minutes later with good news.

"We're good to go, pal. I told him that Ebbets was your mother and that you hadn't seen her in a long time, and that you were trying to get a letter to her. They put the whole thing in a *real* envelope and put a stamp on it, so it's dang sure gonna get there."

"Thanks, man," George said, "I wouldn't uh thought of the mother thing. That was a nice touch. Now I feel like I got all my ducks on the same page."

The switchmen were making up the train as they waited, but they didn't see any empty boxcars for almost an hour. George finally spotted one about three quarters of the way back on the train and the pair made their way to it.

George slid the car's doors open and caulked them with pieces of wood he found lying about, so the doors wouldn't slide closed on them. Sam tossed their gear up into the boxcar. Satisfied that their new home would not become a prison, the two climbed in and made themselves at home.

Sam took the first watch, and George fell asleep right away. He dreamed of running along an empty California beach with Ebbets, pelicans gliding low over the ocean, dolphins playing in the waves, and the sun setting behind the watery horizon.

An hour and a half later, a final bump of the train cars signaled that the caboose was finally attached. This train was longer than the last one, stretching almost two miles. It jerked itself tight as the six engines struggled against gravity to build up the inertia necessary to pull one hundred and seventy-three cars out of San Antonio and into the West Texas night.

Mexico to Texas

As Sam and George were riding the freight train down through Louisiana and into Texas, Diego Jaramillo and his wife, Anarosa were headed north toward the border, having left their home in Las Mariposas, Mexico four days earlier. They had hitchhiked when they could and walked when they had to as they traveled across the desolate Chihuahuan Desert. When they reached the American border, they waited until nightfall before wading across the *El Rio Bravo* just outside of Langtry, Texas.

Travel was slow, due in large part to the fact that Anarosa was seven weeks pregnant. Diego insisted on carrying her belongings as well as his own. Among his possessions was the old leather map that his grandfather, Ignacio had given him. He kept it well hidden in the lining of his bag, afraid of losing it to thieves or highwaymen.

The map had given his grandfather hope after Diego's grandmother passed away, and Ignacio had handed that hope down to Diego, imploring his grandson to use it to find his fortune. Before his grandfather died, Diego promised him that he would hunt for the German cross on the map that marked the location of the treasure.

The couple walked quietly along the side of the freight cars, looking for one that was open. The train had arrived only a few minutes before, and Diego was afraid it would leave before they could find an empty boxcar. It was cold outside and he worried that Anarosa would become sick, though she constantly tried to put his fears to rest by letting him know that she was, in fact, just fine. They found a fallen log beside the tracks and Diego insisted Anarosa sit down while he scouted for an open boxcar.

Langtry

The train passed through Uvalde on its way to Del Rio. The boys expected a layover there but were surprised when they passed straight through Del Rio without stopping. When it reached the western edge of town they climbed back into their sleeping bags and made themselves comfortable atop the pile of cardboard that served as their beds.

The pair woke when the train stopped to drop off some cars and change crews in Langtry. They watched as the new crew of five boarded. Three climbed into the engine: the engineer, a fireman, and a brakeman, and the conductor and flagman were driven to the end of the train, where they climbed the steps up into the caboose. Each man carried a metal lunch pail that would see him through to El Paso.

"Seems like an odd place to change crews," George observed, "You'd think they'd change 'em in San Antonio or even Del Rio. Ain't much here in this little place. Hell, I can't even see a water tower anywhere. I'll bet there's less than a hundred folks here."

"Who knows? It sure don't look like anybody actually lives here," Sam commented.

The sky had begun to lighten in the east as the predawn chill forced Sam and George to put their coats on. They sat in the boxcar's open door, legs dangling over the side, and looked out upon what passed as the town. It was nothing more than a few small buildings, some livestock corrals, and a two lane farm-to-market road that passed through the center of it all, headed in the same direction they were. A scuffling sound caused them to turn around and look back to the door on the other side of the boxcar. A face appeared just above the floor, a disembodied head that seemed to be sitting on the edge of the boxcar's door.

"Por favor," the head said, "Es-cooz may." They saw that the face belonged to a Mexican man, struggling with his English.

"Whatcha need, pardner?" George asked.

"No hay vacíos... I find no eem-tee caros..." the man fumbled.

"Yeah, it don't look like there's any empties on this train. Me and Sam here, we got lucky."

George looked around for a moment, then said, "But hey, you're welcome to share this one with us, amigo," gesturing for the man to climb aboard.

The man stared at them blankly, not understanding George's offer.

"Vamanos up here," George said, indicating the space in the boxcar.

"Ah, muchas gracias!" the man replied excitedly, "Un momento..." He turned away and disappeared from view. George and Sam crossed the car and looked out to see where he had gone. The man was already several cars down and crossing over the tracks to a place where he had stashed his belongings. The boys were surprised to see a woman returning with him.

As they approached, George whistled lowly, "Dang, I think she's gonna have a baby, Sam."

"Yeah, looks that way to me."

The boys helped the couple climb into the boxcar. Neither looked more than seventeen or eighteen, though it was hard to tell because the harsh miles and the fatigue from their travels made them look older.

"I'm George, and this here's Sam," he said, indicating himself and his partner.

"Me llamo.... I am *Diego*," the man said, then pointed to the woman, "y esta es *Anarosa*."

George stuck out his hand. "Well, mighty glad to meet you, Diego and Anarosa."

The boys gave the couple some of their cardboard scraps to use as cushions. George offered to lend the woman—a girl, really—their duffle bag to rest against, but Diego politely thanked him and declined. The couple took up residence at the other end of the boxcar, and as they settled in the boys could hear the wave of energy that flowed down the length of the train, through each car's couplings, and on to the next one as each was jerked by the forward motion of the car in front of it. The sudden lurch of their own boxcar meant that they were finally on the move again.

"Y'know, if all those couplers were tight, the engines wouldn't be able to pull the train," George said.

"What? Whatta ya mean? What's a tight coupler got to do with it?" Sam asked.

"Well, figure it this way, George answered, "If all the train cars were stretched out so there wasn't any slack between 'em, the engines would start out and they'd have to pull *all* of them at once, because there wouldn't be any play. Those engines would start out having to pull every single boxcar, all at once, all the way back to the caboose. The weight would be so much that they wouldn't be able to pull it all. They'd be like a pig stuck under a gate."

As Sam pondered this, George continued.

"So, they make the couplings loose on purpose. The engine starts out and jerks the first car, then that jerks the second one, then the third, and so on down the line. By the time it's jerked five or ten of 'em, the engines are rolling, and once the engines get moving, the train follows. See?"

"Damn, son," Sam said, "You been readin' the encyclopedia again."

"Well, I reckon I ain't the sharpest cookie in the jar," George replied, "but even I know that you gotta jump on the bandwagon before the jury gets back in." He could see that Sam was skeptical. "I mean it... look it up."

The freight train slowly gained speed as it left the tiny town of Langtry. The eastern sky was beginning to show pale oranges and yellows against the dark blue of the fading night. The sun wouldn't come up for another hour, but the desert light had already begun. The four rode in silence for a while, each contemplating their own place on this train ride.

George stretched out and finally fell asleep. Sam watched Diego out of the corner of his eye. He was sitting next to his wife with his arm around her protectively. It looked as if he didn't really trust anyone right then, especially around his wife, and Sam didn't blame him. Anarosa fell asleep against Diego's chest and dreamed of a newborn baby held tightly in her arms.

Sam crawled over to talk with Diego while his wife slept. He didn't speak Spanish, so he just started talking, describing the trip that George and he were on. Sam wasn't sure if Diego understood him, but he continued to talk anyway. Finally, he asked Diego what they were doing in America.

"No tengo familia. Todos estan muertos..." Diego continued in Spanish, mixed with some broken English, "*I have no family now. They are todos muertos, all dead. We have come to find our fortune here in America, for it is a great land of promise. We will find our salvation here, and then we will return to our home in Las Mariposas, where we will raise many children. I will restore my grandfather's hacienda, and I will raise fine Paso Fino horses.*"

Most of Diego's story was lost on Sam, but he was able to catch the gist of some of it. Diego paused continually to make sure his wife was comfortable, reassuring her in Spanish that everything was going to be okay. It was obvious that Anarosa was the center of his life and that he cared deeply for her. He and Sam talked in broken English and Spanish for a while, until Sam finally crawled back to his own part of the boxcar and left the Mexican couple to themselves.

As they rolled along, Sam was propped against the boxcar wall, eyes mostly closed, when he noticed Diego pull a small binder from his travel bag. He silently slid it under some of the pieces of cardboard next to him. Sam had no idea what it could be. He didn't know that Diego was hedging his bets, thinking that Sam and George might not be who they seemed. Diego was afraid of being robbed, and he wasn't going to lose that binder.

It turned out that Diego had bigger issues to worry about. The train pulled onto a sidetrack just outside the town of Marathon to wait for another eastbound freight. Instead of hearing the sound of an approaching train Sam heard the sounds of vehicle tires on the railroad's gravel bed. The sounds grew closer and stopped next to their car. Within seconds there were men in army fatigues and jackboots, brandishing automatic rifles and swarming in both sides of the boxcar.

"Police! Don't move! Stay right where you are and put your hands over your heads! *No te muevas! Quédate donde estás y pon sus manos sobre sus cabezas!*" one of them demanded.

Suddenly, there were agents all around them. The officer in charge demanded to know who they were and where they were going.

Awoken from a sound sleep, George was disoriented but finally mumbled, "Man, we're just a couple of hippies headin' to Los Angeles. We ain't done nothin' wrong. We ain't got any dope or anything like that," he added.

An agent took the boys' details and gave it to his assistant, who headed to his vehicle to check them out. Sam shot a glance at Diego and Anarosa, still sitting on the boxcar floor at the other end. They were terrified. Diego looked back at Sam with a desperate, pleading look. Then his look changed to one of intent, a purposeful gaze straight into Sam's eyes. He turned with an intense look down at the pile of cardboard he and Anarosa were sitting on, then back at Sam, then down at the cardboard again.

Something's going on, Sam thought to himself. *He's trying to tell me something.*

The assistant returned, looked at the agent in charge and shook his head, at which point the agent turned to the boys.

"Okay, we ought to take you in, but we're gonna let you go. You keep yourself clean or there ain't gonna be a next time. You'll end up in prison, straight away."

"Yessir," George said humbly.

Sam looked over at his friend, surprised by the sudden change in demeanor.

"I'm just tryin' to watch what I say with a fine toothed comb," George explained.

Sam nodded and said, "Yeah, right."

Two more agents climbed into the boxcar and pulled Diego and Anarosa to their feet and handcuffed them. The agents grabbed their belongings and within moments they removed the young couple and all traces of them from the boxcar. They hustled the pair into the back seat of a black Chevy CarryAll, fired the engine up, and sped off down the service road, dust billowing and gravel flying.

Sam pleaded with the officer in charge. "Hey man, those two haven't done anything. He's just lookin' for work up here, and look, she's gonna have a baby. You're not gonna throw them in jail, are you?"

"They're going back to Mexico," the officer answered. "Best they go back to their own country. We don't want 'em startin' any revolutions up here."

As swiftly as they had arrived the police left. The sounds of the jeeps and power wagons grew faint as they sped away, spraying gravel and leaving a long plume of dust that settled slowly in the cool dawn of the Texas morning. The boxcar grew quiet again and the boys sat back down on the stack of cardboard, stunned. They were used to living in a parallel universe, hitchhiking and riding freight trains, out of touch with the real world. But to see that poor couple arrested so brutally was unsettling.

The six locomotives slowly came back to life and powered the train back up, and it began the long, slow climb out of the desert floor and up into the higher elevations of Alpine and Marfa.

Ebbets Returns

It was a short walk to Ebbets's house from the convenience store that doubled as Boerne's bus station. She was enjoying the summer morning and thinking about George Willow as she walked along the familiar streets.

I don't know what it is about him, but I just keep thinking about him.

When she rounded the corner, the sight of the old house brought a pang of sadness and joy to her. Memories of her childhood and her father washed over her.

She carried her suitcase up the front steps to the porch and noticed that the front door was ajar. She pushed it open and tentatively entered the front hall. "Hello?" she called.

She set her bag down and looked around. Nothing seemed out of place, and Ebbets wondered if her neighbor had been there.

"Well hello, darlin', " a voice said. Startled, Ebbets stepped into the living room, where she saw Wayne sitting on the couch, a beer in his hand, smiling. She felt sick.

"I've been waitin' for you to get home," he said, "I called your cousins up in Vicksburg and they told me you were on your way back down here." Ebbets stared at him and said nothing.

"Well, aren't you happy to see me?" he mocked, "I mean, after the way you treated me, I figured you'd at least be a bit sorry." He got to his feet and came over to her. Ebbets shied away from his touch, but he grabbed her shoulders and pulled her toward him.

"Hey," he said, moving his head around to catch her eyes, "*HEY!*" more intensely, "I'm *TALKIN' TO YOU!*" He grabbed her by her chin and forced her to look at him.

"Ah, now *THAT'S* better," he said, relaxing a little, "I figured you'd be overjoyed to see me," he said, still holding her chin, grinning.

"But I understand, darlin'. Really, I do. I understand. You got feelin's, and you're goin' through some hard times, I reckon. But it ain't got anything to do with me now, does it?"

Behind his smile was the frozen look of a cold, evil stare through bloodshot eyes. Ebbets saw the dilated pupils and smelled the sour breath from the pills and the booze. She knew she shouldn't provoke him, so she remained passive and shifted her gaze downward.

"Well now," Wayne said, his tone shifting to a higher register, masking the threat behind it, "I reckon it's almost lunch time. I bought some groceries, so how about you go into that kitchen there and make us something to eat, and then we can sit and talk about our future, okay?"

Ebbets started toward the kitchen and stopped when called after her, "Hey..." She turned and waited for him to finish.

"Did you think I forgot? You think I don't know what day it is?" The smile on his face accentuated the death in his eyes. "Happy birthday, darlin'," he said.

Marathon to Marfa

It was late morning by the time the freight train's engines accelerated and engaged the cars they were pulling. The clacks and bangs grew louder as each car down the line was pulled tight against the others. Within a few seconds the sounds reached their own boxcar and the two braced against the sudden lurch as it banged against the car in front of it. The train was transformed from a collection of loosely connected segments into a unified whole, a single vehicle stretching along a straight railroad siding for more than a mile.

They passed through Marathon and wished they could get off and grab a cup of coffee in a small cafe there. Both felt the need to connect with people, to talk about what was happening. Sometimes they felt helpless, disconnected from the rest of the world as they were, and they needed to talk to someone other than each other. But the locomotives ground relentlessly on, ignoring the promise of civilization and drawing its cargo through the small town and back out into the wide desert expanse of South Texas.

Sam suddenly remembered the desperate look in Diego's eyes and his insistent looks down at the cardboard that was scattered on the boxcar floor. Against the rattle and heaving of the boxcar, Sam stumbled over to the pile and knelt beside it. He pulled pieces of cardboard away until he spotted the leather binder. He picked it up and called out to his partner.

"Hey, I think the Mexican fella left something. Look at this," he said, holding up the binder.

He made his way back to the front of the boxcar and sat down next to George. The leather thong holding the binder closed was tied tightly, and it took a few minutes of prying and pulling before they were able to open the leather satchel and look inside.

The first thing they saw was the leather map. It was rolled up and tied, but had been flattened inside the binder over the years. Sam untied its leather string and unfolded the map. When he did, a piece of paper fell out. He picked it up, unfolded it, and found that it was a handwritten note. It was obviously very old, like the map it was rolled up in. It was written in Spanish so the boys didn't understand what it said, but they saw the signature, "Fermin Macías," and the date: "1867."

George was excited. "Dang, look at *THAT*! Must be a hundred years old!" he exclaimed, not realizing that he was almost exactly correct. They studied the map and it dawned upon Sam that they were traveling right through the country it showed. They tried to read the note but made little headway with the Spanish. When they finished with it, Sam stashed the map down into his pack and folded the note inside his own diary.

The train climbed slowly through the hills surrounding Altuda Canyon and into the town of Alpine, where it slowed but didn't stop. It wound its way through the hills and back out onto the flat desert plain in a gradual climb to Marfa. They were surprised when the freight train rolled to a stop in Marfa and the switchman uncoupled their boxcar, along with a few others, onto a siding on the east edge of town.

They watched as he disconnected the boxcar three cars ahead of them, and a switcher engine pulled all the cars to another track. Their car and three others were disconnected from the cars behind them. Finally, the remaining cars, including the caboose, were reconnected to the train, and the pair were left on the siding as the train pulled away to the west.

They climbed down from the boxcar to study their surroundings. The nearest buildings were a quarter of a mile away, with the main part of town nearly another mile farther down the tracks to the west. They started walking along the railroad tracks, following the freight train as it receded in front of them. The sky was overcast and signaled an early summer storm. It would cool things down, but the two were exposed to the elements and were ill-equipped to deal with a downpour. They draped their jackets over their duffle bags and lugged their belongings toward town.

One of the first buildings they came to was a general store, where they set their bags down by the front door and headed inside. It was like stepping back into the past. The shelves were full of old items from twenty or thirty years before, but still in their original packaging. There were all kinds of clothes—shoes and jeans, shirts and dresses—still folded and pinned from when they were new. The top ones on each pile had been badly bleached by the sunlight. The shoes were still in their boxes, unlaced and ready to wear.

"Hey," George exclaimed, picking up a card from a shelf, "They've got postcards! I love postcards, especially from out here in the wild west! And look, they've already got stamps on 'em."

George looked through them, chuckling at the pictures of cowboys punching cattle on jackrabbits. There were giant six-foot trout being carried out of the wilderness on pack horses, and pictures of rodeo cowboys riding giant rattlesnakes at a snake rodeo. There were jackalopes—a cross between a jackrabbit and an antelope—and hunters carrying huge grasshoppers, bigger than they were, back to camp.

He picked out several and said, "I'm gonna send one to Ebbets. Man, these things are a stitch in the nick of time."

Sam just shook his head and grabbed a couple of Snickers bars, and the two walked up to the counter to pay. As they waited for the shop owner to come to the counter, George noticed a man crouched outside on the porch who was looking through the window at them. The man quickly got up and walked away. The pair paid for their items and went out to sit down on the bench in front.

Sam put his candy bars into his pack and stopped. Something was missing.

"What the hell...hey! The peanut butter isn't here!" He continued to rummage through his duffle and said, "And the map's gone, too!"

"What? Gone?" George's face balled up into a wrinkled image of confusion.

"You didn't leave it back in the boxcar, did you? We can walk back up there if you need to..."

"Nope, I didn't leave it. It was here."

"Wait," George remembered, "there was a guy outside, here on the porch. Did you see him?"

"No, what did he look like?"

"Ah, I couldn't really tell," George replied, "I think he had dark hair, and maybe a plaid shirt. I just got a quick look."

Sam thought for a minute. His initial anger gave way to resolve. "Oh well, It was just a dumb map. No big deal."

"We could go after him," George offered, "I think he went up that way," he said, pointing back up the road to the east, where they had just come.

"Naw, just let it go. It ain't worth the bother."

"Yeah, I guess the road to hell is greener on the other side."

They continued west down the two lane highway toward the other end of town. They could hitch a ride from there.

It was the day that Vera DeSoto came into their lives.

Milton Rosser

Milton Rosser was on his last legs. At least, that's the way things looked to him at the moment. He was out of cash, out of friends, and out of luck, and he was stuck in Marfa, Texas wishing he had stayed home back in Harshaw, Wisconsin. But damn, his parents were unbearable. His mother constantly reminding him what a failure he was and his father never having a good word to say about him. They could rot in hell for all he cared. Still, right then he would gladly have traded some of that abuse for the predicament he found himself in.

Hitchhiking was painfully difficult for a guy like Milton. He had been beaten up three times since he left northern Wisconsin three months before. Twice he was robbed and left on the side of the road. He never quite got the hang of the whole hitchhiking thing. He would take a ride from anyone who pulled over. He never paused to look at the people in the car, never tried to get a vibe from them before getting in. He simply opened the door and jumped in before asking them where they were going.

It never occurred to Milton to ask the driver, "Whereabouts are you headed?" before getting into the car with them. If they answered with a question ("Where are YOU headed?") instead of a straight answer ("I'm going about twenty miles, to the next town"), alarm bells should have gone off. But they never did for Milton. He was oblivious, and it was a big part of his problem. In fact, it was the root of it all. He wouldn't take advice from anyone. He focused solely on himself and his own needs and ignored everyone else's. He already knew all the answers.

Once he settled into a car with a stranger, Milton commandeered any conversation and made sure the other person knew how smart he was. What started as a friendly exchange would end up in a shouting match, with Milton disparaging the driver, in no uncertain terms, for being a fool and an idiot. Not surprisingly, this would result in a premature exit from the car, often with the driver speeding away before Milton even had a chance to properly shut the passenger door.

And now he found himself on the outskirts of Marfa with no money, no place to stay, and nowhere to get out of the oncoming rain. After being dropped at the far end of town, Milton walked all the way through town, sticking out his thumb and trying to catch a ride.

At the east end of town he came to a shabby little shack that passed as a country store. As he approached the building he thought about finding enough money to eat. He saw two hippie boys up ahead who were setting their bags down on the front porch. They opened the door and went inside the store.

Milton stepped onto the porch and looked at the bags, then turned to look in the window, then looked at the bags again. The two hippies were wandering around toward the back of the store, so he made a move toward one of the bags. He unzipped it and rifled through it but found nothing but some clothes, a sleeping bag, and some writing paper. He pushed it aside and opened the other one.

Inside he found a family-sized jar of peanut butter, which he quickly stashed in his own bag. He rummaged around and spotted a leather notebook, and he took that, along with two small cans of Polish sausages. He got to his feet, glanced through the door window, and saw the pair of them coming back toward the front counter. He quickly zipped the duffle shut and put it back as it was. He threw his rucksack over his shoulder and walked away quickly.

The Map

"Get out of my fucking car, you asshole," the driver shouted at Milton just before the sedan roared off onto the shoulder of Highway 90 and skidded to a stop. It had taken less than half an hour for Milton to infuriate the man who picked him up in Marfa, only a few miles back down the highway.

To be honest, it had taken Milton only a few minutes to piss the driver off. After being called an idiot who didn't know what he was talking about, the man grew silent, listening to Milton's self-possessed ramblings. Seething internally, he gripped the steering wheel until his knuckles were white. He would not leave a man alone on the side of the road out in the desert, but now that they had reached the outskirts of Alpine, he swerved to the gravel shoulder, slammed on the brakes, and came to a stop, then ordered Milton out of the car.

"What the hell, man... you said you were going all the way to San Antonio."

"Get the fuck out," the driver snapped.

"You can't just leave me here, man..."

"Fuck off, asshole!" the man bellowed as Milton climbed out of the car and shut the door. The driver slammed the transmission into Drive and sprayed gravel, spinning the sedan's tires until it reconnected with the two lane blacktop, leaving Milton to contemplate his surroundings.

Texas is full of shitheads, Milton mumbled to himself. *What a godforsaken goddamn place this is.* He picked up his pack and walked toward town.

Alpine, Texas was a small town of some five thousand souls, half of whom lived below the poverty line. It was a mixed population of Anglos and Hispanics, with a few Native Americans, blacks, and other people of color, who existed together in a sort of live-and-let-live community of widely varied backgrounds, styles, tastes, and interests.

Alpine was often described as "quirky." Several small shops lined the highway, which served as the main street where it passed through town. Every establishment played a supporting role to the Holland Hotel, the town's star attraction. The hotel was a grand old venue that had seen better days, but was still regarded as Alpine's centerpiece, it's pride and joy.

Milton carried his rucksack along the road, looking for shelter from the coming summer thunderstorm. He noticed a small shop—what he would call a junk store back home—and made his way across the road and onto the front porch. "Arnold's What-Not-Shoppe," the sign said. A small bell jangled as Milton pushed the door open and entered.

"Are you Arnold?" Milton asked the old man behind the counter.

"Ain't no Arnold."

"Isn't this Arnold's shop?"

"Ain't no Arnold."

"Jeezus Christ. Okay, well how about I talk to you then? Do you buy stuff, you know, like a pawn shop?"

"Depends."

Milton immediately grew impatient with the old man and shot him an annoyed look, "Can't you just answer my question? I got something I want to sell. Are you interested?"

"Depends," said the old man. He turned to spit into a large brass cuspidor on the floor beside him.

"Jeezus," Milton snapped, "this is like pulling teeth."

He unzipped his pack and pulled out the leather binder he had stolen back in Marfa. "I got this map here. It's old." He pulled the map from the binder and held it out to the old man, who took it gingerly in his hands.

The proprietor examined the map, read the place names, turned it over and over and scrutinized it closely.

"Where'd you get this?" he asked.

"It's a family heirloom," Milton lied.

"Whatta you want for it?"

"What'll you give me?"

"You didn't answer my question," the old man replied.

Milton fancied himself a shrewd businessman and a tough negotiator. He braced himself and said, "Well, it's a real old map. Gotta be worth at least a couple hundred bucks."

The old man was unaffected by this and showed no emotion. He seemed to be considering it, lost in thought. Finally he said, "I'll give you ten dollars."

"*TEN BUCKS*? What the fuck? *TEN BUCKS*?" Milton started giggling hysterically. He shook with a desperate laughter that was a mixture of anger, nerves, and rage. It was a shrill, high pitched nervous titter that finally stopped when he said, "It's worth a helluva lot more than ten bucks. C'mon, man. I need the money."

"Ten dollars, take it or leave it."

"You're a fucking asshole! C'mon, man, give me twenty bucks. Don't be such a dick."

"Six dollars," the old man said.

"What? You said *TEN*!" Milton's voice grew louder.

"You need to calm down, son. If your voice gets any higher it's only the dogs who are gonna be able to hear you. Now, like I said, it's six dollars, or get out of my store."

"God dammit," Milton replied, and handed over the leather binder. "Just give me the money, you sonuvabitch."

The little shop bell rang with a vengeance as Milton slammed the door on the way out. The man watched him making his way down the street. He picked up the map and looked at it again, this time more closely. He knew exactly what he would do with it.

Sam and George

Sam Hardwick first met George Willow in Monterey, California in January of 1967. He stumbled into George's life in a run-down hostel situated inside an old warehouse on Cannery Row. It was a flea-infested joint that passed itself off as a boarding house. Rooms were rented by the week or by the night, and Sam suspected they probably even rented them by the hour by the looks of some of the clientele.

Sam had arrived in San Francisco on a bus from Rock Springs, Wyoming that had carried him across the northern plains. He transferred to another that took him down the coast to Monterey. Sam was driven by his love of John Steinbeck. He always wanted to be a writer, and he figured he would explore the world through Steinbeck's eyes. Along the way, he would search for what Steinbeck had seen and meet the characters he had described.

The middle aged woman at the desk looked up through rhinestone covered glasses with pointed sides that made her look like an angry cat. Her hair was stacked in a bouffant so tall that she had to duck when passing through doorways. Sam thought it must have taken an ocean of hairspray to keep it in place. It likely explained the aroma that permeated the lobby, an exotic mixture of olive and citrus, with a healthy dose of rubbing alcohol and farmhand sweat thrown in. It had a distinct hospital smell, with a faint tinge of automatic transmission fluid.

The woman, who Sam later learned was named Zady, showed him to a cot in a small room that housed two other people. They were absent at the time, so he threw his pack down on the empty bed and sat down to take stock of his situation. Zady made it clear that she was not a babysitter for tenants' personal effects so instead of taking a walk, he resigned himself to staying in the room, depressing as it was.

His roommates returned a few hours later and he found that he was sharing the room with a Mexican kid whose name he never learned, and with George Willow, a dock worker. The kid headed south after two days, leaving the room to George and Sam. The January weather was cold, but the days were getting warmer. Many of the itinerant workers were leaving, headed down Highway 101 to Gonzales and Soledad or inland along Highway 99 to pick produce over in the Central Valley.

When George returned from his shift on the docks Sam saw that he was one of those bigger than life people. He had an infectious laugh, a vibrant voice, and a genuine interest in the people around him. Sam liked him right off.

"Howdy," George said, "I'm happy to make your acquaintance. I'm George Willow," and he stuck out his hand.

They stayed for four days in the small room. George worked on the docks while Sam spent his days walking the waterfront and writing. On the morning of the fifth day George decided he had worked long enough. He got out of bed and declared that he was a free man. Sam was dumbstruck.

"What? You mean you just *quit*, just like that?"

"Yeah, man. As the locals say, *'No problemo, hombre'.*" He pronounced it, "No pro-BLAY-moe, HOM-bree."

"But why? I mean, what're you gonna do now?"

"Ah, that's easy, bud. I figure you an' me, we'll head out and see the country. There's places to go and people to meet, amigo."

"But we can't just…"

"C'mon, man. Git yer gear together. We're hittin' the road. You know what they say… If the shoe fits, walk a mile in it."

Fifteen minutes later their belongings were packed into their duffel bags and they were walking through the waterfront toward the highway. After stopping to collect George's pay, they headed north along the main road.

"The bus from Frisco to Monterey was four and a half dollars," Sam said, "so I think it's probably the same going back up there."

"We ain't ridin' the bus, amigo," George replied. "You wanna see the country you gotta get out in it. We'll hitchhike, just like god intended." He grinned and said, "And besides, it's free."

Sam had never hitchhiked before and was having second thoughts about the prospect, but George seemed to know what he was doing, so Sam decided to go along with the plan. They walked past the wharf on Del Monte, then stuck out their thumbs and headed north to San Francisco, or "the city," as George called it.

"And don't call it 'Frisco'," he told Sam, "they don't like that."

The pair spent the next year and a half hitchhiking and riding freight trains all over America. They stopped at love-ins and music festivals, war protests and rainbow gatherings, and stayed in communes and flophouses all through 1967's Summer of Love. Sam saw himself as a sort of latter day Jack Kerouac and spent much of his time writing his thoughts down in the journal he kept.

The two worked odd jobs and tossed their bedrolls down wherever they found themselves each night. They didn't worry about where they slept. If night came before they caught a ride, they simply climbed up under a highway bridge where they felt, more than heard, the cars and trucks that roared past overhead.

They learned that graveyards offered a place to sleep where no one would bother them. They crept into the back seats of automobiles on used car lots, where they usually found the keys hidden on top of one of the tires. They climbed inside the donation bins on the sidewalks outside the Goodwill and Salvation Army buildings. The bins were always full of clothes and bedding and were warm and comfortable, and the two were often able to upgrade their wardrobes.

They shared stories and jokes and talked about women. George never ran out of topics to talk about. He held forth on all manner of things. It might be a twenty-minute discourse on why cheap American beer was superior to the expensive German stuff, or a comprehensive description of the subtle differences between growing cotton in Arkansas and Mississippi. George never had simple opinions about things.

Sam spent a great deal of time trying to write the Great American Novel. He often sat silent and brooding while he was working, and he knew he wasn't very good company, but George didn't seem to mind and never ran out of topics to talk about.

Sam was in awe of George's genuine love for women and the way he held them in such high esteem. Sam wasn't sure when people started calling it the summer of love, but he figured his travel mate was the poster boy for it. George fell in and out of love in just about every place they stayed. One minute he was smitten, the next he was ready to move on. George carried a little bit of each woman in his heart with him, and Sam never saw a woman who was jealous or angry with him. They all loved him because they knew he truly loved them back.

And though Sam made feeble attempts to imitate George, his own personal issues always got in the way and left him frustrated. Growing up, he had never really received any guidance about women. After the death of his brother, both of his parents became distant and cold toward Sam and toward each other. Neither was able to offer any sort of example to their son. He had no other siblings, no sisters to learn from, so he learned about women the hard way, through mistake after mistake.

George taught Sam by his own example, without trying to educate him. Watching his friend, Sam learned a great deal about the way a man should treat women—not as something to claim or own, but as something beautiful to appreciate and cherish. This was all new to him and he admired George's innate perception. He was painfully shy—unlike George, who seemed completely at ease with women—and he never knew what to say or how to act. So, he mostly kept to himself and let George be the life of the party.

Neither of them shared their inner thoughts or any intimate parts of their past. George was more outgoing and less inhibited than Sam was, but even George kept his deep personal feelings locked tightly away and didn't discuss his own childhood at all. He mentioned a falling out with his father, and he often bragged about his younger sisters, whom he adored. Still, when Sam looked back on their eighteen months together, by the time the two of them landed in Marfa he didn't really know George Willow as well as he might have. And George didn't know much about Sam Hardwick at all.

Sam and Charlie 1953

Charlie was seven when he died. Sam was a couple of years older, the big brother who Charlie followed around constantly and watched quietly, in his solitary way. Charlie was consumed with everything his brother did, and he spent much of his young life quietly observing the methods by which Sam accomplished any task at hand. Charlie tried his best to emulate him and was pretty sure that his big brother knew the answer to just about everything.

Sam loved his little brother, but as boys do, he didn't show it. That was part of being older. You didn't let your feelings show. You needed to stay silent and tough, to show your friends that you weren't a sissy. He learned that from his father.

Jim Hardwick worked in the blasting shop at the Clear Creek limestone quarry near their home in Harrodsburg, Indiana. Within its walls were housed some of the most advanced technological tools of demolition explosives to be found in nineteen fifty-three. There were large spools with miles of electrical wire used for detonating the charges that would reduce the local limestone cliffs to piles of broken rock and powder. At one end of the building were stored the magneto motors and batteries, along with tubs of grease and solvents. Layers of oakum, used for packing, and bales of cloth.

Most of the kids had fathers who worked at the quarry. Sam, Charlie, and their friends were all well known to the workmen there and were allowed the run of the surrounding acreage. The boys watched from a distance as the workmen drilled into the stone shelves with their long thin bits, setting the holes at odd angles and carefully pushing the tubes of dynamite into them, nestled next to their blasting caps.

The youngsters enjoyed climbing the 300 million year old limestone cliffs, pretending they were explorers in a wild frontier that seemed to have no end, but in reality came to a stop at the company's property line. As long as the boys didn't attract the notice of the boss, their fathers were happy to look the other way and allow their sons to be boys.

Even the crisp chill of a February morning in Indiana would not impede the work of those fathers as they loaded charges and blasting caps into the drill holes they had bored in long rows down the surface of the limestone verge that ran across the southeast end of the quarry.

Charlie and Sam were playing on one of the frozen ponds, far enough away from the blasting activity that the quarry workers paid them no mind. Two other boys, James Hinton and Stan Thurman, joined them in what they called "ice skimming." They found several small rough-sawn wooden slats and used them to slide across the ice. In order to skim you threw a board down onto the frozen surface and then ran after it across the ice before jumping onto it and gliding far out into the middle of the frozen pond.

The two older boys—Sam and Stan—were able to slide almost all the way across because their size and weight carried them farther. Charlie was the smallest and had the hardest time, but he sat and watched how the rest of them did it and, after countless falls and failures, finally managed to find his rhythm. Once he gained confidence he was able to set the plank down on the ice and take running jumps onto it. He didn't travel very far, but you could see the smile on his face and the light in his eyes from all the way across the pond.

As they played with their skim boards, the boys first felt—then heard—the rumble of the faraway blast. Charlie was by himself, at the far end of the pond, slipping back and forth across the ice in short spurts. Sam was racing with Stan and James, with one boy acting as timekeeper while the other two threw their boards down and raced to jump on them to see who could go the farthest the fastest.

Sam and Stan had just jumped onto their boards when the ground quaked from the force of the blast almost a mile away. As the pair glided toward the center of the ice they heard James call out, and both of them turned to look back at him. He was yelling something and pointing toward the other end of the pond. Sam saw that Charlie had again fallen down and was struggling to regain his feet.

A large black fissure appeared at the shore's edge of the pond and developed slowly, then more rapidly as it gained momentum toward the young boy. It was as if a giant invisible hand were drawing a thick black line across the ice. When the line reached Charlie, he disappeared from view.

By then the boys were off their boards and stopped, neither of them able to make sense of what had just happened. "It's Charlie!" James called, "He's gone under!"

Sam started to run across the ice toward the crack, slipping and falling all the way, desperate to reach his little brother. He reached the spot where

Charlie had gone through the ice, but he could not quite reach its edge for fear of falling in. Jimmy had the sense to bring his board with him and he lay flat on the ice and inched himself to the fissure while Sam and Stan held his feet. He pushed the board through the crack and down into the dark depths of the frozen pool, pulling it back and forth and screaming, "Charlie! Charlie!" hoping that Sam's younger brother would grab ahold.

The board slipped from James's grasp and floated away beneath the ice. He jerked back up and desperately looked around to find that Charlie's board was still on the ice. He grabbed it and repeated the process, poking and prodding beneath the ice as they all called Charlie's name in terrified gasps. Finally, the three young boys just lay there in silent desperation.

Sam's mind was numb, and all that came to mind was how much trouble he would be in with his father.

The Marfa Lights

Vera DeSoto pulled her pickup truck off the highway and rolled down the window to catch a breath of the cool desert air. She turned the truck down an old ranch road about eight miles east of town, near the old army airfield. The field closed down after the war and was now mostly abandoned. Motorists sped past without a second look, making their way to Alpine or farther east to San Antonio, and on to Austin or Dallas. For Vera it was a place of solitude, a spot that offered a tranquil hush to shut out the hectic, perpetual drone of life in the cafe. It was a place for her to voice her thoughts with no one around.

The pickup bounced over the cattle guard as she entered the dirt road that wound its way south toward the hills in the distance. If you knew your way around the area you could follow this road all the way down to the Big Bend country, where it came to an end at the Rio Grande. That is, if you knew your way around. If you didn't, you would likely become hopelessly lost as you tried to figure out which dirt path to take. If you were one of the unlucky ones, you might turn down the wrong road and find yourself in a box canyon or stuck in the sand in a dry arroyo or worse, with your vehicle broken down, no water, and with nothing to protect you from the elements. You took your life in your hands when you went exploring on old wagon roads in this country.

Vera guided the pickup down the two ruts that passed for a road. She stopped after a couple of miles and pulled into a small flat patch of buffalo grass. This was her spot, the getaway she often made after she closed the cafe for the night. She brought along a thermos and a sandwich and just sat and watched the sun go down.

As the sky darkened she looked for the familiar soft glowing off in the distance, but it didn't appear. There was a lot of speculation about the origins of the Marfa Lights. Some thought that they were UFOs and aliens. Others attributed them to top secret experiments at the old Army base. Hardcore conspiracy nuts believed that the government had not really abandoned the base, but instead had built secret underground labs and tested their experiments in the darkness of the dry Texas night. Some even claimed the Army was doing tests on captured aliens. Skeptics dismissed the Marfa Lights as campfire lights or the headlights of passing cars and trucks out on Highway 67.

Vera paid no heed to any of these claims and was content with her sandwich and iced tea as she enjoyed the serenity of the southern desert. In earlier times she would have been drinking beer with her sandwich, with heavy emphasis upon the beer. But she had given up drinking when she took the job at the cafe and surprisingly, she didn't miss it at all.

The evening was mild, so she spread a blanket in the bed of the truck and rested with her back against the cab. She listened as coyotes sang their plaintive cries to each other. The desert was full of life. Just before dark she watched flycatchers and kingbirds flitting about, grabbing insects out of the sky. Later, there were nighthawks and canyon wrens whistling their own songs.

Even though the moon was new, Vera could just make out the silhouettes of the coyotes who serenaded her. She smiled and remembered the time she caught a glimpse of a Mexican grey wolf as it moved stealthily across the desert floor in silent grace. Like all the creatures out here, it had *purpose*, a reason for being. There were bobcats and mountain lions, white-tailed deer and antelope, and all manner of small critters like desert packrats and jackrabbits. Each lived to serve its own purpose. All of them were resolved to fulfill their role in the grand scheme of things.

The evening ritual provided renewal for Vera, a mini retreat to stop and think, to consider, to relax, and breathe. She often wondered where she fit into that grand scheme, what her purpose was, and whether she would ever learn the answer.

She never shared these excursions or talked about them with anyone. She kept them to herself, especially after she made the mistake of mentioning them to Ernie Sands one time. He scolded her for going off on her own in the middle of the night.

"What if somethin' happens to you? How you gonna get ahold of anybody, out there in the middle of nowhere? You need to *tell* somebody when you're goin' off like that!" He didn't mention that he was often guilty of the same thing.

The new moon was only a sliver, high in the southern sky as Vera scanned the heavens for the stars and constellations she knew. She wasn't an astronomer but she was able to pick out the obvious constellations: Orion, Leo, Scorpio, Sagittarius, and the big and little dippers—Ursa Major and Ursa Minor—Cassiopeia, and Aquila the Eagle. She knew the three stars, Deneb, Vega, and Altair, that made up the Summer Triangle. She could pick out Cygnus the Swan, also known as the Northern Cross, with Deneb as its top point. The night sky fascinated her. She knew that it maintained the strongest hold on her of anything in Marfa.

The Lights didn't show that evening, but Vera didn't mind. She let the darkness of the desert wash over her, as if it could cleanse her spirit and somehow set her free. As much as she loved this place—the sense of belonging, the feeling that she was part of a community—she couldn't help but feel alone sometimes. She tried her best to stand firm against the feelings of loneliness that sometimes threatened to engulf her, but she wasn't always successful.

I reckon I might be lonesome, but I'm not lonely, she thought. *I'm doin' just fine as I am. Got my own business. Got lots of friends. I'm doin' great, all on my own. Yeah, sometimes it might be nice to have someone in my life, but I don't need to be pining away for anyone.*

Still, deep down she knew that her arguments didn't really hold water. Sure, she ran her own business. It paid the bills and it kept her occupied, but it wasn't her life's passion. And yes, she knew many of the folks in the area, but there were only one or two she could really confide in, and she kept them at arm's length. The fact was, a man had not come into her life. Hell, she didn't even have a dog. But as the weeks and months and years passed, she came to accept that this was her lot in life. And that was okay. She wasn't unhappy. But as much as she loved Marfa, her life here wasn't really making her heart sing.

Vera and The Boys

"What can I get y'all?"

Those were the first words that Sam ever heard Vera say. Amy was watching him from her spot back in the kitchen. She loved how Vera's words rolled off her tongue in that sweet Georgia accent of hers, and when Sam heard it he sat up like there was an earthquake or something. Amy watched him intently, with a fifteen-year-old's curiosity. She had never seen anyone like him before, at least not in person. The long hair and scruffy, road-worn clothes. He wore a pair of round wire rim glasses that made him look like a professor. His friend George did most of the talking, but it was Sam who grabbed her attention. She thought to herself, *there's something about this guy...*

To Amy's adolescent self Vera was bigger than life. She was a southern belle, a sweet tart with a dash of pepper thrown in to spice things up. Vera had a calm and reserved manner, but she had an edge to her, too. She did her best to hide that southern beauty behind faded blue jeans and a snap down cowboy shirt, but she never really succeeded. Amy figured a person would have to be blind not to see what a knockout Vera DeSoto was.

As she did the dishes and watched the goings-on, Amy was riveted. It was the first time she had ever seen Vera actually *interested* in a man. Sure, she flirted from time to time, but that sort of came with running a cafe. But this was different and Amy could tell straight away. There was something about Sam that really got Vera's attention.

And there was something about him that tugged at Amy, too. It was something she didn't really understand. At fifteen, Amy didn't yet realize that she wasn't a little girl anymore. And Sam had no idea that this would be the beginning of a lifelong crush from a very strong-willed young lady.

He's a lot older than me, Amy thought, *way too old.*

Outside the cafe a few minutes earlier, George and Sam had decided to get a cup of coffee while they figured out their next move. That move should have taken them back out to the side of the highway where they could stick out their thumbs and head west to California. It didn't work out that way.

Amy watched them as they sat down at the counter. She knew how to act around boys her own age and how to handle the truckers and cowboys that came in, but these two were out of her league. And when she looked over at Vera, Amy could see that these two were having the same effect on her.

Vera usually appeared a bit hard worn, gruff, and overworked, but in that instant she suddenly morphed into something Amy hadn't seen before. And she could see that Vera wasn't faking it, wasn't acting girlish. Somehow, she had let down her guard, and that allowed her natural beauty to shine through, the beauty that Amy already knew so well.

Vera had a fierce spirit and as far as Amy could see, nothing was ever going to break it. She always danced to her own tune. Amy saw that Sam was in awe of Vera from that very first day. *I think he's even a little afraid of her*, she mused.

"What can I get y'all?" was all Vera said, and it hit Sam like a hammer. He turned to look at her like she was talking only to him. Amy smiled. Talk about dumbstruck. The poor guy couldn't find two words to put together for an answer. He just sat there in silence. He looked like an armadillo crossing the two lane and caught in the headlights. Sam turned to look at Vera like she had just dropped in from another planet. Then, when he saw that she was staring back at him, he quickly turned his eyes to look down at his hands on the table in front of him. It was lucky for Sam that George was there to come to his rescue.

"I'm thinkin' I need a cup of coffee if you've got one," George replied.

Vera turned back to the kitchen and hollered, "Amy, can you bring up some coffee please?" And then she turned to Sam and their eyes met again, and again he looked down, too shy to meet the gaze of those intense green eyes of hers.

"And what about you, pilgrim? Can I get you something to drink?"

"Oh, maybe just a glass of water for now."

"My name's George, and this here's Sam. Don't pay him no mind. He's just cryin' over spilt beans."

"Spilt beans, huh? Well, that sounds serious." Vera smiled and looked over at Sam, who was watching her through his wire rimmed glasses. She was thinking, *The quiet type... but there's something about him...*

"I'm gonna have a burger and some fries," George said, "better yet, can you make that a cheeseburger?" He turned to his friend, "What are you havin', bud?"

Sam couldn't think of anything and just stared at the menu on the countertop. Finally, he just blurted out, "Do you have a salad of some sort?"

Vera just stared at him, deadpan and unsmiling. "A salad. You want a salad. Are you sure you're in the right place?"

"Aw, sorry... I don't know... I guess I could have a..."

"Just givin' you a hard time. I can make you a salad, if that's what you're after."

"Thanks, I appreciate that. Oh, and maybe some iced tea?"

"You got it," she said and turned back toward the kitchen, "And some iced tea, Amy. Thanks."

Vera went back to the kitchen and George turned to Sam. "I think she likes you," he joked, "Did you see the way she was looking at you?"

"You don't know what you're talking about," Sam replied, "she never looked twice at me."

"No, it's *YOU* who don't know nothin', amigo. Take it from one who has a world of experience in these matters. And you know something? Maybe you ought to do something about it." He had a knack for getting under Sam's skin.

"Yeah, right. And just what would I do? Ask her to go camping? It's not like we're set up for dating, is it?" He turned to look out the front windows, across the highway toward the expanse of desert that extended forever.

"Well, I'm just sayin'... she's a danged good lookin' lady, and I didn't see any ring on her finger. It wouldn't hurt to make a new lady friend, pard."

"Oh, yeah, I'm sure she's into guys with no visible means of support."

"Aw, hell... It doesn't hurt to talk to a girl," George said.

"Yeah, I know. You're a master at it."

"Well, you don't have to marry 'em. You don't have to even live with 'em or date 'em or anything."

"If you're in such an all fired hurry, why don't *YOU* ask her out?

George ignored him and continued, "Look, meetin' a woman like that is destiny, man. It's *destiny*. And y'know, gettin' involved in somethin's not the same as bein' committed to it. That's all I'm sayin'."

"What the hell are you talking about?"

George paused, scratched his chin, and went on, "You and her are like bacon and eggs."

"What? Bacon and eggs?" Sam shook his head.

"Bacon and eggs, *that's* what I'm sayin', amigo. You're either involved or you're committed. With bacon and eggs, the chicken is involved, but the pig is committed."

"What the hell are you talking about?" But Sam already knew.

"Ebbets... I'm talking about you and this lady, and about me and Ebbets."

"Ebbets? Who is tha... Oh, you mean the girl on the bus. She's gone, pardner. What makes you think you're ever gonna see her again?"

"I've been writing to her. Man, I miss her so much." George got up and went to his pack. He rummaged around in it for a minute before returning to the counter.

"I'm gonna write another letter right now," he declared. "You'll see. These things have a way of workin' out. It's called 'Karma', pal. I don't suppose you'd know anything about that."

"Well, I know that you get what you pay for, and that's about it."

Amy went out to their booth carrying a pot of coffee and Sam's iced tea. She set the tea down and picked up a coffee cup to fill, then saw that George had a pen and paper out and was writing.

She was curious, "Writin' a book?" she asked.

"Nope," he answered, "I'm writin' to my true love."

"Wow! THAT'S something you don't hear around here very much."

"He's lovesick," Sam said, "a bit of an idiot, writing to a girl he barely knows. It's a lost cause, if you ask me."

"Nobody asked you, amigo." George said.

Amy turned to George and said, "Well, maybe you should light a candle for Saint Jude." She saw his puzzled look, then smiled and explained, "He's the patron saint of lost causes. It don't hurt to try."

"Might be more than a lost cause," Sam offered, "more like a hopeless case."

Amy thought it was romantic and she told George so, "The world can use a bit more romance, so you just keep on writin'. Don't listen to your grumpy friend here." Sam saw that Vera was taking an interest in the conversation and had stopped to watch.

"You hear that, son?" George responded, "I'm not the only one who believes in miracles."

He turned to Vera and said, "My friend Sam here is too shy to ask you out. There's that, plus the fact that neither he or I have a job or any means of support. So he thinks it would be foolish to try to get to know you, but I've been tryin' to convince him otherwise."

Vera raised her eyebrows and looked at George in surprise. She considered this for a moment while she snuck a quick peek at Sam, who was desperately studying his iced tea. She turned back to George.

"Sorry to say, but your friend might be right. It might be foolish to try to get to know me."

Amy was surprised that Vera's remark made her feel a bit better. She hadn't admitted it to herself yet, but she was already developing a crush on Sam. It wasn't that she was jealous of Vera... she wasn't. The fact was, Amy knew Sam was too old for her. Still, young girls fantasize, and if Vera wasn't interested, then Amy reckoned maybe she'd have a shot someday.

George was not the least bit discouraged at Vera's response and replied, "Well, I reckon I ain't gonna cry over split hairs. We'll just have to take it one step at a time, then."

He turned and looked out the front window. "The sign out front says 'Vera's Cafe'. Does that mean you're Vera?"

"Guilty as charged. Vera DeSoto, at your service," she reached out her hand and smiled.

"Now see? The world's already a smaller place!" George declared, shaking her hand. "We're here in this beautiful little town, in this beautiful cafe, with these two beautiful women. What could be better?" He paused for effect, then added, "It's just George and Sam and Vera, and...", pointing to each one until he came to the girl.

"Amy," she stuttered, "I'm Amy." She could feel her face burning and was thinking she might have blushed so bad she turned purple.

"And Amy!" George continued, "Very pleased to make your acquaintance, Amy," he said, and stuck out his hand. She hesitated, still embarrassed, then took his grip in a handshake.

"Well, George and Sam," Vera said as she turned back to the kitchen, "I better check on your food. How do you like your burger?"

"Well done, please," George answered.

Sam was still looking intently down at his drink, avoiding Vera's eyes. She thought it was cute and she tapped him on the arm, "And how do you like your salad?"

"Well done," he said.

"So, the pilgrim's a bit of a smartass," she muttered as she walked back to the kitchen.

Vera's food was legendary, and seeing as how it was the first cooked meal the two had eaten in days, Vera enjoyed watching them inhale it. She was used to the appetites of truck drivers and ranch hands and it pleased her when her cooking was attacked with such genuine enthusiasm. When they finished she brought out an apple pie from the kitchen.

"How about a piece of pie on the house, boys?" she offered, "It's just gonna go to waste if it doesn't get eaten up."

George's eyes lit up. "Well now, I thought I had died and went to heaven, but no... NOW I've died and went to heaven. Bring it on, little lady!"

Amy watched Vera as she studied Sam's face while the pair ate their pie. He wasn't the normal type who came in. Certainly not a cowboy or a trucker. Vera confessed to Amy years later that she saw something behind those glasses from the very first day. There was something in those grey eyes that held her attention. He wasn't much of a talker, didn't say a lot, but it was obvious to her that he held a lot behind his eyes, that he would have a lot to say if he ever did decide to talk. And over the years, Sam found that if he did want to talk, Vera listened. And yes, Amy had to admit that she was always a bit envious of that.

Finally, George broke the spell and brought up the subject of accommodation.

"Say, I don't suppose there's a cheap motel in town, is there?"

"Nope, afraid not. Closest one is over in Alpine."

"Ah, well... we'll go climb back into that boxcar we just got out of. It'll keep us dry, at least."

"You're sleepin' in a boxcar?" Amy chimed in excitedly. "Wow, that's really cool!"

"Well, ma'am," George said, "you take what you can get in life, don't you?" He smiled at Amy and she grinned and blushed.

Vera considered their predicament for a minute, then spoke up, "Tell you what," she said, stumbling over her words, "There's a room upstairs. It ain't much, but you're welcome to crash there for the night. No charge."

Amy thought, *Now THIS is getting interesting!*

"We're happy to pay you for the room," Sam replied. He pointed at his friend, "Don't let this idiot fool you into thinking we're complete deadbeats."

"No, that's okay," Vera said, "I'd probably get in trouble if I rented it out, so you better just take it. It's fine." Amy saw how nervous Vera was, and how well she was able to cover it up.

"It ain't exactly the Ritz, but you're welcome to it," Vera added.

"That's real nice of you. We appreciate it," Sam said.

Vera and Sam continued to look at each other until Vera finally broke the spell.

"Are you boys thinkin' of stayin' around for a while? I know someone who might be lookin' for some workers." *Gawd almighty...* Vera thought, *am I acting too anxious? What the hell?*

"Well, probably not. We'll be movin' on in the...."

George broke in, "Yeah, we was just sayin' how much we like it around here." He looked at his partner and Sam glared back at him silently. "We could use some work, I reckon."

Vera paused to look Sam over, to allow him to object. When he didn't she replied, "Well then, I'll introduce you to Olive tomorrow. You'll like her. She's a trip."

Amy felt a sudden rush of excitement and didn't know why. All she knew was that she was happy at the prospect of Sam staying around. At the same time, she wondered what Vera was getting herself into. It wasn't like her to take up with strangers like this. Amy didn't understand it at all. But then it occurred to her that she would have to compete with Vera for Sam's attention, and she didn't have the slightest notion of how to go about doing that.

It was pretty clear that Vera had a crush on Sam, but crushes come and go. Vera had the occasional crush on a customer every now and then, though she would never let them know it. But this was the first time she had ever invited any of them to stay.

Vera was silently kicking herself. *What the hell is going on with me?*

Arnold and The Map

Arnold Lambert carefully unrolled the leather onto the kitchen table, revealing the hand-drawn map on it. He placed two coffee cups, a saucer, and a cereal bowl on the corners to keep it from rolling back up again. It was a fascinating piece of work. He had trouble at first, unable to make sense of the map maker's peculiar style of writing, with its ornaments and sweeping flourishes, but he soon became accustomed to them and was able to see beyond the embellishments to the words that were hidden within the script.

Arnold wasn't fluent in Spanish, but he did have a basic working grasp of it and recognized some of the names that were so painstakingly illustrated on the map. *Fuerte de Davis* (Fort Davis) and *Chinati* were places nearby, and he identified *El Río Perdiz, Río Cibola,* and *Montaña de Cabra* (Goat Mountain), but he was unfamiliar with *Muscalero,* and had never heard of *Agujero del Hombre Muerto* (Dead Man's Hole). He saw that the map was not drawn to scale.

In the top third of the map there was a distinctive figure of a cross, embellished to look much like the Iron Cross found in German military history. Beneath it were the words, *Escondite de los Banditos* (the Bandits' Hideout).

Yes, this is an interesting piece, especially since it is obviously a part of the local history. I can turn a tidy profit on this one, he pondered, *and I know just the right person to sell it to. But first,* he thought, *I'll need to prepare it.*

Arnold rolled the map back up and headed for his workshop.

Breakfast

Amy was living in Vera's house now. Vera had given her the back bedroom if she would clear out the junk that Johnny left in it. It was nice to have a real roof over her head and to sleep in a place where the wind didn't blow through the cracks in the walls.

She was excited about the two strangers staying the night in Vera's little apartment upstairs above the cafe. That morning instead of sleeping in, she got up with Vera before sunrise and headed to the cafe. She didn't want to miss anything.

George woke to the sounds of banging boxcars as the diesel locomotives picked up the empties from the railroad siding at the edge of town. Sam was already up, sitting at the window in the flat's living room, watching the empty highway that stretched through town and out into the desert at both ends.

"Well pard, it looks like we're gonna *HAVE* to find a job now. They're takin' away our home," George watched as the empty boxcar and the others were grabbed by the big diesel engine and dragged to the end of the freight train that would soon be pulling away to the west.

"Yep, looks like it," Sam said, "I suppose we'd better go downstairs and have a look around. We'll need to figure out some place more permanent."

"No sense waitin' for the other pin to drop," George said.

They had taken showers the night before, but George wanted another one that morning. He insisted he hadn't gotten rid of all the boxcar grime. As soon as he hopped in and turned the water as hot as he could stand, he was singing loudly. His repertoire was comprised of fragments of various popular songs, but he sang them together in one long, continuous string of lyrics as one song. A son, working for the Daily Mail, but all he wants is to be a paperback writer. This segued into drums, pounding a rhythm to the brain, with a bunch of "la dee dah dee dee's" thrown in.

Afterward, the two gathered their gear and climbed down the narrow stairway into the diner. The cafe wasn't open yet, so the place was empty. Vera and Amy were setting up for the morning rush.

"Good mornin' there, sunshine!" George said brightly. Amy blushed and said good morning. Sam nodded at her and then looked around awkwardly for Vera. He saw her in the kitchen, where she turned to look at him. He quickly turned away.

"You two sleep well?" she asked from behind the serving window.

"Yeah, we slept great, thanks," Sam replied.

"Whatta ya mean, 'yeah, thanks..', amigo?" George demanded, "That's no way to thank an angel sent to us from heaven!" He shook his head and said to Vera.

"I don't know about him, but I slept like a top last night. Sam here has already forgotten that if it weren't for you, we'd have been sleepin' rough in a boxcar again."

Sam cut in, "I didn't mean to... "

"No, you sure didn't," George cut him off. He turned to Vera and grinned.

"But I'm here to tell you, my dear kind woman, that we are forever in your debt. On behalf of myself and my not-so-articulate running mate here, I offer a most sincere thank you."

With that, George placed one arm across his midsection and with the other, doffed an imaginary hat and made a grandiose bow.

Amy's eyes grew wide and she giggled.

Vera laughed out loud and said, "I think you two might be a bit crazy."

"In my partner's defense," George replied, affecting a bad English accent, "it is myself who is crazy. My partner, although somewhat dull, sluggish, and dimwitted, is otherwise completely sane."

Again, with a flourish, he bowed deeply.

"I'll tell you what, you two help me set up for breakfast and yours is on me."

"You have made us both very happy men, my dear," George answered merrily.

Vera was watching Sam. This time he managed to hold her gaze for a respectable time before he felt his face flush and had to look away. When he looked back again Vera was still looking at him and her gaze never faltered. George and Amy both viewed the silent exchange with some amusement. George winked at Amy, who grinned back at him.

As they sat at the counter waiting for their meals, George said, "Hey man, there's something happening here but you don't know what it is, do you Mister Jones?"

Back in the kitchen, Vera heard this and answered without thinking, "Walkin' in like a camel with your eyes in your pocket and your nose to the ground."

They looked at each other and smiled.

Sam looked back and forth between them, confused.

"What are you talking about?" he quipped. Amy was glad she wasn't the only one who didn't understand.

"It's a Dylan thing, man." George said with a grin. "You wouldn't get it, bud." He winked at Vera and told her, "I like the way you think." She nodded and smiled back at him.

From the boys' point of view, they helped Vera set up for breakfast. But from Vera's point of view, they mostly just got in the way. She knew their hearts were in the right place, though. Amy knew that Vera enjoyed having the company in the early hours before the cafe opened.

"If you boys can crack some eggs without breaking the yolks, I'll do you some huevos. Otherwise, it's scrambled."

George spoke up, "Looks like scrambled it is, then. Trustin' us with eggs is like trustin' a raccoon at the poker table."

Amy spoke up, "Hey, I can break eggs for frying!"

She watched Sam to see his response, but he was a tough one to read.

George said, "Well, it looks like Amy here is gonna save the day." And once again she turned red and shuffled back to the kitchen.

Vera grinned, "Over easy it is then. You boys grab that pot of coffee there and help yourselves. Go sit down and we'll be with you in a minute."

It was still dark outside as the boys sat in the corner booth and watched the headlights of the occasional pickup truck go by on the highway outside the window. Amy watched the pair as they gazed out at the desert that extended into the distance to the south. She fried the eggs and Vera made them up into huevos rancheros with flour tortillas and butter on the side.

George concentrated on his food and finished his plate in no time. He used a tortilla to soak up what was left of the red chile on his plate and settled back against the seat, satiated. He looked over at Sam and saw that he was absorbed in watching Vera.

"She sorta grows on you, doesn't she?" George said, turning to wink at Amy and causing her to blush once again.

Sam didn't reply, but kept his eyes on Vera. Her attention was on other things, so he wasn't nervous about getting into a staring match with her. She moved about with a quiet, steady grace, practiced and with purpose. It was something that Amy tried to copy, but hadn't yet gotten the hang of.

The sun was just beginning to show over Paisano Peak in the east when Vera unlocked the front door and let the first customers in. A half hour later the place was filled with men, mostly ranch hands from around the area, and some truckers from off the road who held out for this little diner because they knew it was the best place on Highway 90.

A lot of the early morning customers lived closer to the cafe over in Alpine, but for each of these men, Vera was the reason for pulling himself out of bed in the dark so he could drive fifteen or twenty or even thirty extra miles each way before heading off to work cattle or mend fence. It was all for the chance to catch a glimpse of a goddess—and an unmarried goddess at that.

Each man viewed Vera the same way, as their own goddess, a goddess who might one day belong to him if he could just figure out the right things to say to her. If he could just get up the courage to talk to her. If only the place weren't filled with all those other men every morning. It was a fantasy that kept them coming back day after day, and the proof sat right there in that cafe each morning, at every booth and on every barstool in the place.

Sam was silent as he watched the interactions between Vera and the men. She never wrote a customer's order down—she kept everything in her head—and he felt he was witnessing something profound. The way she balanced plates, cups, saucers, and silverware in her hands and on her forearms while gliding smoothly from kitchen to table was bewildering to him. Vera carried on conversations with a half dozen men at any given time, never missing a beat, listening carefully to what they had to say and responding in kind. No wonder these men loved her.

"Like I said," George teased, watching Sam and giving him a nudge, "she sorta grows on you."

These were men who had work to do, and the cafe emptied out as quickly as it had filled. By eight-thirty the place was empty again. Sam poked his head over the counter and peered into the kitchen.

"Is there anything we can do to help out?" he asked.

"Well, now that you mention it, sure. You might want to scrub some of these plates."

"I can help with the dishes," Amy offered.

"No, you just sit down there at the counter and eat some breakfast." Then she whipped up another helping of huevos rancheros and brought it out to the girl.

Amy watched Sam while she ate. He was standing before the pile of dishes in the sink. She felt nervous when she looked at him, and she didn't know why. She didn't know whether she liked it or not. Part of her was repelled by the idea of being attracted to a man so much older than her. She didn't know how old Sam was, but she guessed that he was *old,* maybe five or even ten years older than her! He was a *grownup* for gawdsakes. And still, another part of her was excited and welcomed her newfound feelings.

Maybe I'm not a kid any longer, she thought. *Maybe I'm a grownup, now.*

George came up beside Sam, pulled an apron from the rack and tied it around his waist while Sam protested. He tied another around his own waist.

"C'mon, I'll wash, you dry, amigo," as he handed his friend a dish towel, "This ain't rocket surgery."

Amy smiled, and her heart swelled. She thought it was the most endearing thing she had ever seen. Two grown men wearing aprons and doing dishes.

Olive Stanfield

Just as the boys were finishing the dishwashing chores Vera came into the kitchen and said, "C'mere. There's somebody I want y'all to meet."

The boys took off their aprons, and Amy followed them as Vera led them out to the same corner booth where they had eaten their breakfast. She knew the woman who was sitting there alone.

Olive Standfield looked to be in her fifties or sixties, but Amy didn't really know how old she was. To a fifteen-year-old, everyone over thirty was old. Olive wore her grey hair in a long braid that hung nearly to her waist. As always, she was immaculately dressed, with a denim cowboy shirt and jeans that were heavily starched and pressed, with creases up the front of the legs the way the older cowboys wore theirs.

A squash blossom necklace hung around her neck and reached nearly to her waist. She was wearing silver earrings, handmade with turquoise and coral stones. A Navajo concho belt was buckled around her waist and several silver and turquoise bracelets and cuffs adorned each arm, starting at the wrists and stacked together so that they extended halfway to her elbows.

Even with all of the jewelry and accessories, Olive did not look overdressed. She appeared quite at ease in her wardrobe. She was a beautiful woman, and the first thing Sam thought when he saw her was, *man, she must have broken a lot of hearts when she was young.*

Olive spoke with an elegant, flowing intonation that hinted at wealthy family roots, probably from back east. Her speech was laced with the faint hint of a Southwest Texas drawl.

"Wonderful scones this morning, Vera," she said as they approached. She looked past everyone and saw Amy standing in the back.

"And there's my favorite girl," she exclaimed, giving Amy a smile and a wink, "Good morning, dear." Amy blushed and said good morning in a quiet stutter.

"Well Olive, I don't make these scones for anyone but you, y'know," Vera replied.

"There are just some things that make life worth living, aren't there?" Olive said.

"That's for sure, and I reckon we have more than our fair share around here." Vera smiled and stepped aside to introduce the pair.

"This here's George and Sam," she announced, pointing to each of them, "and boys, this is Olive Stanfield."

George was quick to shake Olive's hand.

"How do you do, ma'am. George Willow. Very nice to meet you." He motioned toward Sam, "And this is Sam Hardwick." Sam nodded quietly and said hello awkwardly.

"Well boys," Olive said, indicating her booth, "please join me and have a seat." She paused while the pair slid in on either side of her. "And you, Amy, please. Sit down and have a scone with us." The girl obliged and sat down next to Sam, which made her nervous.

"You two appear to be enterprising young men. Vera tells me you're looking for employment."

"Yes ma'am," George replied, "We've been travelin' some, but we'd like to take a bit of time off from the road, maybe find some work, recharge the funds. And you know, maybe get to know some of the folks in this fine place."

When Sam's elbow accidentally brushed against Amy's arm it was like an electric shock, and suddenly she was terrified. She tried to relax and blend in, but knew she wasn't doing a very good job of it. She sat still, unable to speak, afraid to move.

The conversation drifted in and out of different topics. Sometimes Olive or George would look over at Amy and ask her what she thought, to which she would reply, "Uh huh..." or "ummm, I don't know..." The girl remained frozen in place, afraid that if she moved she would brush against Sam's arm again. Her fear was so palpable that she began to think, *If this is what having a boyfriend is all about, I don't think I want any part of it.*

"How are you with tools and manual things?" Olive was asking, "I need someone to perform certain repairs around my place."

"Yes ma'am," Sam answered, "We're both pretty good at using tools and fixing things."

"I think Sam's being modest, ma'am," George offered. "Oh, he's not the mechanic that I am, and sometimes he's clumsier than a bull in a candy store, but he can get the job done. We both can."

"Well, that's settled then," she said with the practiced manner of one who is used to being in charge, "You might want to stay here and visit for a few days, but when you come to the ranch, bring your belongings. There is a bunkhouse for you to stay in." With a quick gesture, she signaled that the meeting was over and went back to spreading jam on her scone.

"Thank you, ma'am," George said as he and Sam pulled themselves out of the booth. Sam nodded his thanks as they turned to leave. Amy stood up to follow.

"Oh, Amy," Olive said as she headed for the kitchen. The girl turned to meet her gaze, "Yeah?"

"Do you want to come spend some time out at the ranch? There are lots of chores that need doing, and you know, those horses have been missing you."

"Sure!" she answered, "I'd love to!"

"Well, I'll have Vera run you out soon."

"Okay!" Amy said, and in an instant, her nerves had evaporated.

Olive Buys The Map

"It is really quite stunning, Arnold," Olive exclaimed as she studied the old leather map. "Quite a lovely piece. Where did you find it?"

"It belonged to a fellow who lived down south of here, near Shafter," Arnold replied with practiced ease. His speech was that of a proper gentleman from New England, not the desert old timer's accent that he used in his store. The tourists who came in wanted to meet a grizzled old desert rat, so he obliged them by assuming that image. But he and Olive were friends, so he didn't have to keep up his façade with her. Still, he was able to move back and forth between his personalities easily. And as he did with his own image, he was used to creating false provenance to attach to his inventory of antiques. This often involved making up complicated, yet believable stories on the spot, and never missing a beat.

He continued, "You may have known him. Henry Martin? Had a small ranch down that way."

"No, the name doesn't ring a bell," Olive said. She didn't know him because Arnold had just invented him. "This was his map?" she asked.

"He passed away a couple of years back," Arnold continued, "and his children moved away years ago." He paused to consider his story, "The ranch was deserted, so now they've come back to deal with the estate, such as it is."

"So, do you have any idea where this map came from, or when it was made?"

"Looks to be early eighteen hundreds, maybe eighteen twenty or thirty, or thereabouts," he answered. He had no idea how old the map was, or whether it was fake or genuine. "But I thought of you as soon as I saw it. I knew it would look wonderful in your lovely home."

Back in his workshop at home, Arnold had placed the map in an old weathered frame behind glass. When he was finished it looked as if it had been that way for many years. He even went to the trouble of gluing a piece of old parchment to the back of the frame, sealing the leather inside. He used a soft pencil to draw several small symbols and some random numbers on the parchment, then smudged them slightly with his thumb. The framed piece looked as if it were done by an archivist or some other professional. Arnold knew that it would not fool an art historian. But of course, there were no art historians in the vicinity. Most likely, there were none in this entire area of Texas. He had done this sort of thing for years now. Olive was his best customer, and he figured he would take his chances.

"How much do you want?" Olive asked.

"I'd really rather not sell it, truth be told," he began, "I know that if I carted it up and took it back east it would fetch a premium..."

Olive cut him off mid-sentence. "How much, Arnold?"

"Uh... as I was saying, I'm sure it would bring ten to fifteen thousand, but then..." he paused for effect, seemingly lost in thought, "...I must say, I don't relish the idea of spending large amounts of time and effort in pursuit of mere monetary gain. As such, I would rather..."

"Arnold! How *much*?"

"Oh... I suppose I could let it go for two thousand... " He paused to gauge Olive's response, then said, "No... wait. For you? Let's say fifteen hundred."

"I'll give you twelve hundred," Olive responded matter-of-factly.

Arnold chuckled nervously, "You drive a hard bargain, Olive. But for you? Twelve hundred it is, then."

"I'll call James at the bank and have him transfer the money to you, as usual," she said.

As Arnold climbed into his car to drive away, he chuckled. *Well, THAT was the easiest eleven hundred and ninety-four dollars I ever made.*

The Boys Move to Olive's

The boys stayed at the cafe for two days. They did their best to help out around the place but mostly just got in the way. George managed to split and stack some cedar logs out back. Sam swept the floors and wiped down the tables, though Amy finally shooshed him away and told him that was her job.

On the third day, after the lunch crowd had gone, Vera went outside to find the others sitting in the shade. Sam was writing in his journal while George whittled on a piece of wood. Amy was doodling in her notepad, but mostly watching Sam. She could tell that he had an eye for detail and didn't miss much. He kept his observations and recollections the way a hoarder keeps stacks of old magazines.

Sam told Amy that he was going to write the Great American Novel one day, and you never knew what small detail might become a critical part of the story. Amy didn't know what a great American novel was, but she saw that Sam spent lots of time sitting by himself and compiling notes on what he saw around him, and this made her even more attracted to him.

At the moment he was writing a narrative about Marfa, with a detailed description of Vera's cafe and how it felt staying in her flat upstairs. He described the cowboys and truckers who came in, and though he didn't say it outright, Amy was pretty sure that he was just slightly jealous of their time with Vera. *Maybe envious is a better word for it*, she thought. He wrote about Vera but wasn't yet willing to admit that he was smitten with her. Still, Amy could tell, even if Sam couldn't.

George had his pocket knife out and was whittling away on a piece of cottonwood.

"What's that you're makin'?" Amy asked.

"It's gonna be a Texas longhorn steer, if I can just get the horns right."

"Looks sorta like a broken bicycle with real big handlebars," she said. She looked over at Sam and they shared a smile. That felt good.

"Ouch, bud," Sam said, emerging from his reverie, "that one had to hurt."

"It don't bother me none," George replied, "I never claimed to be an artist."

"Yeah, and I don't reckon you ever will. Y'know, that thing looks like something somebody dug up somewhere."

"True enough, but you know, you can't change the spots on an old dog. And I reckon by the time I finish it'll feel like I've dug up a nugget of gold."

"Yeah, well there's folks that'll pay you thirty five-dollars an ounce just to get rid of it."

Vera came out and watched this exchange for a few minutes, then finally remarked, "You two fight like an old married couple."

They stopped and looked up at her.

"Time to go. C'mon with me," she told them, "Go grab your gear. I'll take you over to Olive's."

George answered, "You know, I ain't gonna wait forever... even though you want me to."

Vera shot back, "I... can't wait... forever... just to know if you're still true."

They finished it together, "Time won't let me, oh *NOOOO*!" They looked at each other and laughed.

"The Outsiders!" George exclaimed, and Vera gave him a punch in the shoulder, laughing.

Sam still didn't understand it, but Amy smiled and thought it was cool.

Amy was sorry to see them go, especially Sam. She hoped they would be back in town soon, or that she could go out to visit Olive and her horses. It hurt that he was so much older than her. Even at fifteen, she knew it was never going to go anywhere. She sighed softly and resigned herself to those unrequited feelings.

The old Chevy pickup coughed and sputtered a few times when Vera started it, then died.

"Haven't driven it in a while," she explained, "It's a little cold blooded. A bit rough when you first start it."

"Sam here knows about cars," George said. "He can fix it for you." He looked at his partner and Sam glared back at him. "When he's done with it, it'll run like a scalded-ass ape."

"Well, it runs okay for the most part, but if you want to have a look at it, fine by me," she answered.

"Sure," Sam said, and walked around to the front of the pickup, where he reached under and pulled the hood release. He lifted the hood and began to tinker with the engine.

"Came with the cafe," she explained. "I don't drive it very much but it comes in handy every once in a while. And sometimes I like to drive out and watch the lights."

"Lights?" George asked.

"Yeah, you know... the Marfa Lights. I like to go out and watch 'em every so often."

"What are the Marfa lights?" George wanted to know. Sam was curious as well.

"Oh, you drive out toward Alpine a few miles and you can see 'em off to the south. They're just lights out there in the desert. A lot of people around here think they're aliens, but no one's ever found any."

"Aliens? Wow!" George was suddenly excited. "Do you think we'll be able to see any?"

He turned to Amy, "You seen the lights, Amy?"

"Yeah, lots of times. They're pretty cool."

"Wow! I'm envious," he said. "See any UFOs or aliens?"

"Lots of weird lights and stuff, so yeah... maybe there were some aliens there." It felt good to be asked about the lights. She felt proud that she knew something that these two travelers didn't.

"There's no aliens," Sam said from under the hood, "It's just some sort of natural phenomenon. Like a rainbow or something."

"Yeah, that's what some people say," Vera responded. "But rainbows don't happen at night, do they?" She peered through the windshield at Sam and stared at him for a long time, until he began to get nervous.

George seemed lost in thought for a moment, then said, "We should go out and see those lights!"

This stirred something inside Amy, and in an uncharacteristic way she blurted out, "I'll take you to see 'em!" after which she was embarrassed and could feel her face redden.

"It's a date then, Amy," George said, "You and me will go out and see 'em, even if these two stick in the muds don't want to."

She smiled, pleased with herself, and hoping that Sam would want to go.

"Try it now," Sam shouted from beneath the hood.

Vera turned the ignition key, pumped the accelerator and, after a few rumbling hiccups, the truck started. It took a minute before it seemed to decide that it would run, but it finally settled into a smooth idle. The boys piled in and Vera pulled the floor shift down into low gear, feathered the clutch and pulled out of the yard and onto the highway. Amy waved to them as they headed up the road.

"There's no aliens," Sam was explaining, "That's just a bunch of UFO conspiracy nuts, making it up."

"Well, since you seem to know all about it, I reckon there's no more to be said, is there?" Vera took her eyes off the road and turned to look at Sam, and this went on for a long time.

"You might want to watch where you're driving," he said anxiously.

"What for?" she countered, and continued to watch him.

"Look, I don't mind if you want to drive yourself off into a ditch, but I'm not all that anxious to join you," he replied.

"Wouldn't want to join me, eh? Boy, you sure know how to put a girl off," she quipped, looking past Sam to meet George's eye and see him wink.

"Aw, that's not what I meant..."

"Yeah, I know what you meant," she said and turned back to look at the road ahead.

"There's really aliens here?" George asked.

"A lot of people think so," Vera said.

"What about you? What do you think?" Sam asked her.

"Well, I think I'm driving an old pickup truck with a couple of men in the front seat with me. One of 'em likes me. The other, not so much. When you figure out which is which, let me know, okay?" She kept her eyes on the road ahead and chuckled silently to herself.

Vera pulled the pickup off onto a dirt road that turned out to be Olive's driveway. It ran for almost a mile before the house came into view, a sprawling old adobe hacienda that sat on a small rise, surrounded by giant cottonwood trees. A sixteen-foot Aermotor windmill stood to one side and spun its blades into the wind, pumping the well water up into a large metal tank that sat atop a tower on the hill above the house. There was a barn, a large open hay shed, and another structure that was used as a bunkhouse.

"C'mon," Vera said, as they got out of the truck. She led the way up the stairs to the massive porch that wound around the entire house. The faint strains of classical music were coming from the back of the house, so she knew that Olive would most likely back in her sun room, reading.

"HELLO OLIVE, IT'S US!" she shouted, pushing open the screen door. They made their way through the entrance to the hallway that led to the sun room. As they passed the library, Sam paused to look through the open doorway at the shelves of books that reached from floor to ceiling.

What Sam didn't know was that, hanging on the other side of the wall, only inches from him and out of view was the old leather map that had been taken from them.

Vera poked her head into the sun room and said, "Hi, Olive. I hope we're not intruding."

"Of course not!" she replied, "Please come in and make yourselves comfortable. There is some lemonade if you would be so kind as to bring some glasses from the kitchen," she asked.

"I'll get them," Vera said and headed down the hallway.

George and Sam stepped into the room behind her as Vera made her way back out to the kitchen.

"Hello, ma'am," George said as they entered the room.

"What's this 'ma'am' stuff?" Olive demanded. "Call me Olive."

"Okay, Olive," George replied, "Thanks again for offerin' us the work."

"Once you see what needs to be done, you might not be thanking me," she said. She motioned out the window and pointed to a building next to the barn and said, "That is the bunkhouse. There are only the two of you here, so make yourselves at home. It has a kitchen and a shower. Anything else you need, you'll have to go to town for, or else build it yourselves."

"It'll do just fine," Sam said, "we don't need much."

Vera arrived back with glasses and poured each of them a tall lemonade from the pitcher. George grabbed the only other chair in the room, forcing Vera and Sam to share the small love seat that sat across from Olive. Vera caught a bit of a gleam in Olive's eye, along with a very slight telltale smile at the corner of her mouth. She found herself blushing and had to admit, sitting next to Sam was not unpleasant. He seemed oblivious but was secretly sweating bullets.

"Now here's how it works around here," Olive began, "I don't follow regular paydays, so when you need money, you boys just let me know how much I owe you."

"Could I ask how much the pay is?" George asked tentatively.

"Yes, you may ask, but I'm not going to tell you," Olive answered, matter-of-factly. "You're the ones doing the work, so you should know how much it's worth. You figure out what needs doing, then do it and charge me what it's worth. Is that simple enough for you?"

"Wait, let me see if I have this straight," Sam said, "You want us to choose what work to do, when to do it, and how much to charge for it?"

"Yes, that's right," Olive replied, "there is more than enough that needs doing around here and you seem like honest young men, so I'm sure you'll keep yourselves busy. I'll leave it all up to you."

"Well then, I guess we'd better get started," Sam replied, "C'mon, pard. Let's load our stuff into the bunkhouse."

"The Ford three quarter ton pickup truck out there beside the bunkhouse is yours to use. The keys are in it," Olive said as the two stood to leave. They stopped to pick up their packs from the back of Vera's pickup and headed down the hill to their new lodging.

"God love 'em," Vera said when they had gone, "They haven't got a clue."

"I expect that tall one's got his eye on you," Olive said.

"Oh, I don't know about that." Vera blushed.

"And it looks to me like the feeling's mutual," Olive paused, "and all I can say is... it's about time." She looked at her friend and smiled, and Vera turned a deeper red.

Ernie Sands

Deputy Ernie Sands was talking to himself again but that was nothing out of the ordinary. He talked to himself constantly and was much too self-absorbed to realize others overheard him. Even if he were aware that they were listening, it wouldn't have made a difference. The only real opinion that mattered was his, and who else was he going to hear it from but himself?

He was enjoying his favorite pastime, sitting in his squad car—Marfa's only police car—a 1955 Buick Special two-door coupe. He loved the car, a black and white beauty that should have been replaced several years before but somehow managed to hang together with what some of the locals referred to as bubble gum and baling wire.

A two-door coupe was an unlikely and impractical vehicle for a cop car, but it was all the county could afford back in 1961 when they bought it second hand from the Brewster County Highway Department over in Alpine for four hundred and twenty-five dollars. Ernie had wanted a Roadmaster, a four-door with the big block V-8 engine and the four Cruiser-Line Portavents on the sides of the front fenders, but since the budget was only five hundred dollars for a police car he had to settle for the bottom of the line—a used Buick Special coupe—with a small block engine and only three Portavents.

The old Buick was a workhorse though, even if it had not actually carried any hardened criminals during Ernie's tenure as Marfa's deputy. It served well in its capacity to transport late night alcoholics home to their wives, wayward hitchhikers to the outskirts of town, and the occasional last-minute mother-to-be to the maternity ward over in Alpine. The single door on each side made it difficult to put suspects into the vehicle, and Ernie grumbled as he folded the front seat forward and held it while the offenders climbed in. Somehow, it just seemed a bit unprofessional. Ernie was a fan of the TV show *Dragnet*, and this was not the way Joe Friday or his partner Frank Smith would have done it. They had four-door Buicks with big-block engines, and later, shiny Dodges and Chryslers with lots of chrome.

Ernie had not given a speeding ticket since 1964, but it wasn't for lack of trying. On sunny afternoons and weekends he could be found sitting in the Buick, parked on the side of the highway outside of town, waiting for westbound speeders to come up over the small rise. When a vehicle passed doing over fifty-five Ernie fired up the small block 264 V-8 (a *Nailhead*, as mechanics liked to mock), pulled the Dynaflow automatic transmission (those same mechanics called it a *Dyna-Flush*) into low range, and gunned the automobile away from the dirt shoulder and out onto the highway in pursuit.

The engine was called a *small block* because of its small bore and piston displacement, but it was in fact a massive cast iron behemoth, and the sheer weight of it created a handicap that the Buick could never manage to overcome. A decade after the war, American automobiles in the nineteen fifties were still built like tanks and artillery, as if Detroit couldn't shed its wartime military legacy. And though it was the cheapest, least pretentious, and lightest of Buick's line, the Special weighed almost two tons. Unless he was driving downhill, Ernie would never catch a speeder. In fact, most speeders weren't even aware he was chasing them because by the time Ernie managed to pull the black and white up onto the road and gain speed, they were long gone.

The lumbering colossus would shamble off the gravel shoulder, wheezing and moaning as it slowly gained forward momentum, the sound of the Dynaflow building to a high-pitched whine until it slammed into high range and caused the Nailhead to cough as it abruptly dropped RPMs and began its Sisyphean struggle to push two tons of iron along the narrow highway in a futile attempt to catch the perpetrator.

By this time the lawbreakers would be three quarters of a mile down the road and would not be able to hear the old fashioned siren that blasted an atonal cacophony from beneath the squad car's right fender, and they kept driving, unaware. Of course, the locals knew that Ernie was there, but they just ignored him and pretended they didn't see him, often commenting as they drove past, *that damned Buick can't even get out of its own way.*

Still, Ernie was proud of the dual spotlights on the front fenders—red on the driver's side, blue on the passenger's—aftermarket enhancements that he added himself. He also installed backup lights, and he kept the Dagmar bumpers and the massive amounts of chrome polished to a high shine. And even though it had only three Portavents on its sides, it was in fine shape thanks to Ernie's constant attention.

He often drove out into the desert in the evening, especially in the heat of summer when his little Airstream trailer reached the temperature of a Dutch oven. He took the Buick down a dirt road to the southeast, far from town, where he would park and switch off the headlights. Then he would settle in to watch the Marfa lights, those mysterious flashes of blue and green fluorescence that rose in faint wisps from the mesas to the south.

On this particular evening he picked up a carne adovada burrito and a Dr Pepper at the *Big Burrito Shack* on Dean Street, rolled down the windows, and adjusted the wind wings for maximum ventilation, then turned the black and white beast up the highway to his favorite spot, where he sat in the car, reclined the driver's seat, and listened to the AM radio. Radio stations increased their power after sundown, when he usually tuned in to *XERB* from Mexico or to truck driver shows all the way from Fort Worth and Oklahoma City. On nights when the interference from the Marfa Lights was at a minimum, he could even catch bits and pieces of shows from Little Rock and as far north as Denver.

He listened to the music and mumbled along in stilted phrases when he didn't quite remember the lyrics to the songs. He fancied himself a musician—or at least a musical authority—but he could never bring himself to admit that he possessed no real musical talent. Back in school he played bass drum in the Marfa High School marching band, beating out half notes while marching around on the football field or in the Marfa Shorthorns Homecoming Parade. He got the hang of hitting the drum each time he took a step, practicing for hours by walking up and down the street in front of his house, scaring the neighborhood dogs and cats and even causing the death of a neighbor's pet songbird that was so scared it wrung its own neck on the bars of the cage while trying to escape.

His drumming was cut short when he graduated from high school. His parents had chosen to remain in Marfa so that their son could finish school with his classmates. Neither of them liked living there. Ernie didn't either, but they didn't know that, so they stayed in the area for his sake. When he walked across that high school auditorium stage to receive his diploma in 1954, they put their plans for the future into action.

They bought a second-hand Airstream trailer for their son and installed it on the five-acre plot of empty land they owned south of town. They had already installed electricity and had drilled a well on the land. They put permanent plumbing into the trailer, hooked it up to the electrical grid, and presented it to Ernie. They gave him seven hundred and fifty dollars and told him to find a job. They would be leaving.

When he asked where they were going his mother replied, "We don't know yet, but we'll let you know when we get there."

Three days later, they drove off in the family's 1948 Kaiser-Frazer Traveler, loaded with a few belongings. The house was put up for sale and Ernie moved into the trailer. Instead of leaving home when he graduated, Ernie's home left him.

He didn't hear from his parents for more than eight years.

Ernie didn't play the drums (or, more specifically, *drum*) anymore, but he still fancied himself a musician and kept his drumsticks (or, more specifically, *mallets*) with him at all times. He often took the mallets out of his desk drawer at the jail and played semibreves on his desk. This inevitably raised the ire of any vagrant, loiterer, or drunk who happened to be enjoying tenancy in the jail's only cell. Unbeknownst to Ernie, his drumming was the primary reason he was left off the guest list of many parties and local get-togethers. That, and the fact that having the deputy sheriff at your party tends to put a damper on the festivities.

Ebbets Escapes

It was a short walk to the small mom-and-pop store where Ebbets kept a post office box, something she had not told Wayne about. He'd been there almost a week, and she didn't know how much longer she could stand it. She was afraid to call the police, afraid it would end badly, the way it always did back in San Antonio.

There were no sidewalks in this part of town so she walked along the edges of the streets past the frame houses that were shaded by large cottonwood and elm trees. She had made an excuse to Wayne and told him that she needed some "feminine things" at the drugstore. She guessed that he wouldn't want to be involved, which proved correct, and he allowed her to go, with instructions to bring back a six-pack of beer, and a threatening reminder that he still had the urn that held her father's ashes. She tried to remain calm as she walked but soon began to cry silently.

I need to stop this, she scolded herself, *I need to focus.*

So far, it had not occurred to Wayne that Ebbets hadn't received any mail in the time they had been in her house. She didn't want him going through her mail the way he had gone through all of her belongings in the house. If he brought it up she would tell him that her mail was still going to a post office box in San Antonio.

Her jewelry was the first thing he took, and Ebbets assumed he bought drugs with it. It was a terrible invasion of her life, but it had become vindictive when he broke a picture of Ebbets and her father, back when she was 8 years old. In it, she and her dad were standing on the front porch of the house the day they moved in.

Wayne had been drunk and stoned on god knows what when he began his rampage through the house. It ended only after he had destroyed many of her most cherished items, including photographs and mementos from her childhood.

"You won't be needing any of this crap," he bellowed, smashing glassware and tearing up old letters and other keepsakes. Ebbets shuddered when his gaze landed on the porcelain urn that was resting on the mantel above the fireplace.

"No, please!" Ebbets pleaded, "those are my father's ashes…. please"

"We'll make a new life, you and me," Wayne said, suddenly quiet and calm, "just you and me."

Ebbets watched in horror as he gently lifted the urn from the mantel and turned it over and over in his hands, examining it, mocking her.

"I think it best if I keep ahold of this," he said. "Wouldn't want anything to happen to it, would we?" The smile on his face was the picture of evil.

"Please, Wayne... those are my father's ashes. Have you no decency?" she begged.

"Oh, your father's ashes will be fine, don't worry. This is just a little insurance... just so you don't get any crazy ideas about running out on me."

She knew she had to get away from him, but she couldn't call the police. If she did he would be back, again and again. He would haunt her, and he would hurt her. He would destroy the urn. She had to leave, at least long enough for him to give up on finding her. And she had to get ahold of that urn, at all costs.

The mailboxes were set into the outside wall of the drugstore, facing the sidewalk. Ebbets dialed the combination and opened the small metal door to her mailbox. She saw that it was full of mail, most of it forwarded from San Antonio. It had piled up while she was in Mississippi.

Ebbets sorted through various bills and junk mail until she spotted a crumpled envelope. She opened it to find another envelope inside, which she tore open. There was no sender's name or address, but she immediately knew who had sent it. She rushed to pull the short letter from its container.

> Dear Ebbets,
>
> We are in the San Antonio freight yards now waiting for a westbound train. It feels so lonely, being so near yet so far away from you. If I could I would walk from here to Boerne just to see your face again but Sam says I should wait and not barge in on your life without asking you first. And I reckon he's right about that.
>
> I don't have much time here so I just want to say that I miss you and want to see you again. I'll write every day (or every day that I can). I hope you think of me sometime.
>
> love,
>
> George Willow

Tears came to her eyes. *Oh, George*, she whispered to herself, *I wish you would come and barge into my life right now. I really do.*

She folded the letter and slid it back into its envelope and put it to the back of the pile. She noticed another item, a postcard, and pulled it from within the stack of mail. On the front was a photograph of a cowboy riding a giant jackrabbit, with the caption, "Cattle Punching on a Jackrabbit." She turned it over and read the short note:

> *Dear Ebbets,*
> *We made it to Marfa, TX. There are some HUGE rabbits around here. I think Sam and I fit right in. Will write soon. I miss you.*
> *love - George Willow*

She laughed out loud, then looked around, embarrassed. No one was watching. She found one more letter, this time the return address said,

> *From George Willow, General Delivery, Marfa Texas*

Ebbets tore open the envelope and unfolded the letter.

> *Dear Ebbets,*
> *Sam and I are in Marfa, TX. I think we are going to stay here a while. Maybe find some work. It is a beautiful place with lots of interesting people and exotic things. But not as beautiful and interesting and exotic as you. If I can't get back to see you soon maybe you could come here? I think you would love this place. I miss you lots.*
> *love - George Willow*

She was sobbing now, a flood of tears that she couldn't control. She placed the letters from George back in her mailbox, along with a couple of bills, and locked it. She couldn't let Wayne see them. She tossed the rest into a trash can and went inside to buy the things she was supposed to be buying.

Every day was an eternity to Ebbets. The only saving grace was that Wayne was drunk or stoned most of the time so that he wasn't interested in sex. But it didn't stop the physical violence and emotional abuse he handed out. Still, Ebbets would rather endure that than any sort of intimacy with him, and thankfully she was left on her own to sleep on the cot in the small back room she used for storage, where she could remain hidden from Wayne's criminal friends. They showed up every evening like clockwork to imbibe any manner of drug or alcohol that Wayne offered, and to transact the sorts of business dealings that Ebbets didn't want to know about.

The best part of her day was the walk to the drugstore. Since she wasn't gone long, and she always brought back a six-pack of beer, Wayne allowed her this indulgence. Once she was out of sight of the house, her pace quickened and she had to stop herself from running to get there. Her second trip proved fruitless, but two days later there was another letter from George, and she whooped for joy as she tore it open.

> *Dear Ebbets,*
>
> *Sam and I are still in Marfa Texas. We got a job working on a ranch. Can you believe it? Marfa is small but it has a lot of interesting people. I wish you could see it. The desert is beautiful but it's pretty hot during the day.*
>
> *Looks like we're going to be here for a while. The work is good, and we both like it here. Oh and I think Sam likes a girl here but he won't admit it. As for me, I'm still holding out for you. I miss you and want to see you again.*
>
> *I'll keep writing to you. If you want to write back, you can send the letter to me (George Willow) C/O General Delivery, Marfa, TX. I'm pretty sure it will get to me.*
>
> *I miss you Ebbets Fields.*
>
> *love,*
>
> *George Willow*

Ebbets wiped her tears and smiled to herself. She read the letter again and again. Finally, she folded it back into the envelope. She had been working on a plan, something she could do, and for the first time in a long time, Ebbets felt alive. She grabbed George's other letters out of the mailbox before she closed it. She pushed the letters down into her handbag and covered them with makeup and other things so that Wayne wouldn't see them. She went inside to buy beer and on an impulse, bought something else. Then she headed home.

Ebbets took two bottles of beer out of the two six-packs and hid them among the bottles of cleaner and scrub brushes beneath the kitchen sink. She would need them later. Wayne usually drank every drop in the house by the time he passed out at night, so she made sure she would have some beer on hand for what she planned.

Wayne had stashed the urn underneath the bed, knowing that Ebbets didn't want to go into the bedroom. If she did try to take it, he would make her pay. He would use that bed to make her pay, and he would make sure she knew that her father's ashes were sitting right there beneath her while he was making her pay. And it worked. Ebbets was afraid to go into the bedroom, afraid to go near the one thing she cherished more than the house itself. She wouldn't dare touch that urn.

Ebbets stayed back in the storage room until she heard the last of Wayne's friends leave. When she finally came out she found him in the living room, drunk as usual.

"Hey, bring me a beer."

Ebbets went to the kitchen and pulled the two bottles of beer from their hiding place beneath the sink. As she opened them she hoped he wouldn't notice that they were warm. She would just have to chance it. She opened the small bottle of sleeping pills she had bought at the drugstore and poured its contents out onto the counter. She picked up a teaspoon and used it to crush the pills into powder. Then she swept it up into her hand and dumped it into one of the beers.

"What the hell ya doin' in there?" Wayne shouted from the other room.

"Just finding a church key, sorry. I'm coming."

After wiping the powdery residue from the bottle's spout, she tossed the empty pill bottle into the trash can under the sink and took the drinks into the living room.

She crossed over to the couch and handed him a bottle.

"I like it better when it's like this, just you and me," she said, "I don't like it when all your friends are around all the time."

"Yeah, babe," he slurred, "that's what I've been tryin' to tell you. It's you and me… we're gonna start us a new life. That's what I been sayin'…just you and me." He took another long drink from the bottle.

Ebbets didn't know how strong the sleeping pills were, or how big a dose to give, but she figured they wouldn't kill him. *Especially someone with as big a drug tolerance as he has,* she thought.

They took effect surprisingly quickly. Within half an hour, Wayne had passed out on the sofa, knocking over his bottle and spilling the rest of it on the table. Ebbets tried to wake him by shaking him and yelling at him, but he didn't respond. She went to the bedroom.

She pulled the urn from under the bed and made her way back to the storeroom and grabbed the small bag she had packed. As she rushed from the room she didn't notice the envelope that fell out of her bag. It flew toward two boxes resting on the floor against the wall and slid neatly down between them, out of sight. Ebbets slipped out the back door and went to the garage and rifled through a pile of discarded junk until she found a spot to hide the urn from Wayne.

It was a little after two in the morning when she arrived at the bus depot. The bus to San Antonio wouldn't leave for almost four hours, but Ebbets was fairly certain that Wayne would be asleep far longer than that. There was a bench on the side of the building. She sat down, out of the light, wrapped her coat tighter around her, and waited for the sun to come up.

Wayne

Wayne felt the rage boiling up inside again. *She's gone, god dammit... gone!* He had passed out last night and she snuck away like the thieving, conniving bitch she was. But now she was gonna pay for it, god dammit.

She'll pay for it. She'll pay for all of it.

The hangover seized him like a vise when he woke up that afternoon. He stumbled around and called her name, and it took him some time to finally realize the house was empty, that Ebbets was gone. At first, he thought she might be at the store, but an hour passed, and then another. She wasn't coming back.

"God *DAMMIT*," he yelled at the empty room, "Damn her to *HELL!*"

He threw an empty beer bottle across the room, where it bounced harmlessly off the wall and landed on the carpet, unbroken. It fueled his anger and set him to trashing the living room. He flew about in a rage, knocking over furniture and lamps, throwing anything he could get his hands on at the walls. She wouldn't get away with it. No, she'd pay, and she'd pay dearly.

A sudden thought stopped him. *The urn with her old man's ashes,* he thought to himself. He hurried to the bedroom, pushed the bed aside in a rush of impatience and apprehension, and saw that it was gone. *The bitch took it. DAMMIT!*

And then, as quickly as it had come, his fury vanished. A peacefulness swept over Wayne, the sort of dangerous peacefulness that takes ahold of a psychopath when an outburst of anger is suddenly replaced by calm, methodical, evil intent. If Ebbets had been there she would have recognized this to be the calm before the storm, and that Wayne's anger had disappeared on the outside because he was concentrating it on the inside. She would have known that he would soon explode.

Wayne would not make this mistake again. He would put the booze away for a little while, but not because he felt guilty. Guilt is something he had never experienced. No, he would stop drinking because he could not allow himself to be vulnerable. He would not be defenseless against someone as weak as Ebbets. He needed to focus, and for this he would need a clear head. He would become a new man, a man on a mission. And now he had a clear vision of what that mission was. Ebbets would pay, he'd make sure of that.

Wayne managed to keep this resolution for another couple of hours, until he drove to the store for food and cigarettes. He figured a beer or two couldn't hurt so he bought a couple of six-packs and brought them back to the house. He never got around to fixing dinner because by nine o'clock that night he was wasted. By ten-thirty he was passed out on the couch, and by eleven he had slid off onto the floor, where he spent the rest of the night.

He awoke late the following morning with the same hangover left over from the previous day. His anger had subsided, but his purpose had not—he would find Ebbets and he would show her that Wayne Guidry was not a person to be trifled with.

He searched the house, starting with the storage room where she slept. He rummaged through boxes of old papers and personal keepsakes, tossing them aside and scattering their contents as he rifled through her possessions. There were boxes of clothes and bags of memorabilia, old photographs of Ebbets and her father, a small wooden box full of lipstick and makeup, a personal phonebook that he almost kept—until he realized it was her father's, and then he simply threw it aside—and piles of belongings that didn't interest him.

After he had reduced the storage room to a pile of rubbish, with paper and broken belongings scattered all over, he turned to leave. He nearly missed the envelope that was stuck between two boxes on the floor. It caught his eye, and something about it caused him to stoop down and pick it up. He opened the letter from George and read it, looked at the date, and his anger returned, fueled by the words on the page. When he finished reading, he was trembling, but instead of tearing the letter to shreds, he folded it neatly and slipped it back inside the envelope.

"Hmmmm... So you got yourself a boyfriend in Marfa," he said to himself, "Well, little lady.... I got me some friends there, too. This might end up being fun."

Ebbets Goes to Marfa

Ebbets watched the flat west Texas desert roll by and listened to the hum of the tires on the two lane highway. They sang a sort of harmony with the whine of the Greyhound's big diesel engine. The long day inside the big silver vessel had not bothered her at all; in fact, the trip seemed to give her more energy the farther west she traveled.

When she left Boerne she went to her friend Susan's in San Antonio to hide from Wayne. She needed a bit of space to figure out what to do. When he called, Susan threw him off the trail by telling him that she thought Ebbets was headed back up to her cousins in Vicksburg.

Ebbets spent a few days in San Antonio preparing for the journey to Marfa. She had no change of clothes, not even a jacket, so she withdrew the small amount left in her savings account and picked up some supplies for the trip. She bought a few items of clothing from the Salvation Army thrift store along with some other things—a toothbrush, a hairbrush, some makeup, and a large purse to put it all into. She was traveling light and had no wish to be overloaded with belongings.

The bus left San Antonio around midnight and seemed to stop in every little town and village along the way. At this rate the journey was going to take forever, but as anxious as Ebbets was to get to Marfa—to get to George—still, she was content to put up with the interruptions and delays. She was free, and she would let the chips fall where they may. If things didn't work out in Marfa she would keep going. She would head west until she hit the ocean. After that, she would just play it by ear.

The Greyhound reached Del Rio late in the morning, where it stopped to wait for the bus arriving from San Angelo. During the long layover Ebbets stayed aboard to catch some sleep. She was awakened by the shudder of the engine when the driver put the coach into gear and turned back onto the two-lane. The midday light made the desert look all the more lonely and isolated, but she savored it and allowed it to lull her to sleep again.

It was late in the day the first time Amy laid eyes on Ebbets, when the Greyhound pulled up in front of the cafe. She was wiping off the counter and looked out to see a tall woman climb down from the bus. The woman was wearing a flowery dress, with a big floppy hat that seemed more like an umbrella. She reached down to pick up the bag that the bus driver had unloaded for her and she stepped out into the heat of the Texas afternoon.

As the Greyhound roared back onto the road, the woman turned a complete circle, taking in her surroundings, and then she turned and headed in Amy's direction, across the gravel parking lot toward the front door of the cafe.

She came inside and tossed her belongings into a booth seat, then slid in next to them. When she took off her hat and set it aside, Amy saw the shock of red hair that cascaded to one side in a long, shimmering braid that disappeared below the table top.

Amy kept wiping the counter and filling the napkin holders while Vera hollered from behind the kitchen line, "Somethin' I can get for you?"

"Oh! I didn't see you in there," the lady answered. She seemed startled. "Well, hmmmm. I'm not sure... maybe a cup of tea and some toast or something? I'll look at the menu."

"Sure thing." Vera was going through her regular routine, putting together the setup for tomorrow morning's rush. She filled a pot and grabbed a teabag, then took a place setting out to the woman. She made it all look easy, the way she set the table, poured the small kettle of hot water, and added the teabag all in one smooth movement. What took Vera a few seconds would have taken Amy several minutes.

"Well, I don't know... maybe I'll have lunch... but no, it's too late for that. I don't really want dinner, but..."

"Well, how 'bout an English muffin to go with that tea?" Vera replied, more as a statement than a question.

"Oh, you have those? That would be wonderful! Thank you."

"No problem." Vera walked back to the kitchen, pulled a muffin out of the bag, sliced it, and tossed it into the toaster. Amy continued to study Ebbets as Vera worked in the kitchen.

Amy was fascinated by this new arrival and could tell that Vera was, too. Vera enjoyed watching people from back in the kitchen. She didn't exactly spy on them, but she was able to observe the real *them* from her vantage point. After months of watching Vera, Amy eventually picked up the knack herself. She liked to observe the interplay and interactions between people, especially when they didn't know each other. Each one adopted a public persona while they sat in the cafe. Each chose how they presented themselves to the world, and Vera was always fascinated by it. Amy found it addictive and tried her best to study people without being obvious about it and staring at them, and without stopping her work.

Vera and Amy were both watching this woman. She looked to be a few years younger than Vera as she fidgeted nervously in the booth. She fiddled with a scarf, rummaged aimlessly through her handbag as if looking for something, and checked her watch over and over. She might be waiting for someone, but Amy suspected that it was the other way around, that maybe she was running from something.

She was dressed in bright colors—folks around Marfa would call her a hippie—and she wore that floppy hat, so if she were trying to hide from someone, she wasn't doing a good job of it. Amy was instantly attracted to this new woman and loved the way she looked. Amy thought she was the most exciting person she had ever seen, and at that point in her life, she probably was.

As Vera worked in the kitchen Amy overheard her talking to herself as she often did.

"Her handbag could carry half of everything I own," Vera mumbled to herself.

She didn't understand why anyone would drag all that stuff around. But the woman carried it with a certain ease and elegance. Vera probably figured there must not be a lot inside. Ebbets had on a pair of large round horn rimmed glasses that would make most women look like a librarian, but in her case they seemed to showcase the elegance in her eyes, and they lent her the appearance of an eccentric intellectual. Marfa had a few of those types, so she wasn't completely out of place.

Vera didn't take much interest in the lives of others—especially strangers—but Amy could see that she found this woman intriguing. Vera didn't pry—she prided herself on minding her own business—but when she set the tea and muffin down in front of Ebbets she asked, "What brings you to Marfa?"

"Not sure, really. Sort of a dare. An impulse, I guess. Someone suggested I come here, so here I am. I have no idea why I'm here or what I'm doing. Just wanted to look around."

She was afraid to give the real reason: that she came to Marfa looking for a man she barely knew.

"Well, if you don't know what you're doing, you're probably in the right place," Vera said with a grin, "Marfa's full of folks who have no idea what they're doing. You'll fit right in."

The woman laughed, and her face relaxed for the first time. She held out her hand. "My name is Ebbets," she said.

"Pleased to meet you, Ebbets," she replied as the two shook hands, "I'm Vera," she said, then pointed across the room. "And over there is Amy". The girl waved and said hello.

"Hello Amy, nice to meet you," she said with a friendly smile, and then turned back to Vera, "Ah, Vera… so this is your cafe?"

"I'm afraid so."

"I love your place," Ebbets said, "I love a good cafe where you can just sit and have a coffee and read and just sit and think. And yours is just lovely."

"Well, thanks a lot," Vera replied sheepishly, "It's a little rough around the edges, but thanks. I don't get compliments much. The cowboys and the truckers who come in here ain't exactly complementary types." She looked back at Ebbets and smiled.

"You stayin in town somewhere?"

"I just got here, so I haven't really looked."

"There ain't a lot of choice. You can put yourself up over at the Paisano. It's over by the courthouse. They filmed "Giant" here in Marfa and all the movie stars stayed there. And there's the Saint George. They're both nice, but they're kind of expensive."

Ebbets hesitated, looking a little unsure of herself, "To tell the truth, I haven't really thought this through. I guess if I don't find something here, I'll just keep heading west."

"You lookin' for work, or are you just on vacation?" Vera asked.

"I suppose I'm going to be looking for a job somewhere. I have enough to live on for a little bit, but I'm going to need to work."

"What sort of work do you do?"

"Well, lately I've been an art student, so that's not going to get me very far, is it?" She laughed, "I've been a waitress, and I've done other things. I'm pretty good at just doing what needs doing, I guess."

When she mentioned "art student" Amy's ears perked up and she quickly brought a dishrag and started wiping the table next to Ebbets, just to get in on the conversation.

Vera was considering what Ebbets said. Sam and George were living at Olive's now, and the apartment was empty. *Jesus,* she thought, *not again...*

"I'll tell you what... my tenants just moved out, so there's an empty apartment upstairs if you're interested."

Ebbets was studying her tea, stirring it mindlessly with her spoon. She looked up, "An apartment? Gee, that sounds wonderful, but I'm not sure I could afford it and I haven't found a job yet and...."

"Hold on," Vera interrupted, "Why don't you just stay the night and get yourself collected. We can talk about it later. For now, you look like you could use a place to stay, and I happen to have a place, okay? Like I said, the tenants moved out and it's sitting there empty."

Ebbets' eyes began to water and she turned away. Vera and Amy watched her as she was slowly overtaken by sobs, then began to cry.

"I'm sorry, she said, catching her breath, "I'm sorry... I just can't believe I met someone who is so *nice.* Thank you *so much."*

Amy grabbed some napkins from the next table and passed them to her. "Here you go," she said, "it's okay." Amy patted her on the shoulder, then thought better of it and quickly pulled her hand away. She didn't want to seem forward.

Vera said, "Why don't we get your stuff moved upstairs? Things will look better in the morning. And tomorrow there's someone I want you to meet."

Ebbets and Olive

It was mid-morning when Vera climbed the stairs from the cafe to the apartment and knocked on the door. It was an odd feeling, having to knock to enter her own place. No one else had stayed there since she moved in six years before, and all of a sudden it had two sets of visitors within a few weeks. Vera didn't know what to make of it. Amy guessed that maybe Vera was coming out of her own shell a bit. *Stranger things have happened*, she thought to herself.

Ebbets answered the door and she looked slightly bedraggled and confused, as if she didn't quite know where she was. Vera solved her dilemma for her.

"C'mon downstairs and have some breakfast. Like I said last night, I want you to meet someone."

"Okay, thanks," Ebbets said, "I'll be right down. Just let me fix myself up a bit."

"You look fine to me, but suit yourself," Vera told her and headed back downstairs.

It was late enough that the breakfast crowd was gone and there were only four customers in the place—a man and wife at a table, each reading a section of the newspaper and ignoring the other, and two truckers sitting together at the counter, talking. Every once in a while, one of them would ask Amy for a refill on their coffee.

Olive Stanfield commanded the corner booth by herself, as she always did when she came in. After Vera served the men their food, she asked Amy to set a coffee pot down on the counter in front of them and tell them to help themselves. Amy didn't like doing that because she felt they wasted a whole pot of coffee that way. Instead, she just kept filling their cups when they asked.

Vera walked back to Olive's corner booth and sat down to talk with her. "Sounds as if your apartment is becoming quite busy," Olive commented as she stirred her tea.

"When it rains it pours," Vera replied, "I'm afraid I have another stray that needs looking after. She looks like she's had a pretty rough go of it, from what I can tell."

The upstairs door opened and the two women listened as Ebbets stepped slowly down the stairs until finally the stairwell door opened, and she came into the cafe. Amy hollered, "Hi Ebbets!" and she waved back at the girl. Amy had to look twice at her because she was not kidding about fixing herself up. The girl hadn't yet learned the trick, and she was amazed at how some women can completely make themselves over in just a couple of minutes. It's something that continued to amaze her throughout her life.

She had no idea how women did it, or where they learned it, but Amy knew that Ebbets was certainly one of those women. She had not changed her clothes—she just added a few things—a couple of silver bracelets, a pair of earrings, a long tie-dyed scarf, with her big glasses and large floppy hat. Her red hair was braided in a long strand that hung down one side. The change in her was remarkable, and Amy thought she was stunning. And judging by the open mouths and wide-eyed stares on the faces of the truckers at the counter, she wasn't the only one who thought so.

Ebbets paused to look around, her eyes wide with a perpetual bewildered look that took in everything around her. When she spotted the two women, her face broke into a huge smile and her eyes softened, as if she were overcome with a sense of relief and happiness all at once.

"And here she comes now," Vera said to Olive as Ebbets glided gracefully toward them. Vera introduced the two and Ebbets slid into the booth. Vera offered Ebbets a cup of tea, then stood and turned back toward Amy in the kitchen, leaving them to their visit.

"Vera tells me you're thinking of staying around for a while," Olive said.

"Yes, I think so. I'm not really sure what I would do here, but I want to stay. I know I'll have to find some sort of work. Marfa is such a beautiful place... so primitive and raw... so *rustic*!"

"For a minute there I thought you were going to say 'run down'," Olive added, with a smile. "Around these parts we refer to primitive places as being *western.*"

"Oh no, not that! What I meant was, well, it's just so *different* from Boerne, and the green Texas hill country where I'm from."

"Yes, it certainly is that," Olive agreed. "What sorts of things do you like to do, Ebbets?" she asked. "What makes your heart sing?"

"I'm a painter... that is, I like to paint, and to make things, and do creative stuff."

"So, you're an artist?" Olive responded, more as a statement than a question.

"Oh, I don't know… maybe you could call me that, though I'm not a *real* artist, at least not yet."

"Now, why would you say that?"

"Umm, I haven't really had any big shows or anything, and it's not like my work is in any galleries in New York or anything."

Olive looked at Ebbets with an appraising stare, "You should be careful about the things you declare about yourself. Maybe you don't want to brag about your work—braggadocio is such an unseemly trait, especially for a beautiful young woman like you—but self-disparagement is no better. Are you good at what you do?"

"Well, yes… I hope I am. At least, I *think* I am. And others have told me how much they like my art." Ebbets paused, "All I know is that I love doing it, but that it's not such a great way to make a living." She smiled.

"One never knows," Olive said. "There are many paths to follow through life. The pathways we choose will take us to the places we want to be. And those that are thrust upon us, those that take us to the places we don't want to be, well… they help to teach us about those pathways that we do choose. And while I don't mean to pry, you strike me as being on a pathway right now that is not of your own choosing."

Ebbets blushed and was silent for a moment. Olive's words struck a chord somewhere deep within. When she finally spoke her voice trembled slightly, and she seemed to be fighting back tears.

"I don't know how you knew, but it's true. Coming here isn't what I would choose to do—at least, not the way I did."

"Well, we'll leave that discussion for another time," Olive assured her, reaching over to pat her hand. "That's your business and no one else's. But let me ask you, do you have what might be called 'practical' skills? Something you could work at while you pursue your art?"

"Oh sure," Ebbets replied, "I know how to cook. I've waited tables in a cafe. I've done a bit of bookkeeping, cleaned houses. I'm pretty good with little kids, too." She beamed with pride at being able to list her skills.

Olive paused to consider this. "I'll tell you what… Why don't you come out to the ranch for a visit? There is much that needs doing out there." She smiled, looked across the cafe until she caught Amy's eye, and winked, which made the girl blush again.

"And frankly Ebbets," she continued, "I don't want to be bothered with doing it," she said with a chuckle. "There are ranch hands living in the bunkhouse out there right now, so I don't really have a place for you to stay, but maybe we can find you something here in town."

Vera overheard this part and went over, "You're welcome to stay upstairs for as long as you want. It sits there empty all the time and it could use some loving care. Long as you don't mind hearing customers coming in at oh-dark-thirty in the morning."

"Oh, I wouldn't want to impose... I just don't..."

"It's settled then," Olive declared, "You'll stay here and come out to the ranch as soon as you see fit. Between Vera and myself, I think we can fix you up with enough work to keep you out of trouble."

She turned to Vera, "And Vera dear, I do hope you will bring Ebbets along to my party."

"It will be my pleasure," Vera said.

Olive rose to leave. She gave a knowing smile to Vera, then turned back to Ebbets, "And Ebbets, I'll want to have a look at some of your artwork sometime. I'm always interested in seeing the work of new artists."

"Oh, thank you *so much*!" Ebbets cried, and flung her arms around Olive, who stood sort of rigid as Ebbets hugged her, tears running down her face. Ebbets uncoupled from the embrace and turned to Vera and grabbed her in a hug that took her by surprise, too. Neither of them were really the hugging type, but Amy could tell that both Olive and Vera silently enjoyed it, even though they both did their best not to let it show.

After Olive left and Ebbets returned to the apartment, Vera stood at the kitchen sink. The cafe was empty and it was just her and Amy there, staring down at the dishes. Vera was still feeling that hug. Ebbets had given it so freely and easily and it surprised Vera how powerful that was. It had been a very long time since someone had hugged her like that. She stood there, thinking back to when she was a little girl. A very long time, indeed.

And the scene had been a bit overwhelming for Amy as well. She felt the intense feeling of love and closeness that was all mixed up inside her, together with a sense of loss and loneliness that she couldn't seem to shake off.

Wayne Makes Plans

Wayne Guidry held the phone's receiver clamped between his neck and chin and tried to carry on a conversation while writing down the details.

"I don't give a shit what they think, I'll do it anyway," he said. "What the hell, why can't they just let it go? I can run a few bricks, no problem. I'll get it there fast, and it won't cost you a dime."

He was growing impatient and it was all he could do to hold his temper. He hated being forced to wait for the man on the other end of the line to finish what he was saying. But this was a powerful man, not the kind you wanted to mess with, and Wayne knew he had to let him run out of arguments before he could speak.

"Look, I know these guys in Alpine. They're old friends. I need them to do me a favor, and if I can run a load of herb over to 'em it'll all work out just fine, okay? It's okay, man. It'll be cool."

When the phone call ended and the deal was finally made he dialed a number in Alpine and listened to it ring several times before it was answered.

"Lloyd, is that you?"

"Who is this?"

"It's me, Wayne Guidry, over here in San Antone."

"Dang, man! What the hell? Good tuh hear from yuh, brother!"

"Yeah man, same here. Listen. I got a deal for you."

"What's up?"

He related the details of the deal, then waited for Lloyd to reply. There was a long pause on the other end of the line.

"Lloyd? You there man?"

"Yeah Wayne. Sorry, I was just thinkin'." Wayne waited for him to continue, "It's just that, well... I seen your girlfriend over in Marfa. I didn't say nothin' to her, and I don't think she recognized me. But damn, what the hell is she doing out here?"

"What? You talkin' about Ebbets?"

"Yeah man, Ebbets," Lloyd replied, "I seen her goin' into the drug store the other day."

Wayne paused before replying, "Well, maybe that's just one more reason to come see you."

Vera

Vera let her hair down for the party. It fell as a flowing waterfall that cascaded in waves almost to her waist. She collected it in the back with a coral inlaid sterling silver clip that a Hopi friend had made for her. Her white peasant blouse was cut low in front and allowed the antique Navajo squash blossom to take center stage with its silver flutes and conchos adorned with alternating turquoise and coral stones.

Her blouse was tucked into a long broomstick skirt, sinuous and graceful, with its hem only an inch above the floor. It covered a pair of Tony Lama snakeskin boots. A Navajo concho belt gathered the shirt and dress at their intersection to accentuate her figure. The skirt's highlight was its merry-go-round of pleats that caused it to billow and float in graceful shapes when a cowboy twirled Vera on the dance floor. That was something she had not done in a long time. She felt overdressed, but she wanted to make an impression, and she rarely got a chance to dress up.

As she fastened her turquoise earrings, she considered lipstick but thought better of it. She rummaged through her old wooden jewelry box and selected several silver Navajo pawn bracelets and slid them over both wrists. Vera paused to look at herself in the full length mirror. She kept thinking about Sam and couldn't shake the anxiety of seeing him at Olive's party.

What in the hell is wrong with me? I feel like a fifteen year old girl waitin' by the phone for a boy to call.

She barely recognized the woman who looked back. She could not remember the last time she had dressed up like this, and her nerves were suddenly amplified.

What am I doing?

She was interrupted by a tapping at the door.

"Hello? Are you ready yet?" Ebbets called.

"C'mon in. Just have to grab a jacket."

Ebbets stopped in the doorway and stared. "Oh my god," she gasped, "You are *beautiful!*"

Vera blushed. "Well, not so's you'd notice," she mumbled.

"No, I mean... you are absolutely gorgeous! I LOVE what you've done with yourself. And look at all those beautiful bracelets! Oh, Vera!" Ebbets was on the verge of tears.

"Well, I try to clean up every once in a while," Vera paused, "but speaking of gorgeous, look at *you*!"

Once again Ebbets had risen to the occasion. *God, she looks like a model on the cover of a fashion magazine,* Vera thought as she took in the view of her new friend. Ebbets's hair was braided and pulled to one side, with small ribbons of various colors tied through it. Her dress was covered in a sea of yellow daisies of all sizes, with what looked to be an expensive designer belt that made her waist look even smaller than it was. She had on a pair of bright red pumps with colorful stockings that didn't match. Vera thought it was quirky and elegant at the same time.

They headed out to the pickup truck. "I don't know how you do it," Vera said. "You are absolutely amazing."

"Well, I know one thing," Ebbets replied as they climbed up into the cab, "the men at this party don't have a chance. They're not gonna know what hit 'em." The pair laughed out loud.

The Party

The sun was setting and the party was well underway when Vera turned the old Chevy pickup into Olive's ranch road and up the long drive to the house. She pulled up beneath one of the giant cottonwoods that surrounded the house and the two got out and made their way up the steps of the front porch and into the front parlor. Country music filled the evening air. There were speakers strategically placed in rooms throughout the rambling hacienda, and as the two women stepped inside Merle Haggard was singing "Mama Tried."

"C'mon," Vera said, catching Ebbets's hand and leading her down a hallway toward the back end of the house.

They found Olive in the sun room, holding court with a crowd of people. Amy sat beside her, basking in the glow of the atmosphere. The young girl was a loner, but she loved parties and get-togethers where she could sit to one side, inconspicuous, and study the goings-on around her. Sometimes she would sneak her camera out and take a few shots without anybody knowing. She often sat alone on a sidewalk bench in town with pencil and pad, sketching people who passed by. But there at Olive's, Amy had to make do with memorizing them so that she could sketch them later.

The house was filled with folks from around Marfa and Alpine and from the neighboring ranches to the south and west. Olive sat in her chair at the head of the table with a margarita in her hand, describing her newest acquisition. She had purchased an old map that was a piece of genuine folk art. She paused mid-sentence when Vera and Ebbets appeared in the doorway, and all eyes turned toward them.

"Well now," Olive exclaimed, "don't you two look magnificent." Both women blushed deeply. "I expect Marfa's never seen the likes of you. Welcome to the party, girls. We need to get you two something to drink."

Every man in the room—and many of the women—stared in disbelief. Those who knew Vera had to look twice just to make sure it was really her. And as for the new girl, Ebbets lit up the room like it was a spring morning. If Amy was in awe of Ebbets before, she was even more so now.

There was a momentary pause, a sort of collective gasp as the group absorbed the new arrivals. As if on cue, the cowboys jumped up all at once to offer their seats and asked what the ladies wanted to drink. Vera and Ebbets sat down next to Olive, smiles on their faces.

"Why don't you bring the girls a couple of glasses of lemonade," Olive suggested, and several men stampeded just to see who could get to the bar first. Amy watched all of this in wonder and amazement, and the two ladies went up several more notches in her estimation.

"Now, Ebbets," Olive continued, "this is our dear girl, Amy," she said, running a hand over the girl's hair. "Amy has been staying out here with me for a few days, helping me get the house ready for the party."

"Yes, she and I have met. Good to see you, Amy." Ebbets reached across to offer her hand.

"Hi," Amy muttered bashfully, feeling her face turn red. Ebbets smiled at her as they shook hands. She had an almost magical ability to put people at ease, and it was working on Amy, who had a grin on her face a mile wide.

"So, do you like your school here in Marfa?" Ebbets asked.

"Yeah, sorta. It's summer vacation now so I'm not going to school."

"Amy has been an enormous help to me out here on the ranch," Olive said, "she is a very clever and hardworking young lady."

"She certainly strikes me that way," Ebbets replied.

"Yes, we really love our Amy," Olive added. She turned to the girl.

"And Amy? Ebbets will be working out here, so maybe you can give her some pointers and show her around the place, okay?"

"Sure," she responded, turning to look at Ebbets, "I can show you around if you want."

"Wow, this sounds like fun! Where do we begin? Do you have horses here?"

"Yep, wanna see 'em? We can go down to the barn right now!" She was thrilled.

"You bet I do!"

"That sounds like fun, ladies, but first I must take Vera and Ebbets to see my newest acquisition. Come along with us, Amy."

With that, Olive rose to her feet with the elegance of a queen and, with a flourish, guided the three of them to the library.

The Map

Just down the long hall, George and Sam stood in the library and stared at the map that was now framed and hung on the wall. It was the centerpiece of Olive's party. Earlier, she conducted a short tour for her guests and explained the map's history and cultural significance. Some of the guests voiced opinions about what it represented. Those who spoke Spanish were able to translate the place names, many of which were known to the locals. The place marked with the iron cross remained a mystery, however, and after a bit of fruitless speculation about it, the guests retired to the bar to grab drinks, listen to the music, and dance. The two boys listened to the stories about the map, fascinated. Later, they returned to get a closer look at it.

"Pretty danged sure that's our map," George remarked after the others were gone.

"Yep, it is," Sam replied, "but how in the world did it get here? And what's it doin' in that frame?"

"Do you think we ought to talk to Olive about it?" George asked.

Sam thought about it. "Nah. Probably best to leave it. It wasn't ours anyway, and who knows? Maybe it's just one of those things that are made to look old. You know, like those models of old pirate ships, or those fake pictures they take of you with those old west costumes and guns. There's probably hundreds of 'em out there."

"Yeah, Olive's been mighty nice to us. No sense causing her any grief over a stupid leather map."

This was the first chance they had to really study it. If it was a fake, it was a good one. The burled patina of the leather looked old and genuine to Sam. He fell silent for a minute, then finally spoke.

"Some of these words are the same as the ones on the piece of paper I have." He paused, then continued, "You know, the note that was with the map when we found it?"

George nodded, "That note looks pretty real to me. Looks like it might even explain what's on the map. What if this map is the real thing? Maybe the note would tell us where the treasure is. Whattaya think?"

Sam replied, "Yeah, I was just thinkin' the same thing. That Mexican guy in the boxcar—what was his name? Diego? —he seemed pretty worked up about it all, like he wanted to make sure we kept it."

"Yeah, he did," George said, "It seemed like he was real worried, like it really meant something to him."

"Well, I reckon maybe we'll never know. Anyway, it looks pretty good up there on Olive's wall."

"Yep, it sure does," George agreed, "Now how about we go out on the porch and sorta keep an eye on things?"

"You go on," Sam said, "I'm gonna go over to the bunkhouse for a little while."

As Sam and George headed out the back door, Olive brought Ebbets, Vera, and Amy into the library, unaware that they had just missed them.

"Here it is, girls," Olive said, leading us into the room and gesturing toward the map, "my lovely new piece of Marfa history."

Lonnie Tate stood unnoticed in the shadows at the other end of the room while the boys were talking about the map. He pretended to study one of the paintings on the wall while he eavesdropped on everything they said.

He thought, *Hmmmm… a treasure map and a note. We'll just have to see about that.*

When he heard the women approaching in the hallway he slipped out.

Ernie

Ernie Sands was in the sun room, talking with Sorghum Smith and Davy Lilly, two local ranch hands. Sorghum turned to him,

"Hey Ernie, do you *have* to drive that danged black and white to the party? Hell, man... it's a real buzz kill sittin' out there like that."

"Don't know what you mean, Sorghum," Ernie replied, "It's the only car I have. What's wrong with it?"

"Sorta kills the party vibe," Davy responded, "I mean, what if we was to want to go and have a little fun outdoors? You can't very well enjoy the evening with a cop car and those dual spotlights starin' at ya."

"Those spotlights aren't starin' at you," Ernie said defensively, "Anyway, they're turned off. And besides, I've got 'em both pointed down. So they're not starin'. And that's that."

"Well, I can feel 'em starin' at me through the back of my head, like they was piercin' my skull," Sorghum looked at his pal and winked, "But seein' as how you got 'em turned off and lookin' down at the ground, I reckon you won't mind if ol' Davy and me find us a couple of friendly gals and go climb into that black and white and smoke a little weed then, would you?"

"I hope you boys aren't gonna test my patience here," Ernie warned.

Sorghum took a slow pull on his Lone Star before replying, "Well now, that black and white is mighty invitin'. And I'm gonna tell you what. Not sure if we're gonna be able restrain ourselves when it comes to findin' a comfortable spot to toot a little Mexican laughing tobacco." Davy joined in the laughter and Ernie frowned.

"That car doesn't belong to me, it belongs to the county. It's my responsibility and I'll see to it that no one smokes Mexican tobacco or anything else in it."

"That's Mexican *laughing* tobacco, amigo. There's a difference." Sorghum paused, then added, "Say pard, I'll bet the ladies go wild on a date in that thing, don't they?"

"I don't use it for..."

Sorghum continued, "What I'm sayin' is, it's all about timin' and technology, ain't it? Women are just naturally attracted to all things technical, and it seems to me that your black and white there is the epitome of high technology, what with them dual spotlights and flashin' beacons and sirens and all. Hell, it's even got a walkie-talkie in it." Before Ernie could reply, Sorghum cut him off again, "And the women like it when you take your time, don't they?"

Ernie fumbled for words, "Well, I don't know... I guess they do, but..."

"EXACTLY, amigo! They love it when you go slow. You know, just takin' your time with 'em, not in a hurry, movin' slow." Sorghum turned to look at the faces in the small crowd that had gathered. He turned back to Ernie, "And we all know just how slow that ol' Buick goes, don't we?"

The room erupted in laughter. Another joke at his expense. Ernie should have been used to it, but somehow it always stung.

"Yeah, well... you can have your beat up old ranch trucks and yer goosenecks. That car's the best danged car in Marfa or anywhere else, for that matter." He turned and left them to their jokes.

Amy and Ebbets

Amy felt awkward with Ebbets holding her hand as they walked toward the old weathered barn. She wasn't used to that sort of intimacy but she had to admit, it felt good. They watched the sun drop below the skyline to the southwest and felt the heat of the day already beginning to dissolve into the cool evening air. She led Ebbets around the back of the barn to the horse corrals, where there were seven horses standing and eating an evening meal of loosely forked grass hay.

The horses were lined up in front of a long, rough-sawn manger that had turned grey with age and matched the fence posts and the outbuildings nearby. The trough had been hastily tacked onto the cedar fence years before, as a temporary fix, but as with so many stopgap things in this country, it had since become permanent. It reminded Amy of the travelers she often met who were "just passing through" when their cars broke down and forced them to abandon their plans, to wind up shipwrecked, permanent residents in the southwest desert.

The horses stood facing Amy and Ebbets, so it was easy to reach through the fence to scratch the sides of their faces. They didn't care much for the attention, and they turned their heads away the women's attempts to scratch them between the eyes. These were ranch horses, used to cowboys and western saddles, lariats, and saddlebags full of tools of the trade. They were used to a day's work, and when the workday was finished they wanted nothing more than to eat, roll in the dirt, and catch a bit of sleep—standing up or lying down, whichever way suited—and to just be left alone.

The horses were engaged in their pre-meal skirmishes, taking quick bites and kicks at each other, until each animal found its own place in the pecking order and settled in to eat.

"Oh, they are so beautiful!" Ebbets exclaimed.

"Eh... yeah. They're just ranch horses. Nothing fancy about 'em," Amy said, trying to act indifferent about it. But she was excited that Ebbets liked the horses. She had learned early on to guard her feelings, so she did her best to appear unconcerned. Horses were creatures Amy could relate to, one to one. They understood her and she understood them. It wasn't the same with people. Amy spent a lot of time at the corrals whenever she was at Olive's place, and she knew that those horses were the best company a girl could have.

"I love the color of that red one there," Ebbets said, pointing to the young mare at the end of the line.

"That's a sorrel," Amy explained. "High class folks call 'em chestnuts, but cowboys just call it a sorrel. Her name's Charlotte."

"Well, I think Charlotte is beautiful. And it seems like you know a bit about horses, Amy," Ebbets said.

"Spent a bit of time around 'em," she replied, "I guess I like 'em well enough."

"I think they're magical," Ebbets said.

"Hmmm... I don't know about magical." She tried to appear skeptical but in truth, she *did* know they were magical. Horses were mystical creatures, and Amy's sketchpads were full of drawings of them, drawings that she showed to no one.

"But anyway, they're fun to ride," she said.

"Oh, I would *love* to go riding sometime! I've never ridden a horse before."

"Really? You've never been on a horse?" Amy considered that for a moment, then said, "Well, how about we ask Olive if I can take you out for a ride?"

"Oh, I would *love* that!" Ebbets noticed the habit Amy had of fiddling with the gold medallion that hung around her neck.

"That's a beautiful pendant."

"It was my mother's," Amy replied, "It's Saint Christopher, the patron saint of travelers." She paused to take the medallion in her hand, then continued.

"My mother died, so I guess it's mine now. I don't do much traveling, but maybe someday..." Amy let her voice trail off as she thought about how many places Ebbets must have seen.

"Oh, I'm so sorry," Ebbets said, "I didn't know about your mother." She paused to look at Amy, watching her eyes and recognizing the pain behind them.

"I know how it feels," Ebbets said, "my mom died, too."

There was an awkward silence as Amy considered what to say. In the end she just left it there, but finally asked, "Ebbets…. how do you know about all those clothes and stuff? I mean, how do you know what to wear?"

Ebbets looked at the girl and recognized something in the way Amy was looking back at her, inquisitive and curious. She saw a young woman trying to figure out how to *be* a young woman, a girl alone, stuck in a world without other girls around to teach her about her own femininity and how to follow her own path to womanhood. Ebbets recognized those eyes from when she looked in the mirror as a young girl herself, and her heart swelled as she looked at Amy's frail, fifteen year old self.

"Well, at first you *don't,* really. You just try to make it up as best you can. I didn't really have anyone to show me, so I just wore stuff I liked. And I still do, I guess."

"But you look so nice and… well, I think you look cool."

"Aw, thanks, Amy. That's the nicest thing anyone has said to me in a long time." Ebbets put her arm around the girl's shoulders and said, "Hey, let's head back up to the house. We can take a look at your stuff, and maybe I can show you a few things, okay?"

"Sure, that'd be great!" Amy answered. She was bubbling with excitement as the pair turned away from the horses and started back toward the hacienda.

George

George sat alone on the wide *portale* that wrapped around three sides of the stately old hacienda. Most of the partygoers were congregated along the south and west sides, where the last of the sun was being steadily consumed by the growing darkness, and the sky was streaked with wisps of silver cirrus clouds. George sat by himself on the east side of the hacienda, where it was quiet, watching the first stars beginning to show. He needed to think, to reflect upon where he was and what choices he had ahead of him.

For the first time in his life George could not stop thinking about someone—about a girl. He was used to falling in and out of love at the drop of a hat. It was second nature, something he had done all his life. But this... this was something new, something he didn't recognize. He wondered if his feelings for Ebbets Fields were real or if he was just obsessed with her because he couldn't have her. It felt real to him, since the very first time he laid eyes on her, but that sort of thing was just a cliché from the movies. And he wasn't exactly objective about it.

Even on his best days, George was hardly the unbiased type. He acted on impulse. Emotional instinct was the engine that powered his life, and critical thinking didn't often play a large part in it. Logic was more Sam's thing and George left it to him. George did better with feelings and intuition.

And he did have feelings for her—that was obvious. And as Amy walked to the barn, talking with Ebbets, she didn't realize that it was Ebbets who George had been talking about, the true love he had been writing to. He never mentioned her name, so Amy didn't put two and two together. She couldn't have known that, at that very moment, she was taking the girl of George's dreams down to the barn to see the horses.

What wasn't so clear to George was whether or not he was really in it for the long run. He didn't know what to do. Hitchhike to Boerne and try to see her? Maybe, but his thoughts kept running in circles. What if she has someone there? What if she isn't who she seems to be? What if she doesn't really like him? What if she is *married,* fer chrissake? He didn't have the answers. He didn't even have the right questions.

George had always been comfortable with women, and they were with him. He grew up with women all around him—his mother, his two younger sisters, Jennifer and Leslie. They were a tight-knit family, even as his father steadily drifted apart from them, throwing himself into his well-drilling business and doing his best to work himself to death, seven days a week.

The family lived on the edge of Dumas, Arkansas, but George liked to say he was from Pickens, a couple of miles down the road, because he had grown tired of hearing the inevitable "Dumb Ass" comments. The truth was, Pickens wasn't really big enough to be a town, but then neither was Dumas.

George had been a constant disappointment to his father. To Frank Willow, it seemed as if his boy had somehow missed out on the work ethic that normal boys were naturally given, the same work ethic that he had had when growing up. Frank understood why his boy might not want to work in his father's business, drilling and servicing water wells, but there were plenty of other good jobs around, jobs that built character and taught the value of hard work.

The only thing George wanted from the flatlands of Pickens, Arkansas was to see the place in the rear view mirror as he drove away for good. From an early age the boy had a bad case of wanderlust, and by the time Jeannie died, Frank Willow had given up on George and wanted nothing more to do with him.

George was devastated when the cancer took his mother. *She was only thirty-three, fer gawdsakes.* He adored Jeannie Willow. To George, she had hung the moon. Frank knew his son was "the emotional one," so he expected George would fall apart. The irony was that it was Frank himself who became emotionally fragmented, who steadily threw himself further into his work (if that were possible), and who detached himself from his family.

As things turned out, it was George who, after a short and intense period of grieving, came to realize that his two younger sisters needed him and that they were counting on him. Their father continued to pay the bills, but there would be no emotional support, no real sustenance forthcoming from him. At twelve years old George stepped up and took on that role.

As much as he cherished his mother, George grew to adore Jen and Les even more. Jennifer was a very mature ten year old, with Leslie a year behind her. The two were as different as night and day, but they were inseparable. Young Jennifer excelled in math and science, spelling and history, and all things academic. Unlike most of her classmates, she did not study in order to do well on her tests or to please the adults. The fact was, she really didn't care about grades or what her teachers thought of her. Curiosity was the engine that drove Jennifer Willow, and she simply absorbed things. She tried her best to understand what her schoolwork actually meant in the real world. At ten years old she was a philosopher, inquisitive and wise beyond her years.

Leslie grew up to be the wild one in the Willow family, a raven-haired beauty of a girl who broke the hearts of every boy in her class without trying, though it would have pained her to know it. She was the image of her mother, beautiful, outgoing, loving, and carefree. She wore her heart on her sleeve, unguarded and exposed. As a girl, Les would sit and sing to her collection of stuffed animals, making up verses for each of them. She reminded George so much of his mother that sometimes it made him want to cry.

They were a year apart but the Willow girls were often mistaken for twins. They shared a sort of telepathic emotional bond, the kind that twins are said to share. By the time they were in high school—Jen a senior and Les a junior—they had grown so close that George worried a little that they might never grow up and find their own separate ways. They looked to their older brother as they should have looked to their father, and it was George who kept them from reeling out of control in their early teens; it was George they compared any prospective boyfriends to. Without knowing it, George set high standards for them and saved both of them from having low expectations when it came to men.

He encouraged their dreams and aspirations, championed their causes and convictions, and was there when one of them turned up with a broken heart. He kept out of the way and out of their social lives for the most part, but he did supervise their first experiments with alcohol and marijuana. They never went past the harmless experimenting phase, so their big brother wasn't worried about them. And though he never really knew what he was doing when it came to being a parent, he was gifted with his mother's persona and he seemed to come naturally to parenting.

He had a great hankering to leave, but George stayed home for a couple of years after he graduated from high school. He took jobs up the road in Dumas, moving irrigation pipe and loading rigs at the county yards. He had no plans for college—it had never been discussed in his family—so he spent most of his time and money entertaining girls and smoking weed. At times he felt useless, as though he were just going through the motions and trying to realize his father's expectations of him. But he was biding his time until his sisters finished school, and he knew it was important to be there for them. Jen graduated in 1966, just after George's twentieth birthday.

Jennifer knew how badly her brother wanted to leave home, so she made a deal with him: she would stay home for one more year to look after Les, and George would be free to go off to seek his fortune. He fought back tears as he hugged her, and he told her how much she and Les meant to him, and that he would always be there if they needed him.

A ranchera song started playing on the stereo inside the hacienda, bringing George back to the moment. He shifted his gaze to the southeast, thinking he might be able to see the Marfa lights, but it wasn't quite dark enough yet. The music and the party noise were suddenly suffocating, so he put his beer bottle down and stood up from the old Taos style carved bench. He stepped down from the porch and headed down the path to the barn area.

The trail was barely visible beneath the crescent of the new moon, so George kept his eyes focused on the ground and tried his best to stay on the trail. When he reached the barn he walked around it until he came to the far end. He could hear the horses in the corral, the quiet steps of their unshod feet clomping across the hard dirt there, and the soft sounds of nostrils blowing the dust away in short snorts. He turned the corner of the barn and walked smack into Amy.

"Oooof.... what the?" he uttered.

"Hey, wine-cha watch where yer goin'!" she shouted.

He recognized Amy's voice and turned, "Aw, dang, Amy... Sorry, I was just.... "

But it wasn't Amy he saw in front of him. It was Ebbets Fields.

Part 3

Ebbets and Amy

"How do you deal with boys?" Amy asked after working up the courage to ask.

She sat in the dirt cross-legged next to Ebbets, who reclined on a wooden keg full of horseshoe nails. They rested with their backs against the side of the old weathered hay barn and watched the horses in the corral wandering aimlessly inside the makeshift fence of old cedar posts, latillas, and barbed wire. The animals kept up a steady rhythm with their tails in a futile battle with flies as they idled away the lazy summer afternoon.

"Well now, that's a pretty big question. Maybe you could narrow it down a bit? Be a bit more specific?" Ebbets smiled as she watched the girl struggle with her feelings.

Amy twirled a lock of hair between her fingers as she usually did when she was nervous.

"I mean, well.... you probably have lots of boys who, you know, *want* you, don't you?"

"You mean, guys hitting on me?"

"Yeah, like that. Boys who want to be with you all the time. What do you do about that? How do you get rid of 'em?"

"Well first, it depends on whether or not you *want* to get rid of them. They're not all bad, you know."

Amy considered this. "Well the ones around here are. They're all stupid hicks and I hate 'em."

"Oh c'mon, Amy, they can't *all* be bad. I'll bet there's one you like, maybe just a little bit, isn't there? One of those boys must be pretty nice, a boy you don't mind hanging out with, right?"

Amy thought about Ryan Deputy, a boy in her class. She would never admit that she had a crush on him.

"Aw, well... maybe. But then, when he's with his friends, he just turns into a creep like the rest of 'em."

"Yeah, that can be a problem, for sure."

"What makes them do that? Seems like when they get together they turn mean. I hate that."

Ebbets put her hand on the girl's head in a gesture of endearment, "They're afraid of you, Amy. They're scared."

Amy turned to Ebbets with a puzzled expression.

"What? Nah, I don't think so. They gang up on me and *I'm* the one who's scared. They just don't like me because I'm not like the popular girls, like Linda Farentino and Sally Tibbets."

"Maybe not, dear one, but those boys are scared to death of you because you're smarter than they are, you're tougher than they are, and you're darn sure a lot better looking than they are." They both laughed.

"Well, I don't know about that. I know I'm not very pretty and I don't dress nice and I don't fit in. I don't care about fitting in, though. But still, they call me a street rat."

"You know, being a street rat in Marfa might not be such a bad thing. But if it is, well... there are ways to fix that. And I happen to know someone who can help you in that area, someone who knows all about clothes and makeup and stuff."

Amy turned to face Ebbets, "Really? Who?" She stopped to consider, then blurted, "But what about you? I think you'd be better at it than some old lady in a dress shop somewhere."

"I was talking about me, silly. I could help you with your outfits and teach you how to take care of yourself."

This made the girl both excited and nervous at the same time.

"Yeah... I don't know," Amy said, "I don't think I'm much one for makeup and fancy clothes and all that."

"Oh, you don't need fancy clothes, dear girl. And you certainly don't want to start wearing makeup just yet. In fact, it's not about the fancy clothes or makeup at all. It's about knowing who you are on the *inside*, and then making that happen on the *outside*. Does that make sense?"

"I don't know, I guess so. But I don't really know what I am on the inside, though."

"Oh, I think you do. Sometimes all it takes is a little coaxing to draw it out."

"Really?" This conversation was causing all sorts of mixed emotions for Amy, and she began to regret having started it.

"Yeah, really," Ebbets said, smiling.

"You really think I could look as good as Sally Tibbets?"

"I don't know Sally Tibbets, but I'm guessing that she's already the best Sally Tibbets there is, so it's better not to try to be like her." Ebbets put her arm around Amy and pulled her close, and the two of them smiled.

"I do know this, though. You're gonna make a fantastic Amy Hildago. The best the world has ever seen."

Marfa Days

They formed a small, tight-knit group and engaged in lots of activities together. They went to the rodeo and to the movies, had picnics in the hills, and spent many evening hours beneath the portale in the patio at the back of the cafe. Vera made limeade and they all sipped and relaxed in the shade of the building's north side, letting the evening breeze cool them as they talked about their lives, their hopes and dreams, and about what they thought of the world around them.

George had been dumbstruck when he crashed into Ebbets at Olive's party. Since then, they had been joined at the hip, so much so that he had actually begun to get a bit testy about the constant teasing he and Ebbets received. He wanted to spend every waking moment with her, but Ebbets wanted to take it slow. She was still a little gun-shy and didn't want to make the same mistakes she had in the past.

George urged her to find a place with him, but she held her ground and stayed in Vera's apartment above the cafe. She allowed George to spend the night sometimes, but he respected her wishes when she wanted to be alone, even though it nearly drove him crazy. Sam had to ride roughshod over him just to make sure he showed up for work every day. And within a couple of weeks, the couple settled into a routine. They were happy. The others teased them, but George knew that the others were just a bit envious.

Amy bonded with Ebbets over horses, and the pair often took a couple of Olive's cow ponies out riding. They explored lost trails and savored the isolation and remoteness they found in the silent desert around them. Ebbets became the big sister Amy never had.

Ebbets had grown up in the Texas hill country, but her early life in New York City had left its mark and she remained a city girl at heart. In Marfa she fell in love with horses and with cowboys and with the west, and Amy felt a growing pride and sense of purpose in being able to introduce her new friend to it all. It felt good to Amy to be a teacher for the first time in her life.

Amy began to change. It was in small ways at first, but the others noticed, even if Amy couldn't see it. She was rapidly coming into her own as a young woman. She still saw herself as a troubled teenager, an outcast, a mixed race girl who didn't really belong to any of the "cool kids" groups at school. She was still that girl who got free passes to movies and made promises for popcorn and Cokes that were never fulfilled, and she still snuck off occasionally to smoke pot behind the hotel with her friends, even though she risked Vera's wrath.

To her credit Amy went to school every day and stopped shoplifting and committing other petty crimes around town. She was making an effort. Amy's own view of herself changed little, even as the small circle of adults around her were noticing that she no longer seemed to search out trouble. She would always be wild and impetuous, but a great deal of her anger was disappearing, especially when she was with Vera and Ebbets and the others.

Ebbets took Amy on what she called "shopping adventures", visits to the local thrift stores in Marfa and Alpine. She showed the girl what to look for in choosing her wardrobe, and how a seemingly bland and boring piece of clothing could suddenly become a captivating garment when paired with the right accessories. Most importantly, Amy learned that the inexpensive, second hand items that were found in thrift shops were actually *better* than the fancy designer labels that the popular girls at school wore, and that she didn't have to feel ashamed of wearing used clothing.

Vera and George became fast friends, in part because of their shared love of music and quoting popular songs, and because they shared an offbeat sense of humor. From their very first meeting they just seemed to get each other. Their friendship was further cemented by the tight camaraderie that the entire group shared.

The two were constantly singing songs to each other—the more obscure, the better—especially if the lyrics were relevant to their immediate situation. This developed into a casual competition, with each challenging the other to identify both the song and the singer or songwriter. Most of the time George started it off by issuing a challenge and trying to goad Vera. But once in a while, Vera opened the lyrical volley:

"Third boxcar on the midnight train... where's it going?"

"Wait, gimme a sec.. I'll get it," George replied. "Let's see... oh yeah, Bangor Maine!"

"Yeah?" Vera said, "Well, what's he wearing?"

"That's easy, he has an old worn out suit and shoes, and he don't pay no union dues. And he smokes old stogies he finds in the street."

"It doesn't say anything about finding 'em in the street," she argued, "just that they're short and they're not too big around."

"But he's a man of means by no means," George said, and then they both chimed in with, "King of the road!"

And they would smile and chide one another, each claiming that the other cheated. Amy saw that it irked Sam and that he was a bit jealous, mostly because of the way George was able to communicate so easily with Vera. It was so difficult for Sam.

Maybe it isn't so much jealousy as it is envy, Amy thought.

He knew that Ebbets had a firm grip on George's heart, and Sam had no claim on Vera, no matter what his feelings for her were. But what really bothered him was that he hadn't mustered the courage to tell her what those feelings were. After a while it just seemed too late, a lost cause.

Sam and Vera orbited each other, their own inertia pushing them apart while the gravity of their two hearts pulled them back again. They talked now and then, just the two of them. Sam cherished those conversations, but it seemed like every time he tried to connect with her on a deeper level, he blew it. He would say something awkward and embarrass himself, and then he would get defensive and just clam up altogether. He wished he could be more like George.

Vera didn't help matters. Her sarcastic sense of humor was a façade. It was her line of defense against having to reveal her feelings to anyone. So if Sam fumbled when they talked, if he made clumsy attempts at any sort of romantic talk, she pierced him with that biting wit of hers, even though she could see that he was stung by it. She didn't seem to be able to help herself.

Vera had spent her life being a rock, relying on no one, and then Sam came along. Without even trying, he shook her foundations and unsettled her to her core. She had fallen in love with him and she didn't know what to do about it. To Vera, love and dependence were the same thing. And dependence was the kiss of death.

Amy watched them and wondered when the two of them would finally get together. Of course, she had her own misgivings about that. She knew that Sam was too old for her, but she thought, *a girl can dream, can't she?*

They grew close as a group, yet each one spent the summer inside their own head, silently fending off demons from the past and trying their best to hide old scars from the others.

A Conversation

George picked up the phone in Olive's library and dialed the cafe. Sam was down at the barn, fixing the latch on the corral gate and Olive had gone to town, so he took the opportunity to make a call.

"Hi, it's me."

"And that would be?" Vera asked.

"Aw, c'mon Vera. You know... it's *George*."

"Yeah, I knew. I was just seeing if *you* knew."

"You know what, Vera? You're something else."

"Well, I hope so. If we were all the same it'd be kinda boring, wouldn't it?"

"Yeah, I reckon it would." After a long pause, George said, "Hey, can I meet you somewhere? There's something I want to talk about and I don't want Sam or anyone around."

"Oh George... you're not gonna ask me to marry you, are you?" Vera mocked, then started singing a song about putting your sweet lips closer to the phone.

"What? Oh, NO... NO, NO, NO! Whatever gave you that........ Oh wait, you're just tryin' to get my goat, aren't you?"

"Not just *tryin'* to get your goat. I'm pretty sure I *got* it."

"Well, can you get away from the cafe for a little while, say around two o'clock this afternoon? We could meet over at City Drug. I'll buy you a Coke float."

"Well George, what girl could pass up a Coke float? Sure, I'll meet you at the lunch counter there at two."

At ten minutes to two Vera untied her apron and asked Amy to watch the cafe for a little while. She walked down the street and pushed open the screen door at City Drug Store. Spotting George at the end of the soda fountain counter, she walked down the aisle past the shelves full of breath mints, lipstick, and greeting cards, and boosted herself up onto the stool next to his.

"What's up?"

George looked a bit sheepish, like he'd been caught red-handed doing something embarrassing. "Not much," he answered.

Vera could see that he had something on his mind, but she settled back and waited for him to come out with it. No use trying to pressure George into anything. He'd come around to it in his own good time.

His face suddenly lit up, "Hey, you want a Coke float?" he asked, excitedly.

"How 'bout a root beer float instead."

"Sure, that's fine. I like Coke floats, but I'll order a root beer float for you." He motioned to the high school kid behind the counter and ordered their floats.

"Turned out to be a pretty nice day," he remarked.

"Depends on where you're sittin'," Vera said, "I reckon it looks better from this side of the counter than from where that soda jerk kid is."

"Yep, he's got an albacore around his neck, that's for sure."

"So, what's on your mind, George?" She didn't want to push him, but she needed to get back to the cafe. Amy could handle the place by herself, but Vera didn't like leaving her alone for very long.

"Well, it's just that I've been thinkin'..."

"Yeah, that can be pretty dangerous."

"No, Vera, I mean it. I been thinkin' about ol' Sam, and how you and him need to get yourselves together. You two were made for each other."

"Okay, so that's it then. I didn't realize you were the Marfa match maker." She cocked her head and smiled at him, "Hey, that's kind of a catchy title, isn't it?"

"I ain't tryin' to butt in, Vera, but I just look at Sam, and I look at you, and well... you two just sorta go around in circles with each other. It's like you're ridin' the trail next to each other but you're never on the same flight path."

"Not sure what you mean, George, but I think you're mixing your metaphors again."

"Aw, c'mon, Vera. You know what I mean. I *know* Sam. I can read him like the back of a book. He just don't know how to talk to you, know what I mean?"

You know what, George? Sam and I are perfectly capable of figuring out our own love lives, don't you reckon?"

"Well now, I'm not so sure about that. I mean hell, Sam's out there workin' every day and at night all he wants to do is write his stories and his poems and stuff, but he don't realize that unless he has someone to believe in, somebody to share it with, he's gonna run right outta ideas."

Vera paused, cocked her head, and looked at George with newfound appreciation.

"And here's the thing, Vera. I keep tellin' him that he's found something good here, somebody who gets who he is." George turned to look at Vera, "And I keep tellin' him, Sam, don't look a gift horse in mid stream."

Vera laughed out loud, "Well I'll be darned, George. I didn't know you were such a philosopher. I thought that was more Sam's department."

"Well, I'm sayin' that the same thing goes for you too, Vera. I ain't a philosopher. I'm just a romantic fool who wishes his friends had what he has. And all I'm sayin' is, don't sell love short. It can do things for you that nothin' else can."

"You're wise beyond your years, George Willow." Vera smiled and put her hand on his shoulder. "You're a good friend... and not just to Sam." She leaned over and kissed him on the cheek. "We're lucky to have you."

George blushed and turned away.

"Now, don't go all shy on me," she told him, "You're supposed to be the romantic one, aren't you?"

"Aw, Vera. I just hope you and Sam will quit playin' this cat and mouse thing, that's all."

Vera smiled, "Well, the problem is, we can't figure out who's the cat and who's the mouse."

She put her hand to her chin and thought out loud, "How's that Lovin' Spoonful song go? Oh yeah, you're a big boy now."

"Ah, yeah. John Sebastian. He's a great songwriter."

"Yeah," Vera replied, "and he hit the nail on the head. Sam's a big boy.

He'll figure things out, one way or the other."

She took a long pull of the root beer float.

"This thing's danged good. I ought to serve these at the cafe. Trouble is, I'd probably drink up all the profits."

Amy and Sam

"Whatcha doin'?" Amy asked Sam as she was walking toward him. She aimed her camera his direction as he pulled and twisted a stretch of barbed wire around a corner post.

"Aw, nuthin' much. Just fixin' fence. Seems like they break faster'n I can keep 'em repaired."

"Yeah, that's cattle for you," she said, "They break pretty much everything they're around, and the horses ain't much better."

She watched as he grabbed the loose wire with his fence tool and used its rounded claw to pull it tight. He caught the wire with a small cat's claw tool and wrapped it around the post, then reached into his tool bag for a fence staple. He hammered it over the barbed wire and stapled it into place. Amy snapped a couple of pictures as he repeated the process on the other strands of the fence line. She managed to catch his face in an intense grimace as he pulled the wire taut.

"I expect you'll be headin' back to school soon, no?" Sam asked, "What sorts of classes are you gonna take?"

"Aw, don't remind me. I want summer to last forever." She sat down on the pickup's tailgate. "Not sure what I'm gonna take. Most stuff's pretty boring."

"Well, you'll be able to get back with your friends," Sam offered, "I'm guessin' the boys are pining away for you by now."

Amy blushed. "They're boring, too."

"You mean to tell me that there isn't a boy in Marfa that you're interested in?"

She knew the answer to that one but kept quiet. She fumbled with her camera and pretended to be preoccupied.

"Well I'll tell you," Sam continued, "if you had gone to *my* school, we'd have been fighting over you." He grinned.

"I doubt that," she said, turning away so he couldn't see her embarrassment.

"It's true, Amy," he said, "A girl as smart and pretty as you? Dang, most of us would've been scared to death of you, but we'd still be fightin'." He gave her a smile and a wink that took her breath away.

He drew Amy like a moth to a flame. She felt safe with him, and that was something she had never felt around men. Sam had a soft, friendly manner that put her at ease, and she cherished the times like this when the two of them were by themselves, just talking. Sam was really smart— smarter than anyone Amy had ever known—but he didn't make a show of it. He never made her feel small, like she didn't know anything, like she was stupid. He asked her about herself, about what she wanted to do with her life, and that made her feel special, but it also made her nervous. She was afraid of disappointing him, especially since he was genuinely interested in what she thought and in the things she did. Sam cared about her, Amy could see that, and it meant everything to her.

Amy was determined not to let her crush on him show. Not to Sam, not to anyone. She kept that to herself, kept it from everyone, especially from Vera. Any fool could see that Sam and Vera had something going on, even if they wouldn't admit it. And anyway, Sam was nine years older than her. Yeah, she was fifteen, but *nine* years! Sam was *old,* way too old for her. Amy was disappointed, for sure, but that was nothing new for her. Disappointment was a way of life.

Amy did her best to put Sam out of her mind, but she never really managed it. He came to her in her dreams, and oh, how she wished things were different.

Sam and Vera

Sam and Vera found themselves alone on the patio one evening. The light breeze had cooled things down, so George and Ebbets had gone for a walk around town. Amy was out at Olive's place, riding horses and taking pictures. Vera brought out a couple of glasses of lemonade and sat on the bench opposite him.

"Here, we might as well indulge ourselves." she said.

"Thanks," Sam said, taking the glass from her. "Nice evening, isn't it?"

"Sure is. Kinda nice not to be around a crowd for a change."

As always, Sam was nervous being alone with Vera. He didn't want to just make small talk, but he didn't know what to say. There were so many things he wanted to talk to her about, to share with her, and now he was mentally kicking himself for being such a fool. Vera could see that he was uncomfortable, and for some reason, she couldn't leave it alone.

"So, it's just you and me, looks like," she said.

"Yep, I guess it is."

"Y'know, George has been after me," Vera said, "he thinks we're supposed to be a couple." Sam jerked his head suddenly to look at her.

"He can't see why we're not together. I don't know what goes on in that brain of his."

"Well, George oughta mind his own business," Sam mumbled.

"So, you think he's wrong then?"

"No, I didn't mean..."

"Now, don't worry," she interrupted, "I know we're alone here, but I ain't gonna do anything inappropriate. You're safe with me, Sam." She kept a straight face but was smiling inside, enjoying his discomfort.

"Wait, I didn't mean that. It's fine that you're here, I mean..."

"Well, I *HOPE* it's fine. It *IS* my place, y'know."

"No, I meant..."

"I know what you meant," she said.

"I'm sorry, I just wish..."

"Just wish what?" Vera demanded.

"Ah, nothing. Forget it," he said.

They sat in silence for a long time, each one thinking they had somehow missed a chance, missed something important. Finally, Vera gestured to Sam.

"Then here's to us," she said sarcastically, raising her glass. Sam reluctantly clinked his against hers.

Animal Psychics

George whittled a piece of mesquite as they sat on the front porch at Vera's. He and Amy were debating whether animals knew what was good for them. As usual, Sam was buried in his journal, writing about who knows what, and Amy had just finished doing the evening dishes and was taking a break so she could hang out with the boys.

"Animals will always let you know what's wrong with 'em, is all I'm sayin'," George claimed, "You just have to leave 'em alone, y'know? They'll take care of the rest."

"I don't know, George," Amy said, "Horses are really smart in some ways but awful dumb in others," she told him.

"Well, I don't know...you can try to argue what's good for animals, but it's like bein' left in the lurch with a moot point."

Sam looked up again, puzzled. "What the hell are you talking about?"

"I'm just sayin', all these critters have lasted for thousands of years, just roamin' free on the prairie. Reckon they know what it's all about."

Amy replied, "Well maybe, when they're just out there eatin' grass and stuff. But you put a horse in a barn and turn him loose with a barrel full of grain and he'll eat himself to death. He'll either founder or colic or both. That doesn't exactly sound like a critter that knows what's good for him."

"Aw, Amy... you're just bein' difficult." George had a hurt look on his face but she knew he was just teasing.

She said, "Well then, maybe I could find one of those animal psychics. You know, the kind that can talk to animals? They could talk to the horses and let us know exactly how they're doin'."

George stopped to consider this. "Y'know, Amy? That's not such a bad idea." Sam looked up, shook his head, and winked at Amy, then went back to reading as George continued.

"Did I ever tell you about our vet back home in Dumas?" Amy shook her head and Sam rolled his eyes at her. "Here we go again..." was what he meant.

"Well, ol' Doc Brady was the town vet back in Dumas. Actually, he was from down the road in Pickens, but he doctored all the animals in the area. Dogs, cats, sheep, goats, goldfish, you name it. He tended to horses and cattle, and mules. There's lots of mules in Arkansas. We Arkansawyers love our mules." George paused for effect, then continued.

"Anyway, Doc Brady came out to work on my sister's dog one time and told me about an animal talker, a psychic lady who could talk to dogs and cats and horses and such."

George had the others' attention now. Sam looked up from his journal and Amy kept quiet while George spoke. They were both actually interested, for a change.

"A lady brought a cat into Doc Brady's clinic and wanted it desexed, you know, spayed so it couldn't have any more kittens. She said she adopted the cat and that it was depressed and didn't want to have any more babies."

"Whatta ya mean?" Sam asked.

George continued, "Well, Doc Brady asked her how she knew it was depressed and she told him she had taken it to an animal psychic, one of those animal talker folks."

Sam shook his head. "Oh man, here it comes," he said.

"No, just listen," George replied, then went on, "So the lady told the vet that this psychic had talked to the cat, and it was quite a story.

"Seems the cat got knocked up a couple of times and had kittens, which was okay with the cat at the time. But they kept takin' her kittens away before she was ready for 'em to go and it made her sad and depressed." Sam looked over at Amy with a grin and she smiled.

"So then," George continued, "the cat is gettin' even more depressed because she keeps comin' into heat and all these tom cats keep jumpin' on her and rapin' her, or at least that's her side of the story. Anyway, there's nothin' she can do about it."

"What? C'mon, man... this is ridiculous," Sam said.

"Just hear me out," George answered. "So, this cat is all depressed and tells the psychic lady that she wants to have a hysterectomy so she won't have to deal with all of the stress." George looked back and forth, from Sam to Amy, just to make sure they were listening.

"Now all this time ol' Doc Brady is examinin' the cat and listenin' to this woman talkin' about the animal talker psychic and he turns to her and says, sorry lady but I can't spay your cat.

"What? says the woman. Why not? And the doc says well, because it's a neutered male cat. It's not a female.

"And the lady says to him, but… I don't understand. Why would my cat lie to the psychic?"

Rodeo

South Texas was dry through the summer of 1968. June had brought with it a scorching heat that aggravated the long days and still nights. This continued through July, when the rains of the monsoon season normally arrived. They didn't this year, and by August Amy was spending a lot of time at the movies, using her feminine wiles on the lovestruck and unsuspecting Henry for free admission and supplies of plenty of popcorn, candy, and soft drinks.

The monsoon season had been replaced by small summer storms that materialized in the form of light, low pressure squalls and produced very little actual moisture. They did manage to cool things down in the evenings some. Amy welcomed the afternoon breezes, even as they spun the dry dirt up into giant dust devils that threatened to become tornadoes. They left everything covered with a permanent layer of fine silt. Sweeping and dusting were endless and futile pastimes during the Texas summer.

George and Sam were working at Olive's, so Amy wasn't able to see as much of Sam as she would have liked. The boys spent most of their time repairing the perishable things that make up a ranch. The dry heat and the blowing dust exerted unrelenting pressure upon the fences, gates, outbuildings, pickup trucks and tractors, wheelbarrow handles, jackpumps, roof gutters, and all manner of plumbing and water systems. Everything eventually failed under the desert's steady subjugation, especially people, and there were days when Amy saw her own life as one in slow and steady decline.

The two boys helped with the feeding and doctoring of horses and cattle, though most of that work fell to the cowboys. Their "cowboy" jobs mainly consisted of holding a horse or a mule while a real cowboy performed the actual tasks of shoeing and doctoring. Along with their regular chores they tended to a large, overgrown garden that was planted by one of the Mexican nationals who had since returned to his home across the border in Chihuahua. Eventually, they were able to retrieve a few large, dry zucchinis and some summer squash that somehow managed to push its way up through the hard ground.

There were local pastimes to be shared with their newfound Marfa friends. At Amy's urging, Sam and George witnessed their first rodeo. It was a small event that took place every year at the college over in Alpine and was what the cowboys called a jackpot rodeo, which meant that contestants paid to compete and then split the winnings. Each event's jackpot went to the lucky cowboy who stayed on past the whistle and managed to earn the most points from the judges.

The boys, along with Ebbets, Vera, Olive, and Amy, all sat together in the shaded rodeo arena bleachers and out of the hot July sun, where they cheered along with the crowd as local ranch hands were bucked off a wide variety of bareback horses, saddle broncs, and Brahma bulls. Sam and George were amazed at the skill of the team ropers and steer wrestlers. They all cheered the young kids—usually no more than six or seven years old—as they were strapped to sheep and turned loose in the arena for their indoctrination into the world of rough stock.

Sam had no idea that the sport featured so many different and varied skills, and he sat transfixed through the bucking stock events that were interspersed with pole bending, barrel racing, calf roping, team roping, and bulldogging. Ebbets was especially smitten with the cowboys who rode the rough stock, especially the saddle bronc riders because they seemed to embody what being a cowboy was all about.

Vera and Sam shared a smile when she nodded toward George, who was obviously in some distress over whether or not he could ever measure up to those romantic cowboys. But Ebbets paid him no mind and continued to cheer and comment on how brave and wonderful the buckaroos were. By the end of the day Sam wasn't sure if George would ever want to go to a rodeo again, but Ebbets had a way of putting him at ease and making sure he felt loved.

Through it all Vera and Sam exchanged knowing glances, and one time he looked over to catch Amy staring at them intently. She held her Nikon with both hands, with the camera resting up near her shoulder and hoped that Sam would think that maybe she had just taken their picture. The truth was she had taken many pictures of Sam and had shown them to no one. Years later, Sam would see the photograph of him and Vera at the rodeo, and it would bring up strong feelings for him.

The rodeo included acts that were meant to lighten the mood and introduce a bit of levity, especially when a cowboy or an animal was badly hurt and there was a pause in the proceedings. A young woman rode a Roman team, two magnificent black horses that raced through the arena together side by side at a full gallop. The woman stood with a foot on the back of each horse and performed various gymnastic tricks while galloping at top speed around the arena. It was death-defying, and Amy saw that Sam was completely captivated. He in turn saw that Vera was glancing at him while he watched, and he was silently gratified. He was thinking, *"Ah, she's jealous!"* Later he realized that *"amused"* was a better description.

There was a man who looked like an old fashioned carnival barker. Dressed in a top hat and long black coat, he entered the arena sitting on top of a small replica of a pickup truck that he drove around in front of the crowd, towing a small horse trailer behind it while the crowd cheered. After making a couple of laps in front of the crowd, he parked the rig in the center of the arena and climbed off. He started a conversation with the rodeo announcer, who sat in a small tower above the stands and spoke, his voice blaring through the arena's PA system.

Announcer: *"Folks, this is Edwin Mumps, driving his rig into the arena right now. Edwin, what are you doing, parking there like that?"*

Edwin: [says something, but the crowd can't hear in his unamplified voice]

Announcer: *"What? You say you have hired the best cowboy on the range?"*

Edwin: [nods and says something...]

Announcer: *"No, I don't think so, Edwin. There's a lot of cowboys here who'll take exception to that. You say you can prove he's the best cowboy there is?"*

Edwin: [mouths the word, *Yes* and nods vigorously]

Announcer: *"Okay then, let's see you prove it."*

As the audience responded with wolf whistles and jeers, Edwin opened the back door to the miniature horse trailer and lowered the ramp on the back of it. Immediately, several geese emerged and began to waddle around the arena.

Announcer: *"What the heck are you doing with all those geese, Edwin?"*

Edwin: [says something, then points at the geese.]

Announcer: *"You say, those aren't geese, they're cows?"*

Edwin: [nods and points toward the alleyway at the end of the arena]

All eyes turned toward the gate at the far end. As it swung open a dog appeared, running at full speed into the arena. It was a moment before Sam realized there was something on the dog's back. As the dog approached, Sam could see a miniature saddle strapped to it, and a small monkey dressed up like a cowboy riding in the saddle. The monkey's hands were tied to the saddle horn, and it was obviously strapped to the saddle so that it couldn't get away. The poor critter had a complete buckaroo outfit on, including little leather chaps, gloves, jeans, cowboy boots, and a western shirt with a neckerchief tied around his throat. He wore a miniature ten-gallon hat to top things off.

The dog, a Border Collie, ran toward the geese at full speed and proceeded to herd them back toward the horse trailer. He circled and stopped, circled and stopped, repeatedly until he had herded the geese into a tight bunch. Amy had seen it all before, but she still enjoyed it. The monkey appeared to be in control as he rode the dog, and the way the dog moved quickly back and forth made it look as though the two were cutting cattle.

The dog and his rider continued to move the geese around the rig, where they filed into the trailer, one at a time. When Edwin closed the trailer tailgate, the crowd went crazy, stamping and cheering its approval. The dog hunkered down next to the trailer with the monkey still strapped to its back. It was one of the strangest things Sam had ever witnessed. Who knew that Vaudeville was still alive and well?

Just before the bull riding event they turned a big brindle bull out into the arena and a rodeo clown jumped down from the bucking chute fence to face it. The clown wore traditional clown makeup and funny, oversized clothes. The announcer explained that the clown's job was deadly serious, and he was really an athlete who put himself at risk every day in order to save bull riders from the animals they rode. There was a big rubber barrel with hand holds inside of it, for the clown to hide inside when the bull attacked.

The clown jumped inside the barrel, then picked it up and walked around with it while the bull stood inside. The two put on a great show, with the clown taunting and teasing the bull until it exploded in a rage and did its best to destroy the barrel and the human inside. At one point, the bull managed to get its horns into the barrel enough to lift it off the ground and tossed it back over its head with the clown hunkered down inside. The barrel landed with a tremendous thud that elicited a collective gasp from the crowd, but the clown emerged unscathed, to more wild applause.

Later, during the bull riding event, the group watched as the clown saved cowboy after cowboy from the horns of the bulls, jumping in front of them after a cowboy's dismount, or when they were bucked off, and luring the animal away so that the bull riders could escape.

The women in the crowd especially cheered the female contestants, ranch cowgirls who competed on compact Quarterhorses and rode them like lightning in the barrel racing and pole bending events. The rodeo was a shared family experience, and though Sam felt sorry for some of the animals, he could see that this was all a part of ranch life. Ranch families viewed the animals as equals, as partners who were thrust together with them into a world of hardship and adversity.

There were bleachers for people to sit in, but most fans simply stood along the arena fence, and the most hardcore devotees wrangled themselves a position down in the chute area where the rough stock and their cowboy counterparts were released into the arena.

Sam took it all in eagerly, and as Amy watched him she wondered what went through his mind. He got up and walked down to the chutes and watched the action behind the scenes. A cowboy sat on the ground, his back against a fence post, and positioned himself atop a beat-up Ellensburg saddle with his feet in the stirrups. He made minor adjustments to his rig and seemed to be imagining himself on top of the saddle bronc he drew that morning. The scene was repeated over and over, with cowboys practicing their own brand of meditation in a style that in no way resembled the San Francisco hippies that George and Sam had spent time with.

There were professional photographers allowed inside the arena to take closeups of bucking horses and bulls, and many in the crowd had cameras that hung around their necks until the chute gate was pulled open and the next rider took his turn at winning the day money. When a chute gate opened, a chorus of clicking and whirring began as shutters snapped with their lenses focused upon animal and rider.

Amy wandered the rodeo grounds with her camera and took shots of the rodeo environment. She climbed the fence next to the bucking chutes and photographed the faces of what she thought rodeo was all about. She didn't want to take the same picture as everyone else, so she pointed her camera away from the arena. Amy wasn't much interested in the rides, but she did take a few pictures of the saddle bronc riders. Like Ebbets, she was especially enamored of them. Otherwise, her lens was aimed at the hearts and minds of the people who made up the rodeo community.

Even though Amy was only fifteen years old, she was taking pictures of cowboys and cowgirls, ranching families and friends, their clothing and gear, human and animal, and recording their hopes and dreams in the process. She wanted her photos to capture elation and heartbreak, anger and joy, youth and age. Years later, one of the photographs from this day would win a major photography award and would become known as "The Face of the American Cowboy."

But Amy's favorite shot was the one she took of Sam looking at Vera. Amy wished she were her. For Amy Hidalgo, there in Marfa in 1968, photography was a path that encouraged and validated her views of the world around her. She didn't take the same photos that everyone else took, and that was only natural. Amy saw the world through her own special lens.

Life Lesson

"Hey! Whatcha doin?" Sam hollered across the yard in front of the barn. Amy turned and waved.

"Nothin' much. Just takin' some pictures of the chickens."

"If George was here he'd probably sing a song back at you about that."

She laughed, "Yeah, he probably would." George and Ebbets had borrowed Vera's pickup and left to go back to Boerne to take care of her things. They would be gone for a week or so.

"What're you up to?" Amy asked.

"Not much goin' on so I thought I'd take a little drive. Wanna come along? I packed a lunch."

"Sure! I mean, okay... it would be nice to get away for a while." She was excited but tried not to let it show.

"C'mon, let's jump in the pickup and drive down south a ways."

Amy was surprised at how anxious she felt when she climbed into the pickup's cab and sat beside Sam. For a long time afterward, she would remember that it was how that day started. The day would have a big impact on Amy over the years. She would look back on that time as a turning point, maybe even as the point when she became an adult.

Sam turned the truck east onto Highway 90 and headed toward the old Army airfield. He turned off to the south on the old ranch road that Vera had told him about.

Sam explained to Amy, "Vera said it's a good place to hang out at night and see the Marfa lights and the stars and such. We won't see 'em in the middle of the day, but I figured maybe it'd be a nice drive anyway."

About a half mile down the road he pulled over and turned the engine off.

"Is this it?" Amy asked, puzzled.

"Nope, we're only just beginning," he said.

Amy was puzzled. She thought she knew Sam pretty well, and she trusted him, but she was becoming a bit nervous.

"I brought you out here for a reason, Amy," Sam said, "I want to teach you something."

At this point she was really nervous and said, "Uh, Sam…. I don't know…"

"Look, Amy… you talked about not wanting to be a kid anymore, like you wanted to be treated like a grownup. Right?"

She turned away, afraid to face him.

"Do you want to be an adult, Amy?" Sam asked, "If so, I'm going to help you do just that," he said.

He opened his door and jumped out. "C'mon," he said, "get out of the truck."

"What? What're we doing?" Amy stayed in the cab with her door shut.

"We're gonna swap places," he said.

"What?" she said, "What're you talking about?"

"C'mon, slide over here and get behind the wheel," he said, "You're driving."

"Drive? You mean *me*?"

Sam stuck his head inside the driver's window and looked across at her.

"You want to be a grownup? You want folks to treat you like one? Well, first you're gonna learn how to drive. And right here, right now, I'm gonna teach you."

Amy's relief washed over her. At first, relief, and then, a tiny bit of disappointment. Of course, she didn't want Sam making a pass at her, but at the same time, she wanted him to notice her, not just as some little kid.

"Uh, okay… if you're sure I won't get us killed."

She slid over behind the wheel while Sam went around and climbed into the passenger side.

"Now," he began, "the first thing you wanna learn is how to start this dang thing…."

The two spent the next two hours starting and stopping, backing up and turning, with Sam patiently teaching Amy how to feather the clutch and how to shift into the different gears. He coached her on listening to the engine for the right time to shift, as they continued south down the dirt road. It was like being on a carnival ride. Amy was so happy that she wanted to give Sam a great big hug. She couldn't do that, but for the first time in her life she felt just a little bit like a grownup, and when it was over, she was grateful that she hadn't destroyed the pickup truck.

The pair stopped for lunch somewhere in the hilly desert, far to the south. There wasn't much around except for dry bunch grass and tumbleweeds. They saw the odd cow or two that seemed lost. They sat on the tailgate and made bologna sandwiches and popped open a couple of Cokes that were stashed in the ice chest.

"Y'know, just when I think I know you, I realize I really don't know much about you, Amy."

Her defenses immediately started to raise themselves, and she said, "Whatta ya mean?"

"Well, I know you're smart and you're really talented. I'm amazed at the photos you take and the little sketches you make in your notepad." Sam paused and thought a minute, "Vera told me a little bit about your past," then he interrupted himself, "but *hey*, I don't want to pry. I know it's none of my business, but I guess I just want to get to know you a little better. I think maybe we have some things in common."

"Really? Like what?"

"Well, you lost your mother, didn't you?"

"Yeah. She and my brother. There was an accident and I was in the back seat. That was a long time ago... I was ten."

"I'm so sorry to hear that. I can't imagine how tough that is, losing your mom." He sat and looked at her for a long time, long enough to make her nervous again.

"I lost my brother too," he said finally.

Amy was shaken. "Your brother? Oh, I didn't know that." She wasn't much good at offering sympathy or condolences, so she just sat there and didn't say anything, until Sam finally spoke.

"I was nine, almost the same age as you were. My brother's name was Charlie and he was seven. It was winter. We were playing out on a frozen pond."

Amy watched his eyes as he spoke. It was difficult for him to tell this story, she could see. She found herself imagining walking on a frozen pond, something she had never seen.

"The ice broke and Charlie went in." He paused and took a couple of deep breaths. "I couldn't save him."

"I'm really sorry." She reached over and touched his arm, then quickly pulled her hand away. "I didn't know."

"Yeah, you're the first person I've ever told. I haven't even told George. I don't know why. Just seemed like maybe you've been through the same sort of thing."

"My brother's name was Jimmy. He was two years older than me. I never figured out why he died and I didn't." Amy felt the ache rising in her chest and the familiar lump forming in her throat. She willed herself not to cry.

"After that it was just my dad and me," she said.

"So you're like me, no other brothers or sisters?"

"Nope, just Jimmy."

"Me too," Sam said. "It took a long time to get over it... and yeah, to be honest, I guess I still haven't gotten over it."

"Yeah, me too." She stared at her hands, not wanting to meet his eyes.

"It sorta feels like I'm an orphan, y'know? I mean, my parents are still alive, but I feel like I was left alone when Charlie died."

An orphan. Amy had never looked at it that way, but it hit home with her. As hard as she tried to prevent it, she started to cry. Sam put his arm around her.

"It's okay. I don't know if anyone's told you this, Amy, but it's not your fault. I know about the guilt, and I know I would trade places with my brother in a minute, but I guess it's just something the two of us were meant to live with."

They sat there in silence for a long time, listening to the sounds of the desert, the slight breeze blowing through the sagebrush, the wisp of a lizard crawling across a rock, and the sound of a Mexican jay squawking at the world. And it dawned on Amy that she felt like a different person inside.

Something in her changed, and all of a sudden she saw herself as a person who meant something, someone who was worth something. While she was feeling this, she allowed herself to sink into Sam's embrace and she settled her head into his shoulder. Amy was seeing herself from a new vantage point, but she was also seeing Sam differently, too. Not as a boy she had a crush on, but as a friend, as someone she could count on.

They sat there for a while in silence, absorbed in their thoughts and feelings and listening to the desert around them. Finally, they awkwardly disengaged and stood up. After packing up their lunch fixings, they hopped back into the cab of the pickup, turned around, and headed back to the ranch.

Sam insisted that Amy drive, and as the old pickup rolled down the road, she was smiling inside and feeling like it was the best day of her life.

Hatching Plans

When the sun disappeared below the Sierra Vieja Mountains to the southwest, they were often painted with a glow behind them that turned Marfa's summer sky orange, then pink, and finally a deep dark blue as the night began to settle. As they did most days, the boys finished their work at the ranch and drove into town for a bit of socializing.

The pair stood out from the ranch hands and oil field workers around the area. To begin with, they weren't the sorts who tried to make every non-working moment count by seeing who could be the last man standing after the inevitable bar fight. Sam and George preferred less obstreperous pastimes, ones that usually involved hanging out with Vera and Ebbets. George, of course, was glued to Ebbets every non-working moment.

Amy tagged along, not entirely oblivious to the romantic and sexual tensions that filled the space between the others, but not realizing that she was somewhat of a fifth wheel.

They took their places behind the cafe, where they passed the evenings with shared drinks and stories around the old pine table there. Vera usually lit a small fire in the adobe kiva fireplace, though they didn't need it. The fact was, it was nice to sit and stare at the flames and allow the fire to hold sway as they were caught in the flicker and dance inside the small mud kiva. The flames produced magical effects on the small portale there, and Amy loved watching the glow caught in each person's eyes. She liked to think that she could tell what each one was thinking by the way the firelight played on their faces, and she sometimes wondered what her own reflected.

The drinks were usually Vera's homemade limeade or sun tea in tall glasses with lots of ice cubes to fend off the heat that lingered on into the first hours of darkness. It wasn't until Amy was older that she realized the boys had chosen not to drink beer because of her age. They didn't want her to feel left out, which is exactly how she would have felt.

While she was listening to their stories Amy snapped off shots of them with the Nikon. She framed each face in the firelight and managed to capture moments in time that she would cherish forever.

"I'm tellin' y'all, it's *treasure*!" George was saying. He had pulled out the handwritten note and was holding it up for the rest to see.

"Look at this!" he demanded, "I got Francisco to translate it for me.

Here, I'll read it to you."

He adopted a somber and solemn countenance, and they all grew silent as he began to read:

"To whoever finds this map —

I was with a group of soldiers who were transporting the belongings of Emperor Maximilian to the Port of Galveston in The United States. Outlaws attacked us and everyone was killed. I hid and escaped. The wagons contained the fortune of the Emperor. There is gold and silver and jewels. The treasure is hidden in a cave in the badlands of Texas, where I drew this map. I was captured by the soldiers of Benito Juárez and I will soon be sent to the gallows. I pray to Guadalupe that our Emperor is still safe, and I pray that you who finds this will pass this message to him.

When he finished, George added, "It's signed, 'Fermin Macias, June twenty-sixth, eighteen sixty-seven.'"

He passed the note around for everyone to see. Vera knew some Spanish, but the truth was that none of them could really read the Spanish version. It was a sore point for Amy, whose father was a Mexican national but had always steered his children away from speaking Spanish. He insisted they had to learn to be Americans, so Amy really never learned much more Spanish than a few swear words.

"I think it's the real deal," George said. "Man, this is like gettin' up a head of steam for the gravy train! I mean look, why would anybody make up a map and a note like that, anyway?"

"Could be, pard," Sam said. "I'm not convinced, but I'll give it the benefit of the doubt."

The women knew the story. The boys had related how they came by the map and the note, and how the map had been stolen and later turned up on Olive's wall. Vera had urged them to tell her about it but the boys knew how much Olive loved that map and they didn't want to spoil it for her.

"Still think y'all oughta say somethin' to Olive. I think she'd know whether it was real or fake," Vera said. "She's a pretty tough old gal, and I don't reckon you'd be hurtin' her feelings any by telling her that somebody stole it from you."

"Yeah," George responded, "but it wasn't really ours either, was it? I mean, it belonged to that Mexican couple, Diego and his wife."

"Anarosa," Sam added, "I wonder where they are now." He paused, "We don't even know where in Mexico they were from."

"Yeah, it's too bad what those FBI agents did. I hope they got back to Old Mexico okay." George added, "It might be like lookin' for a camel in a haystack, but if we had the map we could go look for that buried treasure.... just a thought."

"Well, we don't, and that's the end of it," Sam replied.

Amy was looking at the old note and thinking about that map when she suddenly blurted, "Well, maybe it's not!"

Everyone's eyes turned toward her, and that made her nervous. All of a sudden she was on the spot, and she turned a deep red. "I'm just sayin', maybe that's not the end of it."

"Whatta ya talkin' about, Amy?" Vera asked.

"Well, you don't really *need* the map, do you?"

"Well, ya kinda do," George replied. "It has the directions on it, y'know?"

The girl smiled at him and said, "Yeah, but you don't need *the map* now, do you? I reckon a *picture* of the map would do just as well, wouldn't it?" The others looked around at each other.

"Ah, our little Amy," Sam quipped, "Girl genius!" He looked down at her Nikon, and then straight at Amy and smiled. The girl's nerves came back with a vengeance. She could feel the heat rising in her face as she blushed again.

"And we wouldn't have to tell Olive, would we?" George offered.

"Nope," Sam replied, "Amy could just take a picture of the map."

George was excited now. "Yep, and I could get Francisco to translate some of the names on it, and then we could go treasure hunting!"

"I'm thinkin' y'all are crazy as loons," Vera said. And then she added, "but I gotta admit, it sorta sounds like fun."

"We need to do it!" George shouted. "Just think, *treasure hunters*!" He thought for a moment, then said, "That's it! The rooster's in the henhouse now!"

"You two are absolutely crazy," Ebbets said, laughing.

Amy was proud that it was her idea, though she might not have been so pleased had she known what they were getting themselves into.

Bovine Clones

Taylor spared no expense and left nothing to chance with the development of the new cloning facilities. With their newly acquired supplemental funding the team made steady advances even before they made the move to Texas. They succeeded in cloning a calf from the cells of a Guernsey cow. The calf lived for two weeks before succumbing to respiratory failure, but the scientists were not discouraged. They considered the calf a complete success and a giant leap forward in their research.

When they were finally settled into their new facilities on the Braun Ranch outside of Marfa, Jordan Hayes and his crew doubled down on their work. The Guernsey cattle they were using in New York were not common in the southwest, so they began to look at local breeds.

The foundation cow they ultimately chose was a maverick, a lost cow that had wandered far north from her birthplace in Mexico. As a calf, she and her mother had crossed the Rio Grande late one night with a small herd while searching for something to eat in the vast Chihuahuan Desert.

The foundation cow's mother was a Mexican Corriente that had mated with a big, stout Chianina bull. Having wandered off with its mother as a baby, the cow hadn't been branded or tagged. Legally, she belonged to no one. She grew up wild, a maverick of the desert.

After she was weaned from her mother, a couple of the Braun Ranch hands spotted the young heifer out on the southern part of the range, grazing with a small herd of the ranch's own cattle. She was gathered up and driven to the holding pens near the lab facility. As soon as Jordon saw the unclaimed cow he knew he wanted her for his research.

The crossbred cow wasn't required to do anything. The scientists collected a few blood and tissue samples from her and then left her to graze with a dozen other cows in a small pasture that had been fenced off for the research project. She wasn't the only cow involved in the project, but she would become their most prized because she produced the first viable clones, exact replicas of her that would live far longer than two weeks.

Of the first six of her clones, four died soon after birth. The other two survived to produce three more clones in the first quarter of the following year. The scientists added growth hormones to the mix, enzymes they had perfected in order to considerably increase the size and weight of the cows. Their average weight quickly grew from 1,100 to over 4,500 pounds at maturity.

Jordan Hayes and his crew were employing a new process they called "RGA" or "Rapid Generational Advancement." This technique caused the gestation period for the cow to drop from nine months to two and a half, which allowed four generations of cattle to be born in a single year. This produced a few unexpected results, some of which were unsavory enough to make the scientists uneasy about tampering with Mother Nature. But a combination of their own hubris, added to an extremely large paycheck, kept the men in the white lab coats on task. In addition, the higher-ups at the home office issued vaguely worded but unmistakable threats to their future livelihoods.

Cow #12 was the first to respond to the new growth hormone experiments. She added more than 2,000 pounds to her weight and more than a foot in height. Even with the significant changes she wasn't huge, at least by the standards that became common later in the cloning program.

Cow #19 was the first cloned cow to birth another live clone. The baby, Cow #23, had been conceived in a test tube and implanted back into #19, who gave birth two months later. The calf lived almost three months and, had she lasted a little while longer, she would have been old enough to give birth to her own calf. As it was, that honor fell to her sister, Cow #28. Being clones, all of the cattle were identical sisters.

One of the anomalies faced by the lab scientists was the problem of "runaway growth" in the cloned calves, caused by the lab's RGA process. Though they were clones and should have been exactly the same size, there was creeping growth in the sizes of each newborn when compared with earlier siblings. By the time the project was into its third year in 1968, the newborn calves weighed over 400 pounds at birth and were growing at a rate of 50 pounds a day, or well over a fifteen hundred pounds per month. They reached maturity at four months old, and eventually weighed in at more than 6,500 pounds. Standing almost 8 feet tall at the withers, they were giants, and they were producing even bigger giants.

The Barbecue

To celebrate the initial success of the cloning program, Taylor organized a private barbecue for the scientists and their families, to be hosted by Jackson and Harper at the ranch. A mature cow was to be slaughtered and cooked.

What better way to produce a proof of concept than a barbecue for the lab employees, using one of the clones? The patents and trademark licenses are already done and dusted, she thought, *and we'll have a monopoly on it all, from the cloning lab to the butcher.*

She smiled as she watched the crew. *Beef cattle*, she said to herself, *who would have thought that beef cattle would make us all rich beyond our wildest dreams?*

A five-ton shiny black truck, decked out with massive amounts of chrome and pinstriping, was parked along the edge of the ranch house's main yard. Attached to the truck was a matching trailer with a built-in meat smoker. It was a top of the line rig, custom built and hauled in for the event. The fancy chrome plated monstrosity was the size of a house, complete with a mesquite-burning fire pit and a polished chrome serving table that was half a city block long and could serve five hundred people at a time. The whole affair was shaded by a huge black awning with "Hogg Brothers" embroidered in blood red on all four sides.

The crew consisted of six brothers, huge men nearly identical in appearance. They wore matching uniforms with the logo, "Hogg's Brothers: Nobody Beats a Hogg's Meat" emblazoned on the front of their aprons. The brothers were giants, the youngest (and smallest) stood over six foot seven and weighed in at a little over two hundred ninety pounds. To Taylor, the six of them looked as if they themselves had been cloned, and their combined sizes made the enormous sides of beef appear almost normal. Between the six of them, they looked as if they could eat the entire cow without help.

The Hogg Brothers were well known in barbecue competitions at state fairs throughout the South and Midwest, and since no expense was being spared, they were the obvious choice for the event. Each of the rig's two large cylindrical smokers could handle an entire beef, though it would take both of them to accommodate a single cloned cow. Two cords of mesquite wood, with another half cord of barn dried hickory, were stacked next to the cookers, which were fired up and allowed to burn slowly for two days.

More wood was added as needed, and as the coals slowly reached the desired level, the team used one of the ranch's tractors to hoist the beef up so that they could butcher it. The sides of beef were placed onto big iron grappling hooks, where each side of beef was set to rotate at the rate of one turn per hour. Thirty-four turns and several gallons of the Hogg Brothers' special barbecue basting sauce later, the cloned meat was ready to eat.

At 3 PM sharp, the lab employees and their families arrived in a school bus that had been hired to prevent alcohol-impaired employees from driving, and to ensure everyone got home discreetly and safely after the party. The rustic setting of the main ranch house and outbuildings had been transformed using several white tents and dozens of plastic chairs. Pots were filled with flowers of every color and were spread around the premises to create a festive setting. A flatbed hay trailer was parked opposite the barbecue, and a western swing band from Austin stood on it, playing "Roly Poly" as the brothers drew their huge carving knives and set to work. In a short time the serving table was stacked high with various cuts of beef, all cooked to perfection.

Whether blood rare, completely burnt, or anything in between, there were cuts to please everyone. Along with the main course were serving dishes filled with greens, fried okra, butter beans, corn on the cob, potato salad, and cornbread. Ice chests were crammed with Lone Star longnecks and margarita fixings, along with iced tea, lemonade, and various sodas for the kids or adults who didn't drink alcohol.

Loaves of white Wonder Bread were placed next to large bowls filled with slabs of homemade butter on all the tables. The bread was not to be eaten, but was instead used to butter the corn on the cob. In true Texas fashion, the diner slathered a thick layer of butter onto a piece of white bread, then wrapped the bread around the corn and stroked it back and forth in a sort of lascivious movement that resembled what is normally a very private pastime. In Texas, the expression, "I've got to go butter my cob" was loosely based upon this activity, although it meant something entirely different. And like everything else the scientists did, buttering your cob was remarkably efficient.

Jackson Braun watched the family members laughing and having a good time, enjoying their day together. He considered himself these people's benefactor, a sort of kindly godhead, a philanthropist. As the figurehead of the company they worked for, they didn't really work for him, but he didn't let that little detail spoil his fantasy. They were here on his ranch, eating his food and drinking his beer, and he loved playing the gracious host. After the guests had filled their plates and everyone was seated, Jackson stood to make the speech that Taylor had written for him. Someone clinked a margarita glass with a spoon until he had the crowd's attention, and they grew quiet.

"We are here to celebrate your hard work in helping to usher in a new era in food production. The beef we are about to eat is just the tip of an enormous iceberg, one that will send shockwaves around the world. The breakthroughs we have made here will ultimately end world hunger as we know it, and will ensure that everyone has access to decent food with a sustainable amount of protein in their lives." He scanned the speech and saw that Taylor had left out the part where the company was going to make a killing because, he thought, *Well, that's really none of their concern, anyway*.

"Today marks a milestone in food technology and research. We are on the cusp of finally conquering nature and bending it to our will, shaping it to benefit people everywhere." *...especially our board of directors,* he smiled to himself.

When the applause died down, the guests stopped talking to each other and dug into their food.

Bad Beef

It wasn't the *taste* that seemed off to lead scientist Herb Cohen. No, it was the *texture* that didn't quite fit. When you bite down into an apple you don't expect it to feel like a banana. Meat was supposed to fight back, to be tough enough to offer some resistance, something to sink your teeth into. Even rare steak should offer opposition when you put it in your mouth and chew it. It wasn't supposed to surrender like a piece of cheesecake.

Herb was surprised by the first bite into the steak, but he soon got used to the spongy feel of the cloned meat. He looked around and saw that others were having similar reactions. No one seemed to be saying anything, but Herb could see their eyes darting back and forth, looking for some sort of confirmation that they weren't alone in their assessment of the beef. And so it was that when the guests had finished the main course there was a surprising amount of meat left on their plates.

The kids gathered around a large table where a clown was making jokes and serving homemade ice cream. The main ingredient came straight from the udders of the cloned cows, and Taylor was especially anxious to see how it would be received by the youngsters. She could smell another revenue stream.

If the children loved the ice cream, their fathers loved it even more. The clown's assistant was a pretty young woman who normally worked for a different sort of clientele, at gatherings very different from this one. These gatherings were, in fact, licentious meetings attended mostly by businessmen who were in awe of the young lady, mostly due to her somewhat "over-endowments".

Many of the fathers jumped at the chance to go and get ice cream for their children. They watched, in no particular hurry to be served, as the well-endowed assistant poured ample amounts of chocolate sauce on top of the generous servings, reassuring the children (and their fathers) with phrases such as, "Ah, I know you like it big, don't you?" or, "Come here and get some sweet love from mama!" The dessert was so popular that many of the fathers went back for seconds, and even thirds.

Later, many of the mothers noticed their kids behaving abnormally. The youngsters ran around aggressively, hitting each other and shouting obscenities. They grabbed chunks of barbecued beef and threw them at each other. At first the mothers passed it off as a result of too much sugar and left the kids to play, hoping they would eventually wear themselves out and calm down. And the kids did finally calm down, when they started breaking out in hives.

Naturally, the parents grew concerned. At first they didn't connect the problem with the food. They thought that some of the kids had come into contact with poison ivy or some other virulent plant. They didn't realize that there were no poisonous plants growing anywhere nearby, and it wasn't until many of the guests—both children and adults—began to suffer from spells of intestinal distress, culminating in bouts of explosive diarrhea, that they began to consider the food as the cause.

Needless to say, the four portable outdoor toilets were woefully inadequate, not even remotely up to the task, and this left many of those in acute distress having to make their way to the haystack located behind the main horse barn. Hay bales were pushed off the stack and made into makeshift latrines, with people sitting on them or squatting between them. Ultimately, the hay had a similar effect upon their backsides as poison ivy would have, and many were in distress for several days afterward.

The trouble was just beginning, however, for the symptoms seemed to get worse as the event progressed. Several of the scientists were medical doctors but only two remained well enough to attend to the others, because they had not eaten the beef or the ice cream. Moans of anguish and torment echoed from the portable toilets as the two doctors rushed here and there in a vain attempt to thwart the oncoming pestilence.

Later, they would discover that the ugly purple rash that covered the children's bodies was a particularly aggressive form of ringworm, made even more hostile by its extremely rapid progression which, ironically, was caused by the Rapid Generational Advancement enzyme that the scientists had themselves perfected.

Cow 26

In the evening the cloned cows always stood expectantly in the corral, staring at the wooden trough as the ranch hands threw hay over the fence and into the manger. While the other cows were watching their dinner arrive, Cow 26 was busy investigating the sliding clasp that kept the corral gate locked. She was an inquisitive young heifer, a rare bovine who raised her head up and took a look at the world beyond the grass and edible plants within her reach. She often stood alone, watching the slow rolling wind play upon the grama grass, or spotting the movement of an animal on a hillside far off in the distance. She paid the other cows no mind and was usually the last cow to return to the barn from the pasture they were kept in during the day.

26 was only three months old but already weighed over four thousand pounds and stood seven feet eight inches at the withers. Like her identical siblings, she had taken on the Corriente brownish brindle color, mixed with shades of grey along both sides of the lower forerib up into the flank. There were patches of white around her eyes and across her brisket. She and her sisters had inherited the long horns of the Corriente, though they were black and hard from the genes of the Chianina side of her family. The horns sloped gracefully down and forward, ending in sharp tips that could impale a coyote or a bobcat, or a human if they presented a danger. The lab scientists had not yet perfected a polled (hornless) version of the breed, and since the cows grew so rapidly, it was a fruitless waste of time trying to dehorn them. So, they were left in their natural state, as unnatural as that was.

She nuzzled the gate latch, having watched the ranch hands working with it when they let the cattle out to graze. She saw a link between the latch and her freedom, and so she sniffed it, then nuzzled it some more. Eventually, the latch slipped away and the gate swung open, helped along by the gravity that pulled at its sagging hinges. Cow 26 walked out into the open desert. Without any thought otherwise, thirty-six other cows left the safety and confines of the barn paddock and followed her through the open gate.

26 glanced behind her and saw the other cows had turned away from the manger and were following her lead, but she didn't really care whether they came along or not. A herd animal is gregarious and will stick with its own kind, but 26 was an anomaly, a loner among herd-bound creatures. A

few days earlier she had seen a cowboy on horseback, far off in the distance, opening a gate and taking his horse through before closing it again. She headed straight for that gate.

The moon was nearly full and was still low in the eastern sky when 26 reached the opening, which turned out to be a wire gate. It consisted of a mesquite post attached to four strands of barbed wire. These were nailed firmly to the permanent post on the "hinge" side of the gate opening. The post on the "latch" side was held in place top and bottom by two wire loops attached to the permanent fence post. A cowboy need only raise the top loop up over the mesquite post and the wire gate would be free. It had no hinges and would fall flat to the ground if it were dropped.

26 spent some time looking at the gate. She knew it was the path through the fence line, but she couldn't figure out how it worked. She first tried to upend the gate with her horns but didn't realize she was working on the wrong end, which was permanently attached to the fence. Finally, she moved over to the other side and began pushing the wire with her horns.

After a few minutes the wire loop popped up over the mesquite post, and the gate suddenly opened and fell to the ground. 26 stepped through and turned toward the big mesa to the south, careful not to get tangled in the wire gate. The other cows, grazing on the creosote and mesquite nearby, saw her leaving and hurried to catch up. Some of them were momentarily caught in the wire and suffered minor scratches, but they all managed to make their way through the fence in the moonlight and into the adjoining pasture.

The thirty-seven sister clones ranged in age from three weeks to eighteen months. To an observer, a three-week-old calf would appear to be a fully mature cow, standing over five feet tall and weighing more than a thousand pounds. But it was the fully grown cows who created the bizarre spectacle in the moonlit desert night. Like a herd of young elephants, these cows dwarfed any other species living in the vast Chihuahuan Desert. As they moved slowly in the moonlight their silhouettes swayed back and forth like sailing ships at sea.

None knew where they were headed, but they trusted 26 as she maintained her slow pace southward. A small pack of coyotes watched them pass but thought better of attacking the band of giants. A pair of Mexican gray wolves considered their prey but turned away to find an easier target. The cows continued, unaware of any danger around them.

The strange lights spoke to 26. The other cows couldn't see them as she did. They weren't aware of the green glow that appeared every night on the horizon to the south, but 26 had seen them every night of her life. They were the first thing she had seen when she was born that evening, three months ago. She didn't know that humans called them "the Marfa Lights," or that they were only able to see them once in a while. She didn't know that she was the only one who not only saw them, but could also hear them. She didn't know that humans were deaf to them.

The lights spoke soft, whispering messages directly into her brain, messages of comfort and security. Humans saw the lights sometimes, but none heard them. Cow 26 was alone in this. Only she could hear the voices of the Marfa Lights. She looked forward to hearing them each day, and they spoke to her now, even though she was out of sight of them. She knew they were hidden behind the mesa, but their soothing message still resonated in her as she made her way south.

She stopped when she came to an east-west fence line that cut off her travel. She didn't see an opening anywhere, so she followed the voice in her head that told her to turn eastward, toward where the moon had risen, and follow the fence. She walked steadily along for a couple of hours, the other cows following her, single file. She came to a stop when a paved road, north to south, intersected her path along the fence.

She had never seen a paved road, but she sensed that it was a path that humans used. The road passed through the open fence, but there were lines painted across it to simulate a cattle guard. She was familiar with cattle guards on the ranch. Her instinct told her not to step into it. She instinctively knew that her foot would fall between the slots in the road and she would break her leg.

But this one was different. It looked like the ones back on the ranch, but 26 sensed she could cross it, and she heard the voices telling her that it was okay to step over it. She stretched down to sniff the painted white lines, then gently pawed the outside one with her front foot. When she felt no resistance, she stepped gingerly onto it and, finding that she didn't fall through the crack, she walked quietly across to the other side of the fence. Without looking back at her sisters, she headed down the paved road south, toward Mexico.

The first few cows attempted to follow her but were afraid of the cattle guard and decided not to risk it. The rest of the herd felt no compulsion to follow her and stayed with the others on the north side of the fence, bawling and bellowing as their sister walked away in the moonlight.

26 followed the road for a little over a mile until it made a sharp right turn westward. She left the road there and continued her southbound journey into the open desert, following the primal voice that told her she needed to keep heading south.

Looking for Clones

At six-thirty the following morning, Dusty Reynolds discovered the cows were missing. He was making his usual early morning rounds, feeding the livestock, when he noticed the empty pasture. The ranch hands were constantly shifting cattle and horses from pasture to pasture, so it didn't register with him at first that the cows were gone.

Dusty drove up to the fence in the small four wheel drive utility quad bike pulling a flatbed trailer that was stacked high with hay bales. Normally, he threw a few bales over into the wooden mangers mounted inside the fence, where the cows waited eagerly for their breakfast. But this morning there were no cows, and the mangers were still full of hay from the previous evening. Dusty looked once more around the empty pasture, then unhitched the hay trailer, jumped onto the quad bike, and drove up to the main barn to tell his boss.

Taylor was up early as always, ready to start the day. She had wasted no time in pushing this project ahead to its full potential. She knew that success required an early start every morning, especially for a woman. Ideas came to her naturally, but she knew that there was no replacement for hard work.

She was constantly envisioning new ways of using the cloned cattle to provide beef, medicine, and other commodities. The scientists called it "pharming," the ability to extract medicine directly from an animal's milk. Taylor knew she would make a fortune from this, once the science was perfected. When that day came, she would be calling the shots for everything. She set up the financial end of the business so that she could easily cut Turner, Jackson, and most of NovaTrine's board of directors out of the real profits that would be made farther down the line. They would all end up working for her.

Taylor was having her coffee on the porch when the cowboy came to report the missing cattle.

"I'm sorry ma'am, but I need to talk with Mister Braun."

She stared at him. With a bare squint in her eyes she looked down at him from her place up on the porch.

"What's this about?" she demanded.

"Sorry ma'am. Some of the cows got loose, and Mister Braun wanted me to keep him informed on anything to do with the cattle."

"Well, he's sleeping, and we don't want to disturb him, do we?" she replied. "Besides, I'm in charge of the cattle operation, so you can report to me. I expect you will need to take some men out and find those cattle."

"Yes ma'am, we're fixin' to head out to look for 'em in a little while."

"Right *NOW*!" she hissed, "Those cattle are worth more than the lot of you put together."

"Yes ma'am." The cowboy turned a deep red, then turned to leave. Taylor added, "I don't want this getting out, to *anyone*. Do you understand?"

Reaching up, he tipped his hat. "Yes ma'am, understood."

The cowboys caught up with the cows a few hours later. They saw the open gate and saddled their horses and rode out to follow the herd. The clones were not difficult to track. Their hoofprints were the size of a draft horse's, so their trail looked like something a bulldozer made. The cows had drifted to the southeast and had covered a little over fourteen miles. It took most of the morning to find them and turn them toward home.

The cows were finally safe and back in their pasture that evening. Not all of the clones had been tagged yet, so when the cowboys and the lab scientists checked their ear tags against a master list, they didn't realize that 26 was missing.

Heading South

Cow 26 had been walking south, slowly making her way toward an unknown place in her mind. She stopped to eat and rest every so often, and after a couple of days she found herself more than ten miles east and twenty-five miles south of where her journey began. She traveled slowly, as cows do, but her size allowed her to cover more ground than a normal sized cow would.

The path she had chosen took her through a mesquite-covered swale between two small mountain ranges. The voice in her head guided her to a small spring where she paused for the first time. She took her time drinking almost thirty-five gallons of water that her enormous body required there in the desert. It was still cool in the pre-dawn light, but the day would be hot and she would need all the hydration she could manage. When she finished drinking, she looked around and surveyed her surroundings, taking stock of her situation. Then she stepped away from the water and continued her journey to the south.

Normally, a cow will follow cattle or game trails, small pathways that are the result of animal habits and the body clocks that control them. A critter will travel a trail back and forth at various times of the day, and these journeys change with the seasons, but they are well-defined maps that reveal much about the hidden lives of wildlife and livestock.

There were a few small game trails that mostly led up the sides of the mesas, down to the watering holes on the desert floor, and back up to safety at the higher altitudes. 26 saw no evidence of cattle here. If cows had ever wandered this land, it had been many years before, long before she was born. The fact that there were no signs of cattle didn't bother her. She wasn't looking for others of her kind. The compulsion that drove her was pushing her toward another kind of animal, one she would know when it appeared. It was fully light out, though the sun wouldn't show above the top of the mesa for a couple of hours as she resumed her journey southward through the long valley.

Taylor

Two days after the barbecue, Taylor was in her room, planning her way out of the mess she found herself in.

I have to keep a lid on this, she thought, *I can't let this mess get out. We're screwed if it does...*

She stood up from her desk and went into the kitchen, picked up the phone and dialed a number in New York.

"It's me," she said to the man who answered, "We've got a problem and I'm going to need your help."

She recited a list of things she required. She listened to him while he repeated them back to her.

"Yes, that's right. And we *cannot* allow headquarters or any of the stockholders to know about this, understood?"

She hung up the phone, paused to take stock of her situation, then headed back to her bedroom to pack. She needed to be long gone before Jackson and Harper returned from town.

This was a first for Taylor. She was always on top of things and in control of any situation she found herself in, no matter how unexpected. But this was a perfect storm of unforeseeable problems that she would not be able to talk her way out of. And as Jackson Braun's administrative savant, his guru and golden girl of high finance, she could clearly see the road ahead, and it was no longer smooth.

As soon as word of the barbecue disaster got out—and who's to say it hadn't already?--NovaTrine's stock would fold like a house of cards and Taylor would be left with the blame, along with a hefty amount of debt. And come to think of it, there might well be some jail time attached to it, too. She would lay the blame on the Hogg Brothers, of course, but that smoke screen wouldn't last long. The banking authorities, the IRS, and the FDA would see right through it. And so would the stockholders.

Like a spy, Taylor always kept a go-bag. It was a duffel she could grab if she had to get away from a bad situation in a hurry. In addition to clothes, her go-bag contained money, fake ID, and multiple passports, lists of addresses and connections, snacks for the road, keys for a stashed car, and a few other necessities for being on the run. To this end, she had created a very extensive financial network that allowed her to shift stocks and bank assets quickly and easily. She already kept sizable sums in various overseas accounts, and now she needed to race to New York to set the wheels in motion for a speedy exit from the approaching tempest.

The proverbial shit was about to hit the fan.

Part 4

The Search

They were camped in a long slade that was hidden in the shade of a small rocky mesa. Chinati Peak could be seen far off to the west as a series of humps that rose up through the landscape like a camel crossing the desert. Occasional rows of cottonwoods marked the dry creeks with names like *Alamito*, *Perdiz*, and *Matonoso*.

A stand of cottonwood, clumped together with a few large oak trees, stood huddled against the limestone cliff of the mesa. The trees signaled water nearby, and within a few minutes the group found a small spring that spouted from the rock. Sam and George set about building a catch basin with rocks and dirt so they would have a ready water supply.

"Just like somethin' out of a John Wayne movie, eh pard?" George said.

"Well, it beats running out of water and having to drink out of the pickup's radiator," Sam replied.

"Not sure I'd want to partake, man, but go ahead and be my guest."

By late morning they had established a workable camp. They kept food and drink in coolers placed under a tarp in the back of the pickup truck, out of the sun.

"The latrine is up around the corner, behind those big rocks," George told them, pointing to a break in the cliff about fifty yards away. "It ain't the Ritz, and I apologize for violating the sensibilities of you ladies, but I reckon it'll get the job done."

"Somehow, George," Sam quipped, "I'm pretty sure these ladies are tougher than you and I put together. I doubt they're gonna sustain any lasting trauma from using the facilities."

The women looked at each other, smiled and shook their heads.

They spent the day hiking down through a draw that was formed by the intersection of two small mesas. As the day grew warmer their progress slowed and the frequency of their rest stops increased. The surrounding sage and mesquite all looked the same to them, and the map's markings were not specific. The treasure could be anywhere. They might very well walk right past it and never notice. By late afternoon they were tired and dirty, and each wanted nothing more than to call it a day and get back to camp.

After breakfast the following day the group spent most of the morning climbing to the top of the mesa. They agreed that it might be easier to spot something from above rather than climbing around in the rocks below.

"Lookin' at this map, we should be right on top of it," George said, pointing to a mark on the map, "This dang sure looks like the canyon there."

"These canyons all look alike," Sam said, "Maybe it's just a wild goose chase after all. I'm not sure what else we can do here."

Ebbets had remained unusually quiet and reserved during the treasure hunt so far. She felt as if she was in over her head. She had no instinct for this sort of thing, so she left the decisions and plans the others to make. They were surprised when she suddenly spoke up and offered a suggestion.

"Maybe we're doing this backwards," she said.

"What do you mean?" Vera asked.

Ebbets hesitated, unsure of how to explain herself. She looked around at the group. "Ah, I don't know... it was just a dumb idea..."

"Go ahead, Ebbets, spit it out," Vera said, "Tell us what you're thinkin'. Heck, it can't be any worse than some of the ideas these two boneheads have come up with," she said, looking over at Sam and George. They looked down at their feet.

"Well, okay," Ebbets answered, "So, if you look at the map, and then read what this guy Fermin Macias wrote, it looks like they buried the treasure somewhere, and then he went *south*, back to Mexico." The others looked at her with blank stares and waited for her to continue.

"I don't know about this kind of stuff, so please don't think I'm stupid or anything, but..."

"You're *not* stupid, Ebbets," Amy told her, "I'm pretty sure you're the smartest one here."

"I'll second that!" George added.

Ebbets blushed, then walked over and gave Amy a hug. "Thank you, my dear girl." She looked around at the others and hesitated before continuing.

"When our boy Fermin was leaving, he was looking *back* at the treasure, not *forward*." She paused, pulling her thoughts together, "He drew his map the way he had *been*, not the way he was *going*."

"Okay," Amy said, "so, what does that mean?"

"Well, I don't know anything about maps or tracking or cartography or any of that stuff, and I'm thinking more like an artist...like a painter. He *painted* that map, and he would have put in the landmarks that he remembered." She saw the blank stares of the others and felt even more insecure.

"We're starting north of the treasure and working our way south. What if we started from the south and worked our way north, and tried to follow Fermin's path backwards? What if we saw the trail from *his* viewpoint, as he was looking back on it?"

The others exchanged glances and Ebbets felt a flush of shame come over her, mortified that she had made such a stupid suggestion.

Finally, Sam said, "I don't know about the rest of you, but I think that's a great idea! If there was a Girl Scout badge for treasure hunting, we'd be pinning it on Ebbets right now."

"You're a genius, Ebbets!" Amy said, grabbing her hand and holding it. Ebbets blushed even further, this time from the embarrassment of joy.

"C'mon, y'all," George shouted, "We're headin' out. There ain't no arguin' with this brilliant woman!"

It took two hours to work their way back down the mesa. They cleaned the campsite and loaded everything into the truck, then Vera pulled the pickup into the two dirt tracks that passed as a road. George sat in the bed of the truck with his arm around Ebbets. They were all smiling and enjoying their newfound hope.

They arrived at the southern edge of the mesa in the late afternoon, after an excruciating ride that left them exhausted. Traveling through the desert in a beat up Chevy pickup was not for the faint of heart.

"Man, that was a rough one," Sam said as they all climbed out of the vehicle. "I thought maybe I'd get used to it after a while, but nope, I don't think you *could* get used to that."

"Not true, pardner," George chimed in, "It's like my grandfather used to say... you can get used to pretty much anything. You can get used to *hangin'* ... if you hang long enough."

Dazed and weary from the drive, the group took stock of their surroundings. They had driven along the west side of the mesa for more than twenty miles, then skirted its southern end and drove back up the eastern side another fifteen miles or more. They were looking at a long valley that ran up the mesa's east side. They couldn't be sure it was the same one they had explored earlier. The desert had ways of fooling you, and just when you thought you had reached a landmark you had seen in the distance, it turned out to be another one that looked the same, and your landmark was still miles away.

"I figure maybe we oughta make camp and get an early start in the morning," George suggested. "Sun's already down on this side of the mesa and it'll get dark soon enough."

He got no argument, as tired as they were, and they unloaded the truck. By early evening they had cooked and eaten hamburgers that Vera prepared and were seated around the campfire that George built.

Treasure Hunters

"Why is it that no matter where I sit, the wind blows the smoke right in my face?" George asked.

Vera looked over at him, "It's karma, my friend. Punishment for whatever you've done wrong in your life. Past sins and all that."

"Well look, I moved over here because the smoke was blowing in my face over there," George said, pointing to the log he had been sitting on, next to Ebbets. "And now, the wind's changed and it's smoke all over again. I'm tellin' ya, that smoke's thicker'n six in a bed."

Vera said, "It's one of life's great mysteries. You know, there's a song about that, George."

George looked at her and shook his head.

"It's all about asking how you knew... that your true love was true," she explained.

"Ah, The Platters!" he said, "Smoke Gets In Your Eyes. You got me on that one, Vera."

"I don't know," Ebbets said, "It seems fine over on this side." The others laughed, and she added, "Oh, and keep your skinny butt over there, okay?" George gave her a forlorn look.

They sat around the small campfire and listened to the desert's night sounds. Sam had been quiet throughout the evening but now spoke up.

"Y'know, we might just be in the wrong place." The others waited for him to continue.

"I was reading a book about Maximillian's lost treasure and I'm pretty sure that's probably what we're looking for."

"Whattaya mean?" George interrupted, "Where's the treasure supposed to be?"

"Well, I'm talking about Emperor Maximillian, the leader of Mexico back around the Civil War. I think we're following the map and we're in the right place, but the book says the treasure was buried pretty far north of here, between Horsehead Crossing and Castle Gap. Horsehead is an old cattle crossing on the Pecos, and Castle Gap is a little ways east of that. They're both up above Stockton, between Stockton and Midland. That's a ways away... pretty far north of what the map says."

"Well no wonder we ain't found anything yet," George grumbled, "We've been barking up the wrong tree all this time."

"No, I wouldn't say that," Sam replied, "Lots of people have looked for the treasure over the years and no one's found it yet. Maybe the reason is because *they're* the ones who've been barking up the wrong tree. What if we've found the right one?"

Amy was sitting still, listening to the breeze blow across the dry prairie grasses, not paying particularly close attention to the conversation, but she cut in.

"I agree with Sam. Maybe we're the first ones to look in the right place. I mean, we do have the map and all..."

"Amy's right," Vera offered, "If this map is the real thing, we might just have a head start on everybody else."

"Well dang, I hope you're right," George said, "It's a lot of country to cover, that's for sure."

"It said in the book that the treasure was worth more than ten million dollars back in the eighteen sixties," Sam said. "No tellin' what it might be worth today."

"Yep," George said, "and we danged sure don't want to let opportunity slip through our fingers like a fish in water."

"Well, I'm surprised there aren't big crowds of treasure hunters out here," Vera added.

"There probably have been, over the years," Ebbets answered. "But look at this place... it goes on forever. Not surprising that nothing has been found."

"Well, who knows? Maybe we'll get lucky," Vera said. "I wonder what I'd do with millions of dollars."

"I know what I'd do," George answered, "Buy a big fancy house for my beautiful woman here. And maybe a new pickup truck."

Ebbets laughed, "I don't need a big fancy house, George. A little cottage with a garden would be wonderful."

"Well then, you shall have it, my dear, and I'll make do with a beat-up old Ford Bonus-Built pickup." George turned to the rest of the group, "And what about y'all? What're you gonna do when we strike it rich?"

"Oh, maybe take a nice vacation somewhere, I reckon," Vera commented. "Mexico… maybe go to Mazatlán or Puerto Villarta or someplace nice." Sam watched her, and sensed a small flicker of longing in her eyes as she smiled wistfully.

Amy sat silent, listening to the others before she offered, "I'd spend mine on helping others. Maybe help kids who have a rough life or orphans who don't have parents. Something like that." She felt embarrassed by her answer and thought that maybe it sounded corny and childish.

"And once again Amy, you've shown us why you're the wisest person here," Sam said. He smiled at her, "Selfless and generous. And smart… smart as you can be. You're a gem, Mizz Hidalgo."

She blushed a deep red and turned away, but Vera put a hand on her shoulder and said, "Sam might be a buffoon, but he's right this time."

Sam smiled and the others laughed, and Amy felt better.

Lonnie and Lloyd

Lonnie pulled the old truck's transmission into compound low, or granny gear as cowboys and truckers called it. It protested with sounds of grinding gears until it reluctantly popped into low range with a loud thunk. He feathered the clutch to keep the rear wheels from spinning too fast. He didn't want them digging themselves deeper into the sand. The old 1946 GMC one ton was struggling to make it along the old ranch road.

"Gawd damn piece uh shit", Lonnie yelled, hitting the steering wheel over and over, "cum-*ON* you sorry sumbitch!"

The truck groaned as it crept forward sluggishly through the sandy ruts until it found purchase and pulled itself out of the dry bog that had captured it. Lonnie bypassed normal first gear and shifted straight into second.

"Whattaya think, Lonnie? Dang, it's a real hell hole out here," Lloyd said.

"I'm thinkin' that this huntin' fer gold is gonna be a lot more work than I figured. Hell, we ain't even out to the highway yet."

The pair had followed Sam, George and Amy one day when they headed out to search for the treasure. Folks around town were starting to talk about how there were millions in gold lying around out there in the desert, just waiting to be found by some lucky sonuvabitch. After overhearing Sam and George at Olive's party talking about the secret note and the map, Lonnie decided it was just too good a deal to pass up.

There was a highway crew working on a farm to market road out past Valentine, so Lonnie figured they would have just the right equipment needed to hunt for the treasure. In order to steal the highway department's machinery they had to grab some tools, log chains, and a few things before they went to the job site.

A few days before, they had driven out to their hideout in Lonnie's pickup truck to pick up the tools. The hideout was an old line shack located a few miles south of Jorge Perea's place. It was just after sunset when they finished loading the gear into the back of the pickup. They drove back toward the highway on the old ranch road, and as they passed Jorge's place his dog ran out in front of the truck and started barking. Lonnie stopped and swore at the dog. He gunned the engine and inched forward, but the dog stood firmly planted in the middle of the road in front of them.

"Get the hell outta here, ya mangy mutt!" Lonnie was losing his temper as he looked around for Jorge, who was nowhere to be seen. Without a word, Lloyd opened the glove box and pulled out a single action Colt .45 pistol.

"What the hell you don' with that thing, Lloyd? Put it away!"

Lloyd reached out the window, pointed the pistol, cocked the hammer back, and fired at the dog. The blue heeler yelped once and collapsed. The sudden silence seemed louder than the barking had been.

"Gawd dammit, Lloyd. What the hell'd you do that for?"

"I never liked that damn dog anyway," Lloyd said, "Always barkin' his head off, nuthin' but trouble."

"Shit," Lonnie mumbled. He put the truck into gear and watched to see that the dog passed between the tires as they drove over it. He took off in a hurry, creating a rooster tail of dust as Jorge stepped out of his house and saw them leave.

Lonnie had already scouted the highway department's worksite a couple of times, so he knew what to expect when he and Lloyd arrived. He searched one of the tool boxes and found the tractor's key, and under the shine of the waxing moon he fired up the old Case backhoe. He drove it up the ramps and onto the flatbed trailer. Lloyd backed the highway department truck up to the trailer and they dropped the fifth wheel hitch and secured it.

Lonnie pulled the rig up onto the two lane highway and headed east, through Marfa and almost to Alpine, as Lloyd followed in the pickup. They turned south off the highway and traveled along another dirt road for several miles, then turned to follow a pair of tire tracks up a small box canyon where they finally came to a stop. Lonnie pulled the rig behind some mesquite brush and out of sight, then jumped into the pickup with Lloyd. They would leave the stolen backhoe there until things cooled down. Then they could go hunting for treasure.

They drove back to Alpine and spent the rest of the evening drinking beer in the Toltec Bar and making plans about how they were going to spend their money when they found the treasure.

Chico

Amy loved the horses at Olive's ranch. Over the years she often thought about all the times she sat on the side of the manger in the corral, watching them chew their hay as they blew the dust out of their noses with their quick, satisfying snorts. They swatted flies away with a switch of the tail and turned their heads back to bite at an itchy spot on their withers. They spoke to Amy in a language of soft grunts, twists and turns of the head, subtle motions of rotating each ear a hundred and eighty degrees back and forth while listening to the world around them.

The horses rolled in the dirt and played their pecking order games, ears back and teeth suddenly bared, then just as suddenly softened. They stood side by side, front to back, scratching each other's back and neck with their teeth, grooming themselves and reinforcing their own herd driven security. They were her tribe, and Amy felt she was part of theirs, too.

Amy didn't come from a ranching family and wasn't trained to ride from an early age the way ranch children were. She didn't get on a horse until she was thirteen, when Vera took her out to Olive's ranch for the first time. She had been working in the cafe, serving Olive her tea one morning, when Olive asked her if she liked horses. Amy said yes and Olive invited her to come out to the ranch. Amy was filled with excitement, but tried not to let it show to Olive or Vera. Of course, they saw right through her guise, but she didn't know that at the time.

Olive encouraged Amy to go into the corrals to be with the horses, and back then she was a little afraid of them. The young girl walked tentatively up to each one to pet it on the nose and give it a carrot from the bag that Olive had given her. In a few minutes there were about a dozen horses following the girl around, poking their noses under her arms looking for treats. Amy was in heaven.

It wasn't long before Vera was taking her out to the ranch on a regular basis. Olive asked one of her ranch hands, Manuelito, to teach Amy to ride. Manuelito was a quiet, patient man who was naturally gifted when it came to horses. In later years he might have been called a horse whisperer, but back then people just referred to him as a good hand.

The first time Manuelito let Amy climb up into a saddle was a watershed moment in her life. She threw her leg over the saddle of a little grulla mare named Nancy. Amy thought he was the most beautiful thing in the world, though when looking back at the photos she had taken of him, the little gelding was a homely little horse that looked like he was put together by a committee.

Nancy was over at the knees, sickle hocked, and had a big Roman nose that ended in a parrot mouth with an overbite that looked like he was perpetually grinning. But what Pinky lacked in conformation he more than made up for in grit, stamina, patience and honesty. He was the love of Amy's thirteen year old life and, truth be told, he remained that way long after she outgrew him.

They started with circles in the round pen, with Manuelito showing the young girl how to sit Pinky's notoriously rough trot, the roughness due to his short, straight pasterns and the aforementioned knee problems. He taught her how to stop and back up, how to change leads, and how to get him to move away from pressure with her leg. Eventually Manuelito allowed Amy to go out riding by herself as long as she told someone where she was headed. She wasn't a real cowgirl, not by a long shot, but the ranch hands accepted her, and Olive watched out for the young girl like a mother hen.

It was late spring and the days were getting longer and the Indian paintbrush was starting to bloom, along with a few bluebonnets down in the lower draws. Amy was out for a ride with Nancy. As usual, her Nikon was slung around her neck. She stayed alert for anything of interest and snapped off a shot every now and then.

When she got to Jorge Perea's place he waved her in. Jorge was Olive's neighbor who had a small section about three or four miles south of her border fence. His little flat roofed adobe sat in the shade of several huge cottonwood trees, an idyllic setting that Amy had photographed again and again on her rides.

The house's vigas extended far out the front and supported the roof over the front porch. The building was mud plastered in the old way, with millions of tiny cracks running through it and small pieces of straw poking out. There was a small barn and a tractor shed, and a few other outbuildings. Just south of the house there was a sixteen foot Aermotor windmill that could pump water up from three hundred feet below the ground. In the gentle breeze it pushed a steady two gallons a minute up into the holding tank that sat on top of a rough hewn tower next to the house.

Jorge had lived there alone for many years, a widower who had not been blessed with children. Amy could never figure out how he managed to subsist, but he always seemed healthy and happy to see her.

On that particular day he looked frail and down, sitting in his old willow reed chair in the shade of the front porch. Amy stepped down from the saddle and tied Nancy to the hitching rail next to the house and joined him on the porch.

"Hi, Jorge. How's it going?"

"Ah, mija.... ees good to see you." He kept his eyes focused on his boots.

"Hey, where's Chico?" she asked. His dog hadn't come out to greet her as he always did. The little blue heeler usually came running up with a constant stream of barking whenever someone came within sight of the house, but now it was uncommonly quiet.

"Como no, he ees not here." Jorge whispered.

"Oh, where'd he go?"

"Ah, lo siento mi jita. Es muerto. He is dead."

"Dead! What happened?" Amy had a sudden dread and a lump in her throat.

"They shot him."

"Who shot him?"

"Los hombres, those men from town. Borrachos. They are bad men."

"Oh no...." Amy struggled to keep from crying as she saw Jorge struggle with his loss. The dog was all he had in the world and she couldn't imagine anyone doing such a thing.

Amy put her hand on his arm, "Who did it, Jorge?"

"Ee-twas los hombres malos, those bad men.... Lonnie y Lloyd." He sighed, "Muy borracho... drunk. They come here, shoot guns. Chico, he bark at them. He run at them. I call to him but eet ees too late. Es por nada... they shoot him."

Amy knew who Lonnie and Lloyd were. She saw them around town from time to time. They lived over in Alpine but they hung out in Marfa sometimes. They were usually up to no good, mostly drunk, looking for a fight, trying to sell dope to her school friends. Not the type of folks you want around.

"Why would they do that, Jorge? Why would they shoot Chico?" Her eyes filled with tears.

"No se, mija." Jorge just stared at his boots, "Yo no se."

Amy had planned a long ride that day, but when she left Jorge's place she turned back toward the ranch. She needed to tell Olive what had happened.

"Oh no, that's a terrible thing!" Olive seemed shaken. She put her arm around Amy's shoulders where they sat together in the sun room. Amy wasn't one for showing emotion, but she began to cry.

"We both know what it feels like to lose someone, Amy," Olive said. "At the time, it looks like a mountain of pain that we can't possibly climb over," she paused to catch the girl's eyes, "but we do, don't we, Amy? We do manage to make it to the top of that mountain, and then down the other side."

That was the first glimpse Amy had ever had of Olive's past, of her personal life outside the ranch, and she wondered who Olive had lost.

"But you know, Amy... there is something we can do."

The girl looked up at her, "Really? What?"

"Let me make a call," she said.

The next day, Amy was sitting in the front seat of Olive's Jeep Wagoneer, driving along the rough road to Jorge's place. She held a puppy in her lap and was doing her best to keep it from jumping up on the dashboard. Olive had called a friend who raised Blue Heelers and happened to have a litter at the moment. She was a ten week old ball of pure energy.

Jorge came out to greet the pair as they drove up. Olive got out and told Amy to stay in the Jeep. She walked over to say hello to Jorge. She gestured with her hands and arms a lot when she talked and, to someone who didn't know her, it looked like she was describing a tall building or maybe the clouds in the sky.... something huge. Finally, she motioned for Amy to bring the pup. It was all she could do to hang onto the squirming little ball as she got out of the Jeep and walked over.

"Go ahead, put her down, Amy," Olive said, "She's not going anywhere."

Amy set the pup down and the dog immediately began racing around in circles, so full of herself that she couldn't stand it. Olive and the girl both laughed, and finally they saw the beginnings of a smile come to Jorge's face.

"I told you, Jorge," Olive said, "I'm not taking no for an answer. You need a dog out here, and this pup's going to make you a good one."

Jorge was torn, it was easy to see.

"And no, she's not going to replace Chico. She's a different dog, and she won't be the same as Chico was. Just remember Chico the way he was, and then take the time to learn who this pup is, too."

"Ah, gracias, Senora Olive. Thank you. Theese I weel do."

"And now...." Olive looked at Jorge, "What are you going to name her?" She paused for a moment before she held up her hand and said, "No, you don't have to come up with a name right now. You'll probably want to think about it."

"Esperanza," he said. "I think I will name her Esperanza. It means hope."

Olive smiled. "I think that's a good name," she said, and Amy thought so, too.

Wayne Heads West

The sky was turning a light grey in the predawn Texas Hill country as Wayne Guidry pulled the '56 Ford Fairlaine into the bay at the gas station in Rocksprings. The station wasn't open yet but he could see a man inside, rummaging around and getting things ready for the day. The car's fuel gauge had been buried on empty for the last thirty miles or more and Wayne couldn't quite believe he had actually made it here. He would have to wait for the place to open and he hoped it wouldn't be much longer, but better to be stopped there beside the gas pump than out on the highway somewhere, out of gas. Rocksprings was a tiny town, just a dot on the map at the intersection of a couple of two lane blacktops, neither of which went anyplace.

There was no easy way to get through the hill country directly. You had to drive the backroads, twisting and turning, up and down through miles of oaks and willows, elms and cypress and all the other trees that grew thick across the country. The roads were not well marked and it was easy to miss a turnoff and get lost. If that were not enough to worry about, Wayne was forced to keep an eye out for the damned whitetail deer that suddenly appeared in the headlights without warning. People hit them all the time, and it usually didn't end well for either the driver or the deer.

In spite of the danger, Wayne didn't slow down as his headlights cut through the darkness. In the trunk of the car, hidden beneath an old tarp and some blankets, were twenty-six kilos of marijuana that he was taking to Marfa. In return for his courier services he would enlist the help of his drug dealing colleagues who operated out of the area around Alpine. He knew Lonnie and Lloyd—"The Muppet Brothers", he called them—from his dealings back in San Antonio. They moved to Alpine a while back to expand their weed business, relocating to the badlands of southwest Texas, a place they referred to as "the wild west".

It wouldn't do to get pulled over with twenty-six bricks of grass stuffed under a blanket in the trunk. The Fairlaine was a wreck. And it was *white,* fer chrissake. *White,* like a narc's car. The driver's door was sprung, so it squeaked and popped every time he opened it. It was a chore just to climb out of the car, but Wayne was glad to be able to stand and stretch after sitting on the exposed springs that stuck out of the gaping hole in the driver's seat. Throwing an old towel over it helped, but it barely kept the springs from eating into his pants. *"Gawd, this car is a piece of shit",* he thought, *"but it's clean with no priors. Can't afford to get jacked by the heat right now."*

The attendant lifted the "Regular" nozzle and filled the tank as Wayne walked inside to buy cigarettes and beer. He grabbed a case of Longnecks and took them to the counter to wait while the attendant finished pumping his gas and checking the oil.

"Anything else I can get ya?", the old man asked as he stepped back through the door.

"Yeah, gimme a three cartons of those Stuyvesants up there," Wayne replied, pointing to the cigarette display case, "I'll take them and a large bag of those Fritos."

"That'll be sixteen dollars and sixty-eight cents, all up", the man said, "I'll be glad to carry these out and put 'em in the trunk for you."

"Naw, won't be necessary, thanks". *"Yeah, that's all I need"*, Wayne thought, *"some yay-hoo checkin' out my stash."*

He paid, grabbed his purchases and headed out to the car. The sun was just making its way over the treetops and the place began to show signs of life. The Rocksprings water tower stood as the central monument to this tired town of migrants and bluecollars. Working with your hands was important here. If you couldn't make things, or repair things, you weren't worth much in Rocksprings.

"What a god forsaken shithole of a place", Wayne thought as he lit one of the Stuyvesants and threw the match out the window in front of the gasoline pumps. He pulled the Fairlaine into low and gunned the car out onto the two lane.

The Raven

Cow 26 stopped in her tracks and listened. She didn't hear any specific sounds, but her senses told her there was something up ahead and that she should be careful. She had passed coyotes and mountain lions earlier and had even picked up the presence of a wolf, but they were of no interest to her. They were not a threat to her. Her size would protect her from predators, but she wasn't sure about what she sensed was ahead of her. In spite of this, her inner voice urged her forward and she continued on her pilgrimage.

The sun cleared the top of the eastern mesa when 26 heard a loud screech from above. She paused and scanned the area and saw nothing of interest. The flapping of wings startled her and she froze in place in a self-protective reflex. A large black bird, a raven, shot down from the sky toward her. Just before it crashed headlong into her it tilted its wings, tucked its tailfeathers under itself and swooped in for a graceful landing onto the cow's back. The bird's landing was so effortless and light that 26 didn't feel it. The raven squawked again to announce its arrival, then walked forward along the cow's spine until it reached the withers, where it issued a few cooing sounds and began to peck lightly at the small hairs that passed for a mane on the top of 26's neck.

The cow resumed its journey with the raven clinging to its withers. Eventually, the bird tried to sleep as they moved slowly along the broken sandstone rocks and sage that ran through the swale. It had flexed the tendons in its legs so that its claws locked onto the cow's thick skin and kept it in position. The cow didn't mind, and in fact could not feel the bird's talons digging into her hide. Her skin was as thick as an elephant's.

26 had seen ravens before. A pair of them lived in one of the ranch's barns, and they often perched on the fenceposts around her small pasture. They were outgoing sorts and usually offered interesting company and conversation. Sometimes they walked around on the ground beneath the giant feet of the cattle, and other times they lit upon the cows' backs as the bovines made their way through the pasture. The birds seemed very confident and sure of themselves, and pleased to be in the company of the cows. They were not at all intimidated by the enormous creatures and in fact, the ravens acted as if they were the same size as the cows.

This raven was obviously trying to say something, but 26 didn't know what it was. The bird continued to squawk and coo and make muffled noises as it pecked away at the cow's withers. Finally, it hopped along the ridge of 26's neck until it stood on top of her head, taking a stance between her horns. It released a great loud caw and launched itself, flapped its wings once, then glided effortlessly to a place a few yards ahead, where it landed in a small pile of rocks and dead grass.

The bird pecked around on the ground, scattering pebbles and sticks until it found a shiny object and grasped it in its beak. Pulling it out of the dirt, the raven turned and hopped along the ground, back to the cow. It stopped in front of 26 and dropped the object, as if offering a gift. With another squawk, the raven hopped up and set itself afloat, then glided back to the cow's withers and settled in, satisfied.

26 lowered her head until her nose touched the object. It had a faint scent of human, though not the like those she knew back at the ranch. This was much older, and different. There was death on this object and as she looked closely at it she sensed a violent history there. The object was round and shiny.

Like her bovine brethren, 26 was partially color blind but she could tell that it was a bright yellow color, or what humans would call "gold". The side that faced her was inscribed with lettering:

"LA LIBERTAD EN LA LEY"

with more writing beneath:

"8E.CA.1863.J.G. 21Qs"

There was a picture of a book and a disembodied arm and hand that held a pen with a cap on it. The hand was writing in the book.

Of course, 26 had no idea what any of these letters and symbols meant, nor did she realize that it was a Mexican 8 escudo gold coin, minted in 1863. She looked at the coin for a long time, memorizing its details. The voice inside her told her this was important. She didn't know why it was important, but she trusted the voice.

Finally, she raised her head and started forward once again. This startled the raven but it didn't fly away. Instead, the bird seemed to settle in for the ride, enjoying the view from astride the giant cow and squawking every once in awhile to voice its opinion on the things they passed along the way. The pair had barely started off to the south, toward their unknown destination, when something stopped 26 in her tracks.

Amy

"Look at this," Ebbets said as she studied Amy's photo of the map. "He has drawn a picture of a peak, with a big crevasse to the side of it. It looks a lot like that," she said, pointing to the mesa on the east side of the swale.

Amy came over to look at the photo. She studied it, looking from photo to the mesa and back again, several times. "Yep, it looks like the same one, doesn't it?"

The others wandered back, one by one, until all of them were comparing the photo of the map to the jagged peak in the distance. They agreed that the two were too similar to be a coincidence.

"That's a ways off," George said. "I can hike back to the truck and bring it up here, and we can drive up that way if y'all want."

"I'll go with you," Ebbets offered.

"Fine by me, darlin'. Any excuse to take a walk with you," he said, grinning. "We'll head back and grab the truck. Y'all hang out here for a bit and we'll be right back."

"Aren't you gonna need some help loading the gear?" Sam asked.

"Nope, amigo," George said, "we'll just grab some water and leave the rest there. Ain't no one around gonna bother it. We can pick it up on the way back."

As George and Ebbets headed back to the truck the others found a shady spot beneath a rock overhang and settled in. Sam pulled his hat over his eyes and reclined against the rock for a nap. Vera settled in next to him, then pulled out a small notebook and began to write in it. Amy, didn't want to bother them, so she stood up with her camera and set out to take some shots of the area. As she was leaving she turned and snapped a photo of Vera and Sam. There was something very peaceful about the two of them just then.

"Don't wander too far," Vera warned, "They'll be back soon, so stay within shouting distance."

"No problem, I won't go far."

Amy had a roll of Tri-X 400 black and white film loaded into her Nikon. There were thirty-six negatives on this roll and she had already used eleven. She knew not to waste film, especially out here where she couldn't buy another roll, so she was frugal about when and where to shoot. For shooting outdoors she had brought along her 50-180 zoom lens. She could take a reasonable closeup and still capture the magnificent panoramas here in the southern desert.

Amy normally liked to look through her zoom lens as she walked, but the rough terrain forced her to walk a short ways and stop. She repeated the routine several times, walking, stopping, and looking through the lens. She snapped pictures of two of the views she liked. She took a last look before turning back. She moved the lens slowly in a 360-degree circle around her. In the middle of the arc she stopped and slowly swung the camera back. Had she seen something?

There. Something in the brush looked out of place. The camera was zoomed all the way, magnifying her movements and making the image shaky. She knelt and rested against a boulder, bracing the camera against the rock until the vibrations were gone. Yes, there was something there. She couldn't tell what it was so she stood up and started walking toward it. It was about a quarter of a mile away.

Amy thought about going back and telling Vera, knowing that the others would be waiting for her. *If I turn around now,* she thought, *it probably won't be there when I come back.* She decided to head toward it and try to get close enough to get a shot of it, whatever it was.

Amy and the Cow

After walking only a short distance 26 stopped suddenly and stared ahead. She swiveled her ears forward to pick up signals that her eyes could not detect. Something was there, something that shouldn't be. Her inner voice urged her to be wary of it. She remained still, scouting the landscape without moving her head, shifting only her eyes.

The raven woke when the cow stopped. He quickly shifted his weight forward and released the lock on his talons. He did not fly, but remained poised until the cow figured out what danger might be ahead of them. He couldn't hear the voice, but he knew that the cow did and he deferred to her sense of self-protection.

The cow and the raven both caught the movement in the same instant. The raven, having a considerable advantage in eyesight, could clearly see the human. It was small for its kind, and was carrying an item that it held up to its face now and again. The raven knew that the human had seen them and was now studying them. This meant danger, and the raven began to coo and caw, pecking the cow and trying to warn her.

26, for her part, was curious. The raven was urging that danger was near, but her inner voice told her that it was safe. The voice was soothing, and made her feel that the thing ahead, which frightened the raven, was actually the reason she had made this journey. The raven sensed the cow's serenity and identified it with the voice. It soon relaxed and settled down on the cow's back to watch.

At first Amy thought the cow was close, but as she walked toward it she realized it was much farther away than she had reckoned. Her eyes seemed to be deceiving her. The cow couldn't be that big! It must be some trick of the light, or the way the landscape made things look. As she walked toward the cow she could see something moving on its back. She stopped to take a look through the camera lens and saw that it was a bird. As she moved closer she could see that it was a raven, and not the tiny black bird it had first appeared to be. The cow was *much, much* bigger than she had realized. *Holy crap,* she thought to herself, *that's some sorta monster cow!*

She raised her camera and took a quick shot. The cow raised its head slightly and said, "moo." Amy wasn't expecting the sound from the cow and it startled her. It was far lower and louder than it should have been, more than an octave below a normal cow's voice. This was, by far, the biggest cow she had ever seen. She studied the animal as she approached it. It stood silently, waiting. When she reached the cow Amy held out her hand and said, "Whoa, girl. It's all right. I'm not gonna hurt you."

The cow did not shy away from the human's hand when it reached out to touch her neck.

"My, you're a big girl, aren't you? Where did YOU come from? Are you lost, girl?" Amy talked slowly and calmly, reassuring 26 while she looked the cow over.

"My god, you're huge! How on earth did you get this big?" She noticed the raven, who hadn't flown away and remained perched atop the giant cow.

"And who are you?" she asked, looking up at the bird. "Looks like you've found a friend here," she said. The raven issued a squawked response and Amy laughed. "Well, you're a real smart aleck, aren't you?"

The sound of a truck's engine startled them all. The cow grew tense and the whites of her eyes showed as she opened them wide in fear. The raven bellowed a loud *"caw, caw, caw"*, urging the cow to run away, but the cow remained still.

Amy heard her friends calling for her and answered, "I'm over here! Stop the truck! Please, stop! You'll scare the cow!"

The Coin

George pulled the pickup to a stop and shut off the engine. He and Ebbets stepped down out of the cab while Vera and Sam climbed out of the back. There was some distance between them and Amy, but almost as a single person, they gasped when they saw her next to the giant cow. When it raised its head it was almost twice her height.

"What in the world is THAT thing?" George asked, to no one in particular.

Vera added, "Is that a cow? What IS that thing? Its as big as an elephant!"

When the group began to make their way toward Amy she cautioned, "Take it slow! I don't want to scare her. She's a bit skittish already."

The others came closer but stopped several yards away when they saw that the cow was getting nervous. Amy petted her neck and tried to calm her. "It's okay, girl. I'm here. These are my friends, and they won't hurt you. It's okay." She continued to talk softly to the beast.

George couldn't contain himself, "Where would a cow like THAT come from? I mean, somebody musta crossed a brahma bull with a rhino. I'll tell you one thing—it don't take too many of THAT thing to make a dozen."

"What's that on her back?" Sam asked. "Looks like a crow or something."

"It's a raven," Amy replied, "Crows are a lot smaller, and their beaks are straight. Not funky and curved like this one's." The raven seemed to know that Amy was talking about him and answered with a deep squawk.

"Yeah, and crows don't make that sound, either," Amy added.

"Dang girl," George said, "you're a regular Marlin Watkins, ain't you?"

"Who?" Amy shot a puzzled look at George.

"You know, the Mutual of Omaha guy... Wild Land, or whatever it's called. The animal guy on TV... aw, forget it."

"Perkins. Wild Kingdom," Sam corrected.

"Yeah, Wild Kingdom."

"I don't have a TV," Amy said.

"Yeah, forget it. It don't matter… it's a raven, okay?" George said.

The raven squawked again and George sneered at it, "I think he's makin' fun of me."

Vera interrupted, "What in the hell is this cow doing here? I wonder who it belongs to. Does it have any brands on it?"

"Not sure," Amy said, "I just got here and I've been trying to make friends. I don't see any brands on this side of her, but I haven't looked at the other side.

Sam and George set off in opposite directions, walking slowing around the cow, keeping their distance and looking for a brand or an ear tag. The cow had none.

"Y'know, here in Texas I'm pretty sure you can claim a cow that isn't branded. It's a maverick, and they're pretty much footloose and fancy free for the taking," George said.

Sam considered this for a moment, then said, "Not sure about that, bud, but maybe we oughta find her owner, no? We can't just leave her out here. There's no water for her, and there isn't much feed, either."

"Well, sure," George replied, "if she's got an owner. I suppose we just go back to town and ask around about who's raisin' giant cattle."

"There's a problem with that," Vera cut in, "Where are we gonna take this critter, and how are we gonna get her there?"

"Oh, that's easy," Amy replied, "We can take her to Olive's. We can borrow one of Olive's stock trailers. I don't think this cow could fit in a closed horse trailer."

"Yep, that's easy enough to do," George replied, "but I reckon somebody should stay here with the cow, so it don't wander off. We can go and get the trailer and bring it back here. Probably need a few ropes to get her in the trailer." He looked around to see if the others approved of his plan. They nodded their heads.

After a short discussion it was decided that Sam and George would drive back to get the trailer while the women stayed with the cow. The men drove back down to the campsite and packed it up, then brought the food, water, and camping gear for the women before driving back to the ranch.

The women set up a makeshift camp in the shade of a nearby

cottonwood tree. There was a small cut into the rock where the ground was damp. Using the camp shovel, Amy was able to dig a cavity that soon filled with water. The women already had plenty to drink but they were concerned for the cow.

A gentle afternoon breeze began to blow as 26 followed the women and watched them as they laid out a campsite. When Amy finished digging, the cow saw the water and walked over to drink. The raven hopped down and gulped down several beakfuls before returning to roost on 26's back. The women took great pleasure in watching the cow and the bird together.

Though she had grown up around them and was used to them, cow 26 had never been petted or talked to by a human, and she was enjoying the attention and the company. She noticed that her inner voice was silent now, and she felt safe with these three humans. The raven hopped down and took a few pieces of bread from Amy as the women sat on the ground cloth and ate lunch.

"This is the darnedest thing," Ebbets was saying, "I come out here to the wild west and I never know what to expect!"

"Ah, you get used to it," Vera said, dryly. "We like our little oddities out here."

"I think she's the most beautiful cow I've ever seen," Ebbets exclaimed. "Of course, I haven't seen all that many cows up close, but still…"

Vera smiled, "Is there anything you *don't* think is beautiful, Ebbets? But yeah, you're right. She is pretty danged lovely."

"I've been trying to take some shots of her but I'm not sure they're gonna show how *BIG* she really is," Amy said. She got to her feet and grabbed her camera again. She walked around behind the cow and framed a shot.

"I'm gonna get one with you two in it. That'll show how big she is compared to you." She took a couple of pictures, then paused to look around for a different vantage point.

At that point, the raven hopped down from 26's back and over to Amy. *"Squawk, squawk, squawk! caw, caw…."* it set up a racket in front of her until she said, "What's with this bird?"

The raven hopped away from Amy, back to the north, the way it had come. After a few hops it turned to squawk at her, then continued hopping back up the swale. It raised its wings and caught the light breeze and glided low to the ground for a few yards before it landed. Then it turned to squawk at Amy some more.

"That bird's tryin' to tell you something," Vera said.

"I'll go see what's up."

"Don't wander far away," Vera cautioned, "You need to stay within eyesight, okay?"

"Okay, I won't go too far." As Amy headed toward the raven the bird turned and flapped his wings, rising a few feet above the ground. It glided another fifty yards before landing again and waited for Amy to catch up. It squawked the whole time. After repeating this process two or three times, the raven settled to the ground and waited.

When Amy reached the bird it squawked once again, then dug around in the rocks and brush until it pulled up a shiny object with its beak. It held the Mexican coin up for Amy to see, then dropped it on the ground and backed away.

"What the heck is this?" Amy reached to pick up the coin. She turned it over and over in her hands, examining both sides. "This looks like gold!" she said to the bird. "What the heck is the deal with you?" she asked, looking at the raven with wonder. The bird sat calmly and looked back at her, curious about what she would do with the shiny object.

Amy hiked back down the swale to where Vera and Ebbets lie in the shade with their backs against their sleeping bags. They both sat up as she approached.

"Where's the bird?" Ebbets asked.

"Don't know. Guess it flew off someplace."

"Well, did you figure out what it wanted?"

"Yep, I sure did," Amy answered, flipping the coin at Ebbets, who reached to catch it but missed. She fumbled around searching for it in the dry grass until she found it.

"What's this?" Ebbets turned the coin over and looked at the other side, then handed it to Vera.

"Looks like some kinda gold coin from Mexico," Amy replied. "The raven just picked it up and handed it to me."

"Oh come on, Amy. No he didn't," Vera said. "Birds don't just hand you a gold coin," she continued, as she examined the piece.

"Well, not exactly *handed* me the coin. More like, dropped it on the ground in front of me."

Vera handed the coin back to Ebbets. Ebbets looked at it again and said, "Dang, this this is from 1863! It's a pretty old coin. I wonder how it got all the way up here."

"Are you thinkin' what I'm thinkin'?" Vera asked, to no one in particular.

"Whattaya mean?" Amy asked.

"Well, what are we doing here in the first place?"

Ebbets replied, "Well, I mean.. we came out here looking for treas...." she paused, "Oh my goodness!"

Vera smiled. "I ain't sayin' it's the treasure, but it does seem like a bit of a coincidence, doesn't it?"

"They're never gonna believe this back home," Amy said.

The three women looked at each other, wide-eyed and excited. Far above them, the raven floated effortlessly in circles on the thermals and looked down on the three humans and the cow below.

Back At the Ranch

When the group got back to the ranch the boys unloaded the cow with the help of a couple of the ranch hands while Olive and the three women headed to the house.

The two Mexican cowboys who helped them unload were afraid of the giant beast but were too proud to let their fear show. After all, the two gringo tenderfeet didn't seem to be afraid of the monster, so the cowboys held their panic in check until they were finished moving her into the corral next to the barn..

Once Sam and George left for the house one of them said to the other, "Hijole cabron! Esta es la vaca más grande que he visto en mi vida!"

His friend nodded and replied, "La vaca da miedo, que no?"

The other cowboy reached inside his shirt and pulled out the San Miguel medallion he wore, kissed it, and made the sign of the cross. They had a story to tell their friends, that was for sure. The cow was a miracle.

Sam and George found the women sitting in the sun room, drinking iced tea.

"That's the damnedest thing I've ever seen," Olive remarked. The others were used to the oversized bovine by now, but she was flabbergasted. "I can't imagine where it came from!"

George joked, "Well, you can blame Amy. She found it." Amy blushed, and Olive reached over to squeeze her hand.

During this exchange Ebbets was thinking about the cow. It seemed like such a freak because of its size, and she knew how that felt. It brought back memories of being the tallest girl in her school, a freak and an outsider.

She spoke suddenly, "I think the cow is beautiful." Everyone turned to look at her and Ebbets looked down, embarrassed. "Well…. it *IS*."

Olive studied her for a moment.

"I agree, Ebbets. She is beautiful. And you know? I think I'll do a little digging around to see if we can find out more about that cow. There's something fishy going on around here, and I have an idea about that."

The others looked at each other and nodded.

"Her name's *Dinah*," Amy announced. The others all turned to her.

"That's what I call her... *Dinah*," she repeated.

"I think that's a beautiful name to go with a beautiful cow!" Ebbets exclaimed, and the others nodded in agreement.

"Well then, *Dinah* it is," Olive said, "And come to think of it, that cow doesn't seem to be the only thing that our dear Amy has found, does it?" Olive mused.

She picked up the Mexican coin from the table and turned to Sam and George.

"She's been telling me about finding this gold piece. I'm thinking this might be worth a bit of money." She turned the coin over and studied it. She said to the group, "And just what were you all doing way out there, anyway?"

They looked at each other sheepishly, not knowing how to respond. No one had told Olive about the map or the letter. Sam and George didn't want her to feel guilty about buying it and they knew she would want to return it to them, so they had all kept quiet about it.

Finally, Sam spoke, "Well, Olive... it's this way," he stumbled over his words, "Um.... well, y'know that map you have on your wall? Well... " and he related the story of how it had come to be in their possession, and then in hers. He pulled the old letter out and handed it to her.

"George and I really want you to keep the map," he urged, "and we think you should have this letter, too. It goes with the map." Olive took the note and read it silently a few times.

"Well for crying out loud, I didn't even know it was a treasure map!" she exclaimed, "And now you're telling me you found that coin out there where the map says the treasure is?"

"Yes ma'am," George replied, "Of course, we didn't find any treasure, but that coin looks pretty good, don't it?"

"Buried treasure and giant cows... That's a lot to absorb in one day." She laughed and handed the coin to George.

"Ma'am, that belongs to Amy. She found it," George said. When everyone turned to look at her, Amy blushed again.

"Just goes to show, every cloud has a silver spoon," George added.

"I think maybe you've done pretty well for yourself, young lady," Olive said with a smile, and gave the coin to her.

"It was the raven who did it," Amy said, "I just followed him to where the coin was. He's the one who found it."

"Yeah, and who knows?" Vera said, "Maybe he'll lead us to the treasure."

"I wish," Amy replied, "But he flew away. I don't think we're gonna see him again."

As she was saying those words, the raven was outside in the corral, sitting on the Dinah's back, enjoying the evening's cool breeze with his new friend.

The Treasure Hunt

They kept at it for several weeks. The group searched for the treasure whenever they could. Sometimes it was all five of them, sometimes just two or three, depending upon who could get away to search. They made a pact that no matter who found the loot, it would be split six ways. They included Olive without telling her because they knew she would refuse any part of the bounty. But they already had an answer in case she refused her share— if she didn't want it they would find the Mexican couple, Diego and Rosalina, and Olive could give her share to them. The group was proud of themselves for being honest and thoughtful, though it was George who actually came up with the idea.

They began at the place where the bird had shown Amy the coin. They conducted a rigorous search that started at what Amy thought was the place where she had picked up the coin, but it turned out to be a dead end. Much as she tried, Amy couldn't be sure she was in the right place because by the time they went back out to search, the terrain had changed.

Nothing stays the same in the desert. At first glance its appearance is static and unchanging and looks pretty much the same. But once you begin to study it in more detail it becomes an ever-changing environment in which everything is in constant flux. And those changes are rapid and many. A light wind or a bit of rainfall will alter the appearance of plants, rocks, dirt, and even the mesas themselves. Just a passing cloud or the angle of the sun can render very different moods to the same place. So when the group returned to take up where they had left off, their tracks had disappeared and none of them was certain just where they *had* left off. It looked different, *every time*. They needed the raven.

The problem was that Dinah now belonged to Jorge and was living at his place. After he lost his old dog, Amy decided that the cow would be better off with Jorge. She mentioned it to Olive, who thought it was a great idea and immediately had Sam and George hitch up the trailer so that she and Amy could take her over.

After Jorge lost Chico, he grew attached to Dinah. His new pup, Esperanza, had taken to hanging out with her in the corral, and the pair had become best friends. So, the group didn't feel right about asking Jorge if they could borrow her whenever they felt like going treasure hunting.

Without the cow and the raven to guide them they were pretty much back to square one. They really had no idea how to go about finding the lost cache, but none of them were quitters so they set about searching in the most thorough and methodical way they could.

They tried spiral searches, walking in ever-increasing circles around a starting point, but that proved fruitless. They covered areas in a rectangular fashion by spacing themselves six or eight feet apart and walking in a straight line, looking down at the ground and trying to find some small indicator that there was treasure to be found. They climbed up to various vantage points and looked down at the desert below, hoping to recognize a landmark or a piece of evidence from the map.

They studied the map and the note over and over and compared the drawings and hand written letter to their surroundings, but that produced no results. They all agreed that it seemed they were in the right place, but nothing materialized. It was frustrating, yet at the same time they found themselves together as a group. None of them liked to talk about their past, so they talked of the future instead, and of the dreams that lie ahead for each of them. Each was learning not only who the others were, but who they were, themselves.

After several weeks of searching, their hopes for discovering the treasure were exhausted. Amy saw that it had taken the wind out of their sails, and she wished she could do something about. What none of them saw at the time was that the search had pushed and driven them all. It united them as a single entity, whole and complete. They were ready to take on the world and the truth was, whether they found the treasure or not, it was the hunting that mattered, not the treasure. The search bound them together forever.

Bad Guys

Wayne slid into in the corner booth in the Casa Blanca Cafe in Alpine, Texas and looked back and forth at the two men across from him. The place was a dump. He wasn't surprised that Lonnie Tate and Lloyd Hodges chose this place to meet. *This is high society to them,* he thought to himself. *What a couple of trailer trash lowlifes.*

On the wall behind the counter was a big hand lettered sign that said, "The Cowboys Are More Than Welcome". It looked like it was painted by a group of high school kids for a pep rally, with different sized letters and fonts, not quite straight, not quite centered. What it lacked in craftsmanship it more than made up for in team spirit.

Yeah, screw team spirit, Wayne thought, *it's every man for himself.*

"Hey, Wayne! How ya doin', man?" Lloyd reached out his hand in greeting.

"Not too bad," Wayne replied, not returning the handshake. He couldn't remember which was which, so he didn't address either by name. He didn't care, but he needed these two so he kept quiet.

"Lonnie here says y'all got some stash for us..."

"Shaddup, Lloyd!" Lonnie admonished in a hushed whisper, "What the hell? You tryin' to get us busted?"

"Aw, damn, Lonnie. Sorry, I wasn't thinkin'..."

"No, you damn sure wasn't," Lonnie replied.

Well, Wayne thought, *at least I know which is which now.*

"How 'bout we grab some lunch and then go outside and talk things over?" Wayne suggested.

When their food arrived Wayne found that he wasn't hungry. Even if he had wanted to eat, just watching the two drug dealers wolf their food down would have put him off his feed. Lonnie devoured his cheeseburger in two or three bites, then seemed to inhale the pile of French fries on his plate. He didn't touch the lettuce and tomato garnish, claiming to be a meat eater and that vegetables weren't good for him.

Lloyd was working intently on a chicken fried steak that had made its way straight out of the freezer and into the cooking grease. The smell of burnt crumbs did not sit well with Wayne. "I'm gonna go out and sit on the porch. Come out when you're done."

"Hey Wayne," Lloyd called after him, "Ain't you gonna eat the rest of your food?"

"It's all yours." Wayne stepped out into the afternoon heat. He sat down on the weathered bench beneath the cafe's front windows and reached for his pack of Stuyvesants and his Zippo lighter. *I wonder if they sell these in this shithole town,* he thought. *I doubt it. Camels and Marlboros are more their speed.*

Lonnie and Lloyd emerged from the cafe in a contest that had them both trying to shove through the front door at the same time.

"God dammit Lloyd!"

"Aw, dang, Lonnie. Sorry, I wasn't thinkin'..."

"You never do," Lonnie chided as he made his way outside, leaving Lloyd holding the door. He sat down on the bench next to Wayne. Lloyd stood in front of them and leaned against the old wooden hitching rail that separated the sidewalk from the street.

"We paid for your meal in there," Lloyd said, expecting an offer to reimburse, or a thank you. Wayne ignored him.

"So, what's up? What's goin' on?" Lonnie asked.

Wayne needed these two, but he wanted them curious and anxious, so he said nothing about his plans. He took a last drag on his Stuyvesant and flicked the butt into the street and smiled, "Oh, just this and that," he said.

The Map

They worked out their deal right there in front of the Casa Blanca. Wayne would take the marijuana in Lonnie's and Lloyd's pickup truck to meet their drug connection. They would meet at a turnout a couple of miles south of town, on the old Terlingua road, where he would transfer twenty-four bricks of marijuana and pick up a drop-off of cash. He'd meet them in Alpine later that evening and give them the cash.

Unbeknownst to anyone, Wayne would set aside two kilos for himself, a small detail that he didn't reveal to the others. *Let 'em think there are only twenty-four bricks*, he thought. Once that was settled, he changed the topic.

"I figure you two can help me with something," Wayne lit another Stuyvesant and dropped his lighter back in to his pocket. "You mentioned that you saw Ebbets here."

"Yeah, I saw her over in Marfa," Lonnie said, "I think she's there at Vera's place."

"And who's Vera?"

"Ah, well... she runs the cafe there in Marfa. She ain't nobody to be bothered about," Lonnie replied. Suddenly his face lit up with excitement as he remembered a detail he wanted to share with Wayne, "Hey listen, there's something I was gonna tell you but it slipped my mind..."

"And she's a friend of Ebbets?" Wayne interrupted.

"Uh... yeah, I think so. I seen 'em together, that's all I know."

Lonnie had something in his mind to tell Wayne, but now he was sidetracked and it left him wallowing around in his own indecision, trying to remember what it was. Wayne's inquiry about Vera had forced him out of his comfort zone and pushed that piece of information back into the recesses of his scattered mind.

"I expect they're friends, but all I know is that she spends time there, and she's out at Olive Stanfield's place a lot, too."

"And who is Olive Stanfield?" Wayne asked, confusing Lonnie even more.

"Aw, well, she's a rich lady who's got a ranch down south of Marfa. And there was something about her that I was needin' to tell you about. Lemme see..."

Wayne wasn't listening. "So Ebbets is staying at a rich rancher woman's place?" he interrupted once more.

"Naw, I don't think she's stayin' there. But hell, I don't know. Maybe she is." Lonnie was flustered and trying to cling to a hazy reminder but just couldn't manage to hold onto it.

"So, you two gonna help me find her?"

"Sure, Wayne. I'll ask around, let folks know you're lookin' for her."

"Nope, you won't be doing that, Lonnie." Wayne's eyes narrowed as he stared the other man down. "This has got to be on the que tee, know what I mean? You gotta keep it quiet."

"Well, sure Wayne, we won't say nothin'. You wantin' to meet up with her, or what?"

"It's the or-what thing that I have in mind," Wayne replied, "Ebbets Fields is gonna take a little trip with me."

"Well, wait, Wayne. I just remembered!" Lonnie slapped his knee and gave a happy grunt, "There's a map!"

"What? Whattaya mean, a map?"

"A map. The lady—Olive—she has this map that leads to a buried treasure. It's hangin' on the wall in her house."

At this point, Lloyd, who by comparison made Lonnie look like Albert Einstein, jumped into the conversation.

"There's buried treasure at Olive's place?"

"No, you dumbass. There's no treasure at Olive's. It's a map"

"Whattaya mean? What's a map got to do with Olive's place?"

"Jeezus, Lloyd. You're as dumb as a fuckin' post, you know that?"

"Aw hell, Lonnie," Lloyd whimpered, "I didn't mean anything by it."

"You never mean anything by anything," Lonnie scolded.

"Break it up, you assholes," Wayne broke in, "What's the deal with the map?"

"Well y'see, she's got this danged map but she don't know that it's a map of buried treasure, but them two hombres do!"

And Lonnie went on to explain about the map on Olive's wall and what he overheard at the party, the two ranch hands talking about having a note that explained it all.

And for once, Wayne listened.

Berserker Cows

The herd milled around calmly in the safely of their pens just outside the lab building. After the events at the barbeque there were no lab scientists around, no ranch hands to clean their corrals. Everyone was sick. Dusty Reynolds was the only hand who showed up at the barn, and he was only there because someone needed to feed the cattle. For the rest of the day things were quiet.

Toward evening the cows began to get restless. For the first time in their lives they began to hear the voice. It spoke softly at first, in whispered tones of reassurance, but it gradually grew more strident and demanding, until the cows were trembling with fear. Finally, they reacted as frightened cattle do—they ran like hell.

There was a bull fence around the paddock that was built for keeping heavy livestock in, but it was no match for the thirty-four head of terrified giants. The first two cows jumped into the fence and sailed through it as if it were not there. The rest of them followed in a thundering wave of dust and destruction, headed for the barn and lab in which they were conceived. Their hooves pounded and they rolled like a tsunami—as a single unit—and there was no stopping them.

At the time, there was no one around to see what the cows saw, a blazing greenish glow that shone like a spotlight on the side of the barn, pointing the way for the terrified bovines to go. The giant clones followed the light without question as the voice urged them on. As they had done to the paddock fence, so they did to the outside walls of the lab.

There were no scientists working in the lab at the time. They were all at home, fighting off continued bouts of explosive diarrhea and battling the giant ringworm fungus that had engulfed their children. The herd exploded Into the lab and once inside, the cows suddenly seemed to realize their purpose. While it couldn't actually be proven that they recognized their own place of conception, the scientists would never stop believing it. For years afterward, even the most strident skeptics among them would admit that the clones were likely out for revenge.

The frightened desperation of the giant bovines subsided and their panicked charge turned into a methodical frenzy in which they destroyed the lab and its contents in what appeared to be a systematic and coherent manner. They left nothing untouched and ripped up the workplace as if it were made of cotton. Freezers were torn open, cabinets with shelves full of jars with samples were destroyed, and the wall of tape machines containing all of the lab's data were crushed beneath the hooves and horns of the berserk bovines.

The demolition stopped as suddenly as it had begun when fire broke out in the building. The cattle turned and fled in terror. This time they took flight back to the south, through the broken fence and across the paddock to the same gate from which they had originally escaped.

This time the gate was locked, but that didn't matter. The momentum of the stampeding behemoths carried them straight through it and took out several hundred feet of fence line with it. The voice in their heads told them to head for the big river to the south. Into each cow's mind was projected a picture of the Mexican Corriente cow who had given birth to the first of the clones. This cow was their mother, and in a vision reminiscent of the Virgin Guadalupe, the voice urged them to return to the land of the mother cow.

The ground rumbled from the thunderous pounding of the hooves of thirty-four giant clones as the barn and lab facility burned to the ground behind them. And in the aftermath of the rampage, the missing Cow 26 was completely forgotten.

Going to the Site

It was Sunday and the cafe was closed. Every now and then Vera closed on Monday, too, and gave herself an extra day off. The group thought it would be nice if they could all get out of town and spend a couple of days together.

Vera was up long before anyone else and whipped up eggs and pancakes for the group. Amy heard the front door open and close when Vera headed out to the cafe, so she dragged herself out of bed and followed a few minutes later.

When Amy stepped into the cafe Vera had a mixing bowl out, stirring up a batch of pancake mix. She said good morning to her boss and started putting coffee grounds into the coffee maker.

"You might want to go upstairs and see if Ebbets is up yet," Vera said.

Amy climbed the stairs and knocked softly on the door to the flat, then pushed it open. Ebbets was still in bed so the girl touched her softly and whispered, "C'mon, Ebbets. Time to go treasure huntin'."

Ebbets raised her head and groaned, then rubbed her eyes and looked up at Amy.

"We're fixin' breakfast. Coffee's on, so c'mon downstairs," the girl said and headed back down to help Vera.

Sam and George pulled up outside in the ranch pickup. They knocked on the front door and Amy went over to unlock it and let them in.

"Something smells good," George said, "I'm hopin' there's a plate for me."

"Sit yourselves down. Breakfast comin' up," Vera hollered from the kitchen.

George answered, "Well now, I'm just gonna grab the bull by the tail and look him in the eye."

Vera replied, "You do that, George, and you're gonna have one foot on thin ice and the other in hot water."

He stopped to consider this. "Well, I reckon you got me on that one, Vera."

"Well, that's easy as fallin' off a piece of cake," she answered. Amy and

Sam looked at each other and shook their heads. Those two...

Ebbets came down the stairs and into the cafe looking fresh as a spring shower.

"Well now, here I am feelin' sorry for myself," George said, "but how can I have the breakfast blues when this beautiful woman is here?" He rose from the table and went over to Ebbets, kissed her, and the two stood there mumbling things to each other. The other three collectively shook their heads again.

Vera began to sing, "And they called it puppy love..."

Sam suddenly added, ""Young love, first love, it's true devotion..." He spoke the lyrics more than sang them.

"Wow, Sam. That's impressive!" George mocked, "You should try out for Arthur Godfather's Amateur Hour." Sam pursed his lips, embarrassed.

"Godfrey," Sam corrected.

"Godfrey? Godfrey who?" George asked. He looked down at the floor, lost in thought, then said, "Ah, Godfrey Daniels!"

"Never mind." Sam shook his head.

Vera appeared with a tray that held a stack of pancakes, a large dish full of scrambled eggs, a pile of crispy bacon and several slices of toast. Amy grabbed the coffee pot and they all sat down in the corner booth to eat. Amy smiled to herself and watched the banter between the others, the good natured jokes and off color remarks that bonded them. They were clearly enjoying themselves, and she felt happy to be in the middle of it all. These were more than friends. They were her family.

After they finished breakfast they piled into Vera's pickup and headed out to hunt for treasure. Amy helped pack food for lunch along with a cooler full of sodas and lemonade. She sat in the pickup truck's bed with Sam, their backs against the cab, and watched the dust billow out behind them as they drove the dirt road to the south. The coolers were on either side of them, so the two were pushed close together. Amy was thrilled, but Sam seemed oblivious. He had no idea what it meant to the girl, to be sitting there with him, sharing stories and talking about finding buried treasure. It took the better part of an hour to reach the site, though it was still early in the morning when they arrived.

The first thing that struck them was that they were not alone.

Confrontation

"Something goin' on out here," George said as Vera pulled the pickup to a stop and shut off the engine. "Looks like they're doing' some sort of construction or something."

"Seems pretty odd, them bein' way out here," she replied. They opened the cab doors and climbed out. Ebbets followed.

Sam and Amy got up and jumped down from the bed of the truck and they all stood together, looking for whoever was working there. They saw black diesel smoke rising from behind a thicket of mesquite and buck brush, and the sound of a tractor engine disturbed the calm desert morning. Amy could barely make out the yellow arm of a backhoe bucket, rising and falling as it scooped up loads of dirt and deposited them off to one side. A moment later, Wayne Guidry and Lloyd Hodges stepped out from behind the brush.

"Howdy," George called, "Wutch-y'all doin' here?" As he spoke, Ebbets clutched his arm tightly, her fingernails digging into his elbow. He looked over at her, puzzled.

"Well, these two..." Wayne indicated Lloyd and then pointed back to Lonnie, who was operating the backhoe, "these two are looking for buried treasure, thanks to the map y'all had." He paused, then said, "And me, well... I've come here to collect what's mine." Wayne looked at Ebbets, who looked away. "Hello, darlin'," he said to her. Ebbets looked as if she had seen a ghost.

Amy had a bad feeling about this. Her stomach began to twist itself into a knot and there wasn't anything she could do about it. She knew that Lloyd was one of the ones who shot Jorge's dog, Chico, and she figured that Lonnie was probably back there on the tractor.

"What are you doing here, Wayne," Ebbets replied. She turned to face him, her resolve had returned, but she still seemed unsure of herself.

"What the hell's goin' on here," George began. It was dawning upon him who Wayne was, and he could feel the anger rising inside himself. He took a step toward Wayne but Ebbets pulled him back.

"It's okay George. It's just Wayne. Leave it alone. Let's just go."

George shrugged Ebbets off and began to walk toward Wayne. "I'm thinkin' you oughta get the hell outta here," George told him.

"Oh, I don't think so," Wayne replied cheerfully, as he reached to pull a pistol from his back pocket. "And I don't think y'all are goin' anywhere. In fact, I think you're gonna stay right where you are, unless you like the feel of hot lead." George stopped when he saw the pistol pointed at him.

"You sonuvabitch…"

"Now now, just calm down," Wayne said in a smooth, mocking manner. "You're gonna stay where you are, without movin'. All of you."

He looked everyone over, and when his eyes fell upon Amy she had to look away. He continued,

"But Ebbets there, now *SHE'S* a different story. You're gonna come over here and stand next to me." Ebbets stood still. "*NOW!*" he yelled.

"Stay where you are," George turned to tell her.

"I reckon that's a bad idea," Wayne said.

George turned and started toward Wayne. "You leave her alone you sonofa…." Wayne fired the pistol. The bullet missed George by less than a foot and buried itself in the soft ground behind Vera's pickup.

"If I'd a'wanted to shoot you, believe me… you'd be gutshot right now," Wayne said. "As it is, I'm not interested in you or your friends. I just want what's mine, and I aim to get it." He turned to stare at Ebbets, "Now, either you come here darlin', or the next shot isn't gonna miss."

"Just who the fuck do you think you are, asshole." Vera stepped out in front. Suddenly, she wasn't the diminutive cafe owner anymore.

"You want somebody? Why don't you try me on for size, big guy." She was taunting him, and Amy was suddenly very afraid for her. Vera raised her hand and pointed her finger at him, "You chickenshit little weasel."

Wayne tried hard to ignore her, but it was hard for his ego to take. He did not take kindly to a woman standing up to him.

"I'm gonna make this easy for y'all," he said to no one in particular, "Either she comes over here or this fellow—George, is it? I read your letters, George. How sweet they were….—her sweetheart here is a dead man, plain and simple."

Wayne gestured at George with his pistol again. "And if George here tries to interfere, well then, I'm afraid his darlin' Ebbets—*MY* darlin' Ebbets—is gonna wind up with a bullet in her head. How's that for makin' it simple?"

Amy was right about Lonnie. It had been him back there operating the backhoe. When Wayne fired the gun, the noise from the machine suddenly stopped. A moment later Lonnie appeared holding a rifle. During this time, Lloyd went back to their truck and returned with a pistol of his own.

"What the hell's goin' on?" Lonnie demanded.

Seeing Lonnie and Lloyd standing side by side caused something to break inside of Amy, and she stepped forward without thinking and pointed at them.

"You're the ones who shot Jorge's dog! You motherfuckers! I'm gonna..." Sam grabbed her as she started for them. "No, Amy!" he whispered to her, "Just leave it."

"Gawd damn pieces of shit!" the girl yelled.

"Leave it, Amy. They're not worth it."

Amy was so pissed off she couldn't think straight, but Sam kept his arm tight around her and she finally calmed down somewhat.

"That's right, little lady. You do what the man says. You just stand there and shut your fuckin' mouth, or I'll shut it for you." Wayne was grinning. "Now, I've asked nicely, but I'm not gonna ask again." He waved his gun at Ebbets. "Come over here if you know what's good for your friend there."

Ebbets walked slowly toward Wayne.

"Ebbets, wait! Don't do this!" George pleaded.

When she reached Wayne he grabbed her arm and spun her around, then wrapped his arm around her shoulders and pointed the gun at her head.

"Now you..." Wayne said, pointing the pistol at Amy. "Get over here." When she hesitated, Wayne shouted, "*NOW*! Get yer ass over here *RIGHT NOW*!"

"God damn you, you sorry sonuvabitch...." Vera hissed.

I'd keep your fuckin' mouth shut if I was you," Wayne snarled.

"Why don't you take me instead," Sam said, calmly. "You're such a big brave tough guy... Are you too afraid to take a man? You have to take a girl?" he taunted.

"Fuck off, hero boy." Wayne swung his pistol toward Sam and fired. The shot went wide.

"Now, come ON, little girl," he motioned toward Amy. She slipped from Sam's embrace and walked over to him.

"That's a good girl," Wayne said, "Now, you two go get in that pickup over there. And don't try anything, if you know what's good for your lover boy friend here," he warned, pointing the pistol back toward George.

"These ladies are gonna take a little ride with me." He nodded toward Lonnie and Lloyd and said, "You two keep 'em covered. You know what to do."

"Gawd dammit, you sonofabitch!" George yelled after them, as Wayne climbed into the driver's seat of the pickup truck. Ebbets into the cab of Lonnie's pickup. "You touch one hair on her head and I'll...." "Shaddup!" Lonnie ordered, and levered a shell into the carbine rifle he was carrying.

As Wayne drove the pickup away Lonnie called to the group, "You, you, and YOU!" he demanded, pointing to each of them in turn, "Start walking that way!" He pointed to the south. "Git! Start movin'!"

They walked slowly, turning to look back at Lonnie's pickup truck as it headed north, leaving a billowing cloud of dust in its wake. A moment later shots rang out and Vera felt Sam's arm around her as he pulled her to the ground. They all ducked behind a boulder. One by one they snuck a look to see Lonnie levering shells into his rifle. He was shooting at the tires on Vera's truck. When he noticed the group had stopped he yelled for them to keep moving.

"Get the hell outta here, or the next one's gonna hit more than just a tire!"

The three made their way slowly southward, though every instinct told them to turn back.

"We gotta go back and get Ebbets," George said. He was distraught. Vera reached out and put an arm around him.

"We'll get her," she said, "We'll get her, George. For now, we've got no other choice. Let's just get ourselves around the bend and out of sight, and then we can figure out what to do."

It was the first time Vera had seen George speechless, without something to say. He was trying hard not to break down.

"C'mon, pal," Sam urged, "We've got work to do."

This seemed to lift George's spirits and he looked up at Sam.

"Let's get ourselves out of sight and then we'll figure something out, bud," Sam said.

The wide canyon curved gradually to the southeast. When they could no longer see Vera's truck Vera called a halt. She directed them to a large acacia tree.

"Let's sit down here in the shade and think things out," she said. "First, one of us needs to go over to that big rock back there and keep a lookout. George, why don't you go and keep an eye on Lonnie. Stay down, and don't let him see you. He's probably got binoculars, so just stay down and out of sight, okay?"

"Yeah, okay." George snuck back to the rock outcropping they had passed. He hunkered down and sat on his heels and watched Lonnie and Lloyd.

"Look, I don't know that there's a lot we can do right now,"

Sam said, "We'll probably have to wait for dark. I don't think there's much of a moon tonight, so we might be able to sneak up on them if they're still there."

"I was thinkin' the same thing," Vera replied, "Our best bet is to just sit here and save our energy. I don't know if your pal there can keep it together, but he'll just have to."

"Don't worry about George. He comes through in a pinch."

They sat together for several minutes, neither one talking, each occupied with their own thoughts. Vera couldn't imagine what George was going through, and she wanted to just go over to him and give him a hug, but she knew it was a foolish thing to do. Instead, she watched Sam as he took a small twig and drew lines and squiggles in the sand. Vera wondered what was going through his mind.

"There's something comin'," George whisper-shouted to them. "Maybe it's Wayne, comin' back!"

Sam and Vera crouched and crept over to George's vantage point. They saw a dust plume coming back toward the treasure site. They couldn't see what was causing it, but it gave them hope.

From their vantage point they couldn't see that it was Ernie Sands driving his black and white cruiser down the old rutted road. It was a miracle that he managed to make it all that way, but it was a testament to his determination that he did. They couldn't see the police car, but they did see what transpired once Ernie arrived on the scene.

Ernie

Ernie Sands had been tasked by Olive, in secret, to keep an eye on Lonnie and Lloyd and to report to her about their comings and goings. He knew they had killed Jorge's dog and that they had stolen the backhoe from the highway department, but Olive implored him not to arrest them or report them just yet. She told him that there were bigger fish to fry, and to just let it go for now.

Driving out to the treasure site, Ernie passed Wayne and saw Amy and Ebbets in the truck with him. He didn't know who Wayne was or why he was driving Lonnie's pickup truck. Ebbets waved to Ernie and he waved back. At first he thought it a bit odd, the way she looked at him and waved so frantically, but Ernie had his sights set on Lonnie and Lloyd and didn't think much more about it. He kept driving down the dirt road.

When he arrived at the site he shut off the squad car and stepped out. He looked around and saw Vera's pickup truck parked on the edge of the draw, but didn't see her or any of her friends.

Now, that's odd... he thought, *I wonder where everybody is...*

Looking across to the other side, he saw the opening of a small box canyon, and coming out of it was Lonnie Tate, holding a rifle. Right behind him, with a pistol in his hand was Lloyd Hodges.

Lloyd was a skittish type, a high strung troublemaker who was always his own worst enemy, and he left a lot of evidence of it in his wake. Jorge's dog was one example.

Ernie saw the two and hollered, "What's goin' on out here?" Lloyd responded by firing his single action Colt at him. The shot went wide and missed Ernie by a couple of feet, but managed to connect with the driver's side spotlight, which exploded into a million pieces.

"Now wait just a darned minute..." Ernie began, but Lloyd fired again, this time putting a hole in the driver's door of Ernie's beloved Buick.

Depending upon your viewpoint, Ernie was either brave or stupid. Either way, he decided to walk toward the two men with their guns pointed at him. They looked at each other as if to say, "What kind of fool is he?"

Ernie was known for wearing black Dehner boots, the kind worn by motorcycle cops. He was constantly kidded about them but he paid it no mind. He loved his Dehners, even if they weren't very well suited to walking in the desert terrain.

In this instance, the heel of his boot caught upon a small mesquite root that was sticking out of the ground. This sent Ernie pitching forward, face first toward a cholla cactus, its bright purple flowers in full bloom. He thrust his arms out in a desperate attempt to evade his painful fate. As he lunged forward, his standard issue Smith and Wesson 5-shot .38 caliber pistol slid from its holster and slammed against a large stone, causing it to discharge.

From their vantage point behind the rocks, neither Vera, Sam, nor George couldn't tell what was going on, but they heard the shots. Ernie and his car were hidden from them, so they didn't know who was firing the guns.

As Ernie landed in the cactus, the bullet from his pistol sailed past the two outlaws, close enough for them to hear it as it whizzed by. A split second later, they heard it ricochet off the side of the sandstone cliff behind them, altering its trajectory and sending it toward a large GI can of gasoline that was sitting on the ground next to the backhoe's truck and trailer. The sudden impact of the hot lead with the metal can caused just enough of a spark to ignite the gasoline fumes inside, resulting in a loud explosion. There was a second can of gasoline next to it, which was detonated sympathetically.

It sounded like a single explosion. From a distance it was more like a muffled "boom" than an ear crashing detonation. Sam, George, and Vera instinctively crouched down, which was lucky for them, because the fireworks weren't over just yet.

Sitting in the bed of the big truck were four cases of explosives that Lonnie and Lloyd had stolen from the old Army airfield. Each case contained eighty-eight sticks of Class A dynamite, along with the necessary blasting caps. The explosives were meant for blasting the tree stumps out on the airfield in order to clear the land for more runways. In this case, they ended up serving another purpose.

All four cases of explosives ignited at once, with a deafening boom that sent out a massive shudder that could be felt for miles around. Vera and the boys were knocked to the ground and didn't see what happened next.

The blast broke apart the sandstone walls of the surrounding mesa and caused an avalanche that brought down both sides of the box canyon. There was flying debris everywhere, and fragments of red sandstone landed all around Vera and the boys. The resulting thunder seemed to last forever, though it subsided within a few seconds.

As the three got to their feet they were coughing and spitting out sand and dust. They struggled to see.

"Ebbets!" George cried. He began to run back to the site.

"George, wait!" Sam called.

Vera put a hand on his shoulder. "It's okay, Sam. Let him go."

They didn't know if Amy and Ebbets were caught in the explosion, and Vera was afraid to find out. They followed George to the scene, dreading what they would find. When they arrived it took a few minutes to piece together what had happened.

They found Ernie, none the worse for wear except for some cactus spines stuck in his hands and face. The explosion had deafened him, and it would take a few days to recover his hearing. The group searched the area but found no trace of Lonnie or Lloyd. Vera looked over at George, who was visibly relieved to know that Ebbets wasn't there, and she was glad that Amy wasn't there.

It was Ernie who they had seen driving, not Wayne.

Ernie's Buick had taken a direct hit from a huge piece of sandstone. Blown off the top of the mesa, it landed squarely upon the car's roof and crushed it down to the height of the seats. Ernie just stared at it, broken hearted.

The four of them climbed through the rubble but they knew that there was no way Lonnie or Lloyd could have survived the blast. The small box canyon was gone, filled with rubble from the surrounding cliffs. There was no sign of the truck or backhoe, no trace that they had ever been there.

"We need to figure out a way out of here," Vera said, once again taking charge. She was examining her pickup truck. "Looks like Lonnie shot out a couple of my tires, but otherwise the pickup looks okay. The spare's up under the bed, and it's okay."

George turned to Ernie, "Looks like we're gonna need one more tire. What size are the wheels are on your car, Ernie?" Ernie just shook his head and pointed to his ears. He couldn't hear a thing.

George went to examine one of the squad car's tires.

"It's a fifteen inch. Vera's Chevy is fifteen inch, but it's a six bolt wheel. The rim's not gonna work. We're gonna need to change a tire." With that, he went to work on Vera's pickup truck.

With Sam's help George pulled the spare from the trunk of Ernie's car and used a twig to let the air out of it. Once deflated, the pair used tire irons, a crowbar, and a flat piece of metal they found to break the tire away from the rim. They had to repeat the process for one of the flats on Vera's truck, but within a few minutes they managed to slip the tire from Ernie's car onto the wheel of Vera's truck.

"Now, we just gotta figure out how to pump this sucker up," George said.

Ernie walked over to the trunk of his car and rifled around. He pulled a box out and brought it over, motioning for George to open it.

"Well I'll be damned... Sam, c'mere and look at this. Ernie's brought us a foot pump!"

"*ALWAYS NEED TO BE PREPARED!*" Ernie yelled, not realizing how loud he was. "*GOT A CANTEEN OF WATER BACK HERE, TOO!*" he screamed.

"Dang, Ernie," George said, slapping him on the back, "You're my new hero."

They took turns stomping on the foot pump, slowly filling the tire with air. George did most of the work and Sam let him. He knew that his friend needed a diversion from thinking about Ebbets. And though he kept it to himself, Sam was worried sick about Amy.

Attack of the Clones

Wayne kept the pistol in his lap as he drove back along the dirt road toward the highway. He would drive back through Alpine and east, to the pre-arranged spot where he would meet his contacts. After he made the deal he would head to Mexico with Ebbets. He could dispose of the teenage girl somewhere along the way. Hell, she might even bring him a fair price across the border.

Ebbets felt a sudden surge of adrenaline when she saw Ernie's police car approaching them on the old ranch road. She quietly reached over and grasped Amy's hand. They looked at each other, uncertain about what to do.

"You just keep still and don't do anything hasty and you'll stay alive. And so will the cop in that car. You hear me?" Wayne had a way of issuing his threats in a smooth manner, mild and friendly sounding. But Ebbets knew the threat was not an empty one.

"I said, *DO YOU HEAR ME*?" Wayne demanded. The two nodded.

As the cars approached each other Wayne held up two fingers in greeting, keeping his hand on the wheel, the way folks do when they pass each other on a country road. Ebbets waved her hand in quick, jerky motions back and forth, with an exaggerated smile, showing her teeth clenched together and her eyes opened very wide. She tried to look afraid, but without letting Wayne see.

Ernie passed them and waved. He slowed down, almost to a stop and ready to talk, but Wayne just drove past and continued down the road. Ernie thought it was odd, but pulled the old Buick down into low range and edged the car forward. His priority was keeping an eye on Lonnie and Lloyd, so he continued on his way.

"That's a good girl," Wayne said, reaching behind Amy to put his hand on Ebbets' shoulder. She shuddered and pulled away. "Aw, now that's no way to treat your man, is it? Especially when you haven't seen him in so long…"

"You won't get away with this, Wayne."

"Oh, I think you'll see that I will, darlin'. I think you'll see that we'll be long gone before anyone knows what happened."

"You filthy piece of shit!" Amy screamed, suddenly coming to the end of her rope. "You're nothing but a god damn piece of sh...." Wayne cuffed her hard across the cheek.

"I suggest you shut your mouth, little girl, or you're gonna find yourself in some deep shit."

"You really think you can keep us captive, Wayne?" Ebbets interrupted, "Do you really believe you can get away with kidnapping us?"

As though he hadn't heard her, Wayne began to talk, "I'm thinkin' Mexico. How'd you like to live in Guadalajara? Or maybe Mazatlán, or Puerto Vallarta?" The two women looked at him, just long enough to catch a glimpse. He seemed to be talking to himself, as though they weren't there.

"Yeah, I'm thinkin' Puerto Vallarta would be a good place. Never been there, but they say you can live like a king on the kind of money I'm making from this deal. And there's more where that came from." He paused to lick his lips, then continued, "Lotsa money comin' my way, and nobody gonna stop me," he mused. "I'll be livin' like a king down there in Mexico."

"I don't know what you're talking about. You sound like you're cra….."

Wayne slammed on the brakes and the pickup truck skidded to a stop. Ahead of them, blocking the road, stood a herd of cattle. They seemed to have come out of nowhere. On second glance, these were no normal cattle. They were giants, and there were more than two dozen of them walking slowly toward the truck. Ebbets and Amy looked at each other. They were surprised, but they both recognized their kind. Amy's eyes widened. Wayne was dumbstruck.

"What the hell is *THAT*!" He rolled his window down and yelled at them, "Get outta the way! Go on, *GIT*!" The cows stayed in the road and slowly advanced toward him. He opened the door and stepped out, then raised his pistol. Seeing this, Amy reached across Ebbets and put her hand on her door handle and waited.

"I'm telling you to *MOVE*!" Wayne fired a shot at one of the leaders.

The .38 special was powerful, and Wayne couldn't believe that the bullet didn't penetrate the creature's skull, but it was three inches thick. The cow simply shook her head and looked more annoyed than scared. The herd began to bellow and bawl, and the girls could feel the vibration from their low voices. The baritone sounds of their calls sounded more like dinosaurs than cattle.

"Gawd dammit, get the hell outta the way!" The girls both knew that Wayne was beginning to lose it.

Amy saw that he was distracted and reached across Ebbets to open the truck's door. She pushed Ebbets from the truck.

"Run, Ebbets! Run!"

Ebbets got to her feet and started running as the herd of cows closed in. Amy slid across the seat as Wayne fired another shot at the clones. He didn't seem to notice that Ebbets was gone, so Amy jumped out and ran after her.

Wayne came to his senses and turned to see Ebbets running toward the cattle, with Amy following. He turned his pistol on them and fired his two remaining rounds. Amy lurched forward and fell to the ground.

Wayne turned back to fire at the cows again but the pistol was empty. The giant cattle were almost upon him. Desperate, he threw the empty firearm at them and jumped back into the truck. He looked around and caught a glimpse of Ebbets outside the of the herd, kneeling beside Amy. He was beginning to panic now, and a small part of him wondered why Ebbets didn't seem to be afraid of the cows.

The sounds of the cattle were suddenly mixed with a new sound, a low rumbling that moved across the desert like an earthquake. The shock from the dynamite blast shook the truck violently and set the cattle off. They stampeded and raced the rest of the way to the pickup. When they reached the truck they seemed to devour it. The cows closest to Ebbets and Amy made their way gently around them, taking care not to hurt them, before becoming aggressive and charging the truck.

Ebbets watched as the truck seemed to evaporate beneath the hooves of the clones. She had no idea that the cows were hearing the voice in their heads. They were following its instructions as they destroyed the pickup truck with Wayne inside it. When they had finished, all the sister cows stood calmly, as if nothing had happened. Ebbets rolled Amy over and cradled her head in her lap, crying reassurances to her.

The giant bovines discovered the twenty-six kilos of marijuana that were under the tarp in the back of the truck. The bales had been split apart and scattered and the cows munched on the weed slowly and calmly, as they listened to the voices grow louder and clearer. They discovered several cartons of Stuyvesant cigarettes and ate them as well. Oddly, they seemed to prefer the Stuyvesants to the marijuana, though they devoured both.

Like their sister Dinah, they could now clearly see the lights and hear the voices, and those voices told them to head south where they would find a great river. Once across that river, they would find a home and safety for the rest of their lives. Slowly, as a single unit, the herd began to move away to the south.

Ebbets couldn't tell if Amy was breathing. Desperately, though tears, she cried softly, "Oh, Amy... oh, Amy... oh, Amy... Please be all right... please..."

Amy was limp and wasn't moving.

Vera's Cafe

They sat in the shade of the portale in the patio behind the cafe. Amy insisted on helping Vera with the drinks, though she struggled with her arm in the sling. It had been three weeks since the run-in with Wayne Guidry. Her friends told her that it was a miracle she was alive. One bullet had narrowly missed her heart and the other passed through her upper arm. While she was in the hospital Vera jokingly told her that she would have an impressive scar on that arm, one she could really brag about later on. Both bullets had gone clean through and left a pair of gaping holes for the doctors to stitch up.

When the group had come upon the scene, Sam performed CPR and chest compressions to revive her. Ernie and George had searched the wreckage of the pickup truck and confirmed Wayne's brutal demise. The clones had left and were nowhere to be found.

They arrived with Amy at the hospital in Alpine where she was quickly swarmed by the medical team, who worked feverishly. Within minutes there were various wires and tubes attached to her. The emergency ward team managed to save her life.

She spent a week in the hospital in Alpine. When she regained consciousness she was grateful that her friends came to see her every day. After a few days, though, she became a bit embarrassed by all the attention. Vera even closed the cafe for a week, just so she could stay in Alpine to be near her.

George and Ebbets came every day and lifted her spirits. George sang songs and told jokes that made it hurt when she laughed.

"It'll stop hurting once the pain goes away," he told her, and she laughed again.

Ebbets sat and held her hand in her calm and reassuring way. She showered the girl with her own special kind of gentle affection, which Amy just couldn't seem to get enough of. Olive came with George and Ebbets several times, and on each visit she brought several huge bouquets of flowers, which soon filled Amy's hospital room.

Sam came every day, too, and Amy loved that he came alone. He seemed to want to reassure her that he was there for her. She knew that he was trying to be a big brother to her, that it wasn't romantic, and that was okay with her.

Vera and Amy set the trays down on the patio table and settled in for the first "back porch get together", as George called them, that they had had since the disaster at the treasure site.

George sat close to Ebbets and kept his arm around her, as he had done for the last couple of weeks. It was obvious that he was afraid of losing her, afraid she would somehow be taken away from him. Amy thought it was cute and wished she had a man who would hang onto her like that. She looked over at Sam and wondered why he and Vera chose to keep their distance. Sam looked back at her and winked, and she blushed.

"Much as I'm glad to be here with y'all," George was saying, "I dang sure had my heart set on finding that treasure." They all nodded and mumbled their agreement. "And now it looks like I'm gonna have to work for a living after all."

Vera started singing, "In this dirty old part of the city...",

George answered with, "See my daddy in bed he's dyin'..." and together they finished the verse. Then everyone sang the chorus in unison,

"We've gotta get out of this place!"

They all laughed and George said, "Not too bad, y'all! We'll make singers outta you yet, won't we Vera?" He turned to Ebbets and kissed her.

Amy watched for Sam's and Vera's reaction but other than laughing with the rest, neither made a gesture toward the other. She don't know why, but Amy found it frustrating. Still, she was laughing and enjoying the company of her friends. It felt as though a great pressure was released and they could all be themselves again.

"I was kinda bein' serious there," George said, "I mean, I don't know about you, but I had my heart set on finding that gold."

"Yeah, it sure woulda been nice," Sam said. "I'm not sure what I'd have done with a million dollars, but I would've found some way to spend it, I guess."

"Easy come, easy go," Vera added, "They say it's nothing lost, nothing gained."

"Yep," George said, "when there's gators in the swamp, it's time to circle the wagons."

Vera stared at him and creased her brow. "Well, in this case I reckon we still have our Amy, and that's what I'm grateful for." she said with a smile.

"Here, here!" Sam said, and raised his glass for a toast, "To our Amy!"

The others cheered in agreement as Amy smiled, embarrassed. Her eyes began to moisten and she quickly wiped them with her sleeve. Sam held her gaze for a moment and smiled, and she smiled back.

Ebbets had been quiet up until now, "I'm just glad it's over," she said, "and I'm so thankful that my Amy is here." She turned to look at the girl as she spoke, "Oh, Amy.... I really thought you were....." she began to shake, and started to sob.

"It's over, sweetheart," George said softly, hugging her to him, "It's over."

Amy was profoundly touched. She had never had people who worried about her before. People who were actually concerned for her. It felt amazing, and she loved them for it. Still, all this attention made her uncomfortable.

Sam chimed in, "I just wish Amy would've gotten some pictures of it all. Well... except for the getting' shot part. It's just too bad we don't have a record of it."

"Well, at least my camera made it through okay," she replied, "Don't know what I'd do without that camera."

Vera smiled, "Y'know, that might be your first camera, young lady, but I'm guessin' it won't be your last... not by a long shot." Everyone agreed and added their own comments, and Amy felt herself turning red again.

"Well, SUM-body besides me came out smelling like a rose," Amy said. The rest gave her puzzled looks.

"I mean, Ernie got himself a brand new cop car. That's something, isn't it?" Amy was suddenly embarrassed again and looked around for approval. Everyone was looking at her, smiling.

"Yep, I'd say that's a lot," Vera added, "Ernie's a hero, and he's got himself a new cruiser. You're right, Amy. He did come out smelling like a rose."

"Yep, ol' Ernie fell into a pile of horse manure and came up with a piano," George said.

And at the same time, they all knew that Ernie had caused the explosion that put and end to their treasure hunting fantasies, but they didn't seem to mind.

The Buick

In the days following what came to be called "Ernie's Big Bust" the group managed to piece together the details of what had happened. Ernie became an instant hero around town, a man who had singlehandedly saved their lives and brought justice to bear upon drug smugglers, kidnappers, dog murderers, and undesirables. Of course, no one mentioned his accident with dropping his pistol. They were just grateful to be alive, and no one saw any need to spoil his celebrity. They were happy for Ernie and glad to be back safe and sound. George even gave Ernie credit for using his own car tire to get Vera's truck back up and running, thus saving them from certain death out in the desert.

Ernie of course enjoyed his newfound hero status immensely, though he was saddened by the loss of his beloved Buick. He hired a wrecker to drive out and bring the old car back to the station in Marfa. There wasn't much he could do for the it.

Much to Ernie's surprise the county offered to buy him a new patrol car, a top of the line 1963 Buick Electra. It was a four door sedan, like the one Joe Friday used in *Dragnet*, but newer. It was five years old, but to Ernie it seemed like a brand new car. And he wouldn't have to hold the seat forward to put prisoners in the back anymore. What Ernie didn't know was that Olive had paid for the car anonymously and convinced the county commissioners to keep it a secret.

He sold the old Buick Special to an auto salvage yard over in Van Horn. The owner of the yard was enamored with the black and white squad car, especially with the roof caved in as it was. Using a large crane and lots of welding equipment, he mounted the Buick to the top of a flag pole as a promotional sign for his company.

The Buick was suspended sixty feet in the air and could be seen for miles along the newly completed Interstate 10. Its red and blue emergency lights flashed constantly, along with the headlights and tail lights and the two spots. The siren cranked itself up every five minutes and blared until it wound down again.

The "Police Car" became a well known landmark along the highway. Kids would hound their parents as they drove, "When are we gonna get to the Police Car?", and truckers used it as a point of reference when chirping back and forth to each other on their CB radios. So many people stopped to see it that the salvage yard owner opened a cafe and gift shop next door, with a sign that read:

HIGHWAY PETROL
GAS – FOOD – SOUVENIRS
STOP AND EAT – OR WE'LL BOTH GO HUNGRY

Ernie was invited to the grand opening, where he autographed postcards and regaled the crowd with stories of his adventures as a deputy sheriff.

Part 5

May 1990 - Berkeley

The cancer was taking its toll but Vera felt better than usual that day. She walked with Amy in her garden and the pair talked about old times. They sat together on a carved bench and Vera recalled the first day they met Sam and George.

"I'll tell you, that day those two came into the cafe, well... I never felt so discombobulated in my life." She paused to study Amy's expression, as if only in that moment she had discovered something she had missed all along.

"I found myself telling them, 'Tell you what... there's a room upstairs and you're welcome to crash there for the night, no charge.'

Amy laughed, and Vera smiled at her, "And then I thought, *Now, where had THAT come from?* She chuckled and said, "And dammit, Amy, I was already mentally kicking myself for letting that wedge get stuck in the door and letting Sam in."

Amy smiled at the thought of it as Vera went on.

"And then he said something to me and our eyes held for just a moment—not very long, mind you. But the silence got awkward." Vera stopped and turned to look out across her garden, lost in thought.

"It was the weirdest sensation, Amy", she admitted, "And the truth is, I didn't care about them being deadbeats or not. Fact was, I was scared of Sam. Just plain scared, that's all."

Amy put her arm around Vera as they sat. She smiled as she listened to her old friend reveal her feelings.

"I was afraid of someone coming into my nice, safe, solitary life and complicating things, Vera went on, "Y'know? But I was also afraid Sam would leave. And so I made up a lame excuse for them to stay."

She stopped talking. Amy was content to sit by her side and listen. When Vera finally spoke she said, "Hell, I couldn't even look Sam in the eye after that. Gawd help me, when it comes to Sam Hardwick I think I've been lost my whole life."

May 1990 - Amy and Vera

They often sat together on the overstuffed couch in Vera's living room, Vera with her now customary Navajo rug wrapped around her and Amy nursing a cup of herbal tea. More and more, Vera showed the signs of her cancer and looked thin and frail. The treatments had taken her hair and she shunned wigs in favor of a bandana that was given to her by one of her cowboy friends.

The cowboy called it a "wild rag", and Amy supposed that it was wild at that. It was bright red, with a montage of yellow and white daisies printed in haphazard fashion all over. Vera joked about it, saying that he had only given it to her was because he couldn't use it.

"He told me it spooks the horses," she said.

"You remember when Jorge's dog got shot?" she asked.

Amy nodded as the memory of it came flooding back. She saw her fifteen year old self riding out to Jorge's place and finding that his little cow dog, Chico, had been shot, and she remembered the knot she had in her gut.

"Yeah. That was a terrible time," she said.

Vera smiled and said, "Well, there's something I learned back then, something about Olive."

She looked over at Amy, "Remember when we used to wonder what the deal was with her?"

Vera paused, and Amy could hear her breath coming in short, quiet wheezes.

"Well, I do remember George saying that he figured she was a spy or something," Amy replied.

Vera shifted, trying to get comfortable. "Do you mind if I just lie down here and put my feet in your lap? I can't ever seem to get comfortable."

"Here, let me help you." Amy reached over and pulled a pillow from the chair beside them and put it behind Vera's head as she reclined. When Vera was finally settled she resumed.

"Well, it turns out that George was right. Olive *was* a spy!" She looked up at Amy, smiled and winked. "I had a talk with her about those two hombres who shot Jorge's dog. I knew she was up to something but wasn't sure what it was. Something about making sure they got their due."

"She called the sheriff, I know that," Amy said.

"Yeah, she called Ernie, and I'm pretty sure she called a few other people, too. Some real heavyweights, I imagine."

"Did she tell you that?"

"Sort of. She and I cleared up a few things when we talked, and I can tell you it was a revelation to me." Vera paused again, her breathing labored. The two sat in silence for a minute.

"Olive told me that she was in the OSS during the war. She was a spy working in England and Switzerland, and she went all over Europe back then. Italy, Germany, France, all of it. Olive was in the thick of things."

"The OSS... is that like the FBI or something?"

"Yeah, it was before the CIA, back during the war. After the war it became the CIA."

"Wow, that's amazing!" Amy said.

"Yeah and there's more," Vera had a bit of a twinkle in her eye.

"I sort of suspected that she did that kind of work somehow, but she filled me in on some stuff that had to do with me."

"With you?"

"Yeah, it's about Johnny. You probably don't remember him."

"No, not really. I know that he had the cafe before you."

"Yep, that's right. And Johnny ended up giving it to me. Y'know, I thought I was buying it from him, but it turned out he tricked me and I was just making payments to myself the whole time. Damn his hide." She shook her head and laughed.

Amy smiled. It was good to see Vera enjoying herself.

"Johnny used to go away for days at a time. Sometimes a week or two. He never said where. I just ran the cafe and didn't ask any questions."

She paused to look out the window at the sunset. The sun had set and the Bay Bridge was beginning to glow from the headlights of the cars carrying their drivers home from work.

"I thought he was a gangster, part of the Mafia or something. I had no idea what went on with him. It was none of my business so I didn't ask any questions."

"So, was he a gangster?"

Vera chuckled, "Johnny? Naw, of course not. But get this... he was a spy, just like Olive!"

"What? A spy? Wow!" *You think you know people*, Amy thought, *you think you know what's going on around you, and then all of a sudden you find that you didn't have a clue.*

"He and Olive worked together during the war. That's how they met. Johnny retired and went to Marfa, probably just to hide from his past. And I guess he convinced Olive to do the same. Funny, huh? Just goes to show, you never know..."

"Two spies living in Marfa? Who'd have thought that? Do you think they were lovers?"

"I think they probably were, once upon a time. But who knows? In any event, we had a couple of spies living right there in Marfa with us and we didn't suspect a thing. Pretty wild, huh?"

"It's mind boggling."

"Yeah, and so when Jorge's dog got shot, Olive sprang into action. Turns out she still had contacts in high places, so she decided she'd get even with those two sons of bitches."

Vera went on to describe how Olive had phoned Ernie Sands, the deputy sheriff, and explained to him what to do. She told him to investigate the dog's shooting but to keep quiet about it, and she would provide some help for him.

"I don't know if you remember, but Ernie suddenly seemed like a new man back then. He was all charged up and ready to take on the world."

"No, I don't remember much about him back then," Amy replied, "but I've often wondered what brought him way out there to the treasure hunt site that day."

"Well," Vera continued, "Ernie had changed back then. He suddenly became upbeat and positive, and he seemed to have a new purpose in life. We were all thinkin' that maybe Ernie had found himself a girlfriend, but none of us saw any evidence of that and none of us really believed it."

She paused to take a drink of tea, "Still, nothing else explained the change in him. He went from being a poor sod who just plodded along day by day, to a pit bull who questioned everyone in town who might have had even the slightest connection to the crime."

"And y'know," Vera said, "It turned out that Johnny finally did retire. According to Olive, he decided to 'go someplace where the sun always shines'. Olive figured he was probably eating seafood enchiladas and drinking margaritas somewhere on the coast of Mexico, but she didn't know where he was and hadn't heard from him. He managed to drop off the face of the earth, as far as she knew."

"Wow!" Amy said. "I wonder where he is now."

Vera went on to describe how Ernie's relentless investigating method did accomplish a few things, though it failed at others. He was able to link Lonnie and Lloyd to shooting Jorge's dog, Chico. Had he been able to apprehend them, Ernie would no doubt have sent them to jail. But circumstances intervened and they got their just desserts, anyway.

And as Vera said, the most important result of Ernie's activity was that it had saved their lives, especially Amy's. And at the same time it caused the explosion that put and end to their treasure hunting fantasies.

June 1990 - Letters

Vera pulled herself up from her chair and hobbled off to her bedroom. "Wait here," she said to Amy.

She appeared in the hall doorway a short time later, struggling to carry a box filled with papers, and Amy jumped up to take it from her. She set it down on the coffee table, and helped Vera back to her seat.

"There's some papers in there I want you to have," Vera said, motioning to the box, "Have a look through there and tell me what you see."

There were old photos with notes and inscriptions on the back, letters stuffed back into their envelopes, and paraphernalia from rock concerts and other events she had attended over the years. Amy picked up a large envelope.

"Yeah, that's the one," she said.

"Looks like a letter from Sam" Amy observed.

"Yeah," Vera replied, "Open it up."

Amy slid the top letter from the envelope and saw that there were more letters folded in with it.

"Yeah, I think some of those are mine. Go ahead and read them, too."

The letter from Sam was dated November 4th, 1984:

> Dear Vera,
>
> Charlotte and I were married for eight years, and when I look back on it I know that we postponed ending it a lot longer than we should have. That was for Emily's sake. When we got married, Charlotte and I acted like our parents and thought that a couple should stay together for the sake of the children. So, we did, for Emily's sake.
>
> I was writing for the Hemet Valley News, a small hometown rag. My job as their number two reporter had me covering everything from lost pets and car crashes to the annual Christmas parade and the local 4-H rodeo. I wasn't turning out Pulitzer material, but it paid the bills. It was a discouraging time for me, but it was worse for Charlotte.
>
> She wasn't cut out for life in the slow lane. Her friends all lived

back east, and she never took to desert life the way I did. She couldn't accept our existence in a backwater town in the middle of nowhere, with no social outlets, no cultural or artistic inspiration. She was trapped. Charlotte was seriously depressed and I had no idea how to make things better for her.

We moved down south and things got better for a while, but then we fell back into our constant arguments and adversarial routines. We kept away from each other most of the time. We were just roommates. The marriage was over, but our roles as parents kept us there. Emily was seven when we finally split up in 1979. She took Emily and moved home to Delaware, as far away from me as she could.

I spent those first years trying to maintain a shaky contact with my daughter. Of course, I failed miserably. Looking back now, I can see that I was doomed to failure from the start.

It's a tough pill to swallow, knowing your child is getting only a twisted, one-sided version of things. And I'll tell you this: the helplessness you feel as you watch her steadily turn away and distance herself from you and your love of her, well... it cuts to the bone.

I tried to make up for it by throwing myself into my work, by trying to write that Great American Novel I always talked about. I was trying my best to make my daughter proud of me, and now that I'm a somewhat well known author, I see that it was the wrong way to go about it.

And so you can see, I crawled inside myself and kept pushing forward, just as I had done with my own parents. As I had with my brother Charlie. If that isn't denial, I don't know what is.

And through all of this Vera, you have been such a great friend. We write to each other, we call one another, and I try to visit whenever I'm in town. I knew you would never visit me while Charlotte was still with me. In truth, you've been the one person I could trust, a soulmate I could confide in.

Charlotte was always jealous of you, and in some ways she was right to be. She knew there wasn't anything physical between us. But she knew that you and I shared a spiritual bond that she would never have. I knew that my wife peeked into my private world, opened my letters in her clandestine moments of insecurity, stole the thoughts from the pages that you wrote *and wished that she had written them.*

I'm sorry to unload on you like this, but I feel better for doing it. Feel free to burn this letter.

With love always,

~ Sam

When Amy finished reading she turned to see that there were tears in Vera's eyes. But they were good tears, the kind that come from happiness that makes you cry. Amy held up the other pages.

"Looks like there are a couple of letters that you wrote to Sam," Amy said.

"Yeah, he was afraid Charlotte would destroy 'em, so he left them here with me. I reckon I better get 'em back to him sometime." She paused, "Go ahead and read 'em."

The first was dated December 23rd, 1977:

Sam,

You have often asked about my childhood, and I know I've mostly avoided sharing it. Funny thing, I haven't been able to stop thinking about my mother this past week and that got me to thinking about you, my dear friend. I don't know... maybe it's just being alone during the holidays, I'm not sure why. Anyway, I decided to share a little bit of my story with you, for better or worse.

I was born in Benevolence, a little backwater Georgia town. Just a spot in the road, a patch of postwar desperation that had nothing to offer a fierce young girl who was searching for her place in the world. I was an only child, inquisitive and curious and mostly left to my own resources.

Molly Anne Roy—that was my mother's name, and I always called her Molly. She was a survivor. She had a rough time giving birth to me and as a result, she couldn't give me any brothers or sisters afterward. She named me Vera Lynn, after the famous English singer from the war.

My old man was a logger named Ben. When Ben Roy found out that Molly couldn't have any more children he took it out on her every single day that I can remember. He eventually left when I was six, and I never heard from him again. Fact is, I barely remember him. I assume he went off in search of someone who could give him the household full of children that he expected. I've always felt more sorry for those children (if they exist) than I ever did for myself.

The old man never beat my mother but he left her with a lot of scars just the same. I hated him for it without knowing why. I was just a kid. I didn't know how a father was supposed to act. The daily intimidation and bullying were normal to me, but I still hated it. And as I grew up I made sure I never adopted those traits myself.

I think what really bothered me most were my mother's reactions to the constant verbal abuse. Molly was obedient, compliant, and submissive, and though I loved her more than anything, I grew to hate those things about her. I never understood why, over all those years of torment and humiliation, she always stuck up for Ben Roy. She never had a bad word to say about him, even after he abandoned the two of us and left us to fend for ourselves.

The year after he left, Molly took me north to Columbus where she found part time work as a seamstress, and a second job waiting tables in a cafe. Columbus, Georgia was the only city I had ever seen and I thought I'd gone to heaven. For a seven year old girl from Benevolence it was the best thing that could ever happen.

As I said, my mother never had a bad word to say about my father, a coward who had chosen his own needs over those of his wife and daughter. I started out as a gangly, nerdy little girl who read books and spent more time alone in the library than I did with friends. Mother Nature took her time with me, but eventually I blossomed into a pretty young woman who had green eyes and a shock of curly strawberry blonde hair who was able to intimidate the boys around her. I kept reading, but I began to make friends. I even had a boyfriend now and then.

As it turned out, many of my friends and most of my boyfriends were unsavory types. I was drawn to them, and I found myself continually sticking up for them—the same way Molly stuck up for Ben Roy—I saw them as "independent types", and was *always attracted to them because they were non-conformists, and I wanted to be a non-conformist, too. My own disappointment in my parents fueled my resolve to depend upon no one, to live my life on my own terms and no one else's.*

And so in 1957, at fourteen years old I chose a new last name— DeSoto—I saw it on the side of a car—and I packed a small satchel with a few belongings. I wrote a short note saying I love you Molly, don't worry about me, I'll call you, and I hitchhiked north to Atlanta. I'm ashamed to say that I never called her. As it turned out, I never spoke to my mother again.

all my love,

~ v.

Amy slowly folded the letter and slid it back into the envelope alongside Sam's letter. She was stunned. Vera's eyes grew soft and she just looked at her friend and smiled. Amy knew that this was her way of sharing her story, the one she had never told, and she could feel tears welling up.

"Go ahead and read the next one," Vera said.

Amy opened the second letter, which was dated two weeks later:

January 4th, 1978:

Sam,

I hope you had a warm and loving Xmas and New Year. I can't say as how it was all that great for me, but I managed to get through it all relatively unscathed. Hoping we can get together sometime soon. Really want to hear how it is, being a bigshot famous writer now. And yeah, I know I didn't finish up my childhood story last time so here goes...

In 1960, three years after I left home, my mother was struck and killed by a car in Columbus as she was carrying two bags of groceries home and trying to cross 11th Street. The letter from the Randolph County Clerk was forwarded many times, with postmarks stamped all over the envelope. It took two years to reach me.

They buried her in the small cemetery at Red Hill. There were no family or friends there. The only attendees were the minister, his wife, and the pimply faced teenage boy who mowed the grass and tended the garden at the church. The county dispersed Molly's belongings at a sale to cover the cost of the funeral. A few personal things were saved and put in a small wooden box that the county clerk eventually sent to me.

In it were Molly's wedding ring (that figures, I thought to myself, she kept his memory right to the end. I would've pawned the damned thing—and in fact, I eventually did!), and a silver neckless with a locket that opened but had no picture inside. And there was a tattered photograph that I had never seen before. My mother was smiling at the camera and holding a very tiny baby in her arms. Molly's eyes were bright, her smile hopeful, and she seemed to glow with the hope and promise that new parenthood brings, with shiny prospects for the future and a newborn child. I remember staring at that picture of my mother and me for a long time. It's the most valuable thing I own.

with all my love,

~ v.

It was difficult, reading the letter out loud. Amy was sobbing as she added it to the others in the envelope.

"Oh Vera," she wept, "What am I going to do with you?"

July 1990 - Orphans

"Remember that first time we went out looking for the treasure?"

Amy smiled. It was good to see Vera in such a happy mood. That was becoming more and more rare as she grew sicker. The therapy took its toll day by day and her good days seemed to come farther and farther apart. This was one of them and Amy was going to make sure it stayed that way.

"Yeah, I do," Amy said, "I remember how excited George was. I mean, he was always like a little kid anyway, but he could barely control himself when we started driving down that dirt road to the treasure hunt." She chuckled at the thought of it.

"I remember sitting in the back of your pickup with Sam, holding on for dear life. And Vera, you drove that truck like a maniac. I remember thinking that it was a wonder any of us survived."

Vera laughed, "Yeah, I guess I was a pretty wild driver at that."

The light seemed to come back into Vera's eyes when she talked about their times in Marfa.

"George and Ebbets were sitting up in the cab with me and I swear to god, I don't think I've ever seen anybody as petrified as Ebbets was. Heheheh… Poor thing was white as a sheet. And then she turned a little green when we were blasting down that old dirt road."

"Well Vera, you were never a timid one." They both laughed again, and it felt good to share some history with her.

"I remember George, spouting those song lyrics all the time, trying to one-up me. And you know? He did a pretty danged good job of it. He knew his music, that's for sure."

"I might know some of those songs now, but I was just a kid then and most of them were way over my head. I had no idea what you two were talking about most of the time."

"Yeah, singin' those lyrics back and forth, tryin' to stump each other. George would come up with something like, 'When you ain't got nothin' you got nothin' to lose',"

"And then I'd answer him with the next line of the song, 'You're invisible now
you've got no secrets to conceal',"

"And then we'd both finish it off together, 'How does it *FEEL*?'"

"And it just went on like that." Vera looked at Amy and sighed, "What a couple of song nerds we were…" She leaned back into the folds of the overstuffed couch.

"That first night we spent out in the desert… what a great time that was. I remember wishing that it would never end."

"Yeah, me too," Amy said, "I had such a schoolgirl crush on Sam. I thought he hung the moon. Of course, even then I could see you two had your thing going on. But of course I was just too young to figure it out."

Vera rested her hand on her friend's arm and smiled.

"Wasn't anything going on between Sam and me except what I called my 'non-relationship'. Probably the most frustrating thing ever." She looked down and acted like she was examining the Navajo rug that was wrapped around her.

"Sam was so in love with you, Vera,"

"Yeah, well maybe he was, I don't know. He sure had a funny way of showing it."

Amy didn't want to upset her so she changed the subject.

"I think George made up for it though, didn't he?"

"He was a kind soul," Vera said, "George would give you anything, and he'd give it freely. You don't come across too many people like that in this world."

"No, not in my experience," Amy replied, "I've met a lot of great people out there over the years. George was one of the best."

"And Jeanie… their daughter. She's what, in her twenties now?"

"Yeah, hard to believe, isn't it? Ebbets told me she named her after George's mother."

Vera gave Amy a little smile and said, "That's a sweet thing. George would have loved it. And he would have loved that little girl."

"Yeah," Amy said with a lump in her throat, "Such a shame. George was such a dear, sweet man."

Vera coughed suddenly and Amy reached for a glass of water for her.

"Thanks. Like I said," Vera continued, "he'd give you anything. He was one of those who gave a lot more than he got." She was looking out the window again, thinking to herself, probably contemplating something that Amy didn't understand.

"Y'know, they say you're either a giver or a taker. I don't know about that, but George gave his heart and soul and fer gawdsakes, he finally gave his life."

They sat in silence for a few minutes, each lost in her own thoughts. Amy pictured George and Sam, walking into the cafe that first day and dropping their packs in the corner. She could hear George's voice plain as day, shaking her hand like she was a grownup and introducing himself: *Very pleased to make your acquaintance, Amy...* The memory brought on a happy-sad feeling that almost made her cry, and she turned to see Vera, humming a tune very softly, as if she were making sure of the melody.

Vera started to sing the words to an Eric Andersen song:

> *"... take off your thirsty boots and stay for a while,*
> *your feet are hot and weary, from a dusty mile.*
> *And maybe I can make you laugh, and maybe I can try,*
> *lookin' for the morning, and the evening in your eye."*

When she finished, Vera said, "You know something? If it wasn't for George we never would have looked for that treasure." She seemed to be talking to herself, thinking out loud. Amy could see that Vera wasn't really talking to her so she kept quiet and let her continue.

"That treasure was all-consuming, wasn't it? I mean, it started out as a lark, but pretty soon we were obsessed with finding it. And I guess, what the hell, who wouldn't be?"

She turned to look at Amy, as if she had just noticed her friend was there.

"George was really the linchpin in the whole deal, wasn't he? Without him, we wouldn't have bothered. But he made it *fun,* didn't he? You couldn't help but love that guy."

Vera paused to reflect, then laughed out loud.

"And it didn't take long for me, and for everybody else for that matter, to get caught up in his craziness. After that first night... that magical night in the desert... well, I think that's when we became a real group of *friends,* and not just passing acquaintances. Know what I mean? Does that make sense, Amy?"

"Yeah, it does. We sorta found our own little family, didn't we?"

"Yes, that's it, *family!* That's what we were... that's what we still *are,* isn't it?"

Amy felt the lump rise in her throat. "I know *you're* family, that's for sure. And yeah, I think of us all as a family. God knows we were all orphans of one kind or another, weren't we?"

"Well now, I hadn't thought about it exactly like that. But you're right, Amy. Every one of us was an orphan of some sort. We were all just searching for someplace to belong."

August 1990 - George

"I sorta lost track of everyone after I left," Amy said.

Vera had decided to spend the day outside. She hated having to bundle up on the couch in the dark living room, and the day was warm enough for her to sit on the patio and visit. She loved her view of the San Francisco bay, with the Bay Bridge below and the Golden Gate off in the distance. The scent of the salt air was invigorating and the warm sun felt good.

"Yeah, I remember... it was just you and me for a couple of years, wasn't it?"

"I look back now and realize how damned *young* I was," Amy said, "I didn't know *anything*, did I?" she grinned.

"Well, you knew enough to get your ass in trouble a few times, didn't you?" Vera quipped.

"I tried my best to get into as much trouble as I could back then."

"And you did a pretty good job of it, too," Vera said with a chuckle.

Amy looked out at the bay. A pair of seagulls were floating in the air, one trying to grab something from the other.

"I don't know what I would have done if it wasn't for you," she said. She turned to look at Vera, who was fiddling with her sleeve.

"Well, I expect you'd have done just fine."

"I'm not so sure about that, Vera. I mean, if you hadn't saved me I probably would have gone down a very bad road."

"Then you would've just been following in my footsteps, wouldn't you?" Vera smiled again and it warmed Amy's heart to see it.

"I suppose I could've done worse than follow you, couldn't I?"

"Let's just say that before you knew me, I had been down more than my share of dark roads," Vera said, "I finally managed to find the right one, so I reckon you would have found your way, eventually."

"Well, like I was sayin', we both sort of lost track of everyone for a while, didn't we?"

At first it had broken Amy's heart. She was a fifteen year old a girl whose whole universe was the size of a small Texas town. She naturally assumed that everyone else's was the same, and it had taken her some time to figure out that that wasn't the case.

Amy pondered, "I guess I wasn't surprised when George and Ebbets were the first to leave Marfa back then. They were so in love, and they couldn't wait to go to California and get married."

"I remember," Vera said quietly. "Nineteen sixty eight was a big year for all of us, wasn't it? Seems like everyone's life changed back then," she seemed to be talking to herself again, so Amy kept silent and let her go on.

"I remember that beat up old Chevy pickup that George bought, the one with the camper shell on it? Remember?"

Amy nodded and smiled, and allowed Vera to go on.

"That damned truck was held together with a whisper and a prayer. I was a little concerned for 'em—especially for Ebbets."

"Ebbets seemed like the fragile one, but she was the strongest of the two," Amy said.

"You got that right," Vera replied, "Ebbets was a rock. And she still is, isn't she?"

"Yep, she's a keeper," Amy said.

"I remember her telling us about going back to Boerne and finding the house a wreck. I guess that ex-boyfriend of hers... what was his name?"

"Wayne," Amy answered.

"Yeah, Wayne. What a sorry sonuvabitch he was...." she paused, then continued, "Anyway, I guess he messed up the house pretty good. Broke everything she had, stole anything that wasn't tied down. Pretty much trashed the place so bad that Ebbets just put it up for sale and left."

Ebbets had had a lot of conflicting feelings about the old house. A happy childhood with her father, but then the place took on a different aura when he died. The experience with Wayne left a bad taste, and Ebbets knew the house could never bring happiness for her. The only highlight of coming home was discovering that Wayne had not found the urn that held her father's ashes. The urn was the only tangible thing she salvaged from her past life in Boerne.

When George and Ebbets left Marfa they drove to California and moved into a small post-war house in Del Mar, near San Diego. A week later they were married by the courthouse judge up in San Clemente. The couple who were behind them in line served as their witnesses.

Amy laughed and shared with Vera, "Remember when they got married? Remember the letter Ebbets wrote?"

Vera nodded and smiled, "I remember they were so *happy*."

Amy chuckled and said, "That letter... it said, '*WE'RE MARRIED!*' Ebbets had drawn hearts and flowers all over it and she kissed it, like she was sending us a kiss, remember?

"Such a sweetheart, that Ebbets," Vera said.

Amy's eyes were beginning to moisten. "You know, I still have that letter. And her lips, with the bright red lipstick... they're still there." They were both laughing softly now, with tears in their eyes as they remembered their friends.

At George's urging, he and Ebbets had driven north to Los Angeles. The Dodgers finished in a dismal seventh place in 1968 so there would be no post-season playoff games for them. Chavez Ravine was quiet as the couple drove up to Dodger Stadium late one evening and parked in the empty parking lot. George got out and walked around the grounds for a while, then came back to get his wife.

Ebbets carried a small cardboard box with her as they squeezed through the opening in one of the gates that George found. Looking to see that no one was around, they snuck through a corridor beneath the stands and found themselves on the ball field.

"My dad would have loved this," she said. She opened the box and removed the urn.

"He liked Duke Snyder the best," she explained, "but he also liked Gil Hodges and Jim Gilliam and Roy Campanella, so I don't know what I'm going to do." She turned to look at the dark field around her.

"Maybe I'll just put some of him on each of their spots, how about that?"

"Whatever you want to do, darlin', I'm with you." George answered.

Ebbets walked out into center field and stopped. She removed the lid from the urn and poured some of the ashes onto the grass there. "That's for Duke," she said, and walked toward right field, where she would repeat the process for Carl Furillo, then to first base for Hodges, home plate for Campanella, and the pitcher's mound for Johnny Podres and Don Newcombe. When she had finished she walked out behind second base, into the grass of the outfield, and shook the rest of the urn's contents out into the air.

"There, that's for the rest of 'em," she said, satisfied.

"I'm pretty sure your dad would be happy."

"Oh, I know he is." She wrapped her arms around her husband and they stumbled together back to the truck, laughing and giggling and loving each other.

Two months later George got a summons ordering him to appear for his Army pre-induction physical. Four weeks after that he was on a bus, bound for Fort Ord in northern California. Neither he nor Ebbets knew it at the time, but that was the last time Ebbets or any of them would see him again. George didn't know that Ebbets was pregnant with his daughter.

He didn't return from Vietnam. He was killed on May 13th, 1969 at the Battle of Hamburger Hill. The fighting lasted almost a week. The infantry soldiers fought their way up a remote jungle-shrouded mountain named Dong Ap Dia, only a few miles from the Laotian border.

The Army never recovered George's body. They sent Ebbets a folded American flag, some medals, and a folder full of official looking papers instead. The papers explained what a hero Private First Class George Willow was and how proud the government was of his sacrifice.

Vera and Amy were devastated when Ebbets called to give them the news. Amy was just beginning to realize how much bigger the world was than she had imagined. It took a long time for her to accept that George was really gone. Part of the light left Vera's eyes that day and, as Amy thought back on it, she realized that that part of Vera had never really returned.

When Ebbets called with the news, Vera closed the cafe for the day and the two sat in the corner booth, just hugging each other. And Vera sang a line from a Pete Seeger song, a plaintive cry for the loss of a kindred spirit and a dear friend,

> "We're waist deep in the big muddy, and the big fool said to push on."

September 1990 - Vera and Sam

The last time Sam and Vera saw each other was in the autumn of 1990, only a few weeks before she died. He knew it was coming, but Sam wasn't prepared for the shock of seeing her when he got to her place in Berkeley. After a couple of quick taps on the front door and a "hello, anybody there?", he opened it and let himself in. This was expected at Vera's house. She hadn't locked the door in years. In fact, she couldn't remember if she had a key for it.

Sam made his way into the living room and found her bundled up on her couch, a brightly colored turban covering her bald head, an old Navajo blanket wrapped around her, neither of them doing a very good job of hiding her frailness. She was a small whisper of herself, and seeing her like that was a kick in the guts to him. He did his best to appear upbeat, to act normal, but of course he failed.

The room was quiet, the shades pulled, a small fan in the corner was on the low setting, circulating just enough air to make the place bearable. It was so drastically different from the brightly lit party house full of people that he had come to expect when he visited. Vera's was a home to artists and musicians, beatniks and hippies, and all sorts of eccentric street orphans and offbeat vagabonds that seemed to be locked in permanent orbit around her. She spent her life collecting strays. Sam could attest to that because he was one of them. But Sam was the only stray in residence that day, because Vera had let it be known that she didn't want others to interrupt their visit.

"You look like something the cat dragged in," she said as he walked into the room. Her voice had the huskiness of a lifelong smoker, though Vera had never smoked. "Pull up a chair and sit yourself down."

"I think I'd rather sit down next to you. That okay?"

"Whatever floats your boat."

He eased down next to her on the couch and did his best to keep from disturbing her.

"How *ARE* you, Vera? No, wait... that's a stupid question..."

"Yep, you're right, Sam. It *IS* a stupid question. But thanks for asking, anyway."

"Damn, Vera... I'm so sorry... I just..." his voice was shaky.

"It's all right, Sam. Look at me... I've got cancer. I'm dyin'. That's about the long and short of it. I'm on my way out. But hey, it's not such a bad thing, as weird as that sounds."

"Yeah, I know all the lines about how we all gotta go sometime, but christ... not *YOU*," Sam said. He could feel a lump forming in his throat.

"Let me ask you something, Sam. How come you never got married again? How come some hot chick didn't snatch you up and domesticate you, once and for all?"

After all those years, she was still searching for answers to questions that probably couldn't be answered, and she still wore that familiar mask of detachment and indifference, stoic to the end.

"You don't really want the answer to that one, do you Vera?"

"Sure I do. Try me."

"Well... I was gonna say, 'It's complicated', but it's not complicated at all. I did find the right woman, a long time ago. Trouble was, she was unavailable. That's about the size of it."

"Oh, really? And who is this woman? Do I know her?"

"Well now, what do *YOU* think, Vera? Sometimes I think you know her really well, and then other times I think, maybe you never knew her at all."

"What are you talking about?"

"Now's not the time to be clever, *MIZZ* DeSoto. You know what I'm talking about. I'm gonna let you figure that one out for yourself."

"Yeah, well, okay. I'll do that. But you know, that sort of thing cuts both ways, doesn't it?"

"How do you mean?"

"I think you know what I mean, Sam, and I'm gonna let *YOU* figure that one out for yourself, okay?"

"Jeezus, Vera. How did we ever end up like this? What the hell were we thinking?"

"Y'know, old friend, lately I've been giving that some thought. Seems like sometimes life just steers us down paths where we don't wanna go," she said, "Maybe we just make our choices and that's that. We try not to be selfish. We just try to do what we think's best for the other guy. And then one day we wake up and find that the old saying is true. No good deed goes unpunished."

"So, both of us were just trying to do what we thought was best for the other one? Staying away, giving each other space? Trying not to be selfish? Trying to be generous?" Sam paused to consider, then continued,

"Were we just trying to stay out of the other's way, so the other one could find some sort of happiness at the end of their own damned rainbow? Is that what all this was?"

As Vera looked at him Sam saw that her face was drawn tight, gaunt and aged from sickness. But he was looking at the same Vera. The same green eyes that burned holes in him every time he tried to match her in a stare down contest. The same suggestion of a smile that showed itself, that said she held a secret that he would never know. She looked at him with that same wily, contented fire inside her. In that moment Sam saw her plain as day, an apron around her waist, a dish rag in her hand, wiping down the counter in a little cafe back in Marfa, Texas.

And she said, "Maybe it was, Sam. And if that's the case, maybe we're just a couple of damned fools."

Sam spent the day with Vera, just the two of them alone with their memories and their feelings. They laughed over moments of their summer in Marfa. They reminded themselves of how lucky they were to live under the spell of its magic. They relived their wild adventures there. Sam filled her in on how Ebbets was doing, and Vera caught him up on Amy's adventures. Amy was down in Los Angeles at the moment and Sam was glad that Vera had her to lean on. He made a pact with Vera that he would get together with Ebbets and Amy and raise a glass to their friend who ran the best cafe in the world.

"I can't come to your funeral, Vera," he said, looking her in the eyes and holding her gaze for once, "I just can't... that's all," he stuttered, unable to go on. He looked away.

"I know," she said, putting her hand on his, "and that's okay. It's fine..."

"No, it's *not* fine," he said, choking back tears, "but I want you to know that I'm gonna be there in my own way." He looked back at her. "I promise."

Vera gave him the framed photograph that she cherished so much, the one with her mother, Molly Anne Roy, holding her newborn baby. She told him that she wanted him to have it, wanted him to have something to remember her by, as if he didn't already have a lifetime of memories of her, as if she weren't a part of every single fiber of his body.

When the tears finally came Sam couldn't stop them. Vera put her arm around him and told him that it was okay, and he continued to cry. And Sam knew that this photograph was how Vera wanted him to remember her. She was Vera Lynn Roy, named after a great singer who inspired the people of England during the second world war. She was Molly Anne Roy's little girl.

And in his mind Sam could hear her namesake singing "We'll Meet Again".

October 1990 - Amy and Sam

She watched as he climbed the stairs, pushed open the large glass door to the gallery and paused as soon as he stepped inside. He wasn't sure what to expect, Amy could see, and it made her smile. She thought, *He probably had an image in his mind of a quaint little shop with a few photos on the walls, and maybe some tables with crafts and folk art on them, the kind of art gallery where there are little red stickers pasted next to the paintings that have already sold.*

Sam certainly wasn't prepared for this. But maybe he should have been, seeing as how it was located right down the street from the Art Museum. The address on La Brea wasn't exactly in the low rent district.

The place was massive, with an open pitched ceiling that rose two stories above, like a cathedral. A lot of money had been spent on this place in order to create the illusion of "comfortable, but not pretentious" for patrons who, by the looks of them, were the very definition of pretentious. The lighting was subdued, yet at the same time it accentuated the feel of open space as it showcased the photographs on the walls.

And it was clear that the photographs were the star. There were very large ones that immediately pulled Sam to them. As soon as he focused on one, his attention would shift to the smaller ones that accompanied it. It was a clever and impressive presentation, a study in the psychological manipulation of consumers.

Sam was absorbed in the collection named "The Terlingua Period", enthralled by an image of Steve Fromholz slinging his Martin guitar and holding court over the patrons in a rowdy Terlingua roadhouse. Every face in the photograph told its own story, some happy, some sad, some contented, some clearly disturbed. But in that instant, Fromholz held each of them spellbound. Sam stood and looked at that picture for a long time.

"Can you believe it? I have a *Terlingua Period.*"

He turned to see the well dressed, smart-looking woman who had walked up behind him. She was sure of herself, and in his eyes, stunning. There were a few people browsing, and all eyes were turned toward her. They knew who she was. *"That's HER... that's Rosa McBride!"* Sam heard one of them whisper.

"Hello, Amy."

"Oh, Sam…" She hurried to him and threw her arms around him and they just held each other for a long time. She knew he could feel her light sobs as she buried her head into his shoulder but she didn't care. He didn't say anything, just kept his arms around her and finally allowed her to break the embrace when she felt ready.

"I'm sorry… it's just so good to see you," Amy whispered. Her eyes were moist and her mouth quivered as she kissed his cheek.

"It's okay. It's been a long time… and I'm so glad to be here", he said, ignoring the stares from everyone. "I'm so sorry I wasn't at Vera's funeral. I just…"

"She told me you went to see her, and that you couldn't bring yourself to be there," Amy said. "I understand, Sam. We all do," she said, squeezing his hands.

He pushed her back slowly and gently and held her at arm's length.

"Well now, look at you… it looks like life's been treating you well."

"Yeah, I suppose it has."

"Still going by your birth name, I see."

"Well, yeah, sort of. You already knew that Rosa is my first name. McBride was my mother's maiden name."

"Ah, I thought maybe it was your married name. So, a tip of the hat to your mother, then."

"Thanks. I think Myra would approve," Amy said, "And no, never been married, in case you're wondering." She smiled, her eyes still moist.

"I'm sure she would. But of course, you're always gonna be Amy to me, dear one."

"Me too," she said, grinning.

"Pretty danged fancy gallery you got here, ma'am."

"Well, I have Ebbets to thank for that. She knew someone who knew someone, who had some bigshot gallery pals. And in case you haven't noticed, I ain't so young anymore."

"Believe me, I noticed. And I hope you keep a big two by four handy, to keep all those lecherous suitors at bay."

"Don't worry 'bout me," she replied with a grin, "I know how to handle myself."

Sam smiled, "Why am I not surprised?"

Amy led Sam through the gallery show, explaining some of the photographs, but mostly just allowing him to experience them for himself. She enjoyed seeing him contemplate each one. Many were taken in music venues, candid shots of performers and attendees alike. She had managed to make a name for herself in the Texas music scene, turning up at every kind of show, big and small, with her cameras around her neck.

The photos were of familiar places like Gruene Hall, The Saxon Pub, The Broken Spoke, and The Armadillo. There were quite a few clubs that Sam had never heard of, like The Linecamp, Poor David's, and the Ranch Bar.

There was a shot of the smoke-filled dance floor at The Motherlode, a honkytonk and dance hall up in Red River, New Mexico. Ray Wylie Hubbard's band could be seen onstage in the background, but the focus was upon the dancers. The place was packed with couples who presented various poses as they two-stepped around the floor. Some were laughing and smiling at each other, sharing a story or a joke as they danced. Some seemed indifferent to one another, each gazing over their partner's shoulder to something in the distance. One grizzled cowboy was lost in deep contemplation, obviously trying to decide where to put his feet. Amy had managed to capture the bar, off to the left, with the bartender, the waitress, and several customers. Each one seemed to be withdrawn into their own world. The scene was a vignette, a complete story.

Sam turned to her, "I feel as if I know each of the characters in it, Amy. You have such a gift."

"Hey, how 'bout we go someplace and have lunch?" she offered, waking them from their reverie.

"Sure, that sounds good. I'm guessing you know all the trendy and cool places, no?"

"Yep, I know just the place," she told him.

They walked to her car, a 1970s vintage MGB convertible. Sam managed to squeeze into the passenger seat.

"Not sure I could get into this thing if the top was up," he said.

Amy was an aggressive driver and shot through the LA streets like a native Angelino. She navigated the streets of West Hollywood, then headed south on La Brea at speeds that she could see made Sam nervous. He figured they were headed to one of the fashionable eateries on Melrose or Santa Monica, but Amy continued south, made a turn onto Olympic, then headed down Western Avenue for several miles.

They passed beneath the Santa Monica Freeway and traveled over various side streets, and by then Amy could see that Sam was completely lost. They were in south-central LA, far from the elite, stylish district he had expected. Finally, she turned at a street in a residential neighborhood and pulled up in front of a small house halfway up the block.

The houses along the street were the small frame stucco types built by the hundreds after the second world war to house the throngs of returning servicemen who chose to stay in California. This one had been converted into a cafe. "Linda's" the sign said. Sam looked at the place, then turned and looked at Amy with a question on his face.

"Well, here we are. C'mon, don't just sit there, let's go get somethin' to eat!"

Entering the cafe was a déjà vu sledgehammer that smacked Sam squarely on the head. He stopped in the doorway, reached to grab the edge of a counter, and paused to look around.

"Yeah, me too," Amy said.

"This is amazing," he mumbled.

"I knew you'd get it," she said, "I'm not religious, but the first time I came here almost made me a believer. I came in by mistake, just sort of stumbled onto the place one day when I was shooting in the area." She looked at Sam and smiled. "At the time, I thought to myself, *this must be the hand of god...*"

"Well, I see what you mean."

A young lady escorted them to a booth in the corner. They sat down and Sam continued to look around. It was Vera's cafe, or something so close that had you been brought there blindfolded, you would have thought you were back in Marfa. He mentioned it to Amy.

"Yep, exactly the same for me," she said, "But here's the kicker. It wasn't the hand of god at all. It was the hand of Vera."

She saw the puzzlement on his face and continued, "Vera built this place. C'mon, even *you're* smart enough to see that, Sam. It's got her stamp all over it."

"What? But how…"

"I found out later that she opened this cafe a little while after she left Texas. She only ran it for a year or so. I think she was just homesick and wanted to have her family around her again."

"Her family? I didn't think Vera had any family."

"Are you kidding, Sam? Think about it. Of *COURSE* she had family."

"Really? But I thought her mother…"

"It's *US*," she interrupted, "*WE'RE* her family!"

"Us… hmmm…"

"Marfa. Marfa was her family, Sam. Hell, Marfa was family for *ALL* of us." Amy reached over and took his hand. "All of us—you, me, George, Ebbets, Olive, Vera… hell, even Ernie. Every one of us lost our own family somehow. We ended up as orphans, or we may as well have been orphans. Marfa was our family, and we had each other."

Sam looked at her, "I never thought about it like that."

"Took me a while to figure it out," she told him, "Taking pictures of people's faces, studyin' thousands of 'em, and tryin' to figure out what makes 'em tick…. well, I think it finally dawned on me that there's more than one kind of family."

"How do you mean?"

"Well, you know. You got your regular wife and kids type family, with the dog and the yard and all that. Then you got the broken family, and the experimental lifestyle family. But all of those are the same. I mean, all of 'em have members that are blood related, you know?"

"Okay," he said.

"But then there's other kinds of family, too. There's the kind that follow a religious leader, or maybe they follow the Grateful Dead. And there's folks who hang out in a honkytonk every night because it feels like home—I know all about those people. I've taken thousands of pictures of 'em over the years. And then there's groups and little pockets of folks, like we were in Marfa. You get what I'm sayin'?"

Sam looked at her and smiled, "You're wise beyond your years, *Señorita* Hidalgo."

Amy giggled and looked away, embarrassed.

"No, I mean it. You're a wise woman, Amy. I am so proud of you." He reached around and hugged her and kissed her cheek.

"It's Vera," she said, "and Ebbets, too. I learned it from them. They showed me how to stand up for myself, how to quit looking at myself as a failure. Hell, Sam, Vera gave me my first camera, and Ebbets? Well, Ebbets taught me that beauty is on the inside."

He smiled, "Yeah, I remember. And I remember you, out there by the horses, taking pictures for hours. And I remember thinking, how many pictures can a person take of a damned horse?"

"Well, I took a lot of 'em, that's for sure. Those horses taught me more about photography than I ever learned from teachers or books. Hell, they were part of my Marfa family, too."

They sat without speaking for a few minutes. In normal company the silence would have been awkward, but it didn't feel that way to Sam. They were family. They would always be family.

Amy looked at him, "She was in love with you all those years, you know."

He fidgeted and turned away and she knew she had touched a sore spot. He didn't know how to respond, so he kept quiet.

"You two were made for each other," she said, "Yeah, I know that sounds corny and cliché, but it's true. I think you were just too dumb or too stubborn to realize it."

He was slow to respond, "Yeah, I guess maybe I was."

She continued, "It's funny, how you picture someone a certain way and you never change that picture. Kinda like you're lookin' at someone in a photograph from years ago, and you can't admit that they aren't the same person anymore. People change, but that picture of 'em doesn't."

Amy stopped, suddenly embarrassed. "Sorry, I'm rambling on and probably not making much sense."

"No, I think you're making perfect sense," he said, "and you know, I'm guilty as charged. I made that mistake with Vera. I made it with my wife. Hell, I even made it with you." He looked at her and it seemed like it was with a new appreciation, "You're damned sure not the same Amy I knew way back then." She blushed and looked down at the table.

After a pause she reached over and took his hand. "God dammit. I miss her," she said, finally.

He sighed, "Yeah, me too."

They got up to leave. Outside, they stood on the sidewalk in front of the cafe, silent and lost in their thoughts. Amy finally broke the spell. She looked at Sam intensely and worked up the courage to say, "She wasn't the only one, y'know."

"What?" he responded.

"Vera. Vera wasn't the only one,"

He looked at her, perplexed.

She looked away and mumbled under her breath, "She wasn't the only one who was in love with you."

And he suddenly saw her with a new pair of eyes.

"Come here," he said, and pulled her to him. They hugged each other for a long time and Amy began to sob. He gently pushed her back and looked down at her, the tears streaming along the lines of her face.

Sam grinned, "I'm thinkin' we have a bit of time to make up for." He studied her face for a moment, then asked, "You interested in lookin' for some buried treasure?"

Amy buried her face into him and pulled him to her, "Yes," she sobbed, "...yes, yes.."

Epilogue

The Raven

At the same time that Amy and Sam were having lunch in Los Angeles, the old raven launched himself from the barn's ridge beam with a great push of his legs and a flapping of wings. He felt the strain these days, but that was not surprising given his age. He was a youngster when he first came to live in Jorge's barn more than twenty years before.

He lifted his wings and allowed the light breeze to carry him up and away from the barn, where he could see his bovine friend in the pasture below. The old human sat in his chair on the front porch of the house and the raven gave a small squawk in greeting as he flew overhead. The cow acknowledged it by tipping its head, and the human merely squinted and looked up.

The cow was the offspring of the raven's original friend, a gentle giant who had passed away some years before. There was a marker near the pasture fence where Jorge had buried her. The simple inscription said, "Dinah".

Jorge had kept the young cow "for milk," he said. In truth, he kept her for company. She was a large cow, but nowhere near the size of her mother. She carried the genes of her father, a normal sized Santa Gertrudis bull who had somehow managed to mate with the giant clone. Jorge called her *Isabella*.

He had not replaced his last dog, the blue heeler named Esperanza, and so Isabella had become his confidante. Olive Stanfield was old now and couldn't come to visit often, so Jorge shared his conversations with the cow and the raven, and that was fine with him.

The raven flew south toward where the great river flowed and created the border with Mexico. Long before he reached the river he came to the place where the lights and the voices always guided him. He passed the sunken canyon and the spot where the humans' machines lie buried beneath an avalanche caused by the great explosion so many years before. He sensed the humans had been looking for the shiny gold pieces, but they had been digging in the wrong place. He made small circles, floating effortlessly above the desert floor, until he identified the spot, a quarter mile south of the humans' machines. He looked down, then descended.

The raven pecked the ground for a few minutes until he uncovered a shiny object—a gold coin, Mexican by nationality, 1854 by date. Alongside it he had uncovered a gold necklace that was inlaid with twenty-four diamond stones. It was a priceless piece of jewelry but the raven disregarded it because it was too heavy to lift.

The bird picked up the coin and tossed it to one side, then set to work covering up the pile of shiny objects. Satisfied with his work, he grabbed the coin and spread his wings, letting the breeze lift him high above the hiding place. For the raven, this place would always be connected to the voices and the lights.

Flying was easy in this country and he allowed the thermal currents to carry him along. Rather than head straight back to the barn, he made a slight diversion and came to rest high in a cottonwood tree on the bank of a dry arroyo a half mile from the old man's barn.

The raven landed on one of the lower branches and hopped along it until he was next to a large hole in the trunk of the tree, hollowed out by a lightning strike long ago. The voices were speaking to the old raven now. They assured him that he was doing the right thing as he dropped the gold coin into the hole and listened for the familiar *clink* as it landed on the large pile of coins beneath.

He jumped from the branch and sailed out of the cottonwood tree, back to the barn. The old raven came to rest on the cow's back and settled in for an afternoon nap.

About the Author

John Egenes has done pretty much whatever it takes to scrape by. He has been a musician, a saddlemaker, a dog catcher, a taxicab driver, and a university lecturer, among other things. He has ridden the freight trains he describes in this book, and he has seen the Marfa Lights. John now makes his home in New Zealand.

He is the author of "Man & Horse: The Long Ride Across America".

Visit John on Facebook:

https://www.facebook.com/TheMarfaBlues/